ABOVE IT ALL

BY CHAZ WM HUNT

§§

1rpm Press
El Cerrito, CA
aia@1rpm.com

Hi
STEVE & TRIECE

ISBN-10: 0615722970
EAN-13: 9780615722979
Library of Congress Control Number: 2012921552
1rpm Press,
El Cerrito, CA

Prologue – Valentine's Day

Five minutes after the business jet should have slammed into Poyanuk Ridge, Ian MacAran and Rashad Rehman were still fighting to keep the Citation flying. Turning north to fly parallel to the mountain ridges had given them more time, but they were still losing altitude. Fire had forced them to shut down the left engine, and within minutes the right engine had shut itself down. Restart had revealed an unusual fuel flow problem, possibly a partially blocked fuel line. The right engine was running, but it wasn't producing enough thrust for them to hold their altitude. Complicating matters was a jammed aileron trim tab that kept stubbornly trying to roll the plane upside down.

Things did not look good. When they'd been two miles higher the full moon had lit up the cloud tops from Denver to Salt Lake City. Now all the pilots could see was gray mist and the view inside the airplane wasn't much better. The Multi-Function Display that should have given a 3D rendering of the surrounding mountains was blank. The Primary Flight Display was also dead and the crew was relying on backup instruments that showed their altitude and heading in relation to a paper chart Rashad had open on his kneeboard. They were trying to reach a small airfield next to the interstate when there was a sizzling 'pop' and the lights illuminating the backup instruments winked out.

"Oh come on!" Ian growled. "What are the odds we'd lose all three electrical busses?"

"Quite remote, but," Rashad pointed to the backup attitude indicator. "We still have emergency power."

Ian sighed. "You had to say that out loud?"

"But we do have…"

The emergency lighting faded to a pale glow, flickered and expired. Rashad had already pulled a flashlight out of his flight bag and he angled the beam so it illuminated the instruments without reflecting off the windscreen. As the plane descended toward the valley floor, a red flag appeared in the corner of the backup instrument showing the attitude indicator was no longer reliable.

"Right," Ian took a deep breath. "Okay, look outside. We're looking for the freeway, or a road or something with lights on it."

"Roger."

Both pilots strained to see something through the cloud as they sank toward the valley floor.

As though it had been waiting for just this distraction, the stuck aileron tab popped free. In less than a second it shot from fighting Ian's effort to keep the plane level to helping him roll it the other way. Shadowy conifer treetops swept over their heads as the plane rolled upside down. Impact was a short sound effect like a crumpling aluminum can.

"You twisted invertebrate bastard!" Ian unbuckled his harness and levered himself out of the left seat. "Jesus!" He strode past the instructor sitting behind the copilot's seat as if the man didn't exist.

"Hey, that wasn't so bad, MacAran." Bert Stroud glanced from Ian to the simulator console. He seemed impressed. "Not bad at all!"

"Up yours, Bert." Ian unhooked the safety chain and stepped from the simulator platform to the walkway 10 feet above the hanger floor. The chain swung like an angry pendulum as Ian marched past another disembodied cockpit on his way out of Simulator Bay 3. Through clenched teeth he growled, "Son-of-a-bitch!"

Fifteen minutes later Rashad caught up with his captain in the cafeteria. Ian was sitting at the table furthest from the coffee bar and the vending machines. The wall behind him held pictures of SimSafety's various million dollar simulators while next to him was a ceiling-high window filled with the majesty of the Rocky Mountains. Outside, between the SimSafety building and the snow capped peaks, an orange 737 was taking off from one of Centennial's runways.

Ian stared into his coffee.

Rashad filled a cup with decaf, added milk and honey and walked over to Ian's table. He reached for a steel-framed plastic chair, but hesitated. "May I join you?"

"Of course." Ian gave Rashad a puzzled look. "Do I look that pissed off?"

Rashad started to nod but said, "Not at all," as he sat down. They were the same height, same build, and both wore white shirts, black slacks and visitor badges with Air Charter Express hand-printed below their names. Rashad's perfectly black hair was cut exactly as short as Ian's dusty blond. Rashad stirred his decaf. "Would you really try to land on a freeway?"

"In real life?" Ian looked up from his coffee and considered. "If there was any traffic you'd be endangering more people than were onboard, but it's flat and paved. Just landing near a freeway puts you close to people who can help." Ian tilted his head, "On the sim I'd go for the freeway in a heartbeat. There's never more than a car or two and most simulators don't treat the cars as physical objects. You can usually taxi right through them."

"Much less complicated than the real world."

"Yeah."

Rashad sipped his coffee, "Would you like to talk about it?"

"No."

Rashad nodded. "It is not like you to swear at anyone, certainly not a check pilot who has just given you a compliment."

"How is 'not bad' a compliment?"

"Coming from Bert Stroud 'not bad' is high praise! He said we made it further than anyone else this year."

"And then we crashed."

"True, but you always crash. You said everybody crashes with Bert. That is why Bert offers a hundred to one odds on a ten dollar bet and that is why everyone thinks he is a sadistic bastard who will never know the love of a good woman."

"I heard that!" Bert Stroud was pouring himself a coffee. His gray ponytail hung down the back of a rumpled white shirt and three gold hoops glittered from his left ear. His brown tie was loose and his collar unbuttoned but his SimSafety ID Badge had SENIOR EXAMINER engraved below his name. "Jesus Ian, when are you going to start teaching your co-pilots the difference between a bastard and an S.O.B.?"

Ian shrugged. "I haven't been able to teach Rashad anything since we started flying together."

"He doesn't seem that dense to me." Bert took the chair between them and sat with his back to the window. "Is he really that bad?"

"No, he's that good."

"Really?"

"Really." Ian nodded. "Ask him anything."

"Okay." Bert looked at Rashad with the practiced analytical scrutiny of a veteran check pilot and pointed at Ian. "Why was your Captain so far behind the airplane today?"

"Hey!" Ian objected.

"You said ask him anything and I want to know why your flying sucks more than usual."

"I wasn't behind the goddamned airplane!"

Rashad looked sympathetically at Ian and said, "It is Valentine's Day."

"What?" Bert laughed. "So get him a box of chocolates!"

Ian sagged back in his chair and looked at the ceiling.

Rashad said, "I do not think chocolate can heal a broken heart."

"That was months ago!" Bert looked at Ian. "Didn't Marcia dump you about nine months ago?"

"It was a year ago yesterday and how'd you know about that?"

"Like you're the only ACE pilots that train here? Everybody loves gossip, especially when it's about their Chief Pilot." Bert looked puzzled. "But if that was a year ago, why are you still pining?"

"For the love of…" Ian looked Bert in the eye. "I'm not 'pining'."

Rashad was nodding disagreement. "Marcia called him this morning."

"On Valentine's Day? Now that's cold." Bert paused, "Unless she's seen the light and decided she wants him back?" He looked from Rashad to Ian. "Does she want you back?"

"No!" Ian shook his head. "Jeff got arrested and she wanted me to post bail."

"Who's Jeff?" When Ian didn't answer, Bert looked at Rashad, "Jeff?"

"The insurance gerbil she left him for."

"Oh, that's *Antarctica* cold!" Bert looked at Ian with genuine concern, "But why call you?"

Rashad explained. "He still owes her the down-payment for her half of their house, so whenever Marcia needs money she calls Ian."

"They bought a house?" Again Bert looked at Ian, "When did you guys buy a house?"

"Just before she met Jeff." Ian sighed. "It's for sale, if you're interested. Four bedroom, three bath less than a mile from the airport?"

"No thanks: wrong airport." An Airbus on final for the runway behind him seemed to pop out of Bert's right ear. "Why have you waited a year to sell the house?"

"Hey, it's the right airport for me!" Ian looked back into his coffee. "And it's the perfect house. I knew it would be a stretch, but I thought I could make it work."

"So you thought wrong. It happens." Bert said matter-of-factly. "But you absolutely have to get over her; especially if it's interfering with your flying."

"Nothing is interfering with my flying! And I am *completely* over her. What I'm not over is a mountain of debt, a real estate market that's wiped out my equity and a demented examiner who thinks trim tab gremlins should be part of an engine failure!"

"Hey, shit happens!" Bert held up his hands, "That's life."

"Yeah? Well it didn't used to shit all over *my* life." Ian glanced out the window. "Look, can we talk about something less painful, like kidney stones?"

"You too?" Bert shook his head in feigned sympathy. "What a pisser."

Rashad smiled and after a moment Ian smiled too.

"Look, Bert, I'm sorry I snapped at you."

"No worries, Ian. Hell, I've had pilots try to strangle me! Forget about it. But you still owe me ten bucks." Bert looked at Rashad. "Each."

CHAPTER ONE

Saturday, 9:01 am – FOR SALE BY OWNER

One week later and two mountain ranges to the west, Ian was trying to tie his robe closed as he stumbled out of the master bedroom and turned down the hall. The doorbell rang for the fourth time and Ian mumbled, "Alright already, I'm coming!" He looked at his wrist to check the time but his watch was still on the floor next to the futon. The bell rang again as he opened the door and before Ian could say anything the man on the porch started talking.

"Morning! How's it going? I saw the for-sale sign and I thought I'd come take a look. You haven't sold it yet have you?" Five foot ten, slim, with windblown brown hair and a silver cross hanging from his left ear, he wore faded jeans, brand new tennis shoes, and a baseball cap that advertised Budget Lumber.

"Hi." Ian was two inches taller, with no earring. He was wearing gray cotton boxers and a white T-shirt under his bathrobe. He tugged the dark blue robe closed and tied a tighter knot. "Uh, no; the house is still for sale."

"Excellent!" He held out his hand. "My name's Mick, well; Michael Dale, but everybody calls me Mick."

Ian looked at Mick's hand, hesitated and then shook hands awkwardly. "My name's Ian."

"Nice to meet you, neighbor! We just moved in across the street, so I'm still trying to get everything settled. It's a totally excellent house, man: lots of room and a huge yard, especially in back." Mick moved to the side so Ian could look across the street at the thirty-year-old house. Not quite off the street, a big red pickup straddled the sidewalk. 'Dale Construction' and a phone number were lettered across the driver side door. Mick looked proud. "It's got a fantastic view of San Francisco."

"It does? I don't remember Rob and Laura having much of a view."

"Oh, I'm going to add a second floor." Mick pointed to the space above the rust-colored asphalt shingles. "When I was up on the roof checking for leaks and shit I could see from South San Francisco all the way around to Alameda and Oakland. Totally beautiful! I'm a contractor, so I figure I can add a second floor for two, maybe three hundred grand and double the value of the house." He looked back at Ian and then past him into the house. "So, anyway, I saw your for-sale sign and I'm thinking maybe I could buy it as a rental, you know? Uh, are you the owner?"

"Yeah."

"Excellent!" Mick smiled. "So, could I take a look?"

"Sure, but could we do this another time, maybe later today? I just got out of bed."

"Oh I can wait, you know if you want to get dressed or whatever. I don't mind. I've got a bunch of stuff to do this afternoon, but I've got an hour right now and I'm a serious prospect, I mean I'm not just kicking tires, you know?

It'll only take a few minutes, right? So, uh…?" Mick looked past Ian into the living room.

"Sure." Ian stepped back and motioned Mick inside. "Go ahead and take a look around. I'll be right back." He closed the door and headed back to the master bedroom leaving Mick to fend for himself.

"Sweet." Mick said to no one in particular. He wandered from the entryway into the living room and then headed straight for the room's only piece of furniture. "Nice entertainment center, dude!" Mick opened a door, punched a few buttons and managed to turn on the radio. For a moment he was surrounded by contemporary jazz, but he switched stations to news talk.

"Thunderstorms are on the way for Monday but the weekend should stay cool and sunny. In other news: researchers at Stanford say they've identified sub-atomic particles that actually travel backwards in time. The physicists said it was doubtful any one could send back tonight's Lotto numbers since these particles only travel a few millionths of a second into the past, but our understanding of time and space is being dramatically challenged by this discovery."

Mick wandered. There was a pool table in the dining room and several balls were scattered across the bright green surface. Mick ran his hand along the bumper, and then rolled the blue two-ball across the green felt. It cracked into the cue ball on the other side. Mick walked into the kitchen as the announcer segued from news to talk.

"And now back to Book-beat. This morning we're talking with Dr. Paul Neault, professor of psychology at U.C. Berkeley and author of: <u>Pain As Pleasure: S&M as a Way Of Life</u>. It looks like we have time for one more call. John, in San Francisco, this is talk radio; talk to me."

"Come on, Don. Isn't this guy even crazier than your usual guests?"

"Now, John," Paul Neault sounded smooth and reassuring. "Crazy isn't a very objective word."

"You think whips and chains are objective? What does tying someone up and whipping them <u>senseless</u> have to do with making love?"

"Now let's be fair. We're not talking about whipping anybody senseless."

"Oh! Well, that makes all the difference then! What's wrong with healthy, <u>normal</u> sex?"

"Well, not a thing, John. The whole point of my book is that the passion and intensity we've been talking about are part of exactly that: healthy, perhaps unusual but still normal sex."

"You creep, that's bull..."

"Doctor Neault, John, we need to pause for a moment and pay those bills. Book-beat will be right back after a few words from our sponsors. When we return, we'll take some more of your calls and later I'll be talking with D. T. Razzel about her latest book, <u>Ethics in the Modern World</u>."

There was a pause in the news talk as Ian changed the station and then jazz replaced the chatter. Ian stepped up to the counter separating the family room from the kitchen wearing jeans and a Runnin' Rebels sweatshirt. He was still barefoot. "Have you had a chance to look around?"

"Yeah, this is a really neat place!" Mick pointed at the carpet. "Weird colors, though. Why pink?"

"It's salmon. My ex-girlfriend picked it."

"Did she pick the paint and the tiles too?" Mick reached out to feel the counter.

"She had this theme: uh…" They were interrupted by a cell-phone rendition of "Take Five". Ian said, "Excuse me," and flipped open his phone. "MacAran."

Ian listened as Mick reached over and took an orange out of the basket on the counter. Mick dug a thumb into the top of the orange and opened the cabinet under the sink. He began tossing pieces of rind into the trash as he pulled them off the orange.

"Did you call Rashad?" Ian saw a piece of orange rind slip through Mick's fingers and fall to the floor. Mick didn't pick it up. Ian walked around the peninsula to the kitchen side, picked up the rind and tossed it into the disposal in the sink. "We still have the Ixtapa trip Monday, right?"

Mick finished peeling the orange and tossed the rest of the rind into the sink. He ate the orange a wedge at a time as he studied the kitchen and listened to Ian's side of the conversation.

"Thanks, Harry. Look, I just got out of bed. Tell Rashad I'll be there in half an hour." Ian closed the phone. "I've got to run, Mick, sorry. Can you let yourself out?"

"Uh, sure."

"Thanks." Ian backed away from the counter. "If you give me a call we can set up a better time."

"Okay." Mick followed Ian. "What's your number?"

"It's on the for sale sign." Ian started pulling off his sweatshirt as he crossed the family room toward the hall.

"Good enough. So, are you a pilot?"

"Uh, yeah. Nice meeting you Mick." Ian turned into the master bedroom, tossed his shirt toward the floor-level futon and stepped into the walk-in. The left side of the closet was crowded with shirts, slacks, and a dozen uniform jackets hanging above dress shoes and a pair of Reeboks. The right half of the closet was empty except for a single paper covered hanger and a laundry hamper.

"Who do you work for?" Mick was standing in the doorway.

"Hey! I'm trying to get dressed here!" Ian was halfway out of his jeans.

Mick backed away from the door and out of view. "Do you work for an airline?"

"No."

"Some kind of charter outfit?"

"Yeah, Air Charter Express."

"Never heard of 'em. Do you go to Mexico a lot?"

"Occasionally; why?"

"I've got family in Guadalajara, my in-laws actually, but we're real close."

6

Ian came out of the closet in a pressed jacket, slacks and a white shirt. He was finishing the knot in a dark blue tie with thin silver stripes. "Look, I've really got to get out of here." He slung a black duffle over his shoulder and headed toward the front door.

"No worries." Mick followed. "Oh, hey: We're having a housewarming party tonight, a barbecue." Mick checked his watch as Ian opened the front door. "Folks should start showing up around four or so and we'd love for you to come over."

"I'm not sure I'll be back in town."

"That's cool, but drop by if you can. We should be going 'til noon tomorrow. I'm hoping it'll turn into a block party, you know? We want to get to know our new neighbors." Mick gave Ian a friendly smile. "Even the ones who're planning on moving."

"If your party lasts through Sunday morning, you'll get to know the neighbors." Ian pointed out the door. "Now if you don't mind?"

"Swing by if you're in town?"

"I'll try to make it, if I can."

"Excellent!" Mick stepped out onto the front porch and Ian closed and locked the door behind him. A cool breeze was keeping the treetops moving and as he walked toward the street, Mick noticed a hummingbird feeder gently swinging below one of the lower branches. Happy with the red sugar-water, a blue and green jewel with blurry wings stayed in perfect sync with the plastic flower. Mick took a few curious steps toward the hummingbird, but it immediately shot through the tree and disappeared.

Mick shrugged and headed home. He was halfway across the street when Ian's garage door rolled up and a 40-year-old Mustang rumbled into view. The royal blue classic sounded healthy but it had a shopping-cart scar in the passenger side door and more than a few rust spots. Ian nodded at Mick as he steered around him and then accelerated toward Doolittle drive. Mick waved amicably as the rattle from Ian's closing garage door was lost in the roar of an Airbus departing one of Oakland's nearby runways.

Saturday, 11:02 pm - Runway 27 Right,
Oakland International Airport

Two hours later, Citation 229 rolled onto the active runway. As it turned west to line up with the centerline, the tan and gold business jet paused over a blocky white 27 almost as big as the plane's shadow. Rotating beacons on the plane's belly and the tip of its tail blinked red every few seconds. Strobe lights on the wing tips flashed and the whine of the turbine engines rose to a roar. The jet accelerated rapidly toward Bay Farm Island and the sky-line beyond San Francisco Bay.

Halfway down the runway, a hawk settled onto the sign for taxiway Golf and watched the airplane approach. For a moment the hawk shifted its weight from foot to foot preparing to defend its territory. Being senior preda-tor in the airport's micro-ecology, the hawk feared noth-ing, but as the airplane's nose lifted and the jet rose from its shadow, the hawk flapped into the air and dodged away from the runway. The Citation thundered overhead, its landing gear rotating up and out of the air stream as the jet banked gently east.

The turbine roar receded, but the faint aroma of ker-osene remained. The hawk swooped back to its perch and glanced over its shoulder at the retreating jet. With a shrug, the bird preened an errant feather back into place.

Traveling at 220 knots, the Citation climbed over two thousand feet every minute, and covered more than a mile of homes and shopping malls every fifteen seconds. As the plane rose above the haze covering Northern California, a line of jagged ski slopes came into view a hundred miles ahead: the Sierra Nevada Mountains.

Rashad Rehman made a note of their ground speed. "So, finish the story. Is this pushy person going to buy your house?"

"I don't know, maybe." Ian adjusted the throttles. "Did I say he was pushy?"

"Everything you described him doing was pushy."

Through their headsets the Oakland Center Controller sounded like he was right in the cockpit with them. "CITATION 229, CLIMB/MAINTAIN 23,000."

Rashad glanced at the altimeter, pressed the microphone button on his yoke, and read back their clearance. "229, through 13,000 for 23,000."

Ian looked back into the cabin. There was no partition between the flight deck and the passenger compartment, and Ian could see all the way back to the restroom door. Their passenger was in the second seat on the right side, behind Rashad. She was reading a report and making notes on a yellow legal pad. Ian adjusted their heading. He whispered into the intercom. "What was her name?"

Rashad whispered back. "Sandra Taylor. Harry said she works for OHI, but she does not look like an engineer to me."

"Maybe she's an architect." Ian raised his voice over the background noise. "Ms. Taylor? We'll be leveling off at twenty-three thousand feet in about eight minutes. There are drinks and, I believe, some snacks in the refrigerator. You're welcome to move around as you like but please keep your seatbelt on when you're seated."

Sandra Taylor looked up from her paperwork. Her hair was held back from her face in a blonde waterfall that cascaded off the shoulders of her gray blazer. Blue eyes glanced down at her notes, then looked back at Ian. She smiled politely and said, "Thank you." She seemed about to say something else, but didn't.

Ian smiled back and a moment passed as he wondered what she might have said. "If there's anything we can do for you, let us know."

"I will." She nodded and her smile was warmer this time. "I do appreciate your interrupting your weekend on such short notice."

"All part of the service. We'll be in Las Vegas in about fifty minutes."

"That'll be great." Sandra nodded and returned to her papers.

As the Citation left Oakland Center's airspace, they were told to contact Los Angeles Center. Thirty minutes later, after stepping them down to 15,000, L.A. passed them on to Las Vegas Approach.

Rashad made a note on his kneeboard and flipped to the 'Before Landing' checklist. Below them the mottled brown desert stretched away to the horizon. The only sign of life was the city ahead. "Las Vegas Approach, Citation 229 is level at 15,000."

"ROGER 229." Unlike the tower controller a few floors above her, the approach controller was seated in a dimly-lit video mausoleum surrounded by the ethereal glow of numerous radar screens. To her, Citation 229 was a phosphor green bar labeled with its aircraft type, number, altitude and ground speed. "CITATION 229, TURN RIGHT HEADING 150. EXPECT VECTORS FOR THE ILS 25R APPROACH."

Ian rolled the plane into a gentle right turn, and Rashad read back their instructions. "Right 150, vectors for the ILS 25R approach, Citation 229."

The controller took a sip of apple juice from the bottle beside her console as the steady stream of radio traffic continued. American flight 1475, a Boeing 757, checked in and she gave it a similar clearance. The airliner was twenty miles further north of the airport than the business jet, but by the time the Citation reached the runway, the faster 757 would be perfectly spaced five miles behind it.

A 737, Southwest 1057, checked in, and a few moments later a Mexicana Airbus called. Southwest 1057 had called first, but the Airbus was in better position for the runway. The 737 was inbound from the South and the controller didn't have enough room to turn it in front of the Airbus. She decided to put the Airbus behind the 757, and turn Southwest 1057 slightly away from the airport to direct, or vector it behind the Airbus. She took another sip of apple juice.

"CITATION 229, TURN RIGHT HEADING 210."

"Citation 229, right 210."

"Approach, uh, Southwest 1057..."

There was a pause and Ian and Rashad could hear background conversation in the 737 cockpit.

"...Sorry Approach, this is Southwest 1057, we've got ourselves a medical emergency on board right now. We're gonna request priority handling into Las Vegas. We've got a little baby on board with a heart problem. Could you have the paramedics standing by for us?"

"WE'LL DO IT." She spoke over her shoulder to the shift supervisor, "Bob, 1057 has a medical; they need paramedics at the gate."

"Right." The supervisor picked up a phone and started dialing. "Get their gate number."

"Okay." Southwest 1057 was now number one to land, even though it was twenty miles out. The controller finished her apple juice and tossed the bottle in the trash. With all the construction and improvements going on, she only had one runway to accommodate the four aircraft. There would be more aircraft in her sector very soon, and she didn't want to interrupt the steady stream of departures off runway 19R unless she had to. All she needed was a little more room... "CITATION 229, CAN YOU GIVE ME 220 KNOTS TO THE OUTER MARKER?"

Rashad looked at Ian.

Ian pressed the microphone button on his yoke, "229, affirmative. We have the airport in sight, request visual approach."

"CITATION 229, MAINTAIN 220 KNOTS, I HAVE YOUR REQUEST." The controller nodded. Flying a visual approach, the Citation could get to the field much faster than an airplane flying the full instrument approach, but the controller couldn't assign a visual approach because she had no way of knowing what the pilots could see. Ian's request had given her enough time to cross the '57 over the '37 and then turn the heavy back toward the airport. "SOUTHWEST 1057 DESCEND TO 5,000. TRAFFIC IS AN AMERICAN 757 RESTRICTED ABOVE YOU."

"Southwest 1057, down to 5,000."

"ROGER, AND SOUTHWEST 1057, TURN LEFT HEADING 340, EXPECT A 90 DEGREE TURN ONTO THE LOCALIZER."

"Left 340, Southwest 1057, and could you tell the medical people: we have a six-month-old baby boy who is now on oxygen and he has a declining heart rate."

"WE'LL DO THAT. WHAT'S YOUR GATE NUMBER, SIR, DO YOU HAVE IT YET?"

"No, but it'll be right there on the end of the concourse, uh C gates. We'll get right back to you on that."

"ROGER. CITATION 229 IS 4 MILES FROM THE OUTER MARKER, CLEARED FOR THE VISUAL APPROACH RUNWAY 25R. CONTACT TOWER NOW ON 119.9 AND THANKS FOR THE HELP."

"229, cleared for the visual runway 25R, tower on 119.9. Our pleasure." Rashad pressed the active/standby button on the upper radio and the frequencies for Las Vegas Approach and McCarran Tower traded LED displays. "McCarran Tower, Citation 229."

A very gruff, very male voice answered. "CITATION 229, McCARRAN TOWER. RUNWAY 25R CLEARED TO LAND."

"Citation 229, roger." Rashad looked at Ian. "Speed brakes at the outer marker?"

"Negative, she'll slow down nicely without speed brakes." Ian reduced power to begin their descent. The engines' whine softened to a purr. Ian lowered the nose to maintain the 220 knots they'd promised the approach controller, and switched on the cabin intercom. "Ms. Taylor, we'll be landing in a few moments. Please make sure your seatbelt is fastened."

Sandra absently checked her seatbelt. She hadn't touched it since they'd taken off.

Ian turned the plane a degree to the right to correct for the slight crosswind. "Before Landing checklist."

Rashad read off each item, "Avionics, radio altimeter, flaps..." and Ian confirmed the condition of each. "Set and checked, set, I'll call for them..." As they crossed the outer marker, four miles from the runway, a steady beep-beep-beep sounded over their headsets and a blue light lit up on the marker beacon panel. Ian pulled the throttles back to idle thrust.

"It's not that difficult to slow this airplane down." Ian pointed to the airspeed indicator, which was already showing a reduction in airspeed. "The trick is to do it gracefully. Flaps to fifteen degrees at 200 knots."

"Roger." At 200 knots Rashad moved the flap lever to the approach setting. "Flaps to fifteen."

"See? She's slowing down nicely. Landing gear at 175."

"Roger." At 175 knots Rashad put the gear down, and said, "Gear coming down." The slight vibration of the actuators joined with the muted howl of the wind over the struts and wheels as the doors and gear swung out into the airstream. Three green lights showed the main landing gear and the nose gear locked into position. The airplane was lined up with the runway, and the speed continued to bleed off as they descended toward McCarran Airport.

Behind them, Southwest 1057 turned toward the runway as American 1475 passed 2,000 feet above it. On the controller's instructions, the Mexicana Airbus slowed to 200 knots and the 757 began a left circling turn that would take three minutes and burn seven thousand dollars of fuel. Southwest 1057 lowered their landing gear, the jumbo-jet turned over Lake Mead, and the comparatively tiny Citation continued its approach.

A mile from the runway, Ian called for full flaps.

Rashad complied. "Full flaps."

The plane touched down at 100 knots. In the cabin, Sandra crossed out a comma she'd added earlier and drew a straight line through two words. She looked up from her notes and noticed that they were on the ground.

Southwest 1057 had been cleared to land and was crossing the outer marker as Ian taxied off the runway. A pale blue van with 'FOLLOW ME' stenciled across its rear doors met the jet at the edge of the taxiway and led them to a parking spot next to a white limousine. The girl that answered Rashad's call on the Eagle Aviation frequency confirmed that the limo was indeed waiting for Ms. Taylor.

Ian taxied up to the Mercedes and closed the throttles. Rashad slipped out of his seat, opened the door and lowered the stairs.

Sandra said, "Thanks again," as she stepped out of the cool airplane and into 102 degrees of desert afternoon.

Ian watched from the jet's cockpit as she crossed to the limousine and gracefully slipped into the air-conditioned Mercedes. He caught a last glimpse of her leg before the driver closed her door and walked quickly around to the other side of the car. The brake lights flashed as the transmission slipped into drive, and then the limo accelerated down the flight line, disappearing behind the Eagle Aviation hanger. The Citation's turbines wound down to silence.

"Very impressive!" Rashad was standing in the passageway.

Ian nodded. "She is that."

Rashad followed Ian's gaze. "I meant your landing: very smooth."

"Oh. Thanks."

"Ms. Taylor was also quite impressive. I think she's a lawyer."

"Not an engineer?"

"No pocket protector."

"Not an architect?"

"Perhaps." Rashad set his clipboard on the right seat. "Either way, it is sad that we have to go home alone."

"True," Ian smiled, "But if she came back with us you couldn't log PIC."

"Good point. I do need eight more hours."

"And then you'll upgrade to Captain and you still won't be able to afford a house." Ian moved aft, into the much warmer cabin.

"Ah, but I <u>will</u> be able to buy a house. You forget the dozens of dollars I make in the Army Reserve."

"Oh, that'll make the difference." Ian laughed. "Unless one of those antiques comes apart in midair!"

"Your fear of helicopters is completely irrational."

"'Irrational' is trusting a loose association of spinning parts held together by something called a 'Jesus' nut!"

Rashad decided to change the subject. "Hungry?"

"Starving."

"Shall we get some lunch?"

"Absolutely."

Rashad followed Ian out onto the hot concrete. Ian pushed up the stairs, and Rashad closed and locked the door. They walked toward the terminal, blending seamlessly into the not-quite-military formality of professional aviation. Their uniforms, identical except for the fourth gold stripe on Ian's epaulets and the silver in his tie, would have made them welcome in almost any cockpit in the world.

Rashad was as tall as Ian, perhaps a little heavier. "In all seriousness, you bought a house on a captain's salary, did you not?"

"No." Ian shook his head. "Marcia and I got the loan based on both our incomes, and she was making about twice what I was."

"Interesting." Rashad considered. "So my income added to Jocelyn's would be enough for us to get a loan?"

"Sure. Hey! You didn't tell me you two were that serious."

"We are not." Rashad shook his head, but then shrugged. "Not exactly, but we are both very tired of renting, and neither one of us can afford a home by ourselves."

As they reached the terminal, the doors to Eagle Aviation's lobby slid aside automatically. Both men smiled at the thirty-degree drop in temperature. They split up. Ian let the line crew know that 229 would only be on the ramp for an hour or so, and Rashad called Jocelyn to let her know they would be heading back after a quick lunch. When they regrouped upstairs at the coffee shop, Ian and Rashad were escorted to a window table overlooking the airport.

As Ian and Rashad sat down, the waitress turned to the two men at the next table and asked if they needed anything. One was a police officer who just shook his head. The other, a tall red haired man in a grey short-sleeved shirt smiled and said, "No, thanks, Jenny."

Rashad watched the waitress walk back to the front of the restaurant, and then opened his menu. Ian's attention was outside. A Korean Air 777 was taxiing to McCarran International's main terminal. The sparkling clean 777 was almost a mile away and it still seemed surrealistically huge, looming magnificently larger than the business jets on Eagle's ramp. When it reached the main terminal, on the other side of the airport, two temperature-controlled jetways extended out from the concourse and pressed against the jumbo's side, connecting it to the hotels and gaming tables of what was once the fastest-growing city in the world.

Something glinted off to Ian's left. A Falcon Jet had turned onto the closest runway and was accelerating past them. Ian watched as the plane shot past, rising smoothly into the hot dry air. Turning his head to follow the Falcon's progress, Ian found himself studying the crush of images in the window glass. He could see outside, but he could also see the reflection of the broad-shouldered man sitting behind him, and the cop sitting across his table. It should have been easy to ignore the two. They weren't particularly loud or dramatic, but there was something about the big man's deep, grumbling voice that made listening seem like the natural thing to do. He had curly red hair on his head and forearms and a dark red beard that didn't quite reach his shirt collar. He looked about forty but he was talking about his life as if it was already over.

"I just want a challenge, you know?"

The police officer laughed amiably. "Last night you bet five hundred dollars on a busted flush! That seemed pretty challenged to me."

"Yeah, but I still had a pair."

"Eights, Orson! You had a lousy pair of eights!"

"But he was bluffing."

"How did you know?"

"I don't know, Casey; I just knew. What difference does it make? It was a card game."

"There was four thousand dollars in that pot!" Casey sighed, "I had two jacks and I folded!"

Orson didn't respond and Ian glanced at his menu. Nothing looked interesting. He looked back outside at the 777. Baggage, catering, and fuel trucks were swarming around the plane, rushing to get it loaded, fueled and fed for its next trip across the Pacific.

Casey broke the short silence. "Look, Orson, something is obviously eating at you." The sarcasm was gone. "What's going on?"

"Nothing; everything is just fine." Orson paused. "Maybe that's the problem: Nothing *ever* goes wrong. I was a cop for six years and everybody I ever arrested cooperated. The only time I've ever fired a gun is on the practice range."

"And that's a bad thing?"

"No! God no. That's not what I'm getting at; I'm not looking to hurt anybody. I've just never actually faced a life or death situation, you know?"

"What about that hostage thing - the bank robbery?"

"Come on, Casey: That was over before it started!"

"You got a commendation for that, right?"

"I told the guy he should give himself up. He looked at his gun for a second, said, 'Okay,' and handed it to me!"

"There were a lot of people in that bank, Orson. You saved lives."

"Nobody was in any danger, Casey, you know that. The only person that fool was going to hurt was himself." Orson sighed. "I've got all this training, all this 'experience', and it's all theoretical. If I never get to use it, how will I ever really know if it's any good?"

"So join the Foreign Legion. Be a mercenary."

"I'm already a private investigator. It's like being a mercenary without the hazard pay." Orson hesitated. "I don't know why I feel like I want to fight, God help me, but it's not for the sake of fighting, you know? I don't think I want to fight so much as I want my existence to have some meaning. I want my life to be about something more than faithful husbands and high tech golf balls."

Orson didn't say anything more, and Ian shifted in his chair a little, trying to focus on the blur of activity outside. He didn't notice the waitress until she repeated herself. "Sir?"

Ian turned his head away from the window. "I'm sorry?"

"What would you like?" Her pen was poised above a pale green order pad.

"Uh," Ian nodded at Rashad. "Whatever he's having will be fine."

"Cheeseburger, fries and a large iced tea?"

"Could I have coffee instead?"

"Coffee it is. Will that be all?"

Ian and Rashad both nodded and the waitress headed toward the kitchen to place their order. The two men at the table next to them rose and followed her as far as the cash register.

"You look very thoughtful." Rashad smiled. "Are you thinking about our beautiful passenger?"

"Not exactly." Ian shook his head. "Do you ever feel like you're ... I don't know, stuck on the wrong track?"

"By 'wrong track' do you mean trapped, purposeless, dissatisfied with life and tormented by the bad decisions that have doomed me to a pale shadow of what my existence might have been?"

"Uh," Ian hesitated. "Okay, yeah."

Rashad shook his head, "Never."

Saturday, 3:03 pm - Yuri Milanov's
Jaguar, 24th St & 17th Ave, Oakland

As the stretched XJ8 turned onto 24th street, there was a loud CRACK, somewhere outside the silver-gray limousine. A young voice yelled, "Hey, the limo's on our team!" and a second later a tattered softball whumped off the hood.

"What the...?" Oscar Jamison almost slipped off the edge of the gray leather seat as he reached inside his jacket.

Yuri Milanov watched Jamison hesitate. "What caliber softball do you think that was, Oscar?" Milanov was sitting relaxed and comfortable with his back to the driver. It gave him a commanding view of the back seat, but he could also see the street beyond the Jaguar's rear window. A tomboyish girl had caught the softball before it hit the ground and her teammates were shouting that the batter, rounding the cardboard box that served as second base, was out. Milanov watched the girl until the Jaguar turned the corner and headed for the Interstate. As the neighborhood slipped out of view, Milanov turned his head slightly to speak to the driver. "Any damage, Travis?"

"A small dent, Mr. Milanov. I'll take care of it before you get back."

"Thank you, Travis." Tall and slender with sharp, angular features, Milanov seemed to have eyes the color of igneous rock. He watched the scenery slip past for a moment and then focused his cold gaze on a point somewhere behind Oscar's forehead.

Oscar fidgeted and cleared his throat. "Look, I'll do whatever you tell me to, Mr. Milanov, you know that. But that don't mean I understand it. Why are we bothering with these punks? They're small-time!"

"I'm aware of that, Oscar, but this isn't about competition. As I've said before: We do not conduct business with *children*."

"But we're not doin' business with them! We cut 'em off as soon as you told us to."

"Yes you did, but if you're no longer providing them with product, how is it possible that these "X-Men" are still moving almost a kilo a month?"

"I, uh..."

Milanov said nothing.

The Jaguar left the freeway and swung past the Oakland Hilton.

Oscar fidgeted some more. "Mr. Milanov they're not buying anything from me. If they're still in business, they must be buying from somebody else."

"Your logic is impeccable Oscar, as far as it goes, but consider this: who imports almost eighty-five percent of the cocaine sold in the East Bay?"

Oscar looked stunned. "We handle eighty-five percent of the coke in Oakland?"

"Almost." Milanov nodded curtly. "Given our ever improving market share, what do you think the odds are that whoever is selling to these kids, is buying from us?"

"Uh, eighty-five percent, right?"

"Eighty-five percent, very good."

Oscar shook his head, confused. "But if they're not buying it from my troops, Mr. Milanov, why do I have to deal with them?"

"Because you created the problem." Milanov smiled. His teeth were perfect. "You brought them into this business, and it is therefore your responsibility to get them safely out."

"Hey! I didn't know. I mean..."

"Enough." Milanov held up his hand. His Berkeley "Class of '67" ring shifted slightly to expose a thin crescent of pale skin, frozen into his dark, even tan. "What I want, Oscar is a quiet and thorough resolution to this little subplot. You will identify whoever is corrupting these pre-pubescent pushers and make our position in this matter clear. We do not buy from, sell to or in any way conduct business with *children*."

Oscar started to open his mouth, but quickly reconsidered.

The Jaguar swept past a long line of cabs and pulled up to the curb in front of Oakland Airport's International Terminal. As Travis stepped out to open the back door, Milanov reached for his briefcase. "I'll be back in two weeks, Oscar, and I do not want to be distracted by trivia. Get the children safely out of our business." He stepped out into the crush of arriving and departing luggage, and nodded to his driver. "Thank you, Travis. Please drop Mr. Jamison wherever he needs to go." Milanov leaned forward to look back into the car. "You've got two weeks, Oscar." He nodded to Travis and disappeared into the crowd.

Saturday, 4:04 pm - Terri Turner's
Townhouse, San Francisco

"Terri? My hands are getting numb." Stacia's wrists were locked into separate pairs of metal handcuffs, one at each end of a black wooden rod fifteen inches above her head.

"You're not being very good." Terri grabbed a wrist with each black leather glove and lifted. "I told you, hold onto the bar or the cuffs will cut off your circulation."

Stacia grabbed on, her bright red fingernails vivid against the white of her fingers and the black of the horizontal bar. "I'm trying to be good."

Terri combed leather-clad fingers through Stacia's long red-brown tresses and pressed the girl's head forward. Kissing her, Terri's tongue forced Stacia's lips apart as the other glove slid lightly down the girl's naked back. Terri pushed the girl's hips forward, pressing her against Terri's black biker jacket and leather chaps. Though Terri was much stockier, they were about the same height, and as they kissed the silver talon that hung from Terri's right ear caught a few strands of Stacia's hair.

Stacia was wearing only the handcuffs, black boots and a harness that held a softly humming vibrator inside her. A triangle of curly brown fuzz was framed in black leather by the belt of the harness and the thin straps that met in a "V" between her legs. Thin chains looped around her ankles and locked them to rings on the floor.

Terri let their lips part just enough to whisper, "Sweetheart, you're going to be very, very good!"

The next piece of the ensemble was a black leather collar that Terri locked around Stacia's neck. Two braided silver chains hung from the front of the collar with a miniature clothespin at the end of each. Terri cupped Stacia's breasts in her hands and massaged each nipple between a gloved thumb and forefinger. Stacia closed her eyes and leaned her head back. She managed to hold onto the bar as her hips pulsed forward to her own internal rhythm.

Terri stopped the circular teasing and reached once more into the case between the girl's feet.

"What's that?"

Terri loosened the laces on the back of the leather mask, and held it by the wide strap that would fasten under Stacia's chin. "It's a hood."

"Please don't. I mean, *mercy*." Stacia shook her head. "I've never..."

Terri pulled the girl's chin down and pushed the end of the strap into her mouth. Black leather fingers gently pushed the chin up, clamping the strap in the girl's teeth. "Hold this."

With both hands, Terri gathered the red-brown mane into a ponytail on top of the girl's head. Holding the hair in one hand, Terri freed the strap from the girl's mouth and passed her hair through a hole in the top of the hood. Terri snugged the hood down over the girl's head and unbuckled the attached blindfold. The padded leather hung to one side as Terri stared into Stacia's brown eyes. "Your eyes are so beautiful."

"Thank you, I...please..."

Terri stepped behind her. "Didn't we have a wonderful time last night?" Terri tightened the laces on the back of the hood.

"Yes, but, we've only just met and…"

"This is our third date already! I know you had a good time the first two; didn't you?"

"Yes, but…"

"And haven't we had a delicious day together so far?"

"Yes!" Stacia nodded enthusiastically, "I mean, yes, mistress."

Terri leaned forward and whispered, "You're right on the edge aren't you?" Terri tied the laces off at the back of Stacia's neck.

"Yes, mistress."

"I thought so." Terri's hands caressed the girl's shoulders, back and hips, "Tell me you didn't want this the moment our eyes met."

"Yes, but…"

"But?"

"I'm scared."

Terri's voice was reassuring, if not the words: "You're supposed to be." She pressed against Stacia's back. "Savor it." One hand traced the curve of each breast, as the other found the center of that triangle of curly brown hair. Terri pinched the girl's left nipple and she arched forward, into the pressure. The other hand danced on Stacia's sex and her hips bucked forward in response. Stacia's feet left the floor intermittently as she struggled, but she held onto the bar above her. Her movements became more intense, more insistent; Terri stopped.

Stacia growled, "Terri!"

"You are so hot!" Terri moved toward the stairs up to the kitchen. "Let me get you something. I'll be right back."

Terri returned a few minutes later with a tackle box, a glass of ice and a bottle of strawberry soda. She set the case at Stacia's feet and opened it to reveal a mobile pharmacy of unlabeled pill bottles. Sorting through the possibilities Terry found a particular bottle and opened it. She grabbed a short blue cylinder, flipped open the top and shook a pill into the little chamber. Closing the top brought a tiny blade down on the pill and guillotined it in half. Terri started to put one half back in the bottle but she shrugged, popped it into her mouth and swallowed it dry. The other end of the cylinder was a screw down pill crusher and in half a minute Terri had the remaining half of the pill reduced to a coarse powder. She sprinkled the powder onto the ice, poured the soda into the glass and stirred it up with the straw she'd carried in her jacket pocket.

"Here, try this." Terri held the straw up to Stacia's lips. "You need to stay hydrated."

Stacia took a cautious sip. "It's Strawberry!" She drank more.

"You said it was your favorite so I got a few cases."

"Cases? Sweet. Excessive, but sweet." Stacia drank some more. "It tastes a little gritty."

"That's the ecstasy."

"Terri!"

"Half a pill! You'll hardly notice."

"I've never tried ecstasy."

"It'll take the edge off. Trust me." Terri held the straw to Stacia's lips until she finished the soda. Terri said, "Very good," as she set the glass on the floor next to her 'medicine box'.

"Terri?"

"Yes?" Terri moved behind her.

"Could you take off this hood?"

"Of course." Terri stroked her back. "If you really want me to." She moved her hands down to the tops of Stacia's boots and up the insides of her legs.

Stacia arched into the pressure. "That feels good."

"It's going to feel a lot better. Things will get sharper, clearer; just give it a little time."

Terri walked around to face the girl, and gazed for a long moment into the heavily lashed brown eyes. There was a tiny tear at the corner of one eye. Terri kissed it. She licked the salty water off her lips as she swung the blindfold back into place and buckled the strap.

In the closet behind the girl, an orderly array of leather clothing and un-clothing shared space with jeans and shirts. The floor was a jumble of boxes, boots, National Geographics and other, more exotic magazines. Terri took out a pair of motorcycle chaps and buckled them around the girl's waist.

"What are you doing?"

Terri wrapped the leather chaps around each of Stacia's legs and zipped the in-seams closed, covering the girl's legs from mid-thigh to the ankles of her boots. "You do have such beautiful long legs."

"What are you doing? I *said* mercy." Stacia turned her head from side to side. "Please talk to me. Terri?"

Stacia's mouth was the only part of her face not covered by the hood. Terri reached into the case, stood, and kissed the leather-framed lips. "I'm just making you presentable, but we can stop if you really want me to." With her free hand Terri teased Stacia's sex. "Do you want me to stop?"

"Uh…" Stacia moaned. "No mistress."

"That's my girl." Terri kissed her again. She pressed her tongue into Stacia's mouth, opening her wider and whispered, "Open a little more."

When Stacia complied Terri slipped the flat leather gag in place. The girl objected, but the gag blocked all but her sense of indignation. Terri pushed the gag in tight and buckled it to the hood.

Reaching into the closet, Terri took a faded brown bomber jacket and draped it over the bar next to the girl's hands. She released Stacia's right wrist and the girl struggled, trying to free herself, but there was little hope. Terri had two free hands to Stacia's one and Terri could see what she was doing.

"It's okay to struggle. I like it when you struggle." Terri slid the right sleeve of the jacket over the girl's arm and re-cuffed that hand to the bar. When Terri got the other sleeve on Stacia's left arm she cuffed both wrists together behind the girl's back. Terri unhooked the chains from the floor but left them wrapped around Stacia's ankles. Grabbing the two chains that dangled between Stacia's breasts, Terri walked her captive out of the bedroom and down the hall toward the garage.

The motorcycle was black with black trim and black chrome wheels. The letters and numbers describing the bike had been removed and the mounting holes filled, sanded and painted over. The only thing that acknowledged the motorcycle's Japanese heritage was the KZ-2000 maintenance manual next to the two helmets on the workbench.

Stacia tried to resist but she couldn't see what she was resisting, and Terri quickly maneuvered the girl onto the back of the motorcycle. The chains on the girl's boots were looped around the passenger foot pegs and clipped back to the boots, tying her feet to the bike. Terri curled Stacia's fingers around the bar at the back of the seat.

"Hold on tight." Terri used a small padlock to fasten the handcuff chain to the bottom of the backrest, and another padlock to attach the girl's collar to the top of the backrest.

A gloved hand brushed across Stacia's breasts, teasing first one nipple and then the other. Her breathing was shallow and rapid and her nipples stood out tense and excited. Terri squeezed Stacia's breasts, pinching and tugging her nipples. When the first miniature clothespin clamped onto the girl's right nipple, she moaned into the gag. Terri pulled on the chain and the girl screamed; the sound muffled and indistinct through the leather. Terri steadied Stacia's heaving chest and clamped the other clothespin to Stacia's left nipple. She checked its grip and zipped the brown jacket closed.

Terri slid one of the helmets over the girl's head and buckled the chinstrap under her chin. The helmet was black, except for a white, rough-sanded patch on the back, just above the neck. Terri pushed the smoke-gray visor down, and stepped back. From only a few feet away, her passenger looked like any other motorcycle rider. The chains around her boots looked like decorations. The long sleeves of the jacket hid the handcuffs and the padlock at her neck was lost in her ponytail. The thin lines of thigh that the chaps didn't cover weren't even noticeable.

"Perfect!" Terri patted the top of Stacia's helmet. "You're completely camouflaged. Now don't go away." Terri went back into the house. She returned a few minutes later with a pair of empty saddlebags. She hooked the bags over the luggage rack at the back of the bike and reached for her own helmet. The initials TNT were set in black on a gold triangle on the back of the helmet. Terri buckled the chinstrap and slid in front of her passenger.

The garage door opened with a press of the remote mounted on the motorcycle's fairing. Terri started the engine, toed the bike into gear and rolled across the sidewalk, into the street. She pressed the remote and waited to make sure the garage door closed all the way before twisting the throttle and roaring east toward the Bay Bridge.

Saturday, 5:05 pm – MacAran Residence:
FOR SALE – ALAMEDA REALTY

Back in the East Bay, the sun was about an hour above the South San Francisco hills when Ian returned from the airport. While he'd been gone the Real Estate Agent he'd called the day before had replaced his cheap 'for sale by owner' sign with a solid wood sign of her own. There were cars parked everywhere. The front door to Mick's house was open and "Veteran Cosmic Rocker" was echoing off the surrounding houses. Ian had to park on the street between a BMW and a Volkswagen that was blocking his driveway.

Once in his kitchen, Ian opened a Henry's and took a healthy swallow before tossing the cap in the trash. He swept an errant bit of orange rind into the sink and ran the garbage disposal to get rid of the debris from Mick's visit. He tried watching TV but he had to keep adjusting his volume to keep pace with the erratic noise from across the street. Weather it was the Moody Blues, H2O or Grumpin Fearcat the music would be barely audible for a while and then it would suddenly pound through the walls as though the speakers were in the next room. The intensity would ease off for a few songs and then blast back up to full volume. Ian looked at his watch, looked at the ceiling and sighed, "How bad could it be?" He picked up his keys and his beer, locked the front door on his way out and headed toward the party.

As Ian started across the street, a black motorcycle roared around the corner. The bike looked like it was floating sideways as it leaned into the turn, the knees of the two riders barely an inch off the pavement. The motorcycle started up Mick's driveway, then cut to the right and swerved to a stop on the sidewalk. Both riders wore black boots, black leather chaps and black helmets with smoke-gray visors. The driver's jacket matched the rest of her ensemble, but her passenger's jacket was brown leather.

The engine died with the turn of a key, and the driver pulled off her helmet and impaled it on one of the handlebars. She had short brown hair that she straightened with her fingers as she swung the kick-stand out and slipped off the seat. Leaning close, she said something to her passenger and then walked to the back of the bike. The saddlebags she took from the luggage rack were heavy, and she used both hands to swing them up and over her left shoulder. She walked the way Ian imagined a bullfighter might walk and disappeared into the din of Mick's house. Her passenger didn't even take off her helmet.

Ian crossed the street and paused by the woman on the motorcycle. He smiled at the smoke-gray visor. "Nice bike." He couldn't see any model or company emblems. "What kind is it?"

She kept her hands on the backrest behind her, ignoring him.

"Right." Ian smiled awkwardly, "I'll just head inside." He nodded politely to his reflection in the visor and headed toward the music.

Mick's living room seemed smaller than Ian's, but it also held a lot more than fireplace tools. Several chairs and a couch were arranged around a coffee table that held at least a dozen remotes. Shelves lined the two walls opposite the entryway, and were packed with records, tapes, CDS, and a dozen or more audio system components.

Several people were standing near the open window trying to hear each other over the music coming from speakers in every corner of the room. A man and a woman seated on the sofa were talking in sign language, and another group was admiring the sound system. The huge video screen was tuned to MTV but the music was coming from one of the CD players. A rock group Ian didn't recognize danced around the screen amid silent explosions while the audio system pumped out <u>Sell</u> <u>My</u> <u>Soul</u> by Midnight Oil.

Ian walked through the living room and into the hall, where he was tackled by a little boy with short black hair, dark brown eyes and a very embarrassed smile. Unwrapping himself from around Ian's leg, the boy said something Ian couldn't quite hear and rocketed off into the living room. The stereo volume, both inside and outside the house, dropped by half and the boy returned, slipping past Ian to head toward the kitchen. Ian followed. The little boy continued through the kitchen and out into the back yard, but Ian stopped to watch the action in the kitchen.

"Budweiser is not a soft drink!" The woman had black hair, dark brown eyes and a golden brown complexion. She was winning a tug-of-war with an older version of the boy Ian had collided with in the hall. The prize was a can of beer, and both of them were laughing. "You can try it when you're twenty-one, if you live that long!" She tickled the kid's stomach with one hand and wrested the can free with the other. "There's Coke on ice outside."

"Coke?" The boy grimaced dramatically. "Curses, foiled again!" He slunk toward the sliding-glass door like a thwarted arch-villain but slipped out of character at the threshold and ran outside. He dodged around several grownups and dug a dripping red can out of a large blue ice chest.

Ian looked back to the woman with the liberated Budweiser. "He's cute."

"Thanks." She smiled.

"My name's Ian."

"Clara Dale." She passed the Budweiser to her left hand and extended her right. Ian did the same with his empty Henry's and they shook hands.

"Ian MacAran. I just met Mick this morning."

"Oh! You're the pilot from across the street, right?"

"Right." Ian was holding the bottle on its side. "Welcome to the neighborhood."

"Thank you. Would you like another beer?" Clara started to give Ian the beer in her hand but changed her mind. "Let me get you one that won't explode." She took Ian's empty and pulled a calmer Budweiser out of the fridge.

"Thanks. Have you..."

Ian was interrupted by the high-speed return of the former arch-villain. The boy did a vocal rendition of screeching brakes and crunching metal as he came to a stop. "Ken needs some more stuff."

"Okay." Clara opened the fridge and pulled out a large cookie sheet covered with shish-ka-bobs and another full of chicken. When she turned around, her son was gone. "That's helpful."

Ian laughed. "Can I give you a hand?"

"Thank you." Clara gave Ian one of the trays. He followed her out into the yard and the loudest part of the party. Speakers in several windows and on the lawn seemed to turn the whole outdoors into a sound studio. There were a few people Ian had seen in the neighborhood and a lot of people he'd never seen before. They mixed together in groups that changed and shifted as people got beers or sodas from the coolers, made sandwiches at a long table on the patio, or just got tired of that moment's conversation. A gas grill was set up on the far corner of the patio and a short blond guy with a dark tan was cooking chicken and shish-ka-bobs. The arch-villain and his younger look-alike were watching the transformation of "stuff" into dinner.

Clara introduced Ian to Ken, the chef at the grill, her older son Xavier and her younger son Zachary. Xavier was very polite, "Pleased to meet you, Mr. MacAran." Zachary just said "Hi." They both shook Ian's hand when he offered it, and then blasted away at full speed as soon as Ken handed them each a shish-ka-bob.

Clara gathered the empty trays that Ken had stacked on the grill's fold-out shelf. "Make yourself at home, Ian." She headed back toward the kitchen, stopping several times along the way to chat or to make sure everyone had enough to eat.

Ken handed Ian a shish-ka-bob. Ken was a carpenter who had been working for Mick for about a year. He was the foreman and did all of the day-to-day supervision on Mick's job sites. Ian finished his Budweiser and several shish-ka-bobs while they talked about houses and Ken's desire to move to a neighborhood like Bay Farm Island.

Ian put his empty can into a trash next to the grill. "Do you want a beer or something?"

Ken shook his head. "No thanks, I'm fine. You could get me some more barbecue sauce, though."

"In the kitchen?"

"Ask Clara, no big hurry." Ken held up a bottle with an inch or so of thick paste in the bottom. "I've got enough for now."

"Back shortly." Looking for a beer, Ian found himself in the middle of a heated discussion about someone's fitness to be a teacher. Most of those debating the issue were teachers who worked with Clara and the teacher in question. They were grouped around the coolers and Ian had to step between them to get a beer. He pulled a Michelob out of the big red ice chest and listened to the different arguments.

Those on the hinged side of the beer cooler favored a sympathetic we-learn-from-our-mistakes approach. Those on the other side argued for immediate dismissal. A thin woman wearing a black blouse with red and green roses over a black skirt covered with big white circles was pressing for termination. "He was arrested for smoking marijuana! *Marijuana*, for God's sake!" She said the last directly into Ian's left ear.

Ian took a sip of his Michelob. "Is marijuana really that different from alcohol or tobacco?"

The woman in the roses and polka-dots looked at Ian as though she'd found something crawling through her cat's litter box. "Marijuana is a drug!"

"Isn't alcohol a drug? For that matter," Ian pointed to the cans of Coke in the blue cooler. "Isn't caffeine a drug, too?"

"Don't be ridiculous. That's different!" She looked to make sure her point wasn't being lost on her original opponents. "Marijuana is illegal!"

A thin man with red hair was shaking his head. "But that's just the point, Marge, it shouldn't be illegal. Prohibition didn't work with alcohol, and it's not working with drugs."

"Drugs are destroying our families and our communities." Marge turned away from Ian. "They're eroding the moral foundations of this country and you want to make them legal? You're a bigger fool than I thought, Robert."

"Maybe" Robert shrugged, "but are the drugs the cause of our problems or the comfort people turn to after the erosion has destroyed their dreams?"

Ian retreated to the buffet.

A picnic table next to the house was covered with everything a barbecue gourmet could ask for. Chips, dips, crackers, and condiments shared the red and white-checkered cloth with shish-ka-bob, chicken, hamburgers, buns and a vast assortment of fixings. A couple on the other side of the table was adding shredded cheddar cheese to two huge hamburgers. Ian wasn't sure but he thought he'd seen them in the Safeway. "Hello, my name's Ian."

John Fouches introduced himself and his wife Betty. Ian sipped cold Michelob and enjoyed a piece of really good barbecued chicken while the two Fouches listed the places in the neighborhood they hadn't run into him. "Remarkable!" John Fouches' concluded. "We've lived only four houses away from each other for over a year and we haven't met until today!"

Betty agreed with her husband. "Remarkable!"

"My schedule can be pretty strange sometimes." Ian looked around. The party was beginning to thin out but there were still eleven or twelve people in the back yard. "Have either of you seen Mick?"

"Who?" John Fouches looked puzzled.

"Mr. Dale, silly," Betty put her arm around her husband. "Our host!"

"Oh! Right! Kitchen, last I saw."

Ian thanked them and headed for the kitchen. He didn't find Mick but he did find a recycle bin for his beer bottle and paper towels to clean the traces of barbecue sauce from his face and fingers.

Mrs. Fouches had said that the bathroom was the first door off the hallway. Ian found the right door but had to wait for someone who'd had the same idea, only a little sooner. Standing in the hall, he realized that the music had gotten much quieter.

Around the corner of the L-shaped hall, a door slammed. Ian looked toward the sound and saw the motorcycle rider heading toward him. She was looking back over her shoulder and ran right into Ian at a fast walk.

"Jesus fucking Christ!" Terri took a short step back. "Watch where you're going!" She didn't wait for him to let her past. Terri was much shorter than Ian but she put all of her strength into pushing him out of her way. Ian took a step back to keep his balance. The empty saddlebags Terri had draped over her arm swung gently into Ian's crotch, adding a bizarre element of intimacy to the encounter.

"Excuse you!" Ian said it jokingly as he smiled down at the short brown hair, brown eyes and pale white skin.

"Fuck you!" She walked past him.

"Another time." Ian said to her retreating back. "Maybe when hell freezes over!" The music went quiet for a moment and he heard the motorcycle start, rev and then accelerate through smoothly shifted gears.

The wall of sound returned, the bathroom door opened and Robert, the man with the red hair, emerged. He and Ian nodded to each other and Ian took his turn. A poster of penguins wreaking havoc in an upright freezer hung in a frame over the toilet, and there were penguins on the towels and the shower curtain. Through the wall, Ian could hear a man and a woman arguing. He couldn't separate their conversation from the song on the CD player, until the woman shouted, "Not in the house, Mick!" It sounded like Clara.

"I didn't know she was coming!" sounded like Mick. "And I *never* told her to come *here*!"

Rushing water made all the background noise unintelligible and when Ian turned the faucet off the argument had stopped. He dried his hands on a terry cloth montage of amorous penguins and went back to the party.

Clara wasn't in the kitchen but there was a full bottle of barbecue sauce on the counter. Ian took it out to the patio.

The teachers had moved their debate to a picnic table on the grass, leaving the beer and soda coolers un-chaperoned. Ian looked at the selection of bottles and cans and pulled a root beer out of the soft drink cooler. Ken was watching ground beef become hamburgers. Ian set the barbecue sauce on the folding table next to the grill.

"Thanks." Ken tossed the empty sauce bottle into the trash and set the new bottle next to his tea.

"No problem." Ian moved away from the thin smoke rising off the grill.

"Hey pilot!" Mick had a Budweiser in one hand and a chicken thigh in the other. He cleaned the thigh down to the bone as he walked over to the grill and threw the bone in the garbage bag behind Ken. "Great chicken, Ken-meister, you're gonna make somebody a fine wife someday."

"Piss off!" Ken laughed and turned the burgers over.

"Cook some more chicken, will ya?" Mick headed away from the grill. "Ian, come here and take a look at this." Mick went to a ladder that was leaning against the side of the house and started climbing. Ian watched him step off the ladder and onto the roof. "Come on up!"

Mick's head and shoulders were outlined against the reddening sky.

Ian went on up.

The roof was covered with asphalt shingles that sloped gently up to the ridge. In the fading light, the roof and the trees around it were beginning to share the same shades of gray. Mick had gone to the very edge of the ridge and was looking out toward San Francisco. Ian stopped next to him and took a sip of root beer.

"Beautiful, isn't it?" Mick swirled the last few ounces of beer around the bottom of his can.

The usual Northern California coastal fog could be seen pressing against the hills from just north of San Jose all along the coast to San Francisco. The towers of the financial district were beginning to light up under the fog, while the sky above was a swirl of orange, blue, grey and red. Colors combined in a mad palette that formed and faded as the earth turned away from the sun. Streetlights seemed to get brighter, office lights became visible and soon the spectacle was of mostly man-made light under innumerable stars.

Mick shook his head. "Is this a view or what?"

"It's definitely a view."

"Look at all those planes." Mick pointed toward the southwest. Over a dozen points of light, too bright to be stars, were strung out in a line that ended at San Francisco International Airport. "You know, I've done hundreds of takeoffs, mostly in helicopters, but only a couple of landings."

"How's that?"

"101st Airborne. We jumped out, but I've always wanted to learn to fly."

"I've always wanted to try skydiving but I've never had the time." Ian shook his head. "Besides, why would anyone want to jump out of a perfectly good airplane?"

Mick laughed. "Because it's a total rush. I'm telling you, Ian, it's better than sex."

"Better?"

Mick considered. "Well, it depends on who you're with."

They both laughed.

"Jumping off the roof, on the other hand, I don't recommend." Mick started back toward the ladder. The ladder was easy to see against the floodlit backyard and Mick walked down with his back to it as though the rungs were stairs. He waited at the bottom for Ian to come down the conventional way. "What would it cost to get a pilot's license?"

"About ten grand, but it makes more sense to think of it as a few hundred an hour, depending on the airplane, and an hour of flight time costs the same the day after you get your pilot's license as it does the day before."

"What's your point?"

Ian smiled. "You've got to enjoy it. Otherwise you're wasting your money no matter what it costs."

Mick tossed his empty beer can in a long arc that fell just short of the trash can next to Ken and the grill. "Ten grand is nothing. Want another beer?" He headed for the cooler.

Clara Dale stopped Ian before he could follow her husband. "Ian! What in the world did you say to Margaret?"

"Who?"

"Margaret Stevenson," Clara looked around but her coworker had already left. "The thin woman in that terrible flowery blouse with the black and white skirt."

"Oh!" Ian took a Budweiser from Mick, who had brought two. Mick took Ian's empty root beer can and tossed it in Ken's general direction. The can flew high and wide but Ken hit it with his spatula and it dropped into the trash.

Ian shrugged. "I just said that I didn't see any difference between legalizing marijuana and legalizing alcohol."

"That explains it." Clara pushed Mick's hand away from her waist. "Marge likes a martini or three for lunch but she thinks illegal drugs are destroying America. I don't think comparing the two is something she's ready for."

"I don't think having an I.Q. is something she's ready for, either." Mick looked disgusted. "She's such a bitch."

"She's not a bitch!" Clara glared at Mick and turned back to Ian. "She has some personal problems and I think that clouds her judgment sometimes. She does put a lot of time and effort into drug prevention programs. She just takes the war on drugs very personally."

"Do either of you think this 'war on drugs' is getting a little scary?"

"What do you mean?"

"Well, first the government suspended the rights of *suspected* drug dealers with a so-called 'state of emergency'. Now they want to shoot down airplanes that they think might be carrying drugs."

"Wait a minute." Mick held up his beer as though that would make the conversation clearer. "You can't shoot a suspect without provocation."

"That's what pilots' groups have been telling Congress every time a law like this gets proposed. The latest version would allow the Air Force or Coast Guard, or whatever authorities are involved to just shoot down any aircraft that fails to follow their instructions, or fails to respond when hailed."

"Sounds like 'Halt or I'll shoot!'" Mick smiled as Clara finally let him put his arm around her waist.

"Exactly," Ian nodded. "But what if you're yelling at someone who can't hear? What if the plane you're hailing is on the wrong frequency, or has radio failure. Do you shoot him down? You'd be handing out a death sentence without trial for equipment failure!"

Clara shook her head. "Drugs aren't a national security issue, they're a health problem. We should be spending all this time and money on education and health care."

Mick chuckled. "Spoken like the quintessential educator."

"You turkey!" Clara gave him a playful punch in the ribs. "What do you know about education?"

"Hey I remembered 'quintessential'!"

"Only because I used it beating you at Scrabble!" Clara kissed him.

A little girl with Clara's dark eyes and black hair ran up and tugged on Clara's dress. "Zach is asleep under the picnic table."

"He is?" Clara picked up the little girl. "Ian, this is our daughter, Yolanda."

Ian smiled. "Hi, Yolanda."

"Hi." She turned away and wrapped her arms around her mother's neck. The shyness only lasted a moment, and then Yolanda leaned back to look at her mother. "Xavier says the ants will take Zach away unless we rescue him."

"Okay." Clara sounded serious. "We'll rescue him right away." She set Yolanda back down on the bricks. "Excuse us, we have to rescue Zach." Clara followed her daughter over to the far picnic table.

Ian looked at his watch. "Mick, I'm about to crawl under a picnic table myself." He extended his hand. "Thanks for inviting me. It was fun."

"Thanks for coming." Mick shook Ian's hand and held onto it. "When can we go flying?"

Ian considered. "If you're serious, I'm off tomorrow. We could go then."

"That would be great!"

"How about noon?"

"Uh, noon should work. I've got a couple errands to run, but yeah, I'm there man. Excellent!" Mick hesitated, "Where is *there*?""

Ian told Mick how to get to the flight club, waved goodbye to Ken and headed back through Mick's house toward home. The music in the living room was less deafening, and the couple Ian had seen using sign language earlier was necking on the couch.

Ian's house was dark and quiet. He locked the door, turned on the hall lights, and tossed his keys next to the phone on the kitchen counter. There was one message on the ancient answering machine:

"MacAran? What's wrong with your goddamn cell phone?" Ace Quintero called all his employees by their last names. Ian's cell was still plugged into the wall recharging its battery. "I'm still in Hawaii, God Dammit! Looks like I'm stuck here through Tuesday. My *sixty-seven year old* wife wants to go *scuba diving*! Can you believe that? I'm telling you boy, the sharks are in for some competition!" Quintero laughed. "Thanks for flying this morning, Boy-o. Take tomorrow off. Monday, I want you in Vegas to pick up the whole OHI group and take 'em to Chicago. You'll bring 'em back to Oakland Tuesday night. They want you at McCarran at eleven. Okay? I guess Harry could've told you all this; I just wanted to say hi." Ace coughed. "I'll talk to you Wednesday. Bye."

"You got it, Ace." Ian reset the machine, turned out the lights and went to bed.

Sunday, 2:06 pm – Shooting Thru 3,500
Feet, Fourteen Miles North of Oakland

"Whoa! *Level* flight, Mick!" Ian's seatbelt dug into his lap as Mick pushed the wheel forward and the plane dove for the ground. "Don't chase the altimeter; just look outside and put the horizon two fingers above the nose." Ian held two fingers above the glaresheild to give Mick the picture. With his other hand he opened the vent by the right wing to bring more cool air into the cabin. "Try to loosen up a little. The more you look outside and enjoy the view, the easier this gets." Ian's hand was poised inches from the wheel but he wanted Mick to get the plane under control on his own. "Just relax."

"I am relaxed!" There was a gap of several inches between Mick's Death Records T-shirt and the beige leather seat. He had both hands clenched around the yoke and his knuckles were as white as the underside of the four-seat Cessna. As they nosed over the top of another Mick-induced roller coaster, Mick forced himself to look outside and ignore the altimeter. He tore one hand away from the wheel long enough to raise two fingers up to the windscreen. He held his index finger even with the horizon and pulled the wheel back just enough to bring the engine cowl up to his ring finger.

With the nose of the plane two level fingers below the horizon the red and white 172 settled into straight and level flight.

"There ya go!" Ian was looking for other airplanes and taking in the scenery. The storm front that was due to hit late Monday evening was already affecting the Bay Area. Winds had blown the urban haze east, and San Francisco shone like a picture postcard under high layers of puffy cumulus clouds. San Pablo Reservoir and Contra Costa County were spread out below them like a satellite photo. Ian was wearing one of his white uniform shirts but he'd left his tie at home. "That's looking good, Mick. Let's try a shallow left turn. Use..."

Mick twisted the yoke to the left and the plane banked left, but the nose jerked a bit to the right before it swung into the steep left turn.

"Use some left rudder, Mick... "

Mick stepped on the rudder pedal and the plane's nose lurched to the left.

"Gently! You have to use rudder and ailerons together if you want a coordinated turn. That's better. Now, hold this bank and pull back a little to hold your altitude." Ian nodded as the plane began to respond to Mick, rather than the other way 'round. "Watch the horizon, and ease off on the rudder. That's it. You only need rudder to start the turn."

Mick was leaning toward Ian as if to keep from falling out, but he wasn't hunched so far forward.

"You're doing fine, Mick. Just drag the nose along the horizon." Ian looked at his watch, and waited until the plane was turning through southwest. "Let's level off and head southeast; fly a heading of 140. We'll refuel at Hayward and then go back to Oakland."

"Okay." Mick watched the gyrocompass as it swept toward 140. "I want to start the roll out about fifteen degrees early, right?"

"That's right."

Mick started to level off as the plane passed through south. He remembered to use the rudder and rolled smoothly back to wings-level.

"That was better." Ian smiled. "That was much better."

"Thanks." Mick stopped leaning toward Ian and glanced down at the reservoir. "What would we do if the engine quit?"

"We'd figure out why it quit and restart it." Ian pointed to another plane, three miles away, headed toward them. "Always keep looking for other aircraft."

"Right." Mick nodded. The other plane moved to their left and passed within about a mile. Mick watched it carefully. "What if you can't restart the engine?"

"Well, we'd have to land."

Mick looked outside. "Where?" Ahead of them, the rolling hills surrounding the reservoir gave way to the homes and power lines of Orinda. The suburban town with its rural charm was bisected by eight lanes of freeway with train tracks in the center divide. Beyond the freeway lay more hills and a chain of small lakes.

"Best place we can find." Ian looked down to his right, and then across Mick at the terrain to their left. "Take a look; where would you land?"

"There's a parking lot..."

"Yeah. What about the light poles?"

"The freeway?"

"That's where I'd go." Ian nodded. "Though that would depend on the traffic. Your best bet is a dry, open field, but I don't see one we could glide to. The freeway would be okay if there aren't too many cars and they're all moving at the limit, but then you're counting on the other drivers to see you, and planes don't have brake lights. Hell, somebody might think you're trying to merge and cut you off!"

Mick nodded. "There are a lot of idiots loose on the freeway!"

"Tell me about it!" Ian nodded too. "On the way to the airport this morning I got passed by a Porsche going about a hundred and twenty and we weren't even on the freeway!"

"Where were you?"

"Passing FedEx on Doolittle Drive."

"When?"

"About 11:45."

"Brand new, jet black Cabriolet?"

"It was black…"

"Dude! That was me!"

"What?"

"Yeah, I picked it up yesterday. Sweet car, man. I'll let you drive it when we get back."

"What were you thinking driving 120 on a city street?"

"130, but Doolittle isn't really in the city." Mick shrugged. "It's hard to drive 55 in a Porsche."

"Are you crazy? You could have killed someone! Jesus!" Ian glared at Mick for a second but forced his attention back outside the plane. "Look, this isn't the time, or the place. See that lake just ahead?"

"Yeah."

"That's Lake Chabot. Head for it."

"Okay."

Ian adjusted the radio frequency to Hayward airport's automated terminal information service, or ATIS. "First we find out what runway Hayward is using and what the wind is like. Reduce your power to 1800 rpm, and let the plane descend so our airspeed stays at 110 knots."

Mick pulled the throttle back too far and the tachometer dropped to 1000 rpm. He shoved it forward and the engine revved up to 2100 rpm.

"Gently!"

Tweaking the throttle back and forth, Mick eventually got the needle to stop near 1800 rpm. Their rate of descent smoothed out to 500 feet per minute. "Can I do the landing?"

"No!" Ian said it harshly, but in a friendlier voice he added, "It's a little early for that, but you can do the takeoff."

"Excellent!"

Ian clenched his jaw and pointed to their left, toward Lake Chabot. "Turn left and head for that lake."

Mick pointed through the faint blur of the propeller. "But Hayward's straight ahead."

"I have the airplane." Ian used the controls on his side to turn the plane to the left. Mick resisted for a second, but quickly let go of the controls. "Oakland Airport is also straight ahead, Mick and that's class C airspace that we haven't been cleared to go into."

"Oh." Mick nodded.

Ian rolled the wings back to level. The C-shaped lake was centered in the windscreen. "You want to run into a 737?"

"No." Mick shook his head.

When they reached Lake Chabot, Ian let Mick start flying again. He reported their position and Hayward Tower cleared them to land. Ian talked Mick through the approach, but when they were a mile from the runway, Ian took over and demonstrated a normal landing. He taxied to the fuel island and showed Mick how to follow the shutdown checklist. Suddenly the only sound in the Cessna's cabin was the hum of the gyroscopic instruments as they slowly wound down.

Ian took his headset off and set it over the right side of his yoke. "That was interesting." He reached in front of Mick, pulled the key out of the ignition and dropped it into his shirt pocket.

"That was great!" Mick followed Ian's example and hung his borrowed headset over the yoke in front of him. "I want to do it, man; I want to get my pilot's license!"

Ian had opened his door and was stepping out of the plane.

"Where are you going?"

"Restroom." Ian waved at the guy pumping avgas into the plane ahead of them.

The attendant waved back. "It'll be about fifteen minutes."

"Okay." Ian walked across the ramp toward a hanger with large signs that advertised B & B Electric and Seagull Aviation.

Mick had a moment's trouble with the door but he quickly caught up with Ian. "What's next?"

"Take a break. I'm going to the bathroom."

"Right." Mick followed Ian toward the hangar. "What do I have to do to get my pilot's license?"

"Technically, it's a certificate, not a license, and all you need to do is learn to fly."

"How long will it take? How many hours do I need?"

"One step at a time, Mick. Relax. Let yourself enjoy it." Ian sighed. "Stop trying to conquer everything in your path!"

Mick shook his head. "I'm not trying to conquer anything!"

"You're not listening!" Ian stopped walking. "You're charging into this as if anybody could just hop into an airplane and become an instant expert! That's not going to happen. You have to learn how to fly, and that means you have to let me teach you, but I can't teach you anything if you don't listen! If I tell you to turn left, trust me, you want to turn left! Ask me why we're turning left after you start the turn."

"I just..."

"And you're still not listening!" Ian stepped toward Mick. "If I tell you to head toward Lake Chabot, I expect you to head toward Lake Chabot! I do not expect you to fly into Oakland's airspace without a clearance!"

"I..."

"Don't equivocate, don't rationalize; just listen!" Ian stepped closer and glared into Mick's eyes. "There's more to being a pilot than making turns and holding altitude!

Any Chimpanzee can do that! You have to think about the safety of everyone in and around your plane. If you can't take that responsibility seriously, you can't be a pilot!"

"Okay, okay!" Mick looked at his feet. "I see your point."

"I hope so." Ian pointed his finger at Mick's chest. "Because if you try to fly airplanes the same way you drive your Goddamned Porsche, I have an obligation to make sure the FAA never *issues* you a pilot certificate!"

They were interrupted by an old man in a new cowboy hat. "Hey, Sky-king!" Under the fancy Stetson and gray hair he wore a faded bomber jacket, blue jeans, and brown boots. Short and wiry, he walked toward them with a slight limp.

"Hi, Wally!" Ian held out his hand and Wally shook it enthusiastically.

"Not interrupting anything, am I?"

"Not really." Ian glanced at Mick. "Wally, this is Mick Dale; Mick, Wally Prescott."

"Glad to meet you, Nick." Wally nodded absently toward Mick. "Ian, you've got to take a look at my new GPS!" Wally pointed to a large black seaplane that had its nose and left wing in the B&B hangar. The seaplane was much larger than the Cessnas and Pipers tied down outside the hanger. Its right wing extended out over a Cessna 182 parked next to the airport fence, and its tail rose several feet above the top of the hanger doors. Small white numbers under a greenhouse-like window read N1292W.

Wally smiled. "This Global Positioning System is the neatest gizmo I've put into her yet! With all the satellites operational, you can pinpoint your position to within a few feet, anywhere in the world!"

"Why do you keep putting new equipment into 92-Whiskey? I thought you wanted to sell her."

"Where'd you get that idea? I don't want to sell!" Wally was a little shorter than Mick with thick grey hair and a matching mustache. "Okay, I have to sell eventually, but I can still fly her until you're ready to buy her."

Ian laughed. "You're as bad as I am! I know I have to sell my house, so I bought a new lawn-mower!"

"Sell the house!" Wally cuffed Ian on the shoulder. "Then you can sell the lawnmower to whoever buys the house and then you'll have enough money to buy 92 Whiskey. Did I mention it has a brand new G.P.S.?"

"Wally, if I sell my house where will I sleep?"

"Sleep in the Catalina!" Wally lowered his voice, "I do. You know, when Carol gets *particularly* pissed off at me."

Ian shook his head. "You'll have to wait till I hit the lottery, Wally. I'll be lucky if I can sell the house for what I owe on it!" Ian and Mick moved into the hangar and walked around the nose of the big seaplane.

Wally walked next to Ian. "But you do *want* to buy her, right?"

Ian looked at the wing. His eyes traveled along the leading edge to the engine nacelle. "Oh yeah, I want to, but..."

"Good! I wouldn't trust her with anyone else!" Wally looked away for a second and then his face lit up with inspiration. "Tell you what: just buy half! We'll incorporate or whatever as partners!" He nodded to himself as if that settled it. "How'd the interview with Virgin go?"

"Except for my being forty-two instead of twenty-two, I thought it went great!" Ian shrugged. "They said they might call me."

"So you've got a chance. That's a start!"

Mick walked over to get a better look at the seaplane. "What kind of plane is this?"

"PBY-6A Catalina." Wally pointed to a patch on his jacket that said 'Black Cats' above an angry cat carrying a bomb. "My Granddad flew the 5A in the war."

Mick nodded. "I think I've seen it before; do you do air shows with this?"

Wally smiled. "Whenever I can."

Mick nodded. "I thought so. How much are you selling it for?"

"Depends on who's buying."

"Why?"

"Well, I don't want to sell her to just anybody." Wally stroked the side of the plane affectionately. "This is a classic World War Two Warbird in *better* than new condition. I want the person who buys her to take good care of her."

"Give me a ballpark." Mick put his foot up on the main wheel. "How much, approximately?"

Wally glanced at Ian and then studied Mick for a moment. "Three million, five hundred twenty two thousand, eight hundred thirty dollars."

"Three..."

"Plus tax."

Ian smiled. "Approximately."

"Approximately." Wally looked at his watch. "Oh, she's gonna kill me!" Wally turned to walk away and then turned back. "Gentlemen, I gotta go. I'll see you later, Ian." He turned away again. "Nice meeting you, Nick." Wally walked through the hangar and out the other side.

Mick turned to Ian. "Is he for real?"

"Oh yeah. Wally was one of my flight instructors, one of the best. I got my commercial and seaplane ratings with him." Ian looked at his watch. "Let's hit the restroom and then get back in the air."

"Okay." Mick started to follow Ian, but Ian stopped after a step and turned to face him.

"Mick, I meant it when I said this is supposed to be fun, but I also meant what I said about responsibility. The number one killer of perfectly good airplanes is the pilot's bad attitude."

"I'll work on it."

"Good." Ian nodded and started walking again.

The restrooms were in a suite of offices attached to the other side of the hangar. Ian led the way through the hangar and around the airplanes parked inside. Most of the planes had access panels removed and there were technicians working on a few of them. Mick stopped to look through the side window of a tan and gold business jet. He whistled. "This is plush." He pointed to the ACE logo on the door. "Isn't that the company you work for?"

Ian hadn't stopped and Mick had to run to catch up. "Ian, how much weight can one of those carry?"

"One of what?" Ian pushed open the Men's Room door. "Depends on the plane."

"That PBY-6A we just looked at or a jet like that Lear in the hanger."

"Lear?" Ian thought for a moment. "That's a Citation. Cessna makes those. Same company that built the 172 we're flying. With full fuel, that Citation can carry about 900 pounds."

"Is that all?"

"Full fuel is almost 6000 pounds of Jet A. That'll carry five people almost two thousand miles! You can carry more cargo if you carry less fuel, but then you can't go as far without refueling."

"Makes sense. Is that Citation one of your jets?"

"One of Ace's. It's down here getting the autopilot fixed." They washed up and headed back through the hanger. Ian paused to look at his favorite plane. "She sure is beautiful."

"Yeah." Mick walked over to look in through waist turret. "Are you going to buy it?"

Ian shook his head. "Not on my salary."

"You never know." They started walking toward the fuel island. "Do you have to file a flight plan if you're going to another city?"

"It's a good idea, but no, you don't have to."

"What about Mexico?"

"You have to file to cross the border and you have to go through customs, but it's not complicated."

"How long does it take them to search the plane?"

"Well, usually they don't."

"They don't?"

"Not really. We check in with customs in Oakland, they go over the paperwork and we're on our way. Usually the same story on the way back." Ian shrugged. "We always end up with a bottle of tequila or something over the duty-free limit. They never check that closely."

"I thought you had to stop at the border."

"Not if you have an over-flight exemption." The fuel attendant handed Ian a clipboard with their fuel slip attached. Ian signed the form, tore off the top copy and handed the clipboard back. "Thanks." He folded his copy in half and slipped it into his shirt pocket.

Mick waited for the attendant to move on to the next plane. "What's an over-flight exemption?"

"It lets you cross the border without having to land and go through customs at the first available airport. We fill out a lot of paperwork and tell customs all the details of each flight and they let us check in with them in Oakland or Chicago or wherever. That way we don't have to waste time descending, stopping, and then climbing out of someplace along the border like Calexico." Ian got into the right seat of the red and white 172 and buckled himself in.

Mick got into the left seat. "You could bring in a whole plane load if you wanted to."

Ian laughed. "Yeah, but who needs that much tequila?"

"I was thinking about something with a much higher resale value."

"What, Dos Equis?"

Mick buckled his seatbelt. "Cocaine."

"No." Ian shook his head.

"It would be completely safe."

"And completely illegal."

"Technically, you could say that." Mick sounded serious.

"Technically you could lose your certificate! Hell, you could go to jail!"

"But think of it: you could make two hundred grand on a single trip."

Ian shook his head again. "No thanks." He took out the checklists but stopped and looked directly at Mick. "Have you ever done anything like that?"

"Smuggle a plane into the U.S.?" Mick smiled. "No."

"Good." Ian turned the pages to the before-start checklist. "You can't even get a medical certificate if you've had anything to do with drugs." He slipped on his headset. "Ready to do a takeoff?"

Mick pulled his own headset over his ears. "You bet!"

Ian handed him the checklist. "Let's go."

Back in Oakland, Mick's cell phone rang just as he and Ian finished connecting the tie down chains. Mick looked at the caller ID and then pressed the call button.

"Ken-ster! What's up?" As Mick listened his expression swung from amiable to furious before settling on annoyed. "Okay. I'll be right there." He closed the phone and turned to Ian.

"Thanks again, man; that was an absolute blast! How much do I owe you?"

"Let's go inside and get you signed up."

"Can I just give you the money and do the paperwork next time? I've got a crew burning daylight and two concrete trucks waiting for a replacement pumper."

"Sure. The plane will be $140. Ground and flight instruction totaled three hours for $150, so, $290."

Mick's eyes widened in disbelief. "You're only charging fifty dollars an hour?"

Ian nodded, "That's the club rate."

"Jesus! That's less than my carpenters make!" Mick pulled a mass of bills from his left front pocket, counted out $140 and handed it to Ian. "That's for the plane." He peeled three hundred dollar bills off the back of the stack and handed them to Ian. "And that's for your time."

Ian laughed. "What's this, a tip?"

"A raise."

"Uh," Ian hesitated, but folded the bills in half and slid them into his shirt pocket. "Thanks."

"When can we fly again?"

Ian considered. "Same time next week should work for me."

Mick shook his head. "What about tomorrow?"

"I'm working tomorrow. Besides, you've got some reading to do before we go up again. I gave you the booklist, right?"

Mick patted his back pocket. "Got it."

"Good. How about Wednesday?"

Mick nodded enthusiastically. "Yeah, I can arrange that. That's the nice thing about being the boss. Noon on Wednesday?"

"I'll be on call in the afternoon. Better make it earlier: nine o'clock?"

"Damn! That's way too early!" Mick shuddered but nodded agreeably. "But alright. I'll see you at nine."

CHAPTER TWO

Monday, 4:07 pm – Roof of, A#1
Market, East Oakland

Jamaal watched the white and red airplane as it crossed the freeway a thousand feet above East Oakland. It was headed right for another plane, going the opposite direction toward the airport. The second plane was white and blue and Jamaal liked it better because it looked less boxy and with its wheels retracted it looked more like a jet. The red plane's wheels hung out from its sides and made it look like a drunken seagull. It wasn't until they seemed to touch that Jamaal realized that the blue plane was much lower than the red one. He watched, fascinated as the wheels extended under the blue plane's wings. He still thought it looked cooler than the red one, even with its Tonka Toy wheels out.

The cell phone in his left hand buzzed and Jamaal pressed 'talk'. "Lookout one."

"Baby Jay, how's it look?"

Jamaal rolled his eyes. "I don't know who you think you're talkin' to, Richard, but I ain't nobody's *baby.*"

"Damnit Jamaal! Don't say 'Richard' on the phone!"

"You call me 'X-ray' like you promised."

"Okay, what's your status?"

Jamaal didn't say anything. Although he was two years younger than his do-it-or-else fourteen year old half-brother, Jamaal was smarter. Richard was bigger, faster, and stronger; he could outrun and out-slug Jamaal and he won all their fights, but Jamaal won most of the arguments. He waited.

"Okay, oh-goddamn-kay! X-ray, what's your status?"

Jamaal looked around. From the roof of the boarded-up grocery store he could see anything that happened on the corner and down streets in four directions. "I'm hungry."

"Little X-ray, I'm gonna kick your 'A', if you don't answer right away!" Richard rapped it cool, but there was passion in the lyric that Jamaal knew he'd better take seriously.

"I'm cool, everything's cool."

"Good."

Jamaal looked around for something on the roof to kill the boredom, but a minute later a black Camaro turned the far corner and stopped across the street. Jamaal watched it. There were three guys in the car. The one in the back seat handed what looked like a shotgun to the guy next to the driver. The car rolled forward, picked up speed, and turned down the street toward the Royal Oak Apartments. Richard and the rest of the gang were closing a deal in the condemned Royal Oak building in the middle of the block. When the Camaro slowed down, Jamaal sounded the alarm. "Doctor D! Doctor D! There's a black Camaro stopping outside." He looked at the phone, but the call had dropped out. He hit redial and listened through four long rings for Richard to answer. The black muscle-car bounced up onto the sidewalk in the middle of the block and two guys with guns jumped out. They ran into the building where Jamaal's gang, the X-Men were buying five thousand dollars worth of cocaine.

Finally Richard answered, *"Yeah?"*

"There's guys downstairs, they're going' inside! They got guns!"

"Everybody out of here!" Richard yelled. *"Jamaal, run!"*

One shot was fired. Jamaal heard the shot echoing from down the block and then heard it over the cell. There was another single shot and then Jamaal heard frenzied gunfire. Thunderous blasts from a shotgun were connected by strings of firecracker pops from something automatic. Jamaal shoved the still open phone into his pocket and jumped off the roof onto an overflowing dumpster. He bounced sideways, but landed on his feet in the alley behind the gas station. The staccato gunfire slowed to intermittent shots, then all was quiet. Jamaal looked around the corner and up the sidewalk. A last shot within the building echoed from the cell phone a heartbeat later.

The Camaro sat half on the sidewalk and half on the street with the motor running and the passenger side door open. The two men ran out of the old building, and the first one, probably about twenty, dove headfirst into the back seat of the car. He was carrying some kind of machine pistol and the gym bag Richard had brought the money in. The second one was older. He pulled the door shut as the driver pressed too hard on the accelerator. The Camaro screamed through a smoky U-turn that left an oily cloud and the stink of burning rubber in the air. As it headed back toward East 14th Street, nobody noticed Jamaal crouched in the alley beside the liquor store.

Jamaal ran toward the Royal Oak Apartments, but turned down a breeze-way between the condemned apartment building and an old dry cleaners. The narrow path ended at a chain link fence, which Jamaal leapt onto with practiced ease. He pulled himself up, and was almost over, when he got hung up in the barbed wire at the top. Jamaal jerked himself free and jumped to the narrow sidewalk between the fence and the worn brick building. The barbed wire left several cuts on his arms and a deep gash in his left leg. Jamaal pushed a half-sheet of battered plywood to the side of one of the boarded up windows and slid into the first floor apartment. He took out the cell, folded it shut and slid it back into his pocket.

Something scurried around a corner and into the hall. Jamaal listened for a moment as his eyes adjusted to the boarded-up darkness. Nothing else moved. He went into the kitchen, climbed onto the counter and levered himself up through the hole they had made in the ceiling. The rear apartment on the second floor had been the perfect place to meet and the best way to get to it was through the first floor unit.

They had called themselves the X-Men, first after the comic books and then, when they got a little older, after Malcolm X himself. The oldest, Keenan, was sixteen. He had even talked about changing his name to Malcolm.

Now he was laying half in the kitchen and half in the hall with his revolver in his hand. A track of bullet holes wound around his body like lights on a Christmas tree.

Jamaal had seen dead people before, but never someone he knew. A long minute passed before Jamaal could step over Keenan and into the hall. He picked up Keenan's revolver, sliding it out of the dead boy's fingers. The hand rose a bit and then thumped to the floor when the fingers let go. Jamaal jumped away from Keenan's body and almost dropped the gun. It was heavy for the twelve year old. He held it in both hands, the way Richard had showed him.

Chris was on his back on the dining room table. Jamaal only knew it was Chris because he was wearing Jamaal's old Oakland Raiders sweatshirt. Jamaal had outgrown the shirt but it still fit Chris, even though Chris was four years older. It had been his idea to sell crack. He had set up the buys and figured out the best ways to sell the stuff. Chris had made all of their families' lives a lot easier, and his mother had been very proud of him. Most of Chris' face was missing. Jamaal wiped a tear from his cheek and choked back a wave of despair.

Jamaal didn't recognize most of the boys in the living room. The only one who belonged to the X-Men was Keenan's brother Lonnie. All were dead. Keenan's gun pointed absently toward the floor, holding Jamaal's hands together as if in prayer.

Richard was in the hall. The two cell phones he'd used to talk to the lookouts had fallen behind him. They started a dashed line that ended in wet red circles from his left thigh to his neck. He hadn't been able to outrun the bullets.

Jamaal set the gun on the floor and lifted Richard's head off the dirty green linoleum. He gently rolled his brother over onto his back. Air escaped from the dead boy's lungs in a rattle that blew away the last of Jamaal's cool. He leaned against the wall, sank down next to his brother and began to cry.

A siren wailed far away. When another siren went off much closer, Jamaal picked up the gun and stood. He looked down at his brother as his sock soaked up the blood from the cut on his leg. When he heard voices outside the apartment, Jamaal glanced down the hall. "I gotta find Jesus." He slipped the gun into his pocket. "Goodbye, Richard."

Tuesday, 1:08 pm – New Meigs Field, Chicago

"I think she likes you." Rashad drank the last of his iced tea as he looked at Ian through the bottom of the glass.

"Right." Ian laughed.

Rashad leaned forward and put his glass down on the short table between their chairs. "I am serious! I think she really likes you."

"She's said 'Hello' three times, 'Thank you' twice, and 'See you in the morning.' I don't think she's interested in me. What interests Ms. Sandra Taylor is International Crane and Rigging."

"But you are interested in her, are you not?"

"No!"

"Then why are you keeping track of how many times she says 'hello'?"

Ian smiled.

"She has just been busy with those suits we picked up in Las Vegas." Rashad leaned forward. "But I think Ms. Taylor could manage a corporate takeover and a corporate pilot at the same time."

"You think?"

"I know!" Rashad nodded enthusiastically. "This could well be the woman of your dreams!"

"You're talking about a client." Ian shook his head. "Besides, I don't know anything about her."

"So get to know her!" Rashad winked.

"What is it with you? First you set me up with your girlfriend's sister and now you're playing matchmaker with the passengers!"

"She was my sister's girlfriend, and you should have given Pam a second chance."

"How can I go out with someone who hates to fly?"

"She was just a little uncomfortable."

"Pam hated the takeoff, the landing, and every hint of turbulence in between."

"That is true. But, Ian, you have to give *someone* a chance. You and Marcia broke up over a year ago."

"And your point is?"

"You need to move on. You have not even purchased any furniture!"

"What's that got to do with...? Hey! I've got furniture!"

"A couch and an old pool table?"

"That pool table is an antique! Besides, what else do you need?"

"You are sleeping on the floor!"

"I've got a bed..."

"You have a mattress!"

"It works." Ian shrugged. "Besides, I don't need any more bills."

"What you need is a life, and Sandra Taylor would be an excellent start."

"Be realistic! What chance do I stand with a woman like that? She probably makes more in a week than we do in a year."

"Which means you do not have to worry about supporting her. You should go for it, dude!"

"Dude?"

"I am trying to expand my command of the vernacular. Go for it Captain? Go for it your Eminence? Your Airworthiness..."

"Okay, okay," Ian smiled, "I'll think about it."

"Enough thinking." Rashad nodded toward the terminal's main entrance. "Here is your chance to do something about it."

Ian looked up in time to see Sandra Taylor step through the automatic doors. He glared at Rashad, "I meant I'd think about getting furniture!"

Wearing a red skirt suit with a cream blouse, Sandra was obviously the only passenger in a room full of pilots. The only other people in the terminal not wearing dark slacks, white shirts with striped epaulettes and dark ties were behind the service counter. Most of the pilots wore nondescript black shoes that blended in with the rest of the uniform, and even the women had short hair. Sandy recognized Rashad first and then saw Ian sitting next to him. Both men stood as she walked toward them, but after nodding 'hello', Rashad turned and headed out toward the airplanes. Ian met Sandra in the middle of the lobby.

"Good afternoon, Ms. Taylor." Ian pointed to her briefcase and the garment bag she had purchased in Las Vegas. "Can I carry those for you?"

"Thank you, Captain, and please, call me Sandra." She handed him the garment bag but kept her briefcase.

"If you'll call me Ian."

"It's a deal." She noticed Ian looking toward the loading zone beyond the automatic doors. "Oh, everybody else is staying. It's just me back to Oakland. I'm sorry I'm late. It's been a complicated day."

Ian smiled. "You can't be late, M... Sandra. The plane isn't scheduled to leave until you're on it." He pointed toward another pair of automatic doors with 'AUTHORIZED PERSONNEL ONLY' stenciled across the glass and they started toward them.

Sandra shook her head. "I appreciate that, but I did say I'd be here at eleven o'clock."

"It's eleven o'clock in Oakland." The doors slid open and they walked through.

"That's true." Sandra looked at her watch. "It's always the right time somewhere." The outside air was humid and smelled of Lake Michigan with a hint of jet fuel.

Rashad was looking inside the tan and gold cowling around 229's left engine. He gave Ian a thumbs-up when he saw them approaching and walked around to check the right engine.

Inside the Citation, Sandra set her briefcase on the right front seat and Ian put her garment bag in the forward closet.

"Do you really just type in a destination and let the autopilot do the work?"

Ian turned around. "What?"

"On the trip out from Las Vegas, John Geaque from ICR was saying that airplanes today are all automatic. He said it's easier than driving a bus."

"You're kidding." Ian looked at her for a moment. He couldn't tell if she was serious or not. Her professionally friendly smile could have meant anything. "Is this 'Geaque' a pilot?"

"No." Sandra sat down opposite her briefcase. "He's a soon-to-be-*former* Vice President."

Ian thought her eyes looked like the winter sky just before sunset. "Your trip was successful?"

"Phenomenally successful." Sandra grinned. "International Crane and Rigging will soon be an OHI subsidiary."

"Congratulations!"

"Thank you."

"Would you like to see what driving a bus like this is like?"

Sandra nodded. "I'd like that very much."

Ian opened the closet and pulled an extra headset out of his flight case. "This will let you hear what we're saying, and," he rotated the microphone down off the headband, "if you have any questions you can ask." He handed the headset to her.

"Thank you." She held it up and the cord dangled almost to the floor. "These earmuffs must not be very well trained, if they need a leash."

Ian laughed and showed her where the jacks plugged into her armrest.

Rashad stepped into the plane and brought the ladder up behind him. "Exterior preflight complete, Captain."

"Thanks, Rashad. If you'll brief Ms. Taylor, I'll get started up front."

"Yes sir." Rashad described the door mechanism as he closed it and reminded Sandra to keep her seatbelt on whenever possible. Rashad kept it short since it was the third time he had recited the passenger safety briefing for her. Sandra listened because it would have been rude to ignore him.

As Rashad slid into the right seat, Ian turned to check on Sandra. "Can you hear me okay?"

She shook her head. "Not through these."

Ian twisted his hand next to his left ear as though he was tightening a screw. Sandra found the volume knob on her own headset and adjusted it. She noticed that Ian's headset was much lighter, like a Walkman headphone with a lightweight microphone boom attached.

"Can you hear me now?"

Sandra nodded. "Yes, much better."

"Great. Rashad has done the exterior preflight inspection. Our next step is to start the engines."

Sandra watched and listened as the two pilots went through the Before Start and Engine Start checklists. It was obviously a familiar routine; a routine they took seriously. Each engine started with a muted whine that got louder and louder before stabilizing at an impatient whir. Rashad said, "Passenger advisory light: passenger safety," and switched the seat belt sign on.

While Rashad asked the tower for permission to taxi, Ian turned to look over his shoulder. "Once we start to taxi, we'll keep our attention completely on flying until we reach ten thousand feet. After we pass through ten thousand feet, you can come up and take a closer look, if you like."

Sandra nodded, "Great."

The tower cleared them to taxi and the plane began rolling forward. Sandra could see the masts and sails of boats on Lake Michigan, white triangles tossing under puffs of scattered clouds. Most of the boats were on tacks toward the shore, fighting the same wind that was pushing the clouds out over the lake. The plane turned toward the lake and stopped, waiting its turn for the runway.

Ian and Rashad went through the crew briefing and before takeoff checklist. Sandra watched the cloud shadows as they swept across the buildings on Lakeshore Drive and then they were moving as well. The thrum of the engines rose as the plane rolled forward to line up with the runway and then the turbine whine roared to full power. Sandra couldn't see much out the front but the view from her window was extraordinary. Mottled in sunlight and shadow, the Chicago skyline looked like a postcard. The John Hancock building and the Sears Tower dominated a vast collection of architectural styles and statements that were each state-of-the-art construction projects in their own time.

Ian banked to intercept the course they had been assigned by Clearance Delivery. "After takeoff checklist."

Rashad read down the list and Ian acknowledged each item as they climbed into the clouds.

Startled, Sandra pulled back from her window as the view of streets, cars, buildings, and people suddenly blanked to featureless white. Patches of scenery returned, visible in flashes through breaks in the cloud layer. The towering office buildings that had dominated her cab rides and strategy meetings were dwarfed by chunks of cumulus scattered across the landscape, each puff the size of a dozen city blocks.

The tower controller broke the silence in the cockpit. "229, CONTACT APPROACH."

"229, good day." Rashad switched frequencies. "Chicago Departure, Citation 229 is level at 4,000, request flight level 330."

"CITATION 229, PROCEED ON COURSE, CLIMB-MAINTAIN FLIGHT LEVEL 260. EXPECT HIGHER IN FIVE MINUTES."

Ian pulled the yoke back as he pushed the throttles forward. Rashad acknowledged the clearance. At ten thousand feet, Ian lowered the nose and set up a cruise climb at 300 knots. He glanced back at Sandra. "We've been cleared to 26,000 feet. There will be some clouds below us but nothing at our altitude. We'll be in Oakland in about four hours and they're forecasting the usual late afternoon fog with temperatures in the low fifties, and a chance of rain." Ian flipped a switch and the seatbelt light went out. "You can move around as you like. We restocked the fridge this morning, so please, make yourself at home. If you'd like to take a closer look up here, I think Rashad could be persuaded to loan you his seat."

"Thank you." Sandra released her seatbelt and moved to the refrigerator. The cord on her headset was just long enough to reach across the aisle. "Would either of you like something to drink?"

Rashad looked back. "Could I trouble you for an iced tea?"

"Sure. Ian?"

"Tea would be great thanks."

Sandra took three bottles out of the little refrigerator and started forward but the headset cord tugged her back toward her seat. She balanced the bottles in one hand for the few seconds it took to take off the headset. In two steps she was standing in the cockpit. The view forward was an intense white until they flashed out of the cloud into a bright blue sky.

Sandra handed them their drinks. "Are we at 26,000 feet yet?"

"Almost. We should get a clearance to 33,000 pretty soon." Ian glanced at the green and yellow label on his bottle as he opened it then looked at Rashad. "Diet?"

Rashad shrugged apologetically. "It was all they had."

"As long as it's not decaf." Ian took a drink, recapped the bottle and put it in the cup holder by his elbow.

Looking first out Ian's window, then Rashad's and then straight ahead it seemed like Sandy was trying to see around the scattered clouds below them. "It hardly seems like we're moving."

"Do you have to be back in Oakland by any specific time?"

Sandy looked at Ian. "No, why?"

"I thought we might take a closer look at those clouds."

Sandra looked outside and smiled. "Okay."

"Rashad, could you let the lady borrow your seat for a while?"

"Of course." Rashad unbuckled his harness.

Sandra stepped into the main cabin to let Rashad out and then squeezed into the right seat. Rashad leaned forward to show her how to attach the five-point harness. He retrieved his tea and then relaxed into the aft-facing seat behind the cockpit.

Ian keyed his mike. "Chicago approach, Citation 229 climbing through 24,000, request a block altitude of 22 to 23,000 for training."

"CITATION 229, MAINTAIN 24,000 FOR NOW, I HAVE YOUR REQUEST."

Ian pushed forward to take the plane back to 24,000. "229, leveling at 24,000." He looked at Sandra. "Have you ever flown a plane before?"

Sandra smiled. "No."

"Want to try?"

Sandra looked at the dozens of instruments and switches in front of her and back at Ian. "Okay."

"It's pretty basic. Turn the yoke and the airplane turns." Ian demonstrated by gently turning left. "Use your feet to smooth out the beginning of the turn." He pointed at her feet, "The rudder pedals are on the floor, like two brake pedals. Push right and the nose goes right, left and the nose goes left." Ian demonstrated using just the rudders and it felt as if they were skidding right and then left. "You can turn just using the rudder, but it isn't very graceful. To get a coordinated turn you need to use both the rudder and ailerons together."

"Ailerons? In French that would be 'little wing.'"

"Exactly, they're little panels on the wings. That's what you're moving when you turn the yoke. As long as you leave the plane in a bank it keeps turning. To stop the turn you twist the yoke the other way to bring the wings back to level." Ian took his hand off the yoke. "Try it. Turn right a little to bring us back on course."

Sandra held the yoke with both hands and turned right. Ian could feel her pressing the right rudder, but the nose was still lagging behind the turn.

"Try a little more right rudder as you start the turn." He tapped his left foot and Sandy felt it as a tapping on the bottom of her right foot. She tapped back. They were just above the upper layer of scattered clouds. White bands and clumps of water vapor raced past, an uneven screen through which other layers of cloud below and the Illinois countryside were intermittently visible. Sandra smiled. "Now it looks like we're moving!"

"CITATION 229 DESCEND AND MAINTAIN 22 TO 23 THOUSAND."

"Citation 229 down to 22 to 23 thousand." Ian pointed at the altimeter. "Push the wheel forward and we'll start descending."

"What about the clouds?"

"Go through them." Ian pointed to the gyro compass. "Just keep us headed west."

Sandy pushed forward and the jet descended into a clear trough between two ridges of cloud. She looked up from the gauges in front of her. "Wow!" The scenery had become three dimensional. Sheer cliffs and impossible mountains were sculpted from innumerable shades of white. A mottled white and grey cliff loomed in front of them and suddenly all they could see was featureless fog.

"Oh my God!" Sandy kept one hand on the wheel and ran the other through her hair. "The clouds seem so far away, even though you know you're headed toward them. They don't move. Then, all of a sudden they just leap out at you!"

They burst back into the real world with blue sky mostly above and dappled ground mostly below. The plane was in a climbing right turn. Sandy brought the wings back to level.

"It's easy to lose your bearings when you can't see outside. Let's go back down to 22,000." Ian pointed at the altimeter. "Try to keep us pointed west. You can skip along the tops of the clouds, or dive back in. Just stay between 22 and 23 thousand heading west."

Sandra pushed them back toward 22,000. "This is fantastic!" She guided the plane along the tops of the clouds and then along the sheer face of a ridge that seemed to stretch to the horizon.

Ian pointed to the compass. "Let's turn five degrees to the right and try to correct for the crosswind." The compass card smoothly rotated from 270 to 275. "You're good at this."

Sandra nodded. "Thanks."

They shot out of the clouds to find themselves between layers that looked more like impressionist paint than the collision of air-masses.

Sandra looked at Ian and saw the same look of child-like wonder that kept playing across her own face. "Do you ever get tired of this?"

"Not yet." Ian kept watching the clouds. "Sometimes I think I'm getting tired of the routine, but no two flights are ever really the same. The weather changes, the client's plans change and the sunsets are always different."

"Always?"

"Always." Ian smiled. "Besides, I love to fly."

"I can see that."

As they chased the setting sun, Sandra asked questions about air traffic control and instrument flight rules. Ian explained the basics of radio navigation and aerodynamics.

Over Denver, they left the clouds behind, and began crossing the real mountains.

Sandra did her best to stifle a yawn. "I'd better go back to my seat. I feel like I've had about four hours sleep in the past four days." She slid out of the co-pilot's seat. "Thank you, that was really great!"

Ian nodded. "Anytime."

Sandra headed aft and Rashad reclaimed his seat.

After they climbed up to 33,000 feet, Ian went aft to the restroom. Sandra was asleep.

She was still asleep when they taxied to a stop in front of Business Jet's Oakland terminal. Ian watched her for a moment. She had turned her back toward the window and her hair curved down across her face. It was raining and as the engines wound down, the background noise became the gentle patter of raindrops.

"Sandra?"

She opened her eyes, "Huh?"

Ian smiled. "Welcome to Oakland."

Sandra brushed her hair back. "Thank you."

Ian pulled her garment bag out of the forward closet and Sandra picked up her briefcase. While she checked to make sure she hadn't left anything on her seat, Rashad opened the door. Thunder rumbled overhead and the rain intensified. Ian and Sandra stepped down onto a wet square of red carpet rolled out by the line crew, and dashed the fifteen yards to the Business Jet Terminal.

A limousine was waiting in the loading zone and the driver took Sandra's garment bag from Ian. Sandra stopped just inside the open doors and looked at Ian. "Thanks for letting me fly. That was a lot of fun."

"My pleasure." Ian reached into his shirt pocket. "If you'd like to learn more..." He handed her his card. "You've got a real talent for it."

Sandra took a gold business card holder out of her jacket pocket, slid out a card and handed it to Ian. She smiled. "I'd love to learn more."

Wednesday, 11:09 am – Surrounded by
Squawking Seagulls at Princeton-By-The-Sea

The little white airplane floated on two long pontoons and bumped against the short, floating dock every third or fourth time a wave passed under it. Ian and Mick watched from the fishing pier along the breakwater as the pilot and his three passengers boarded, each additional person pushing the floats a little lower into the water. Once everyone was belted in, the pilot swung the fabric covered door closed revealing big green letters that spelled out "Whale Watchers". He used an oar to push off, and the catamaran with wings drifted slowly away from the dock. The engine started with a grinding, ragged cough and the plane taxied west toward the less crowded side of the harbor.

A sleek Beech Debonair with its wheels down and locked passed a few hundred feet overhead. On final approach with its engine at idle it seemed silent compared to the float plane. The Debonair disappeared behind the line of trees that separated the marina from Half Moon Bay Airport.

When the Whale Watchers reached the breakwater the plane turned into the wind and the throttle roared to maximum. The float plane accelerated slowly at first, but when the floats rose partway out of the water, the plane began to pick up speed. The tourists lifted off in their boat turned airplane, and headed out to sea.

"God! That's fucking excellent!" Mick kept watching the plane. "What do you have to do to fly something like that?"

"You need a seaplane rating." Ian was looking at the harbor as well, his elbows on the rail. The pier was only eight feet wide but it stretched several hundred feet out into the water, ending in a large fishing platform. Ian and Mick had stopped when Mick first noticed the float plane. They were about halfway between the end of the pier and the shore.

"Is that an add-on to the private pilot?"

"Usually. Hey, look!" Ian pointed to a pelican much closer to the pier. The awkward bird was flapping its wings and paddling its feet in an all-out attempt to get airborne. It gained a little altitude and for a moment, looked like it was running across the surface, its wing tips making tiny splashes in the dark, oily water. Still running, the pelican turned away from the pier, lifted its webbed feet and became suddenly graceful.

"I wish I'd been born with wings." Ian smiled philosophically. "To answer your question, you *can* get an airplane single-engine-sea rating without getting the single-engine-land, but most people get the land rating first."

"You said 'single-engine'. You'd need a twin-engine seaplane rating to fly that PBY we saw at Hayward, right?"

"Yeah, but they call it a multi-engine rating. Anything more than one is multi."

"And you have one?"

"Oh yeah, I couldn't fly the Catalina without it." Ian looked out across the rows of sailboats and motor yachts that rose and fell with the movement of the water. "There's nothing like flying into a mountain lake, shutting down the engines and feeling all that silence just rush in around you."

"You know..." Mick turned around and leaned against the railing. He was wearing blue jeans, a sweatshirt with an F-14 on it and the same style sunglasses Ian had worn the week before. "One trip to Guadalajara and you could buy that PBY."

"Christ! Give me a break, Mick! You've been pushing this thing all afternoon." Ian pointed his finger at the fighter on Mick's chest. "I'm tempted. I'm ashamed to admit it, but I'm tempted, okay? But we're not just talking about jail, Mick. If I get busted," Ian pointed at his own chest, "they tear up my pilot certificate."

"That's not going to happen!"

"That's easy for you to say." Ian shook his head. "I still can't believe you're actually serious."

"Oh, I'm totally serious, Ian." Mick turned toward Ian. "It's too God-damned perfect a deal to pass up. And it's totally safe: we can't be in any danger because we're not going anywhere near the bad guys."

"Check your score card Mick; if we do this, then we *are* the bad guys."

"That's open to interpretation." Mick considered. "Do you drink?"

"What do you mean?"

"I know you don't smoke, but you drank more than a few beers last Saturday night. Does that make you a criminal?"

"Not as long as I don't drive afterwards."

"Right. You're a responsible adult. You take responsibility for what goes into your body and you act responsibly by not driving or flying under the influence. Alcohol used to be illegal, now it's a staple part of the American diet. Nicotine has never been illegal. Why should any other drug be different?"

"Because they're addictive."

"And nicotine isn't?"

"You're rationalizing."

"Maybe a little." Mick shrugged. "Look, if drugs weren't illegal, they wouldn't be worth a million times what they cost to produce and nobody could make obscene amounts of money selling them."

"That's not the point."

"It's one point. An even better point is you could pay your bills, pay off your mortgage and buy that PBY."

Ian shook his head. "Wally wasn't kidding when he said it's worth three million dollars."

"So make a down payment! You have to owe money on something or you're not living the American dream."

"Mick..."

"Work with me on this, will ya? The airstrip is in the middle of a ranch that's owned, and I mean body-and-soul *owned*, by Clara's father." Mick made a tight fist for emphasis. "We'll have absolutely no problems on the ground. Coming back: everybody else, good guys, bad guys, everybody, is sneaking back and forth across the border trying not to get noticed by the other guys. *We* cross the border at thirty *thousand* feet, on radar; talking to everybody we're supposed to. They won't even look at us twice!"

"Mick, it can't be that easy." Ian shook his head, but asked, "How long is the runway?"

"About a mile." Mick hesitated. "Well, it's at least 5,000 feet."

"And what's the surface like?"

"What?"

"Is it paved, or are we talking about somebody's cornfield?"

"Oh, it's paved. They fly airplanes in there all the time."

Ian watched another pelican flying along the edge of the pier. "It could work." The bird rose a few feet and then dove into the water. "It could actually work."

Mick nodded. "Of course it will work."

The pelican surfaced with a fish caught sideways in its mouth.

"I don't know: everything fits together so neatly." Ian thought for a moment, "I keep thinking there has to be a catch..."

"There's no catch." Mick moved closer to Ian. "We're at the right place at the right time, and we have the right plan. It's perfect."

The pelican tossed its head several times to turn the fish around. Ian sighed. "Not exactly something to tell the grand-kids about, but it sure would be a kick..."

"Your share would be about $250,000."

Ian looked at Mick, stunned. "That's a quarter of a million dollars!"

Mick relaxed back against the railing. "Approximately."

The pelican swallowed the fish head first, and shook itself as if to settle its meal.

"Wow." Ian chuckled. "I had no idea." The pelican paddled languidly past a long yacht whose skipper was getting ready to Bar-B-Que. Tall flames were shooting out of a tiny hibachi bolted to the stern rail. Gold letters below the lighter-fluid blaze spelled out "Carpe Diem!"

As Ian watched the blaze in the hibachi burn down, two women and a little girl were walking toward them from the shore. The little girl had a grown-up finger in each hand and was pulling the women toward the end of the pier. Just before they passed Mick, one of the women swept the child up into her arms and posed next to the railing. The other woman took their picture.

"I love this place." Ian nodded toward the line of hills to the east. "It's hard to believe all that concrete and Bay Area noise is just fifteen minutes away."

"Yeah." Mick smiled at the little girl. She smiled at Mick and stuck her tongue out for the camera. As soon as she got her feet back on the well-worn timbers of the pier, she started tugging her photo crew toward the end.

Ian watched her for a moment and then looked at Mick. "I'll do it."

"Really?" Mick only let his surprise show for a moment.

"You only live once." Ian shook his head, but then nodded, as if convincing himself. "Yeah. Let's do it."

"Excellent! It'll take me a few days to get the gear I need." Mick started walking back toward the shore and Ian walked with him. "What about the jet?"

"I'll check. We haven't been that busy, so there'll probably be one available whenever we need it." The Debonair passed not quite silently overhead, on final for another practice landing. Ian and Mick walked toward the point in the tree line where the plane had slipped from view.

"This is gonna be fucking excellent!" Mick went first across the little footbridge to the airport. "I'll call Carlos, that's Clara's brother. He'll need a day or so to get set up too."

Ian considered. "Is the runway on the sectional charts?"

Mick shook his head. "I don't know. I don't think so."

"Okay, have your brother-in-law get the latitude and longitude for a point near the middle of the runway." Ian dug the airplane keys out of his pocket and handed them to Mick. "Meanwhile, show me another 'excellent' preflight."

Back in Alameda, Ian turned into Mick's driveway and stopped the car. Mick opened his door and set one foot on the pavement. "Thanks again, man. That was excellent! Did I really do that last landing by myself? You didn't help at all?"

"I didn't need to."

"Fucking excellent!"

"For someone who's only had two lessons, you're doing really well. That last landing wasn't bad at all." Ian shifted the car into neutral. "Next time we'll work on keeping the plane over the centerline."

"Right." Mick nodded. "How long were we gone?"

Ian looked at his watch. "Three hours."

Mick pulled a mass of bills from his left front pocket, counted out six hundred-dollar bills and handed them to Ian. "Here you go."

Ian laughed. "Mick, you already paid for the plane at the club, remember?"

"I know."

Ian tried to hand the money back but Mick wouldn't take it.

"Come on, Ian. My mechanic charges two hundred an hour, why shouldn't you?" Mick stepped out of the Mustang. "When can we fly again?"

"Uh..." Ian hesitated, then shook his head, and slid the bills into his shirt pocket. "Are you free Friday?"

"Yeah, I can arrange that. What time?"

Ian considered. "Ten o'clock?"

"What is it with you and the crack of dawn?" Mick shuddered. "Okay, I'll see you at ten." He closed the door and walked up the driveway to his house.

Ian let the Mustang roll back to the curb, pressed his garage door opener and checked for traffic before backing across the street. He stopped in his driveway and pressed the remote again. It worked the second time. Once the door was open, Ian backed into his garage. He tried the remote again, and found that he had to hold it down for several seconds before the door moved to shut out the rest of the world. Ian left his flight bag in the car but carried the remote inside with him.

There was mail in the box next to the front door, and Ian picked it up on his way to the kitchen. There were no calls on the answering machine, but Sandra Taylor's business card was pinned to the bulletin board above the phone. Ian set the mail and the remote on the counter, got a root beer out of the refrigerator, and pressed the speaker button on the phone. When the dial tone came up, Ian touched in Sandra's number.

The mail was mostly small envelopes with clear plastic windows that let Ian's address show through. "Bills, bills..." He sorted it into three stacks: bills, junk and everything else.

"Good afternoon, OHI Engineering." The voice was professional, but friendly: the perfect receptionist.

"Hi, can I speak to Sandra Taylor?"

"Certainly, one moment." Rapid clicking was followed by recorded music, something classical.

Ian tossed the bills into a drawer in the counter and the junk mail into the trash. That left two flying magazines, an aviation catalogue, a stockholders' report from Virgin Atlantic and a letter from Citibank. Ian opened the Citibank letter. "Dear Ian A. MacAran: Thank you for your recent request for an increase in your credit line. We regret..." Ian crumpled the letter into a tight ball. "Yeah, yeah; same to you."

On the phone, a real person replaced the classical music. "Legal, may I help you?"

"May I speak to Sandra Taylor, please?"

"May I tell her who's calling?"

"Ian MacAran." He opened the cabinet below the sink and tossed the paper ball into the trash.

"One moment." The music returned.

Ian pushed the flying magazines to one side and opened another drawer in the counter. From an assortment of batteries he selected a little rectangular 9-volt, and started taking the garage door opener apart.

The music stopped. "Sandra Taylor."

"Hi, this is Ian." He unplugged the old battery.

"Hi."

"I'm sorry to bother you at work, but I have a question I don't think anyone else can answer." Ian plugged in the new battery.

"I'll give it a try."

"Do you like vampire movies?"

"Well..." Sandra smiled and started to draw a face on the pad of paper by her phone. "That depends on the movie."

"Have you heard anything about <u>Fair Game</u>?"

She made the face long and thin, and drew in sharp fangs. "I know there are a lot of good people in it. There was an article in <u>Time</u> that said it went way over budget. Why?"

"I have two tickets to a sneak preview. I was hoping you could join me." Ian couldn't get the remote closed because the wires to the new battery were pushing the cover out of alignment.

"That would be fun. I didn't think <u>Fair Game</u> was due out for another month." Sandra added a drop of blood to the end of one fang. "When is the preview?"

The remote snapped shut and Ian could hear the garage door opening. "Saturday night at seven."

"In the city?"

"Which city?"

"San Francisco?" She drew a heart below the vampire face.

"Right, uh, yeah. It's at the Kabuki."

"I live near there. It's right across from Toraya, on Post Street." Sandra made the heart a tattoo on the vampire's chest. "Would you like to get something to eat before the movie?"

"Good idea."

"Meet me at Toraya at, say, five o'clock?" She softened the vampire's expression into a smile. "Five is a little early but we'll beat the rush."

"Five o'clock would be great."

"See you Saturday." Sandra smiled back at the cartoon.

"Bye." Ian pressed the speaker button to disconnect, and groaned. "'Which city?' Like she could've meant Hong Kong! I'll bet she's really impressed now!" He pressed the remote and the garage door started rumbling up.

Saturday, 8:10 pm – 7ᵗʰ row, Kabuki
Theater #4, San Francisco

Emergency floodlights over the stairwell door made bright circles on the north elevator and the ceiling above it. The only other light on the floor came from similar emergency lights at each end of the long hallway. Between the spot-lit paths to safety and their green EXIT signs, the corridor was dark. Regularly spaced shadows marked the doors to offices along the hall.

The door to the central stairwell opened and Zach Hunter stumbled into the lobby. On another floor somewhere below, a fire alarm was screaming. Zach staggered a step and then slouched back against the faded yellow wallpaper. He shook his head groggily and took a deep breath. A tall man with dark hair and a carefully trimmed mustache, Zach wore black military-style fatigues and a headset that held a small microphone below his mouth. He pushed the microphone up with his bloody left hand and pressed the earphone tight to his left ear.

"Trev, I'm on eight, headed for the south stairs. Meet me on the roof." Zach put his hand back over the bullet hole in his right side. "Trev?" Below the hole, his fatigues were soaked with blood all the way down to his right thigh pocket. Resting against that pocket was the Beretta he held in his right hand. "John, can you hear me?" He sighed. "Shit."

98

Zach took another deep breath and started down the corridor. When the doors to the north elevator opened behind him, he stopped and turned toward the sound. There was no car, just the dusty, unpainted walls of the elevator shaft. Zach aimed the Beretta at the opening and backed cautiously away from the elevator.

As if launched from a silent catapult, a grey figure rushed up and out of the shaft . Zach fired before the apparition landed on the pale green carpet. The bullet grazed his target's shoulder. Zach fired again as the figure rushed toward him, and fired again. Both bullets hit their mark square in the chest. The expensively dressed demon grabbed Zach's wrist as Zach pulled the trigger yet again. The last bullet hit the fire extinguisher mounted between the two elevators and a stream of fluffy white powder began shooting out of the red bottle.

"You're not having a good evening, Mr. Hunter. Your 'surgical strike' seems to have become a suicide mission." As tall as Zach, but with white hair and pale skin he sounded genuinely sympathetic. Of the three bullet holes in the grey suit only the hole in the shoulder of the jacket, close to the man's neck, showed any blood. Zach stared into the pale blue eyes for a moment and then drove his free hand, fingers straight out, into the man's chest. His fingers hit just below the center-mass bullet hole and there was a sharp crack.

"Shit!" Zach hugged his left hand to his own chest. The man took the Beretta out of Zach's right hand and smiled sympathetically. Behind him the lobby was swirling with white haze.

"Usually a good target, the solar plexus." The man tapped his chest with the Beretta and it made a dull plastic sound. "Kevlar. Takes the sting out of getting shot." He grabbed Zach's left hand and looked at it for a moment. The middle finger was bent at an odd angle and was beginning to swell. "Works pretty well against fingers, too." He let go of Zach's hands and Zach sagged back against the wall. "Allow me to introduce myself, Mr. Hunter. My name is Archimedes." He pushed his jacket back and tucked the Beretta into the back of his slacks. "You and I have a great deal to talk about."

The door at the south end of the corridor burst open and a police officer appeared briefly in the emergency spotlight. He ducked back out of any possible line of fire, but the door stayed open.

"Do you want to talk to the police?" Archimedes looked over his shoulder. "I don't." He grabbed the front of Zach's fatigues and pulled him away from the wall. "Let's take the elevator."

Zach started to go with him but then raised his right knee as hard as he could and connected solidly between Archimedes' legs. Archimedes punched three stiff fingers into Zach's solar plexus and Zach went limp. Archimedes bent over a little, *pinning Zach against the wall with one hand. He gingerly rubbed his crotch with his other hand. "Gods that hurts!" Archimedes shook his head, straightened up, and dragged Zach into the white haze, toward the elevators.*

The police officer reappeared at the south end of the corridor. "Police! Stay where you are!"

Archimedes swung Zach up and over his shoulder as if he were a child. He nodded toward the cop and then turned and jumped into the shaft. They fell about four feet before landing on the roof of the elevator car. Archimedes set Zach down on the dusty sheet metal and leaned him back against the support beam that ran over the center of the car. A screwdriver was jammed between the eighth floor and the bottom of the elevator's right door. When Archimedes pulled it out, the doors slid shut, powered by the same circuit as the emergency lights. He set the screwdriver next to a work-light that was plugged into the service panel and pressed the panel's up button. Relays clicked, machinery hummed and the walls started sliding down around them.

Ian moved his left foot off his right knee. The theater seats were comfortable, but when he leaned back, his knees pressed against the seat in front of him. He crossed his right ankle over his left knee and looked at Sandra. She was wearing glasses and a hint of perfume. Ian inhaled slowly. Sandra's face sparkled as the images shifted on the screen. She glanced at him, smiled, and rejoined the story.

There were floor numbers painted on the doors. The top of the elevator passed the 12th floor and stopped, eight feet from the top of the shaft. Above the doors to the 12th floor, someone had painted "Watch Your Head!" with an arrow pointing up. Archimedes whistled three notes and a panel of sheetrock receded into the west wall. He grabbed Zach by the collar and pulled him to his feet. Zach hung limp from Archimedes' hand.

"Oh dear." Archimedes pressed two fingers against Zach's neck. He moved them slightly, nodded, and slapped Zach lightly across the face. "Time to wake up, Mr. Hunter."

Zach's eyes opened halfway.

"Do I have your attention, Mr. Hunter?"

"Yeah." It was almost a whisper. Zach looked around.

Archimedes slapped him harder. "Your full attention?"

"Yes, God-Dammit!" Zach stared into Archimedes' brilliant blue eyes.

"Good." Archimedes looked at him for a moment. "How do you feel?"

Zach glanced away and shook his head weakly. "I've felt better."

"I'm sure you've looked better."

Zach looked back at Archimedes. "Fuck you."

"Really?" Archimedes stepped into the passage, across the gap between the car and the wall, and pulled Zach after him. He flipped a light switch to reveal a room the same size as the elevator shaft. It had a bed, a desk, and a short counter with all the essential elements of a kitchen. Archimedes pushed Zach toward the bed and sat him on the edge of it. He whistled again and the panel slid shut.

Archimedes unzipped Zach's tunic and pulled it off. "How bad are you hit?"

"I might live." His headset was connected to a transceiver in the tunic. Zach pulled off the headset, clumsily, and let it go with the jacket. His head nodded forward. After a moment, he straightened up.

"You've lost a lot of blood." Archimedes pulled off Zach's black T-shirt. "You're certainly dressed for sneaking around in the dark. Is your underwear black, too?" Archimedes examined the bullet hole in Zach's side, and then looked at his back. There was no exit wound. "Looks like the bullet will have to stay where it is, for now." He looked into Zach's eyes and placed two fingers against Zach's neck. He seemed to be listening. "Zachary - may I call you Zachary?"

Zach shrugged.

"Zachary, if you don't get medical attention very soon you'll die." Archimedes stepped away from the bed, slipped out of his jacket and hung the *expensive silk over the desk chair. "You might die anyway." He started unbuttoning his vest. "My personal feelings on this are unusually sympathetic: given the people you've murdered, I shouldn't mind letting nature take its course." He laid the vest on top of his coat and started unbuttoning his shirt.*

"I haven't murdered anyone." Zach said it quietly.

"No?" Archimedes laid the shirt on the chair and took off the thick Kevlar vest. "You've certainly killed enough of us. If not 'murder', what do you call it: sport?" His T-shirt was white with a ragged, red line across the top of his left shoulder, close to his neck. The blood was dark, drying, but when Archimedes pulled the shirt off, bright red welled up from the reopened wound. "Do you call it hunting, Zachary? Do you think of us as animals? Is that how you rationalize pillage and murder?"

"You're vampires."

"Oh, I see." Archimedes stepped toward the bed. "That makes us fair game, does it?" He wiped his right thumb across the cut on his left shoulder, and leaned forward. "You have a lot to learn, Mr. Hunter." In one smooth motion, Archimedes grabbed the hair at the back of Zach's head with his left hand and pushed his bloody right thumb into Zach's mouth.

Zach tried to resist. He pulled on Archimedes's wrist with both hands but couldn't break the connection. After a few seconds, he stopped trying. Zachary stared into Archimedes' eyes and swallowed. Archimedes pulled his thumb out of Zachary's mouth and ran it again through the blood on his shoulder. Zachary's mouth stayed open and Archimedes' thumb slid easily inside. His hand was pale against the flush of color returning to Zachary's skin.

Archimedes pulled his hand away and leaned closer. He gently pulled Zachary's head toward the wound on his shoulder. Archimedes nodded as Zachary lapped up the blood. "Yes, that's it." He let go of the dark brown hair and dropped his hand down to Zachary's back. Zachary closed his lips over the wound and drank. Archimedes sighed. "You have a lot to learn Mr. Hunter."

Two hours later, Ian and Sandra made their way out of the theater toward the noise and commotion of Post Street. After holding the door for Sandra, Ian put his hands back in his jacket pockets. "You think it was erotic?"

Sandra was wearing a gray blouse, black jeans and suede boots. She carried a suede jacket over her arm. "You don't think so?" They walked away from the line of people at the front of the theater. A few hundred feet above them, fog was moving in from the ocean.

"I didn't say that." Ian stopped by the movie poster that advertised <u>Fair Game</u>. An almost naked woman was leaning back into the bite of a tall, shadowy figure. "I thought Kim Kelly had a certain erotic quality."

"Oh, she was hot! She even died sexy." Sandra shook her head. "I'm talking about something else. I thought there was an erotic tension underlying the whole movie." Sandra shivered and put on her jacket. "I'll never get used to summer in San Francisco."

Ian zipped up his own jacket. "You said you walked over here; can I give you a ride home?"

"That would be nice. Thank you."

Ian pointed west. "I'm parked in the next block." They walked down the street toward the ocean. "I don't know about erotic tension. There was a lot of suspense but I thought the movie was more about death and destruction."

"It had that, all right." Sandra nodded. "Even so, didn't you think there was a celebration of life in the movie? I thought it had a real passion that was intensified by the violence."

Ian shook his head. "What do you mean?"

"Think about the scene at the top of the elevator shaft, when Archimedes saved Zach's life. What were you thinking when Zach drank the vampire's blood?"

"Well, I was thinking there are diseases you can catch doing that."

"Seriously?" Sandra laughed. "How pragmatic!"

"Hey, I don't know. I thought he was turning Zach into a vampire." They arrived at Ian's old Mustang and he opened the passenger door. If she noticed the freshly waxed dents and dings she didn't say anything. She just slipped in and as Ian walked around to the other side she leaned over to open his door for him.

Ian said, "Thanks."

"My pleasure." Sandra pulled her seat belt across her lap and adjusted the shoulder harness. "Didn't you feel the tension between Zach and Archimedes? The way Zach resisted at first, but then wanted the blood? It was so passionate! I thought their desire for each other gave the whole movie a very powerful subtext."

"Desire?" Ian shook his head. "I noticed their desire to kill each other!"

"But Archimedes could have killed Zach any time he wanted!"

"True..." Ian nodded. Two different streetlights shown into the car and he could see Sandra very clearly. He leaned a little closer to her. "Your eyes are the same color."

Sandra tilted her head slightly. "What?"

"Your eyes are that same incredible blue as Archimedes'. They're beautiful."

"Thank you." She smiled and they spent a moment studying each other's eyes.

"Uh..." Ian turned to start the engine. "Where to?"

"1711 Gough. It's right off California."

"1711 Gough." Ian pulled away from the curb and headed toward California Street. He cleared his throat. "All in all, I thought it was a pretty good movie."

"I thought it was tremendous." Sandra's face brightened and faded with the passing streetlights. "I've never seen a vampire movie that had so many interesting levels to it!"

Ian stopped at a red light. "Would you like to stop somewhere for a drink or something?"

Sandra shook her head. "I'd love to, but I've got to work in the morning."

"Work?" Ian made a right turn onto California. "On Sunday?"

Sandra nodded. "I'm going out of town Monday, and I need to wrap up some loose ends before I leave."

"Are you going to New Orleans?"

"No, why?"

"I've got a charter Monday morning to New Orleans. I thought it might be you."

"That would be nice, but..." Sandra smiled. "I'm taking Lufthansa. Sorry."

Ian turned onto Gough. There was a parking space several houses past 1711 and Ian pulled into it. Half the block was taken up by one big apartment building, the other half by a row of Victorian houses all brightly painted to highlight the details of their trim. 1711 was right next to the apartment building. Ian turned off the ignition. "May I walk you to your door?"

"You're such a gentleman, Mr. MacAran." Sandra opened her door and stepped out.

Ian met her on the sidewalk and they walked to her house together. Sandra had her keys out by the time they reached the door. She slid the key into the lock but didn't turn it. "I'm leaving for Copenhagen Monday. I'll be gone for almost two weeks."

"Another merger?"

"I wish." Sandra shook her head. "I'm visiting my folks."

"Sounds like fun."

"You haven't met my folks."

"I'm sorry."

"Me too." Sandra smiled. "Can I call you when I get back?"

"I'd like that very much, Sandra."

"Call me Sandy." She stood up on her toes and kissed Ian on the mouth. Before he could react, Sandra turned the key and pushed the door open. "Maybe I'll call you before I get back." She smiled at him as she stepped through the doorway and pushed the door closed.

"Sandy..." Ian looked up at the elaborate patterns in the stained glass window over her door. He nodded his head as he turned back toward his car. "I like it."

Thursday, 1:11 pm - Sixteen Hundred
Miles Southeast of San Francisco

A day after returning to Oakland from New Orleans, Ian was in the same plane but not on company business. Green trees and brown rock flashed below the tan and gold Citation as the jet's shadow dove into a deep arroyo. A second later the shadow shot to the top of a ridge, twisting and contorting as the plane sailed smoothly above it. Citation 229 snapped into a steep left turn 1500 feet above a road that ran along the top of one of the ridges.

"Mick, God-damn it! That's not a runway!" Ian rolled the plane to wings-level and flew west, parallel to the two-lane road. "And it's sure as hell not five thousand feet long!"

Mick looked out his window and then tried to see out Ian's side. He looked at the map in his lap. "The runway is the straight part of the drive from the highway up to the Hacienda. Are you sure you're looking at the right road?"

Ian brought both throttles back and the jet slowed to 120 knots. "I'm looking at the only pavement within ten miles of your coordinates!" He made another steep 180 degree turn to the left and followed the road, this time heading east. "I don't see any cars, or people, but there is a windsock. Looks like a light breeze out of the west." Ian shook his head. "Dammit, Mick! Putting a windsock next to your driveway doesn't make it a runway!"

Mick shrugged. He was listening to his cell phone and looking at the notepad he had brought with him. He put his finger next to one of the lines as he listened.

He read back the next line. "Muy bueno. Como esta su padre?"

At each end of the high flat plateau, the road dropped down to lower terrain and meandered away. Ian looked at his watch as they passed the west end of the 'runway' and checked it again as they passed the east end. "At 120 knots we cover about twelve thousand feet a minute. Fifteen seconds gives us about three thousand feet." Ian glanced at the altimeter and then at the outside air temperature gauge. His frustrated expression softened. "Okay, that isn't five thousand feet, but it'll work."

Mick stuffed the phone into a satchel behind Ian's seat. "They're on their way. Carlos says everything is ready and the coast is clear."

"Okay." Ian lowered the landing gear and turned back toward the road. He set the flaps at full, deployed the speed brakes and brought the throttles back almost to idle. As the jet descended toward the narrow strip of pavement, it crossed and re-crossed the road that cut back and forth in its struggle up the side of the arroyo. The Citation sank toward the edge of the mesa. Ian raised the nose and reduced power to idle.

Looking out his window, Mick was surprised to see treetops reaching above them. The yoke in Ian's hand started shaking to warn him he was too slow and a high-pitched horn sounded as the plane touched down. As soon as the wheels started rolling on the 'runway', Ian pressed the brakes. The engines roared up to full power as the thrust reversers directed the engine exhaust forward and both men were pressed forward against their seatbelts. The jet came to a stop halfway down the road as Ian throttled the engines back to idle.

"Holy shit!" Mick looked pale.

"Now *that* was fun." Ian brought the flaps up and retracted the spoilers. "This road is a lot wider than it looks from the air."

"Good." Mick starred at Ian with newfound respect. "That's good."

Ian turned the plane around and taxied back to the point where they had touched down. He repeated the tight turn and set the parking brake. "Welcome to Bumphuck nowhere." He shut down the engines and put the checklist back in the pocket behind Mick's seat. They headed aft and Ian showed Mick how to open the cabin door. Mick clomped down the stairs and Ian followed him out into the quiet, sunny afternoon.

"It's hot." Mick was wearing camouflage fatigues and heavy boots. He looked down the road to the west and then turned around to study the road's erratic course east.

"Yeah." Ian wore the blue slacks and white shirt he always wore for ACE. "At least Guadalajara had a restaurant." He followed Mick's gaze. "You're wondering if this is the right road, aren't you?"

"No, this is the right road."

"You don't sound too convinced."

"Well..." Mick sounded worried but his mood brightened when he looked back to the west. "Here they come." He pointed to movement in the haze over the roadway. A mottled brown and tan Hummer shimmered into focus and rapidly closed the distance between them. The big uber-purpose vehicle rolled down the center of the road, its knobby tires set almost as far apart as the Citation's. A taller, thinner Land Rover followed the Hummer as it swung off to the side of the road. The Land Rover was a solid, dark green.

The young man driving the Hummer stepped out and nodded at Mick and Ian. Maybe 16, probably younger with black hair and dark eyes, he wore a white shirt, tan slacks and a shoulder holster that held a large automatic pistol. He waited by the Hummer's open door. He had left the radio on and the Lawmen were singing "Boiler Plate Rag."

A short older man with a white hat and an assault rifle slung over his shoulder walked around from the Hummer's passenger side. The Rover's driver stepped out with a similar assault rifle. He leaned back against the Land Rover and watched the two Americans. A fourth man wearing white slacks and a pale green sports shirt walked around from the other side of the Land Rover. He didn't appear to be armed, but he seemed quite comfortable with the guns and the caution. He looked a lot like Mick's wife, Clara.

Mick walked over to meet him and they embraced. "You're looking good, Carlos!" Mick patted his arm. "You've added some muscle!"

"Honest labor, Mickey. We've got 30,000 acres. We're raising cattle!" Carlos held Mick at arms length and looked at the shorter American's fatigues. "Jesus, Mickey, you look like a commercial for the Army Reserve!" They both laughed, and Carlos clapped Mick on the shoulder. "How is the family?"

"Good. All good. Clara sends her love."

Carlos looked past Mick's shoulder at Ian and the Citation. "My, my. You are definitely moving up in the world."

Mick shrugged. "It's a rough life, but somebody's got to live it." They walked the few paces to where Ian was waiting. "Carlos, this is my friend, Ian MacAran. Ian, Carlos Orozco, my brother-in-law." Ian and Carlos shook hands.

Carlos was looking at the Citation. "That's a beautiful airplane, Ian. Can I look inside?"

"Of course." Ian led the way toward the door. "I like your airport."

Carlos laughed and turned toward the kid who had been driving the Hummer. "Juan Carlos! Help Arturo bring the packages."

Mick looked back as the Hummer's driver walked around to the rear doors. "That's Juan Carlos?"

Carlos nodded.

Mick held his hand level with his waist. "He was only this high the last time we were down here!"

"They grow up when you're not looking. He's in high school." Carlos lowered his voice. "He has a girlfriend!" Carlos followed Ian and Mick into the airplane. "It's been too long, Mickey. You and Clara should bring the kids down this summer. It would be nice to have the whole family together for a week or two. Just a visit, no business."

Mick nodded. "As soon as school's out, we'll come down." Mick sat in the right front passenger seat and waved Carlos forward. "Check it out."

Ian slipped into the co-pilot seat and let Carlos sit on the left. "Make yourself comfortable."

"This is nice." Carlos studied the instruments. "What kind of plane is it?"

"Citation Five."

"I like it. I've flown some big twin-engine planes, but never anything with turbines."

"You're a pilot?"

"Oh yes." Carlos pulled the yoke back a little and turned it from side to side. "We had a Cessna 310 for a while but we didn't use it enough to make it worthwhile."

Ian nodded. "Flying can be expensive."

"I suppose. For us it was too conspicuous." Carlos put his right hand on the throttles. "How fast will this go?"

"At 45,000 feet, we get about 425 knots."

"Nice." Carlos smiled. "Beats walking."

There was a thump in the cabin behind them. Carlos and Ian both looked back. The short man with the white hat pushed a wooden crate into the plane and then disappeared. Mick pulled the crate in between the seats opposite the door and pried off the lid with a small flat-bar. Juan Carlos set a second crate on the floor and pushed it up next to the first. As soon as he got out of the way, the white hat reappeared with a third crate. The crates had pictures of red and green bell peppers on their sides.

Carlos slid out from the pilot's seat and Ian followed him aft. Mick unfolded a large olive drab bag and started filling it with small bags of white powder from the open crate.

Carlos nodded toward a pile of green straps and green nylon ropes in the seat behind Mick. "That brings back some memories."

"Yeah. The guy at the surplus store was in Kosovo the same time we were. He sounded like he was just as crazy, but *he* was a supply sergeant." Mick laughed. "He stayed in after the war. Guess where he got all this stuff?"

"Your tax dollars in action." Carlos turned to Ian. "Were you in Kosovo?"

Ian shook his head. "I was in junior high."

Carlos nodded. "Kosovo was also an education."

"It was a party!" Mick handed him the emptied bell pepper crate and gestured for another one. "Speaking of parties, you guys going to have a big celebration tonight?"

Carlos pushed another crate toward Mick. "No. Why?"

"Cinco de Mayo!" Mick opened the crate with the flat bar.

"Oh yeah." Carlos shook his head. "That's an American thing. It *is* a national holiday and they *do* celebrate pretty seriously in Puebla, but we don't get into it much."

"Isn't Cinco de Mayo independence day?" Ian watched Mick strap the dark green duffle bag closed.

"No," Carlos shook his head. "That's in September. Cinco de Mayo honors the victory of our troops over the French in Puebla."

Juan Carlos returned with another crate and Carlos gave him an empty one. "Estan todos, papa." "Bueno."

Carlos stepped out of the plane and Ian followed him. They stood a few meters from the door and Carlos studied the leading edge of the jet's wing. "I would really like to fly one of these someday."

Ian nodded. "If we had more time, I could take you up. It handles a lot like the 310."

"Really?"

"Well, the acceleration is a little better."

Carlos laughed.

"Heads up!" Mick threw an empty crate out the door. Carlos put a foot out to keep it from bouncing up at him.

Carlos looked thoughtful. "Ian, are you married?"

"No."

"Do you have a girlfriend?"

"I'm working on it." Ian shrugged. "I don't know, maybe. Why?"

Carlos waved his hand at the chaparral around them. "This is a beautiful place to rest and relax. We have a swimming pool, tennis courts, a stable; you name it. I thought you might want to bring Mick and his family down this summer, along with your girlfriend of course."

"Gee," Ian smiled. "That would give us a chance to take the Citation up for a little air work, wouldn't it?"

Carlos pretended to be surprised. "What an excellent idea!"

Mick tossed two more empty crates at their feet and stepped out of the plane. "Do I have to do all the work?" He walked over to join them. "That's the last of it. Two hundred keys?"

Carlos nodded. "Two hundred kilos."

Juan Carlos grabbed two of the crates and the white hat picked up the other. They carried them back to the Hummer.

Mick extended his hand to Carlos. "Thanks for backing me."

Carlos shook Mick's hand. "There are very few people in the world I would trust with so much money, Mickey. You and Clara are two of them. But I will need to hear from you within two weeks."

Mick held up his index finger. "One week."

Carlos smiled. "You have two." He shook hands with Ian. "A pleasure to meet you, Ian."

"You too, Carlos." Ian stepped up into the jet and waited for Mick to board before pulling up the stairs and closing the door.

Carlos walked over to the Hummer as the jet's engines came to life. Juan Carlos was sitting behind the wheel, and he shook his head sadly. "He didn't even say hi."

Carlos looked at his son. "This was business, hijo. Too much time on the ground can be fatal. Besides," he tapped the automatic in Juan Carlos' holster, "you probably scared him off."

The boy smiled at his father and they both laughed.

The jet inched forward a little and then stopped as its engines spooled up to full power. Ian released the brakes and in less than a minute the Citation had lifted off the road. From the side of the road it seemed to climb straight up until it turned north, toward America.

Thursday, 5:12 pm – Backroom,
Andy's Appliances, Oakland

Surrounded by washing machines, refrigerators, assorted odd appliances and seven guys with guns, Oscar stood quietly, nervously; waiting. Oscar's cousin Farzad was also supposed to be standing quietly, but Farzad couldn't keep still. He crossed his arms, shifted his weight from one foot to the other, uncrossed and then re-crossed his arms. He kept looking around and moving from side to side as he tried to find an exit that wasn't blocked by somebody with a gun. When the fidgeting got too irritating, the guy behind him poked him in the back with his own shotgun. "Knock it off, Farzad!" That stopped the squirming, but only for a little while.

Neither Oscar nor Farzad paid much attention to the kid by the roll-up door in the too-big Cal Berkeley sweatshirt, but Jamaal watched them both. He could feel the gun he had taken from Keenan resting comfortably in the holster Jesus had given him. Oscar had been the one with the Uzi, the one who had jumped into the Camaro carrying Richard's gym bag. Jamaal had heard someone say Farzad had been driving.

Jamaal had been waiting at the appliance store since school let out. He'd gotten most of his homework done by the time Oscar showed up. They had pushed Oscar into the warehouse through a side door and told him to make himself uncomfortable. Jamaal was sure the four guys all worked for Jesus, but you'd never have known they were together just by looking at them. They had different styles, wore different clothes, and one was white, but all of them had guns, and all the guns had been pointed at Oscar.

A little later Farzad arrived, cursing and screaming that he was going to kill them all. The three guys who'd brought him just laughed. Even Oscar shook his head; amazed that Farzad could be so stupid. Farzad was describing exactly how he was going to kill them when they dragged the dead guy out of an industrial dryer. He looked baked.

Things stayed pretty quiet until the roll-up door to the alley went up and Jesus' maroon Oldsmobile drove into the loading area. Jesus stepped out but then a cell phone rang somewhere inside the Intrigue. The first few bars of Funk It Up cut through the silence just as Jesus reached back inside to grab the phone. Oscar and Farzad watched Jesus, the guys with the guns watched Oscar and Farzad, and everybody waited for Jesus to get off the phone.

The shop was filled with hundreds of used and refurbished appliances. Washers, ovens, freezers, and refrigerators covered the walls several rows deep. Haphazard walkways had been left to let people move from the showroom up front to the large open space next to the roll-up door. The big door closed with a solid mechanical finality.

"Yeah, right; I'll call you back when I can, okay?" Jesus Ruiz leaned back against his car and looked at the ceiling. Average height, medium build, flawlessly dressed, he looked like a lawyer on vacation. He switched the phone to his left ear. "Right... No. I said *I* will *fuck-ing* call *you* back!" He tossed the phone into the car and walked around to the dead guy. He bent over slightly and looked into the still open eyes. Jesus smiled. "The things we do for love, eh?" He shrugged and walked over to Oscar. "How you doin', Oscar?"

Oscar smiled, nervous. "I think you probably know better than me, Mr. Ruiz."

"I do." Jesus chuckled as he patted him on the shoulder. "You're in deep shit, Oscar."

Oscar nodded.

"Mister Ruiz!" Farzad rushed forward. "You've got to listen, man. We were just..."

Jesus slapped him across the face with the back of his hand. Farzad fell back but came up with his fists raised. He froze, staring at the nickel-plated .45 pointed at his nose. Two guys moved in and each grabbed an arm. Jesus had pulled the gun from a shoulder holster, but instead of maneuvering it back into the brown leather he just tucked the gun into the waistband of his slacks. Clenching his right hand, he raised it to punch Farzad, but paused, looking over the shorter man's shoulder. Jesus smiled as he opened his hand and pointed toward the wall of appliances behind Farzad. The guys holding Farzad dragged him backwards toward the wall and Jesus followed a few paces behind.

"Farzad, I think you need to take a moment to cool off." Jesus pointed to a large green chest freezer and Farzad was quickly levered into it. Jesus leaned over the freezer and grabbed the lid. As he smiled down on Farzad, his voice sounded calm, almost soothing. "Just relax for a minute, dude. Get a grip on your impulses."

Jesus closed the lid and motioned the two guys closer. "Have a seat." He patted the top of the freezer. Both men looked puzzled but lifted themselves up onto the big avocado-colored box. Jesus leaned in close and whispered, "He'll probably try to get out when he runs out of air. Don't let him out." One of the guys smiled. Both nodded.

Jesus walked over to Oscar. "I had a very informative discussion with your buddy." He gestured to the dead guy. "I know Farzad set it up, and that you went along with it, against explicit orders direct from Mr. M. I know you sold the coke to the kids and then stole the coke back along with the money the other kids brought to buy it." Jesus was standing right in front of Oscar, and he stared into his eyes. "What I don't know is why you killed them. You sure as hell didn't have to; so why did you kill them, Oscar?"

"Who?"

"The kids, Oscar, six <u>children</u> gunned down in East Oakland. It's been all over the news the last few days! You must have heard about it?"

"Yeah."

"Yeah? I've got cops who'd never <u>seen</u> East Oakland until two weeks ago crawling all over my turf! Some smartass said it's increasing property values, but it's hurting my business." Jesus turned his head to one side, still looking straight into Oscar's eyes. "So?"

"What?"

"Why did you kill them?" Ruiz shook his head. "Can't you take candy from a bunch of babies without shooting them full of holes?"

Loud thumping, and a succession of muffled curses came from under the two guys sitting on the freezer. There was a pause and then one solid thump lifted the lid, two guys included, almost an inch.

"Come on, Jesus, let him out." Oscar took a step toward the freezer, and all the loosely-held guns in the shop swung toward him. He stepped back. There was another loud thump from the freezer. "Why you doin' this, man?"

"Because you killed those kids!"

Thump

"And I want to know why!"

Thump

"Actually, technically; I could give a shit, but Mr. M. wants to know why."

Oscar shrugged and shook his head.

Thump

Jesus stepped right up to Oscar and screamed into his face. "Why?"

"They shot first!" Oscar yelled back, and then quietly, "Besides, they were witnesses."

"Witnesses?" Jesus was astonished but he felt no need to lower his voice. "You stupid bastard! How could they go to the cops?"

Thump

Jesus turned toward the freezer and then looked at his watch. He chuckled. "I guess there's more air in there than I thought!"

In one swift move Oscar grabbed the .45 from Jesus' belt and stepped behind him. With his other arm, Oscar grabbed Jesus around the neck and then pointed the gun at his temple. Oscar turned to put his back to the big door and Ruiz between himself and the rest of the men in the garage. "Drop your guns!"

Everybody froze. Faint, desperate pounding sounded from the freezer.

"Put the guns down or I'll blow his fucking head off!" Oscar moved the gun away from Jesus' temple and pointed it at the guys on the freezer. "Let him out!"

The single shot was deafening in the enclosed space and the sound seemed to echo through the room for a long time. Jesus felt Oscar go limp and sag against him. When Jesus stepped aside, Oscar fell face down on the concrete. Blood oozed from the hole in the base of his skull, and more blood pooled around the much larger wound where his forehead had been. Jamaal had waited until he was right behind Oscar before he fired and the bullet had stayed well away from Jesus. As Oscar had fallen, however, he'd slid against Jesus' back and the whole left side of Jesus' suit was smeared with blood.

Jesus bent down and pulled his gun from Oscar's hand. He looked at Jamaal and Jamaal met his gaze. He slipped his .45 back under his shoulder, and shrugged out of the jacket. Jamaal pushed his revolver back into its holster. Nobody noticed he was shaking. Jamaal clenched his teeth together and managed to look cool and unaffected as he tugged Jesus' old sweatshirt down over the gun.

CHAPTER THREE

6:13 pm - Final Approach, Oakland Runway 27R

B arely an hour later, just two hours after Ian had crossed the Mexican border, the Citation's landing gear swung down and locked as it lined up for the right runway at Oakland International. Ian hadn't slept the night before and he'd been flying for almost ten hours straight but he was too hyped on adrenalin to even feel how tired he was. The jet passed a blue Twin Star that was on final for the parallel runway and touched down just past the runway numbers. Ian slowed to taxi speed with a touch of reverse thrust and halfway down the runway he turned onto Taxiway Golf.

From behind the tinted windows of Air Charter's office, Custom's Agent George Scott watched the business jet taxi toward him. He drank the last of his complimentary coffee and tossed the big paper cup in the trash. "Here it comes."

His partner looked up from the March issue of Popular Science, and checked his watch. "Right on time." He tossed the magazine on the glass tabletop. "Come on, Tala! Let's go to work." Beside the table, the Belgian Malinois' ears turned up and she lifted her head off her paws. The dog rose as her human stood up, and the three Customs agents walked out to the ramp.

They met the plane as it rolled to a stop between a Lear and another Citation. They waited next to the lineman while the engines were shut down and the lights on the underside and tail of the jet stopped flashing. George checked his watch as they closed on the door. His partner and the dog seemed more patient. Eventually the door opened and Ian lowered the stairs to the pavement.

"Hi, Ian." George extended his hand as Ian stepped down.

"Hi, George." They shook hands. "How are you?"

"Can't complain." George nodded toward the other agent. "This is Keith Axelrod. He's checking Tala out for field work."

"Hi, Keith."

"Hi."

Ian glanced at the dog. "Will this take long?"

George shook his head. "No more than usual. Anything to declare?"

"Nope." Ian watched as the other agent pointed into the plane and the Belgian Malinois bounded up the stairs and disappeared inside.

"Traveling alone?"

"Ah, yes." Ian watched the agent follow the dog into the plane. "It was a one-way charter this time."

George nodded and filled in another part of the form. He handed the clipboard to Ian. "Check the details for me. I filled out most of it at the office."

Ian read over the form. "Everything's right." He signed the bottom of the form and handed the clipboard back.

George tore off the bottom copy and handed it to Ian. "Here you go."

"Thanks." Ian folded the canary yellow sheet in thirds and slid it into his shirt pocket.

The Belgian Malinois jumped out of the plane to the pavement and waited for her master. Keith used the stairs and then directed the dog to look under the airplane. Tala sniffed around the landing gear and inside the landing gear bays. She did it carefully, methodically, and then trotted over to butt her head against the agent's thigh. Keith rubbed the dog's head and nodded to George. "All clear."

George nodded back. "Have a good afternoon, Ian."

"You too." Ian smiled. "Thanks for coming out."

"Hey, thank you for not arriving at two in the morning." The three agents walked back toward the ACE office. The dog barked and Keith answered her, "Yeah, yeah. Come on." They got into an unmarked blue sedan that was parked next to the building and drove away.

Friday, 10:14 pm – 15ᵗʰ Floor, Hilton
Hotel, San Francisco

Des Pierrot swung the door to 1528 wide open and stepped back to admire his visitor's fancy clothes. The silk shirt, three-piece suit, and polished leather shoes were totally out of character. "Who the fuck do you think you are?"

"The name is Dale. Mick Dale." Mick suavely adjusted the knot of his silver tie and waited for Des to get out of the way.

The barefoot business major whistled as he stepped back into the room. "I must say, you are looking very sharp Mr. Dale."

"Yeah, yeah, I wish I could say the same for you." Mick carried his blue hard-shell suitcase into the room and Des closed the door behind them.

"Hey, I'm on vacation!" Des combed his fingers back through his thick, black, shoulder length hair. "So what's with the suit?"

Mick carried the heavy suitcase over to the king-size bed and balanced it on the bed's edge. "Would you believe camouflage?"

Des shook his head. "No."

"We went to the symphony. I'm meeting Clara at a party later." Mick pushed the Samsonite further onto the bed and started to open the combination lock.

"Hold on. Not here." Des nodded his head toward a door by the window. "Let's go next door."

Mick picked up the suitcase. "Why?"

"Trust me." Des led Mick through the connecting door into the next room. Room 1530 was a mirror image of 1528, with the same furniture in exactly opposite positions around the room. Des closed and bolted the door behind them.

Mick shrugged and set the suitcase on a bedspread identical to the one it had rested on before. "I think I liked the other bed better. What's up?"

"Applied paranoia." Des smiled. "This room is checked out to a Memphis car salesman and his wife. If any cops wanted to use this room to get next to us, they'd quietly move the tourists to a different room."

Mick nodded. "And we'd know something was up."

"If I didn't know already." Des grabbed a black cell phone from the round mahogany table by the window. He dialed as he pulled back the curtain and peeked out the window at the city. While another cell rang somewhere in the lobby, Des glanced back at Mick. "There's beer in the... Hello? Yeah, it's me." Des listened to the phone for a moment. "Okay. Later." He hung up and dialed another number. As he waited for the call to go through, he nodded toward a tall mahogany colored cabinet with a television in its middle. "There's beer in that video thing. The bottom is a refrigerator." Des looked at the ceiling and back out the window.

Mick got a soda out from under the television. The can popped softly when he opened it.

Des glanced at the front door and dialed the number again. "Come on Ross." He listened for a moment and then yelled. "What the fuck took you so long? ... Yeah?" He flashed Mick an 'okay' with his left hand. "You must have been in a bad area. Stop moving around down there!" Des tossed the phone next to the Samsonite as he walked over to the head of the bed. He leaned down, pushed his hand under the mattress and pulled out a brown leather briefcase. "I'll trade ya."

"That's the deal." Mick took the briefcase from Des and opened it on the table. One of the bundles of hundred dollar bills had shifted out of place and lay sideways at the bottom of the case. Mick set that bundle on the table first, and started stacking the others on top of it.

Des unlatched the blue suitcase and let it fall open on the bed. Each side of the case held ten lumpy brown paper lunch bags, twenty in all. Des took two bags from the left side and one from the right and set them on the table. Mick moved the empty briefcase to the side to make more room while Des retrieved a gray camera case from the top drawer of the ornate mahogany dresser. He sat down across from Mick and opened the paper bags.

Inside each brown bag was a large Ziploc bag filled with a kilogram of coarse white powder. Des folded the paper bags flat and set them aside. He opened the camera bag and took out a tall thin glass cylinder with an orange plastic base, a rectangular mirror, and a small bottle of bleach. The cylinder was marked in milliliters. Des poured bleach into the graduated cylinder until the fluid reached the 250 ml line.

The little phone on the bed rang and both men looked at the door. Mick slid his hand under his jacket and Des pulled a revolver out of the camera bag. They glanced at each other as Des reached over to pick up the phone. "What?" He listened for a moment and then slid the gun back into the camera case. "Hi, Doc. What's up?" Des leaned back in his chair. Mick started counting the money.

Des shifted the phone to his other ear and balanced it on his shoulder. "Uh huh." He reached into the camera bag again and took out a straight razor and a long-handled teaspoon. "Sure. Nine o'clock sounds fine." He took off his watch and set it on the table next to the cylinder filled with bleach. "Okay, okay! Don't worry, I won't set up anything until I hear from you. No ... I'll take care of it, don't worry!" Des shook his head as he put the phone back on the table. "Christ! I thought I was paranoid."

Mick put each bundle of money into the briefcase as he finished counting it. He drank some of the soda. "Who was that?"

Des looked at Mick suspiciously for a second, then shrugged. "Somebody who's not going to be happy your prices are better than his."

"Life can be rough."

"That's a fact." Des opened one of the bags and dug into its center with the long skinny spoon. Des dumped the spoonful of pale yellow cocaine in the center of the mirror and tapped the glass to shake off the tiny flakes that clung to the spoon. He spread the tiny translucent crystals into a thin layer on the mirror, and glanced up at Mick as he pushed all but a pearl-sized sample to the left side of the mirror. "How is the apartment building coming?"

Mick smiled. "Pretty good. The parking structure is finished and we've got the first floor framed in."

"And when you're done in what, a year? You can sell it and make less than you're making on this deal in one night, right?" Des used the razor to chop the little sample into a fine powder.

"I'm not going to sell it." Mick placed the last bundle of hundreds on top of the rest and closed the briefcase. "It's real. That's why they call it real estate."

"Whatever." Des used the straight razor to pick up a tiny sample of the finely ground cocaine. He held the sample over the cylinder of bleach and tapped the blade against the glass until the powder fell onto the surface of the bleach. It rested on the liquid like snowflakes on clear, smooth ice and for twelve seconds, nothing happened. Des looked at his Rolex. As the second hand swept through thirteen seconds, the cocaine began to drift lazily down into the bleach, trailing white, milky tendrils in its slow-motion wake. The trail ended halfway down the cylinder as the last of the cocaine dissolved. As they watched the tendrils, they faded like smoke, and disappeared.

Des leaned forward and looked at the top of the bleach. "Holy shit!" A tiny oily spot floated on the surface. Des looked at Mick. "I haven't seen shit this good since... Holy shit! This is good stuff, Mick."

"Better than the crap you were selling me?"

"Hey, that wasn't bad..."

"It just wasn't as good." Mick picked up his soda.

"You never complained." Des took a pinch of the powder between thumb and forefinger, held it to his nose and inhaled.

"Nobody complained to me, why should I bother you?" Mick shrugged. "I made enough money."

"Looks like you're going to make a lot more." Des carefully slid the rest of the cocaine off the mirror and back into the plastic bag. Some of the powder clung to the mirror. He wiped that up with a finger, then rubbed his finger tip along his gum-line. "Wow. That is good. You know, it sure is weird buying shit from somebody I used to sell to."

"You think it's weird? I think its fate."

"Fate? Like *destiny*, fate?"

"Exactly. I've been trying to figure out how to make this connection for years and then this pilot just drops into my life. Bam! It all comes together." Mick finished his soda and set the can on the table. "It's just like you said: destiny."

Des zipped the first bag closed and opened the second. He spooned some crystals from the second bag onto the mirror and started chopping a small sample with the razor. Des tapped the powder onto the surface of the bleach.

Des watched the little vapor trails fade away. "This *is* really good shit, Mick!"

"Unbeatable product at unbeatable prices." Mick smiled. "Does that mean you can use more?"

"At the same price?"

"Same price."

Des nodded slowly. He pulled his cigarettes out of his shirt pocket. He offered the pack to Mick but Mick shook his head. Des nodded with more enthusiasm as he lit a cigarette. "I like destiny." He glanced at the curtains covering the window. "Can you get me forty keys? Same quality?"

"When do you want it?"

"Next week."

"Done." Mick stood up and the two men shook hands over the razor and the mirror.

Saturday, 4:15 pm – Mick & Clara's Den, Alameda

"It couldn't have gone any better!" Mick was sitting in a leather executive-style office chair in his not-quite-unpacked-yet den. He turned the chair to one side and put his white trainers up on his desk. The floor of Mick's office was a cluttered mess but the desk itself had been kept clear. "Hell, I figured, even if we missed the drop zone entirely, I could hike to the truck and drive back for the stuff, right?" Mick laughed. "Man, I almost landed on top of it!"

"That could have hurt." Ian was standing on the other side of the large walnut desk. There were two armchairs in Mick's office, but one held a big cardboard box, with Ian's root beer on top, and the other was overflowing with Guns & Ammo Magazines. The party had started several hours ago, and though it wasn't as loud as the first barbecue, the Beatles were still audible through the wall.

Mick put his feet on the floor, leaned forward and held up his hands. "I'm hanging there, right?" He pretended to curl his fingers around the lines of a parachute. "I'm steering for the truck, but it looks like I'm drifting, like I'm going to overshoot so I spill a little just to even up the line. Christ! All of a sudden, I realize I'm going to hit it! I'm trying so hard to save myself the walk that I'm about to drop forty keys and my steel-toed combat boots right through the roof of my brand new Chevy!"

"Did you hit it?"

"No, but I came damn close. The rest of the stuff came down along the side of the road. I just picked everything up and came home."

"Sounds like I had more trouble than you did."

"How's that?"

"Remember I told you they hardly ever search the plane when we come back from Mexico?"

"Yeah?" Mick grabbed his Budweiser from the desk top and put his feet back up on it.

"This time they checked it inside and out. They even brought a dog."

"Really?" Mick had been about to take a sip of his beer but he paused. "Why this time?"

"I don't know." Ian shook his head. "Sometimes it's random but they also look at a lot of different factors..." Ian considered and then snapped his fingers. "I do know. We flew direct to Guadalajara, but we didn't fly back direct."

"How do they..." Mick held up his hand. "Wait a minute; our flight plan is in a computer somewhere, right?"

Ian nodded. "Several computers."

"And they still found nothing!" Mick laughed and raised his beer. "A toast! To the perfect execution of the perfect plan!"

Ian retrieved his soda from the top of the packing box. "To perfection." They clunked their cans together and drank to their success.

Still smiling, Mick pulled a black briefcase from under his desk and pushed it across the walnut surface toward Ian. "The market is a little soft right now and I've still got to pay Carlos. Can you give me a few days to get the rest to you?"

"Of course." Ian opened the briefcase. Bundles of twenty, fifty and hundred dollar bills filled the case in neat rows. "Wow!" Ian stared at the money. "How much is in here?"

"One hundred thousand dollars."

"Oh my God!" Ian closed the case. He laughed. "I think that'll tide me over for now."

"Be careful." Mick tapped the briefcase. "The only way we can screw up now is with the IRS. Don't put it in the bank. Don't pay off your debts or change your spending habits. Be discreet. Don't look rich."

Ian feigned disappointment. "That takes all the fun out of it."

"Yeah." Mick shrugged. "Life sucks."

They both laughed and Ian picked up the briefcase. "I should probably put this somewhere. I'll be back in a few minutes."

"I'm serious." Mick sounded every bit of it. "I know it sounds crazy but trust me; the money is fabulous, but the most valuable thing you have right now is anonymity. Right now nobody knows who you are and trust me; you want to keep it that way. Don't draw attention to yourself."

There was a knock on the door.

They both turned to look at the door as Mick hollered, "Yeah?"

"Mickey?" It was Clara, "Bernie Selleca is here to see you."

"Who?" Mick looked at Ian. "Get the door, will ya?" Mick pulled the desk's middle drawer open enough to slip his hand inside, while Ian unlocked and opened the door.

Clara smiled at Ian, waved at her husband and headed back to the party. Bernie had dark brown hair and hazel eyes. She was wearing blue jeans, a red blouse and a black leather jacket. "Mr. Dale?" She looked up at Ian and held out her hand. "I'm Bernie Selleca; we talked on the phone about a job?"

"Hi." Ian shook her hand. "I'm Ian MacAran."

She looked puzzled, saw Mick sitting behind the desk, and then let go of Ian's hand. "I'm sorry."

"I'm not."

"Hey come on in." Mick let go of his .357 and closed the desk drawer. "You're the architect, right?"

"Someday. Right now I'm an Architecture student."

"Are you hungry?" Mick stood up and walked around the desk to meet her.

"A little, I guess." Bernie took a step into the room. "I appreciate your talking to me. I uh," She glanced at Ian, and then looked back at Mick. "I don't want to interrupt anything."

"Don't mind me. I was just leaving." Ian nodded to Mick. "I'll be back in a bit."

"See ya." Mick ushered Bernie down the hall after Ian, but where Ian turned right, they turned left through the kitchen and headed for the backyard.

Ian had never hidden a briefcase full of money before and it took some time for him to find a place that he felt was safe. From the top shelf in the bathroom closet to the dead space behind the vanity, every place he tried seemed like the obvious place someone would hide a lot of money. Eventually he ended up burying the briefcase next to an air duct in the fuzzy pink insulation that filled his attic. Throughout the search he couldn't stop smiling. At one point he stopped in the hall and opened the case just to look at the neat bundles of bills hidden inside.

When he got back to Mick's, most of the guests were in the back yard. They had formed a big circle around a papier-mâché elephant that hung from the yard's only tree. A young girl at the center of the circle was trying to break the big elephant open with a baseball bat. She was wearing a blindfold and the crowd was yelling instructions and cheering each time she swung anywhere near the piñata.

Ian fished a bottle of tea out of a cooler of ice and leaned back against one of the picnic tables. The crowd quieted down while they transferred the bat and the blindfold to a fresh contestant. They spun him around three times and sent him wobbling toward the elephant. Two men holding the other end of the elephant's rope pulled the piñata up and away from the swinging bat, and the crowd cheered.

"He needs a bigger stick." Bernie Selleca sat next to Ian and put her feet on the bench. She had taken off her jacket and her hair seemed to catch some of the red from her blouse.

Ian nodded. "Taking the blindfold off might help." He pointed to the cooler behind him on the table. "Would you like a soda or a beer or something?"

Bernie nodded. "A beer would be perfect. Thanks."

Ian pulled a bottle of Schlagmeister out of the cooler and twisted the cap off. He passed the bottle carefully under his nose and sniffed critically. "Late April, I believe." He handed Bernie the bottle. "A very good week."

Bernie nodded and sniffed the bottle as Ian had. She then examined the label as she held the bottle up to the not-quite-setting sun. She took a drink and swished the beer around in her mouth for a moment while making critical, very sophisticated faces. She nodded, looking satisfied, and spit the mouthful into the grass at the edge of the patio. "Impetuous, but reserved: very satisfying." She took another sip with her little finger carefully held away from the bottle.

Ian stared at her for a moment and then started laughing.

Bernie laughed with him and took another drink. She swallowed. "Thank you."

"My pleasure." Ian drank some tea. "Bernie, right?"

She nodded. "And you're Ian."

"Except when I'm Mick."

"Right." Bernie looked down at her boots for a second. "I'm sorry if I interrupted you guys earlier."

"Hey, don't worry about it. I was pleased to meet you. I am pleased to meet you." Ian smiled. "Did you get the job?"

"Yep."

"As a carpenter?"

"Apprentice carpenter. I'm going to be an architect, but I don't want all my experience to be theoretical."

"That sounds smart." Ian raised his tea. "Congratulations on your new job."

"Thanks." Bernie clunked her bottle against his can, then took a sip of beer. "I like your shirt."

"Uh." Ian was wearing an ordinary blue dress shirt. "Thank you."

"It brings out the blue in your eyes."

Before Ian could reply, Zachary Dale ran up to him. "Can I have a beer?"

"Sure." Ian turned around enough to reach the ice chest and pulled out a can of soda. He held the top between his thumb and three fingers and used his index finger to open the pop-top. "Here you go." Ian handed the can to Zachary. "You know, I saw you in the movies last week."

"No way!" Zachary looked doubtful.

"Yes, way! I saw Fair Game and the hero is named Zachary."

"Really?" Zachary grinned.

"Really." Ian smiled back.

"Cool!" Zachary started to walk away but looked back long enough to yell, "Thank you!"

"He's cute." Bernie watched the boy disappear into the crowd. "I feel like I'm the only one drinking beer."

Ian glanced from his tea to Bernie's Schlagmeister. "I'd join you, but I'm on call 'til midnight."

"Oh. Do you turn into a pumpkin or something?"

"Uh, what?"

"Midnight, turn into a ..." Bernie shrugged, smiling. "Never mind. Are you a doctor?"

"No, pilot."

"And you're on call? What airline?"

Ian shook his head. "I work for Air Charter Express. We're a charter company, so we have to keep a crew available just in case somebody calls. Today it's me and Rashad."

"Rashad?"

"My copilot."

"'Till midnight?"

Ian nodded. Planes had been flying over the neighborhood every few minutes, and Ian looked up as another small Cessna passed overhead.

Bernie followed his gaze. "Do you fly those?"

"Sometimes."

"They look so delicate." Bernie shook her head. "I've never flown in anything that small before."

"Oh really? Never?"

"Never."

"I'd be happy to take you flying sometime."

"I think I'd like that."

There was a whump and a cheer as the stick made contact with the elephant. A crack appeared along its side but it held together as the boy swung again.

The crystal earring in Bernie's right ear glittered in the sunlight, and then swung forward as Bernie turned to look at Ian. "When?"

"How about now?"

"I thought you were on call?"

"We won't be more than twenty minutes away and I've got my cell. If they do call, they'll just want me to go to the airport. Come on." Ian glanced at the western sky as he moved away from the table. "Maybe we can catch the sunrise."

Bernie raised an eyebrow.

"You haven't lived until you've seen the sun rise in the west."

"I haven't lived?" Bernie followed Ian across the street to get his car.

Thirty minutes later he was showing her how to buckle the shoulder harness in a tiny blue and white Grumman Lynx. From the outside, the little trainer's low wings and clear, tapered canopy made it look like a miniature World War II fighter. From the inside, it looked like a convertible with one too many steering wheels, and it seemed very short. Only the tail of the little plane was taller than Ian or Bernie, and not by much. Bernie glanced at the other, larger planes tied down around them. "Isn't this plane a little small?"

"Kind of." Ian reached up between them and slid the Lynx's canopy almost, but not quite, closed. "Actually, the Lynx is about the same size as a Cessna 150." Ian pointed to the high-wing trainer that was parked right next to them. "That's a 150 right there. They both have two seats and the same size engine. The Lynx just seems smaller because of the low wing. Without the wing in the way you can see a lot more, and the Lynx handles better."

Bernie tugged her shoulder harness a little tighter. "What do you mean, it handles better?"

"Well, it's more responsive." Ian strapped a folding clipboard to his left leg, just above his knee. "Cessnas tend to be very stable, which is good, but they can seem a little stiff. The 150 handles something like a Volkswagen with wings. Solid, dependable, you know: boring. Now the Lynx," Ian twisted the control wheel slightly and nodded approvingly. "This handles more like an MG."

"Oh great!" Bernie laughed. "I used to own an MG."

"Cool." Ian clipped the plane's engine start checklist to his kneeboard. "Did you like it?"

Bernie nodded. "When it ran."

"I see." Ian used the primer to start the flow of fuel to the engine, looked outside to make sure no one was standing near the plane and shouted through the gap between the canopy and the windscreen. "Clear prop!" With one hand on the throttle, Ian waited a moment for any reply and then pressed the start button. The two blades of the propeller cranked a half turn, hesitated, and then swung around and around for six or seven seconds. The starter stopped grinding when Ian released the button, and the propeller stood motionless, almost straight up and down.

"It's just cold." Ian pulled the primer back, waited a moment for the little pump to fill with fuel and then pushed it back into the instrument panel. He gave the engine three more "shots", yelled "Clear!" and pressed the starter again. The propeller ground around for six long seconds, hesitated, and then whirled into a blur as the engine growled to life. Wind, whipped back by the propeller, rushed into the cabin through the slightly open canopy. Ian tapped the oil pressure gauge and the needle swung smoothly into the green.

Bernie said something to Ian but it was lost in the rush of air and engine noise. He closed and locked the canopy and switched on the avionics. The intercom came on with the radios and Ian asked what she'd said.

Bernie smiled. "Just like my old MG!"

Ian laughed and called ground control. The ground controller cleared them to taxi to runway 33. Ian checked that everything was working properly in the run-up area, and then asked the tower controller for permission to take off. When the tower gave them clearance, Ian taxied onto the runway, and lined the little plane up with the center-line. He glanced at Bernie. "All set?"

Bernie looked down the long strip of concrete that seemed to lead straight into the bay. "Too late to change my mind?"

"Of course not." Ian smiled reassuringly. "We can go back."

"Can't you tell when someone's kidding?" She pointed down the runway. "Let's go!"

Ian pushed the throttle forward. With redoubled noise and vibration from both the engine and the pro-peller, the Lynx accelerated down the runway. Bernie nervously watched the end of the runway and then laughed, delighted, when the plane lifted off the pavement.

They climbed away from Bay Farm Island, and the barbecue at Mick's house to fly along the estuary between Alameda and Oakland. They flew past the old Navy base and Bernie studied the traffic and the long shadows of the

Bay Bridge. Ian flew into the setting sun and soon they were over the steel towers and concrete canyons of San Francisco's financial district.

Bernie pointed ahead to their right. "Look! You can see Medford Plaza!"

"Where?"

"See the five buildings just east of the Transamerica building?"

"Not yet." Ian turned left so he could see out Bernie's side of the plane.

"See the two tall towers with the three shorter buildings connecting them.?"

"Oh yeah." Ian turned back to the right to get closer to the brick-red group of buildings. "Is that where you live?"

"No! We built it!"

Ian banked left for a moment and then started a gentle right turn around Medford Plaza. Bernie watched the complex rotate below them as the plane turned around it. "It looks just like my model!"

"I thought you were still in school?"

"Grad student. I interned the last two summers with Osmund-Harris-Ikaki. They designed Medford, and I built the model they used for the presentation."

"It looks neat." Ian kept his eyes moving, always looking for other airplanes. "If I may ask, why are you working for Mick?"

"I want to build something. I learned a lot interning, especially working with Lisa Harris, but an office that size is all paperwork and theory. I want to do something practical. I think Architects have to work with materials and contractors and such if they're going to be any good."

"So you're going to work for Mick as a carpenter?"

"Well, an apprentice. You think I'm crazy?"

"Hell no! Sounds like great experience." Ian adjusted the trim. "I liked working construction."

"Were you a carpenter?"

"I was learning. I used to help on remodel jobs to pay for flying lessons." Ian pointed past Bernie. "Take a look at the bridge." He turned toward Alcatraz and the south tower of the Golden Gate Bridge hovered above the plane's right wing. Ian kept turning and the world slowly revolved around the tip of the wing and the top of the tower.

Bernie looked down at the cars and trucks crawling across the thin strip of concrete suspended between the sky blue airplane and the dark blue bay. To the east, the last rays of daylight reflected off thousands of windows in the East Bay Hills. To the west, the sun was the bright spot in a thin band of orange and red that stretched across the horizon. Above it all the sky was dark blue streaked with wisps of orange cirrus clouds. Below, street lights and porch lights had begun to supplement the fading sunlight and as the sun disappeared, more lights came on. The dark blue of early evening advanced.

"Pretty." Bernie watched the deep reddish-pink fade from the darkening clouds.

Ian was looking toward the west as well. "See that line of gray way out there on the horizon?"

"Oh yeah." Bernie smiled. "It looks out of focus."

"It does, doesn't it? That's the fog that'll cover the whole bay in a few hours." Ian rolled the plane level, heading south. "If you look very carefully, you might be able to see the Farallon Islands."

Bernie searched the fuzzy space between the distant fog and the dark water. Ian gradually eased the yoke back as he pushed the throttle forward. The drone of the engine became more labored and the rush of air past the canopy less shrill. The Lynx started climbing. Out past the elusive Farallons, the sun appeared as a faint sliver and then gradually rose out of the west as the Lynx continued to climb. Bernie watched the setting sun rise in a cobalt blue sky and set fire to a whole new horizon. The fog glowed orange and pink and the black ocean stretched from the reborn sunset to the electric-lit city below. Bernie glanced at Ian, her eyes wide with wonder. "It's beautiful!"

Ian nodded. He reduced power, leveled off, and the sun resumed its descent into the sea. "Did you want to try flying?" He pointed to the yoke in front of Bernie.

Bernie smiled, shaking her head. "No, that's okay. You're doing fine."

"Ready to head back?"

"Sure." Bernie watched the last of the sunlight slip away again and the sky faded to darker and darker shades of blue. She sighed. "This is so beautiful."

When Bernie and Ian had left for the airport, only a few cars had been parked on his side of the street. When they returned, the whole block looked like a parking lot and an old green Lincoln Continental and a dark red Chevy truck were each blocking about a third of Ian's driveway. There might have been enough room to squeeze through, but Ian decided not to try. He parked several blocks down the street, and they walked back toward Mick's house.

After they'd passed a few tidy lawns and crossed a few driveways, Ian broke the silence. "You seem thoughtful."

Bernie nodded. "Just thinking about sunsets and old friends."

"Good thoughts?"

Bernie shrugged. "Yeah." She glanced down to fit the two sides of her jacket together and then zipped it up. "Well, mostly."

Ian hadn't brought a jacket, but he hadn't noticed the chill either. He pushed his hands into the pockets of his jeans. "Kind of a mix of good and bad?"

She stopped on the sidewalk in front of Mick's and Ian stopped beside her. Bernie looked at him. "Yeah, I guess. I miss..." She turned away, toward Mick's, and started walking toward the house. Ian started to follow, but Bernie stopped after a few yards and turned around to face him. "I miss more opportunities..." Bernie stepped toward Ian, looked up into his eyes and slid her hand up his chest and over his shoulder. She brushed her fingers through the hair at the back of Ian's neck and pulled him toward her.

Ian leaned forward and brushed his lips across hers. They kissed, gently, with their lips closed and their eyes open.

Mick's stereo played Mariachi music, very loud Mariachi music.

Ian put his arms around Bernie's waist and they kissed again, slowly. Bernie opened her mouth just enough to touch Ian's lips with her tongue. Ian parted his lips, but Bernie pulled back and traced the edge of Ian's jaw with her finger. Her voice was husky. "Could we go someplace quieter?"

"My place is quiet." He glanced across the street, and then smiled as he stared into her eyes. "It's a long walk, though."

Bernie grinned. "The longest journeys begin with a single step." She slid an arm around Ian's waist and hugged him close. Ian put his arm on her shoulder and they crossed the street together.

They kissed again when they reached Ian's porch. Ian pulled his keys out of his pocket while Bernie started unbuttoning his shirt. Ian rubbed his cheek against Bernie's as he tried to fit the right key into the lock. His breath was warm against her neck. Bernie nibbled on his ear as she unhooked the last button and slid the shirt down off his arms. The door swung open.

They stumbled inside and Bernie tossed Ian's dress shirt in toward the living room. Ian kicked the door closed with his foot, and his keys jangled, forgotten in the deadbolt. Ian unzipped Bernie's jacket and she let it drop to the floor. Ian ran his hands across her shoulders and down to the small of her back. She pressed into him, biting his neck, and he pulled the back of her blouse free from her jeans.

Ian's T-shirt was sky-blue with four Navy jets on the front. Bernie grabbed a handful of Blue Angels and tugged the shirt up and over his head. She dropped the T-shirt and started to unbuckle Ian's belt. "Do you have any roommates?"

Ian tore the last button off her blouse. "No."

"Good." Bernie kissed his nipple as she squeezed him through his slacks.

Ian pushed her blouse off her shoulders and it dropped to the floor. Bernie put her arms around his waist and rubbed his back. She teased his nipples with her tongue and kissed the skin between them as he tried to unfasten her bra. The clasp snapped and a small piece of black plastic shot across the living room and into the fireplace. "Sorry." Ian pushed the thin straps down off her arms. Bernie bit him, gently, and Ian bent down to bite her neck.

Ian combed his fingers through her hair and tilted her head back. "You smell good!" He traced the outline of her mouth with the tip of his tongue as he slid his other hand down her stomach and unzipped her jeans.

Bernie licked her lips, her tongue retracing the line that Ian had drawn. "Mm." She bit his neck, and then kissed and nibbled a zigzag path down his chest and stomach to the curls of hair above his belt. She looked up at his face as she crouched in front of him and unzipped his slacks.

Ian stared into her eyes and rubbed his hands across her shoulders. Bernie brushed her lips across his stomach and began pushing his slacks and underwear down. She teased her fingers through his pubic hair and took him in her mouth. Ian leaned his head back, closing his eyes. He moaned, softly, but then opened his eyes and pulled back. "Wait a minute."

Bernie turned her head away. "What's wrong?"

"Nothing's wrong." Ian smiled and kneeled down next to her.

Bernie looked down at the floor.

"Hey, nothing's wrong, nothing at all!" Ian put his arms around her, and she pressed her head against his chest. "We just need to get something out of the bedroom."

Bernie looked up and Ian kissed her, softly, and then forcefully, their tongues playing in a new space they suddenly shared. Ian stood, tugging his slacks up so he could walk, and pulled Bernie to her feet. He led the way down the hall, flicking the hall light on as they passed the switch.

There was an end table in the corner of the bedroom, but Bernie tackled Ian before he could get to it. They fell in a tumble onto the double sized mattress and Bernie maneuvered herself on top. She moved down to Ian's slacks and he kicked off his shoes. She pulled his slacks off, shorts and all, and tickled his foot as she kissed her way up to his thigh.

Ian pulled her up next to him and slid her jeans down to her boots. She held still long enough for Ian to get the boots unzipped, but once he'd pulled them off, Bernie kicked off her jeans. The jeans landed in the hall but her red panties separated from the jeans in flight and landed in the doorway. She pushed herself up and crouched like a cat at the foot of the bed. She growled, her face framed in the fiery brown halo of the hall light shining through her hair. "En garde!"

Ian sat up, laughing, and Bernie pushed him over on his back. She straddled him and slowly slid herself down his stomach. He held her arms to keep her from sliding down further and kissed her. "Let me get something out of the drawer."

Bernie brushed her hand through his hair. "Okay." She kept kissing him.

Ian twisted toward the night stand and Bernie moved with him, kissing and playfully biting the smooth skin of his back. The top drawer was empty. "Damn!" The bottom drawer was also empty. Ian leaned down to look under the night stand. "I thought I unpacked..."

Bernie pulled him back. "If we're looking for condoms, I've got some in my jacket."

Ian nodded. "Where?"

Bernie looked out toward the hall.

"Damn." Ian pushed her over, rubbed his hand through her hair, and slowly down her side. "I'll be right back." Their lips met again. Bernie moaned a growl from deep in her throat. She pressed herself against Ian, feeling him hard against her thigh.

She stopped kissing him for just a moment. "I've got you now." She pushed her tongue deep into his mouth and Ian matched her passion.

"I'll be..." His voice was rough. He kissed her neck, biting her not quite hard enough to leave a mark. "... right..." Ian pushed himself away and rolled off the bed. "...back."

Bernie followed him down the hall. Ian found the black leather jacket on the entryway floor, but Bernie tackled him as soon as he picked it up. They rolled together on the plush living room carpet and landed with the jacket between them.

Bernie pulled a foil packet out of the inside pocket, tossed the jacket to one side, and tore the packet open with her teeth. Ian stroked her back and tousled Bernie's hair as she gently nibbled and kissed the insides of Ian's thighs and stroked the condom onto him. Ian tried to change their positions but Bernie stayed on top, kissing his thigh, his stomach, his chest. "I love the way you taste!" She kissed him on the lips, searching out his tongue with her own. Seductively, teasingly, she began to lower herself onto him.

Ian thrust up to meet her and Bernie cried out.

"Sorry." Ian froze. "Are you okay?"

Bernie ground her hips and shoved back, impaling herself on Ian's erection. She grinned at him, as she rocked forward slightly and squeezed his hips with her knees. Ian moved a little to match Bernie's motion. Bernie changed the tempo and soon they were lost in a steady, insistent rhythm.

Bernie leaned back, her hands on Ian's chest. He slid his hands up from her hips and brushed his palms across her breasts. Bernie put her hands on his and brought his fingers to her nipples, squeezing them. Ian rolled the hardening buds gently between his fingers.

"Harder." Bernie gasped as Ian followed her instruction, but she nodded her head. "Yeah, just like that."

Bernie's breath came in short ragged gasps. She rocked and twisted as she drove herself onto him, her hair flying around her head.

Ian's breathing matched hers; his eyes locked on her face. Washed in shadows, they moved against each other in the middle of the curtainless living room. The yellowish bulb in the hall cast less light on them than the street lamps outside. Their rhythm increased for a moment, and then Bernie closed her eyes and screamed, hammering herself against Ian with frantic intensity. She screamed again and Ian followed her over the edge, arching his back and lifting both of them off the floor.

Bernie held onto him, squeezing him, and he shifted inside her. The blue-white glow from the streetlights washed through the windows, casting squares of light and shadow across their bodies. Music from across the street mixed with their breathing. They smiled at each other and Bernie leaned forward to rest on his chest. Ian wrapped his arms around her, and gently stroked her back.

Bernie rested her head on his shoulder. "Wow." She raised herself a little so she could see him more clearly. "That was fantastic."

"You're fantastic." Ian stroked her back.

"No, you're fantastic." She kissed him softly. "I love the way you kiss." She kissed him again, hard, and Ian matched her passion. They broke away when they ran out of breath. Bernie looked into his eyes and then down at the few curls of hair scattered across his chest. "I liked that. How'd you get to be so good?"

Ian laughed self consciously, "Well," He hugged her close. "As Woody Allen said: 'I practice a lot when I'm alone.'"

"Oh yeah?" Bernie smiled. "Then how'd you get so good at kissing?"

"Licking the hair off my palms."

She laughed and lifted herself off him to lie beside him on the carpet. Except for the paintings and the fireplace tools, their scattered clothes were the only other things on the living room floor. Ian slid the condom off and, after a moment's consideration, tossed it into the fireplace.

Bernie laughed. "What ever will the maid think?" She rubbed her hand slowly across his chest. Ian slid his hand from her shoulder down across her chest and along her side. He drew feather-touch circles around her nipples and then brushed his hand across her ribs and down to her stomach. Several inches to the right of her navel was a small round scar.

Ian touched it. "What's this?"

"That's a scar." Bernie was teasing him.

"That would never have occurred to me." Ian tickled her stomach and Bernie tickled him back. They rolled across the floor and ended up kissing again. After a few minutes Ian asked her again. "Come on, what kind of scar is it?"

"I got shot. There's a bigger patch on my back where the bullet came out." Bernie twisted around to show him.

"What?" Ian sat up to look. "Wow." Tenderly, he traced around the circle of rough skin with his finger. "I, uh... What happened?"

"It's kind of complicated." Bernie hesitated. "Well I guess it's not complicated at all: It was an accident, of course. T.J. didn't mean to hurt me; he just wasn't a very good shot."

"Who's T.J.?

"My brother."

"Your brother shot you?"

"I was fourteen. He was aiming for my father." She sighed. "T.J. is very protective."

Ian started to say something more but Bernie put her hand over his mouth. She kissed him, softly at first. They fell back to the carpet. Ian rolled on top of her and stared into her eyes. "You are so beautiful."

She smiled up at him, reaching down between his legs. "You're pretty scenic yourself." She grabbed him, gently, and began rubbing him the right way. "Hand me my jacket, will ya?"

Monday, 10:16 am – Espresso Rasputin, UC Berkeley

"Sweet sizzling shiest!" Tony Johnson dropped his backpack next to the waist-high, ivy covered fence that separated the cafe's patio from the sidewalk. "If I'd known Bookbinder was going to cancel class, I'd have stayed in bed!" Tony was a wiry young man with short, occasionally combed brown hair and clean, rumpled clothes. He pulled a white plastic patio chair back from the matching white table and slumped into it.

Des Pierrot stole a chair from the next table and sat next to him. His long black hair was tied back in a ponytail. "Don't worry, Tony. I'm sure you're getting enough sleep in class."

"Who said anything about sleep?" Tony leaned over and opened his backpack.

Des looked at his watch. "You could go back. You've got an hour before your next class."

Tony shook his head. "Nah, Cindy's probably gone by now." He pulled a shiny metal-and-plastic hand out of the backpack. "Check this out!" The hand was mounted on a dull metal case with a row of switches on the side. Tony set it on the table and flipped a switch. There was a faint hum of servo-motors and the fingers curled slightly. Tony took an infrared remote out of his shirt pocket and pressed a few buttons. The hand rotated its knuckles toward Des as all but the middle finger curled down, flipping Des off.

"Hey! That's pretty cool." Des leaned over to examine it. "What's it for?"

"Depends." Tony grinned. "My engineering professor gave it a B minus, but my art teacher called it "Techno-Impressionistic" and gave it an A." He pressed the remote and the hand brought thumb and forefinger together to signal "okay".

While Tony showed Des the range of obscene gestures the hand could sign, Brian Nguyen set his Wall Street Journal on the table and took the chair across from Des. "Morning, gentlemen."

"Hey, Brian."

"Morning."

As they exchanged greetings, a waiter came out of the cafe, smiled politely and offered to take their orders. The waiter wore faded jeans, a rumpled white shirt and a green apron. With his hair pulled back in a ponytail and earrings in both ears he looked more like a student than the three younger men at his table. The waiter took their order for three cappuccinos while the mechanical hand waved at him. He waved back and went inside

Brian opened the Journal to the stock report. "Tony, did you buy any TVX?"

"No, I think it's maxed out. Why do you bother with hard copy? Don't you get the market reports on line?"

"Yeah, but I like to read the Journal."

"It's the feel of the newsprint, right?" Des brushed the paper with the back of his hand. "Some kind of ink fetish?"

Tony chuckled but Brian just shook his head. "Get real."

Des nodded knowingly to Tony. "No sense of humor."

Brian folded back the top of the paper and pointed to a line of fine print. "TVX rose two points over the weekend."

Tony's engineering project rotated palm up and Tony shrugged. "You were right, I was wrong; sue me."

"Can't." Brian turned to the next page. "Stupidity isn't a civil offense."

The hand's thumb and fingertips came together, pointing at the almost cloudless sky.

Des nudged Tony with his elbow. "What's that mean?"

Tony smiled. "It's a bouquet of these." The hand flipped Brian the finger.

"And to think we used to be such good friends." Des laughed. "Brian, what's with TVX?"

Brian was still looking at the paper. "Erica said she left you a message."

"I haven't checked my messages."

"You lead a disconnected life, Des." Brian turned to a different page. "TVX is at 37 but they just got the FDA's go-ahead for a new product. Their stock will go through the roof over the next few days. I think we should buy as much as we can."

Tony shook his head. "I talked to Erica this morning." The hand wagged a warning finger. "They're still testing. Even if they complete the trials without a hitch, they still have to convince consumers to trust another genetically-engineered product. Every source I've heard says TVX is as high as it's going to get, and a lot of analysts think it's already priced too high. Besides, I want to focus on something else."

Their waiter came out of the cafe with a tray of cappuccinos and was almost knocked over by a tall woman with long red hair. He adeptly recovered his balance and graciously motioned for her to go ahead of him. She walked over to the impromptu board meeting and looked down at Des. "Hi, Des. Can I sit next to my fiancé?"

"Sure, Cindy." Des stood to give her his chair, "Whoa! Since when are you guys are engaged?"

"Since yesterday." Cindy sat down and leaned over to kiss Tony.

"Congratulations!" Des took the chair next to Brian. The waiter set the three cappuccinos on the table and tucked the serving tray under his arm. "Can I get you gentlemen anything else? Something for you, miss?"

Des looked around the table. Brian shook his head and the mechanical hand twisted from side to side. Cindy pulled away from Tony long enough to say, "No, thanks."

Des took some bills out of his pocket. "That's it. Thanks." The waiter departed, promising to return with Des' change.

Tony smiled at Cindy. "I didn't expect to see you so soon."

Cindy smiled back. "I just saw you guys over here and thought I'd steal a kiss." She kissed him again.

Brian rolled his eyes and Des sipped his coffee.

"Come on, Tony." Brian set his glass down. The hand waved at him. "What 'something else' do you want to focus on?"

Tony leaned back. "Can't you see I'm a little distracted here?" Cindy drank some of his cappuccino.

"Yeah." Brian sighed. "Get a room, will ya?"

Cindy said, "Got one?"

Brian opened the paper and lifted it like a wall. The top of the paper folded away from him in a gust from the otherwise gentle breeze. Brian snapped it back upright.

Tony watched Cindy take another sip of his drink. "Are you sure you don't want some coffee or something?"

She put his glass down. "No, thanks. I've got to go. I've got a flight lesson at eleven."

Des looked up from the foam in his glass. "Don't you already have a pilot's license?"

Cindy nodded. "This is for my instrument rating."

"Is that any easier?"

She shrugged. "Sometimes. Most of the time it's a huge challenge."

"Hey!" Tony held his empty glass accusingly toward Cindy.

"Gotta run!" Cindy gave him a quick kiss, stood and stepped right into the waiter. Des' change scattered across the table but Cindy and the waiter kept each other from falling down. Cindy straightened her sweater. "I'm so sorry!"

Though he was obviously thinking something else, the waiter said, "Excuse me," and stepped aside to let her pass. Des gave him a five-dollar tip, and gestured for another round. The waiter departed, Brian went back to reading his paper, and Des reached over and handed Brian's cappuccino to Tony. Tony drank some of the foamy coffee as he slid his empty glass in front of Brian's paper wall.

Brian lowered the paper and reached for his coffee. "Hey!"

Tony leaned forward and put his forearms on the table. "You've got to keep this quiet, even if we don't go for it." He looked around cautiously. "This isn't based on market analysis or computer projections, okay? This is totally inside information."

Des smiled. "That's great!"

Brian sighed. "It's illegal."

Des nodded. "Even better."

Tony looked from Brian to Des. "My brother works for Daga Kabt Incorporated. His team has been working on a file server that he thinks will be the hottest, fastest, whatever-est file server ever."

"Your brother the lawyer?" Brian tilted the empty glass to one side and looked into it.

"No, not John; Rob. He's an engineer, like me."

"Like you wanna be."

"You want to hear this or not?"

"I'm listening." Brian set the glass down.

Tony sighed. "Okay. A primo file server is good for your product line but even the best file server isn't going to rocket you to fame and fortune by itself. What's important about this one is the computer it's being designed to work with. Rob and his team just got some of the revised specs on it. It's totally new."

Brian snorted. "Everything out of Silicon Valley is always 'totally new!'"

Tony shook his head. "Yeah, but this is different. Rob thinks they're working on a different kind of computer chip.

He's been there for two years and this is the first time he's ever told me to buy their stock."

"I thought we bought some DKI." Des had finished his cappuccino and was playing with the spoon.

"We did. We've still got 2,000 shares." Brian turned through the Journal to the page he wanted. "We bought it six months ago at about 25, I think. It was at 22 last week and, uh, here it is. It dropped to 21 and a half over the weekend." Brian closed the paper. "The company is losing market share, it's heavily in debt and has no assets to speak of. How much of this dog do you want us to buy, Anthony?"

"All of it."

Des chuckled. "The whole company?"

Tony shook his head. "We can't raise that much money, but if we liquidate everything we have, we can buy enough DKI stock to get controlling interest."

"Are you serious?" Brian lowered the paper to the table. "You want to put everything we've made over the last three years into one declining stock?"

Tony nodded. "Everything. Rob is going to mortgage his house to buy as much as he can. I think we should do the same."

Des shook his head. "I don't want to bet everything on one stock, no matter how good the information."

"It's lousy information." Brian wiped cappuccino foam off his paper. "DKI is going into the toilet."

Tony shook his head. "I don't think so. I do think DKI is in danger of a takeover."

"This is sounding better!" Des leaned forward. "If that happens, the stock could go ballistic."

Tony added. "That's a fact, but there's an even better option."

Brian rolled his eyes. "What's that?"

"We engineer the takeover." Tony's art project formed a fist. "Instead of buying stock in the company as an investment, we line up some other investors and buy the whole company."

Des set his spoon in his empty mug. "You're serious?"

"Full on." Tony nodded.

Des leaned forward. "How much money are we talking about?"

"A lot, maybe forty million dollars. I figure between the four of us we can raise almost sixteen million. With that kind of commitment, I'm sure we can borrow the balance."

"Commitment? You should be committed." Brian leaned back in his chair. "Count me out, okay? You're fucking crazy!"

"I'm fucking crazy *inspired*, Brian, and it's kind-of your fault." Tony turned toward him. "You've been gung-ho to make it big ever since we started trading! You were the one who got us together! You keep saying you can't wait for us to start our own company - well here's our chance! We could walk from graduation ceremonies right into the boardroom of the next Intel."

"Have you seen Intel stock this morning?" Brian shook his head. "It's too risky. We've made a lot of money over the last three years and I don't want to blow it."

"You want to be cautious now? Jesus!" Tony looked at Des. "We can dissolve Conquistador Ltd. anytime, right?"

"Yeah." Des shrugged. "We're way past needing to pool our money, but..." He glanced at Brian and then looked at Tony. "Do you really want to break up the partnership?"

"Of course not!" Tony leaned forward. "Three years ago, we said we were going to build a Fortune 500 company and I still want to do it! What we have here is a company with a revolutionary new product and an outdated corporate culture. What DKI needs is new management, our new management." The mechanical hand was still clenched in a fist. "Why should we start at the ground floor when we can buy the penthouse?"

"Buy? At what cost?" Brian considered. "Take the long view, Tony: we're not at the bottom! You said it yourself: Conquistador owns stock worth almost sixteen million dollars. Actually I think we just topped that. Why should we gamble that on a bankrupt company? We'd be pissing our futures right out your penthouse window!"

Des chuckled. "Since when did you get so conservative, Brian? Didn't you used to say, 'You've got to risk money to make money'?"

"Not everything you've got!" Brian looked angrily from Des to Tony.

Tony smiled. "Brian, DKI is not bankrupt. Let me get some more information from Rob, and I'll prove it. Let's get together with Erica tonight to talk it over."

Brian shrugged. "We can talk about it all you want."

Des nodded. "It wouldn't hurt to know what DKI is worth. Can we get a stockholders' report? I'd like to..." Des stopped talking when a woman with short brown hair and a black leather jacket walked up behind Tony. "Hi, Terri."

"Hey, Des. Dudes." Terri leaned on the fence. "Where's Erica?"

"Grading papers, I think." Tony turned sideways so he could see her. "How's the Tae Kwon Do class going?"

"Great!" Terri slid her sleeve up to show a large bruise on her forearm. "I've got bruises all over. You should have stayed with it."

"No way! I didn't want to get killed, I just wanted some exercise." Tony laughed. "I switched to tennis."

Terri nodded, and turned to Des. "I'm headed over to Shaggy's. You guys hungry?"

"God!" Brian grimaced. "Isn't it a little early for pizza?"

"Never." Terri looked at Tony. "You?"

"Nah. Thanks but," Tony shook his head. "Nah."

Des slid his chair back. "I'm up for pizza." He stood up. "Tony, let me know when and where you guys want to get together."

"Will do." The mechanical hand waved as Des turned and walked into the waiter. The laid-back dude with the ponytail was carrying a tray of coffees in his right hand. He lifted the tray over his head and stepped back to stay under it. He and Des said, "Excuse me." at the same time, and Des watched as the waiter regained his balance without spilling a drop.

Des gave him a thumbs-up. "That was pretty good."

"Thanks." The ponytail bobbed as the waiter nodded his head. "Didn't you want your cappuccino?"

Brian waved at the waiter. "I'll take it."

Des walked out through the gate and came back on the other side of the fence. "Later, guys."

Tony nodded. "Bye." Brian was paying for the cappuccinos.

Des took a cigarette out and lit it as he and Terri walked down Bancroft Street toward Telegraph. Terri's black jeans, dark blue T-shirt and black leather jacket clashed with the tan slacks, pale yellow shirt and pullover sweater Des was wearing. They stepped apart to let a person with silver nose rings and a purple Mohawk pass between them.

Terri looked back over her shoulder. "So how's life with the Four Musketeers?"

Des blew smoke at the sky. "All for one and one for all?" He laughed. "Not very. Tony wants to bet everything on one company and Brian wants to crawl into a hole and live off the interest."

"What about you and Erica?"

"Haven't talked to her yet. The more I think about Tony's idea, though, the more I like it."

"Sounds like a breakup to me."

"Yeah, well, we've lasted longer than a lot of marriages. Maybe it's time for a change."

"It's time for a lot of things to change." Terri stepped to one side to get past an old man who stepped to the same side as Terri, forcing her to stop.

Wearing a rumpled gray suit and carrying a huge Bible under his arm, the geezer flashed his few remaining teeth. "Are you saved?"

"Yeah, but I'm earning lousy interest." Terri dodged around the grinning old man. The eagle talon hanging from her ear brushed against her cheek as she shook her head. "Jesus! There are entirely too many idiots on this planet!"

Des laughed. "You've been talking to Paul."

"Exactly the scum-encrusted fuck I wanted to talk about. How'd you guess?"

"Simple." Des shrugged. "You have his Graduate Psychology Seminar on Monday mornings and every Monday afternoon you go ballistic."

"Yeah, well, the seminar is great. It's Doctor Paul head-up-his-ass Neault who pisses me off. There are at least two students, in my group alone, who are already better qualified to teach psychology than that worthless asshole!" They waited at the corner for a car to stop and then crossed Bowditch Street. "Christ! He pisses me off!"

"Did you manage to get another professor to be your doctoral advisor?"

"Yeah, I think so. Once I get that bastard out of my academic life, I'm taking my people and my contacts and I'm going into business for myself."

Des shook his head. "Paul's not going to like that."

"Fuck what he likes! He doesn't even handle the stuff anymore! We're doing all the work, taking all the risk, and he makes all the profit!"

"Not all the profit." Des smiled. "We're doing good."

"That's easy for you to say; you don't have to take any classes with the bastard! Slimy, fucking prick!" Terri shouted the last expletive and people around them looked to see what was wrong. Terri lowered her voice. "I needed the fucker's signature on one lousy letter of recommendation, right? He makes me wait for almost an hour while he talks about women paying him to let them do his housework, naked! It's total bullshit! I mean, who does he think he's kidding? Even if I did believe the twisted old shit, why would I want to hear about it?" A car honked as Terri stepped into Telegraph Avenue. She backed up onto the curb. "And he keeps hitting on me! I've only been telling him I'm gay for the last four goddamned years!" The light changed and they crossed the street.

"You realize, of course, that we go through something like this every week?"

"Fuck you!"

"Hey, come on!" Des took a puff off his cigarette. "I'm on your side, I agree with you! Paul has been getting weirder, and he was pretty strange to begin with. He needs to see a shrink himself, but we still need him. Half the cops in the East Bay end up talking to him or somebody he knows."

"We don't need to know which cops are having mid-life crises, just what the narcs are doing." Terri headed down Durant and Des followed. "He gives us valuable information, but it's not worth paying him half the profit! Besides, Doctor Neault-Nuts is not the only source."

Des flicked what was left of his cigarette into the gutter as they turned off the sidewalk into Shaggy's.

The restaurant was almost empty, but they went upstairs to the second floor, and picked a table next to a window. "What other sources did you have in mind?" Des handed Terri a menu. "I'm open to suggestions."

"Jesus."

"What?"

"Jesus Ruiz."

"What about him?" Des looked at the menu.

"He's tired of dealing with Neault, too. I've talked to him about getting rid of the Doctor and he's up for it." Terri glanced around the restaurant. "Jesus has some really good contacts, he could easily replace Neault. We're buying from Jesus anyway. If we stop dealing with Neault, we make a better profit, and Jesus gets a tighter operation with a more progressive management team. What do you think?"

"You've got the right idea, but I had a different supplier in mind."

"Yeah?"

"Mick Dale."

"The contractor? He buys from us!"

A waitress rushed over to the table and apologized for not noticing them sooner. They ordered coffees and a combination pizza and the girl hurried off with their order.

Terri leaned forward. "Mick buys from me."

Des shook his head. "Not anymore. He's got connections in Mexico, and he's figured out a foolproof way to bring the stuff across the border. I just bought twenty keys from him at sixty percent of what Milanov has been charging Neault."

"But he was my customer!" Terri raised an eyebrow. "Is it any good?"

"Premium." Des leaned forward. "I mean pure, uncut Bolivian."

"Uncut?"

"Straight from his source." Des cleared his throat as their waitress returned with two glasses of ice water. "So, uh, how did you do on Stoddard's pop-quiz?"

Terri smiled. "Aced it."

"Really?"

"It was easy." Terri shrugged. "I'm more worried about my Tae Kwon Do test."

"When's that?"

"Tomorrow." Terri drank some of the water and watched the waitress walk away.

"Good luck."

"Thanks. I should be a brown belt next time I see you."

"I'll try to be more polite." They both laughed.

"It seems weird that Mick was buying from us, and now all of a sudden he has a better source than we do."

"You sound suspicious."

"Of course I'm suspicious. Aren't you?"

"Yeah, but we knew he had family in Mexico. The only thing that's changed is that now he has a guy who can get him in and out."

"That's true." Terri considered. "Sixty percent?"

Des nodded. "Forty percent off."

"I'll need ten keys as soon as possible."

"No problem."

"Did you tell Neault?"

"I had to, but I gave him as few details as I could."

"Hell, money talks." Terri smiled. "We can forget about Jesus, string Neault along to keep tabs on the cops and buy most of our product from Mick."

"We'll buy some from Mick. We have to do this gradually; Neault and Milanov are too tight for us to switch suppliers overnight. And I don't want to get Milanov pissed off."

Terri nodded, "Amen."

The waitress brought their coffees over and the conversation shifted back to school.

Thursday, 12:17 pm - Ian's House, Alameda

Mick rang Ian's doorbell and stepped back, away from the door. He was wearing a green bomber jacket over a black spy plane T-shirt, and he had a shiny black leather flight case in his right hand. Standing with his back to Ian's garage, Mick could watch the street without turning his back to the front door itself. He jerked his head away from the street when Ian opened the door.

"Hey, Mick. How's it going?" Ian let the door swing open, and Mick stepped into the entryway.

"Good, real good. Hey, I'm sorry I'm late, man. I got a little hung up."

"No problem." Ian closed the door and they walked into the family room. "Do you want a root beer, or something?" Ian continued into the kitchen. "We need to do some ground school before we go to the airport."

"Root beer would be great, thanks." Mick set the flight case on the breakfast bar and sat up on one of the new barstools. "Hey this is nice."

"Thanks." Ian brought out two sodas and handed one to Mick. "They delivered it yesterday."

"Zach said there was a big truck over here. Cool." Mick looked around. The new dining room chairs matched the new bar stools and the new recliner went very well with the new couch. He opened his soda. "So, am I going to need any of my gear for this 'ground school'?"

"You'll need that red and white regulations manual and your logbook." Ian pointed at the case on the counter. "Isn't all your stuff in there?"

"No, that's yours." Mick pushed the case toward Ian. "You said you needed a new flight case, remember?"

"Yeah, but..." Ian opened the top and looked inside. "Jesus!" The bottom of the case was covered with neat rows of bundled bills. Ian closed the top and snapped the latches shut.

Mick smiled. "I know we agreed on a quarter mil, but the market wasn't as soft as I thought and I made a lot more than I planned. I couldn't have done it without you, man, so I threw in an extra fifty." He shrugged. "It's only fair."

"An extra fifty thousand?" Ian shook his head, started to take a drink, realized he hadn't opened the can yet and put it down. "'Thank you' doesn't cover it."

"Don't mention it."

"But I mean it. Thank you." Ian looked around at the newly furnished rooms. "Two weeks ago I was trying to sell this house because I couldn't afford to keep it. Now..."

"I noticed the 'for sale' sign was gone."

"Yeah, but they left the hole in the lawn." Ian put his hand on the case. "How much is in here?"

"The hundred and fifty I owed you, plus your 'bonus' makes two hundred thousand dollars."

"Two..." Ian looked at the ceiling. "Well, obviously I need a bigger house."

Mick set his soda on the counter. "Are you going to buy a bigger house?"

"No!" Ian laughed. "Hell, no! This one's perfect."

"So what are you going to do with this?" Mick tapped the case of money.

Ian considered. "I think I'll buy a new car."

"For two hundred grand?"

Ian shook his head. "Between Marcia and the bank I owe a hundred and eighty thousand on the house, and about forty five on credit cards and student loans. I'll pay that off, gradually like you said, but I think I'll buy a new car. That leaves about sixty thousand to put in the bank."

"Sounds very practical." Mick shook his head

"You sound disappointed. What are you going to do with your share?"

"I have a wife and kids to spend whatever Dale Construction doesn't eat up." Mick looked around the room. "You don't have that problem. You could buy that PBY. You could buy Air Charter Express and be your own boss! What do you want, man? What do you dream about?"

Ian considered. "I'd like to fly 787s, but those jobs are hard to come by. It would be great to own a charter company, especially Air Charter Express, but it wouldn't be A.C.E. without Ace Quintero. Besides, he's not about to sell his multi-million dollar company for sixty thousand."

Mick shook his head. "No, but with a few more trips..."

"I don't think so."

"You could make a lot of money."

"I made a lot of money and it was way too much fun; my adrenaline was pumping all the way back - hell: it's still pumping but I don't want to press my luck." He drank the rest of his soda and stepped over to set the can next to the sink. There were two red and green coleus plants on the windowsill. Between them, Ian could see his new patio furniture sitting on the faux flagstones. "I can't believe this is all paid for." Ian turned back to Mick. "I'll never be able to repay you..."

"Sure you can."

"How?"

"Do it again."

"No, thanks."

"How can you turn down a quarter of a million dollars?"

"How can I not? My bills are paid, or will be; same with the house. I don't need the money and I sure as hell don't need the risk!"

"Risk? What risk?" Mick turned his hands palms up. "What could be safer than going through Customs with an empty airplane?"

"Mick, there are a lot of other things that could go wrong. It's an excellent plan, we proved that. But why risk everything I have on something I don't need?"

"I hear your words, man, but I think your heart is saying something else. You're the one always saying flying should be fun, admit it! Wasn't last Thursday a rush? Don't you really, deep down, secretly, want to do it again?"

"Dammit, Mick! It was a once-in-a-lifetime experience that I will never forget." Ian's tone turned thoughtful. "Or ever be able to tell anybody about, but I'm not doing it again!"

Mick watched Ian hesitate and a wry smile seemed to make his eyes sparkle. "Name your price."

Ian just shook his head. "Let's talk about ground school. This would be a real good time to talk about Federal Aviation Regulations."

"Name your price."

"Come on Mick, let's quit while we're ahead."

"Name your price."

Ian studied Mick's eyes. "You're serious."

Mick nodded. "Name your price."

"Okay," Ian threw up his hands. "A million dollars."

"Done."

"What?"

"Done." Mick held out his hand to close the deal. "But you have to let me fly the Citation."

"One million dollars?" Ian shook his head in disbelief. "Just like that? How much is this stuff worth?"

Mick shrugged, his hand still extended. "Enough to buy a block of houses and build an apartment building. Enough to buy an air-charter operation."

"A million dollars?"

Mick nodded. "One million dollars."

"This is uh…" Ian cautiously reached out and shook Mick's hand. "This is the last time."

Mick smiled. "I'll call Carlos."

Friday the 13th, 10:18 pm – 169 Fair
Haven Court, Alameda

Mick armed his new truck's alarm, and the red Chevy 4x4 answered with an electronic chirp. He had parked across the cul-de-sac from a large two-story house with bright lights in the front and side yards. Mick dropped his keys into his pocket, and swung his backpack up onto his shoulder as he crossed the street toward the house. A sign next to the front door proclaimed, "The Houghton's", in large ornate letters. Mick had to press the bell three times before a short man, with more hair on his chest than on his head, answered the door. Don Houghton was wearing a towel and dripping on his entryway's hardwood floor.

"Hey, Mick! Glad you could drop by!" He stepped back and Mick followed him into the large foyer. "How you doin'?"

"Good, Don. You're dressed for success."

"Hey, I told you it was a hot tub party."

"Oh, yeah." Mick could see people in swimsuits at the other end of the corridor.

"You bring the stuff?"

Melissa Etheridge was singing, "Ain't it Heavy" at party volume. Mick tilted his head back toward his backpack. "Of course."

"Great." Don walked toward the white-carpeted stairs that curved up to the second floor. Mick was right behind him. On the way up, they passed a young man in a bulging thong swimsuit who bounded down the stairs two at a time. Don led the way to an expensively furnished office overlooking the front lawn. Floor to ceiling shelves on the eastern wall were filled with law books. Mick closed the door as Don opened the top drawer of his desk and took out a key to open the bottom drawer. Mick swung the backpack off his shoulder and set it on the desk next to a calendar still turned to Thursday the 12th.

The blinds over the window behind the desk were only halfway down and Mick stepped over to close them as Don pulled a steel apothecary scale out of the bottom drawer. Looking out the window, Mick could see his pickup, brawny and clean in the bright circle cast by the streetlight next to it. He started to close the blinds, but noticed a man across the street walk over to the side of his truck and crouch beside it. Mick looked down the street and saw a powder-blue sedan roll to a stop a few houses away. He looked back at his truck but couldn't see if the man was still there. The sedan's headlights switched off but no one got out of the car.

Mick stepped away from the window and pulled a pair of leather gloves out of his jacket. "We've got trouble, Don."

"Where?" Don dropped the scale back into its drawer with a loud clunk and shoved the drawer closed.

"Outside. At least one unmarked car and a guy on foot." Mick pulled one of the gloves on.

"No worries." Don moved toward the door. "Sit tight. They're probably after Hal Stifely, next door. If not, I'll get rid of 'em." He tugged his towel a little higher. Mick pulled on the other glove, grabbed his pack and followed into the hall, but when Don turned toward the front door, Mick headed the other way.

He could hear water running in the bathroom, and he opened the door to look inside. Steam from the shower filled the room and wafted out into the hall. A couple were making love under the hot spray of the shower. Completely engrossed in each other, they didn't even notice him. Mick smiled and whispered to himself. "Perfect."

He stepped across the hall into the guest bedroom, shut the door, and emptied his backpack onto the bed. Using a corner of the bedspread, Mick carefully wiped any possibility of fingerprints off each of the four plastic bags. He then lifted the mattress, and shoved the bags as far back as he could reach, spacing them out so they didn't make too obvious a lump in the mattress. Standing, Mick zipped his pack closed and hung it in the closet next to a pink ski parka. Back in the hall he took his gloves off and stuffed them into their pocket in his jacket.

The concussive of the front door crashing open was almost as loud as the music from the CD player, and the impact seemed to shake the whole house. Mick stepped into the bathroom, lifted the lid on the toilet and unzipped his jeans. The woman in the shower had her eyes closed and her partner had his back to the door. Mick cleared his throat as he watched the pair, and the woman opened her eyes to look at Mick. She raised her eyebrows slightly and smiled. Mick smiled back and shrugged. She closed her eyes.

Listening to the faint cries of "Cops!" and "Police!" and watching the mounting passion in the shower, Mick found it hard to concentrate. As the shouts drew closer, and the clomp of heavy boots became noticeable through the floor, Mick still hadn't been able to relieve himself. He reached down, flushed the unused toilet, and turned so his right side was toward the door. He reached for his zipper as the door flew open.

"Police, freeze!"

Mick turned his head slightly to look at the cop. The blue uniform and cherubic face seemed far away behind the department-issue 9 millimeter. The barrel of the blued-steel cannon that hovered a few inches from Mick's right eye completely eclipsed the young cop's expression.

Mick tried to smile. "Can I zip my pants?"

The woman in the shower screamed and the officer swung his gun toward her. Her partner saw the gun and moved to shield her with his body.

"They're not armed!" Mick zipped his jeans as the gun swung back toward him. The cop was about the same build as Mick but a lot younger. "It's okay." Mick sounded like a doctor reassuring a patient. "Everything's okay."

The officer looked at Mick, the couple in the shower, and the water swirling around in the bowl of the toilet. He focused on Mick. "Hands on your head and face the wall!" As Mick carefully turned toward the wall and put his hands on top of his head, the officer kept the big gun pointed at Mick's ear. "What did you flush?"

"Uh," Mick smiled, "borrowed beer?"

The officer grabbed the collar of Mick's jacket and hammered his face into the wall. "Wrong answer!"

"Ow!" Mick moved his hands toward his nose, but the cop jabbed the gun into his back.

"Interlace your fingers!"

Mick linked his fingers together and let himself be pulled backwards into the hall. There were three other policemen in the hall and the officer dragging Mick out tilted his head toward the bathroom. "There's two more in there." One officer raised his gun and headed into the bath. The other two headed down the hall. Mick was shoved into the wall again, leaving a bloody nose-print on the off-white wallpaper. "Put your hands on the wall and spread your legs!" Mick complied.

The officer searched him with one hand, using the other to keep his gun pressed into the back of Mick's neck. "I asked you a question."

"I, uh..." Mick tried to exhale through his nose but only blood came out. It landed in thick red gobbets on the white carpet. "I think you broke my nose."

The cop found the .38 revolver under Mick's T-shirt. "Gun, partner!" The cop in the bathroom stepped out into the hall while his partner pulled Mick's gun out of its belt holster. "What's this, huh?"

"If I get the right answer, will you stop hurting me?"

The cop drove an elbow into Mick's back. "Don't fuck with me, asshole!"

"That'll do, Thomas." The voice was calm, professional, and very much in charge. Looking down to his right, Mick could only see pressed gray slacks and polished gray cowboy boots.

The gun eased away from Mick's neck. "Okay, Captain." Mick's hands were cuffed behind his back, and then the officer spun him around and leaned him back against the wall.

The gray pants belonged to a large unfriendly looking man, with mottled pink skin. An open, tan overcoat that looked a size too small covered some of the gray suit. The captain looked at Mick carefully, as though he'd seen him before but couldn't remember where. "We'll have plenty of time to talk after we book 'em." He moved down the hall, as the officer started reading Mick his rights.

CHAPTER FOUR

Saturday, 4:19 pm – Gate 81, SFO

Ian looked first at his watch then at the closed Jetway doors and then beyond the terminal windows at the tarmac. An Airbus was taxiing past but it was the wrong airline to be Sandy's plane. He'd gotten to SFO early and Sandy's flight was delayed by weather, but Ian wasn't feeling put out. He was actually grateful and he was savoring the opportunity to watch the ebb and flow of people and airplanes. Harried business people rushed past excited families: nervous first timers eavesdropped on gossiping flight crews and the busy employees of a hundred different airport franchises all contributed to the thrilling vitality Ian loved so much about airports. Beyond the human drama, just past the soundproofed glass, the descendants of Clipper ships and Pullman Sleepers swept past with names and livery that spoke of thrilling adventures and faraway places.

Ian was leaning against an arch that shot up to the ceiling like the buttress of a glass and steel cathedral. It was the perfect spot from which to see everyone coming off flight 143, and Ian would have seen Sandy deplane except that just as her plane turned toward the gate, Ian was distracted by what sounded like a dozen arguing ring tones. The strange music wasn't coming over the PA and Ian looked around to find the source on the other side of the concourse. Four musicians and an actor with a harmonica had formed an impromptu jazz ensemble. They were having trouble getting in synch, but faced with the tedium of waiting for their delayed flight they were determined. When they finally found a groove it began to sound really sweet. The harmonica mixed with violin, flute, sitar and drumsticks on a hard-shell suitcase in a variation of Lucky Joy's "Ecstatic Pomegranate Ballet". Ian wasn't familiar with the tune, but when they all busted up laughing and had to start over from the top, he was tapping his foot by the third bar. The Jetway doors opened behind him.

Third off the plane, Sandy turned toward baggage claim as she reached the concourse. She had her cell phone out and when she heard Ian calling her name, she stopped and gave the phone a puzzled look before turning back toward the gate. Ian was running and she waited for him to reach her before saying, "Hi! What are you doing here?"

"Picking you up!"

"I know, I mean, thank you, but I thought we were meeting at baggage claim." She hugged him. "It's good to see you."

"And you."

"How'd you get past security?"

Ian pointed to the FAA ID clipped to his belt. "Pilot, remember?"

"Right." Sandy nodded. "I'm sorry we're so late. Were you waiting long?"

"I have no idea; I love airports!" Ian pointed back toward the ensemble. "They even arranged some live music in your honor."

Sandy listened for a moment. "Sounds familiar. What is it?"

"No idea, but I like it."

Sandy grinned. "Me too."

As they walked to baggage claim Sandy explained about coming home through Chicago to clear up some merger details. The Vice President she'd had trouble with turned out to be a fantastic help and so John Geaque was now President of OHI's newest subsidiary. Before the brief stopover in Chicago, of course, she'd been in Copenhagen and when Ian asked about her parents Sandy said she really liked having a close, loving family on another continent.

Twenty minutes later they'd claimed Sandy's luggage, stowed it in the back seat of Ian's new Mustang and the convertible was whisking them north along the edge of San Francisco Bay. With the top down and the bay behind her, Sandy looked like she was flying over the water. Her hair danced in the turbulence behind the windshield and she had to raise her voice to be heard over the road noise. "What a great car! I love convertibles!"

"Me too!" Ian nodded enthusiastically, signaled and moved into the center lane to pass an empty airport shuttle. He had the cruise control set at 75, but there was plenty of room to get around the few cars moving closer to the 65 mile an hour speed limit. They quickly left the cluster of slower vehicles behind and had all five north-bound lanes to themselves. The afternoon was cooling off and tendrils of coastal fog were beginning to push across the ridge from the other side of the peninsula. Ian looked from the fog, to Sandy's hair, whipping and pulling at her headrest as though trying to escape the car altogether. "It's not too windy, is it?"

"It's wonderful!" Sandy stretched up to catch more of the wind in her face and her hair went wild. She raised her arms and the sleeves of her sweater rippled and popped in the wind. "Absolutely smashing!"

Ian kept most of his attention on the road ahead, but he glanced at his passenger a lot. "Do you have any plans for this evening?"

"No." Watching him smile made Sandy start to smile as well. "Any suggestions?"

"I thought you might like to get some dinner."

"With you? I'd love to." Sandy nodded enthusiastically. "Could we stop at my place to get rid of the luggage?" The Mustang had a tiny trunk, which was why her bags were in the back seat.

"Of course. Do you like Italian?" Looking from Sandy, back to the road ahead, Ian checked the rear view mirror. "What the...?"

Sandy didn't see his smile disappear. "Italian would be perfect. How about..."

Ian stomped the accelerator to the firewall and the convertible surged forward as he yelled, "Hold on!" The engine had enough torque to press them back into their seats but the car couldn't accelerate fast enough to stay ahead of the dirty green Galaxy catching up with them.

Seconds before impact, the Galaxy's driver noticed them and swerved to the right. The big car almost slipped past, but rusty chrome dug into red plastic and the Mustang swerved toward the center divider. Ian steered into the skid and got the car straightened out in the far left lane.

Sandy turned to look behind them. The Galaxy's brakes were locked, the worn tires had lost their grip on the pavement and the car was spinning around as if it were on ice. After several revolutions, the wheels regained enough traction to stop the rotation. Moving north, but pointed south, the big car's front wheels were still cranked into a tight right turn. As the wheels took hold and the car started to track backwards, it swung toward the south-bound lanes and slammed trunk first into the concrete center divider.

Ian slowed down, signaled, and crossed the empty freeway to the gravel shoulder. He stopped the car and looked at Sandy. "Are you okay?"

Sandy held up her hands, nodding. "Yeah, fine. Are you okay?"

"Yeah, I'm fine." He took a deep breath and they studied each other carefully for a moment, as though making sure. When Ian looked back at the Galaxy, it was sitting sideways across two lanes of the freeway. The cluster of traffic Ian and Sandy had passed was squeezing past the rusty green car a vehicle or two at a time.

"What an idiot!" Ian left the car running, but released his seatbelt and opened his door. "Let me see how bad it is." He stepped out and walked around to the right side.

Sandy reached into the back seat and pulled her cell phone out of her purse. Dialing 911, she watched Ian as he checked the side and rear of the car.

He looked surprised. "This is amazing!"

"Is it bad?"

"No, not at all! Looks like it just bent the bumper a little. There's a scratch in the quarter panel, but basically it's fine." Ian looked back at the other Ford, crumpled against the center divider. The driver's door was still closed. "Christ! I hope he's okay."

A steady flow of traffic was squeezing past the green roadblock and accelerating north toward San Francisco. Ian got back in the convertible, shifted into reverse and started backing up along the shoulder. Sandy was still describing the accident to the 911dispatcher when the Galaxy lurched away from the center divider and started rolling toward them. Ian shook his head. "What the hell is he doing?" Sandy looked back and then relayed the new situation over the phone.

As the Galaxy got closer, inky black smoke began pouring from the rear wheel wells. The car's rear end was scrunched up against its tires and the crumpled metal was burning through the smoking rubber. By the time it reached Ian and Sandy, the back of the car was engulfed in a thick oily cloud.

Ian stopped the Mustang and stood up on his seat. He yelled, "Hey, stop!" as the smoking green sedan limped past.

With a loud "POP", the right side of the Galaxy dropped several inches. The distorted metal had burned through the rear tire. Incredibly, the Galaxy kept going.

Ian looked down at Sandy and shrugged, embarrassed. "God, I'm clever."

"I'd have stopped." Sandy pointed to the phone still pressed to her ear. "I'm on hold."

"Right." Ian slid down into his seat, shifted into first gear and followed the smoke.

"God, that stinks!" Sandy wrinkled her nose.

"Burning rubber." Ian looked at the speedometer. "This guy is making his getaway at eighteen miles an hour!"

The Galaxy left the freeway at the exit to the old football stadium and Ian followed. A second "POP" announced the failure of the sedan's left rear tire. The Galaxy limped through a red light on its rear rims and died a block later at the top of a short hill. Ian stopped and waited for the light.

When the light changed, Ian drove up the hill and parked on the left side of the road, a few hundred feet from the Galaxy. The Galaxy was stopped on the right side of the road just before a circular cul-de-sac. A very thin man in pale yellow pants and a tattered sport coat was staring at the crumpled rear end of his car and shaking his head.

As Ian stepped out of the Mustang, he asked Sandy, "Are the police coming?"

She listened to her phone for a moment and then nodded.

Ian walked over to the thin man, stopping about 15 feet away. "Are you okay?"

The sport coat shifted as the man swayed back on his heels. He seemed about to fall over, but then turned to face Ian. He was in his forties, had a week's growth of stubbly beard and smelled like landfill after a rainy day. Pale rheumy eyes tried to follow Ian as he moved around the man to get upwind. When Ian stopped moving the man's eyes narrowed. "Did you hit me?"

"No." Ian pointed to himself and then back toward the freeway. "You hit me and then you hit the divider. You did this all by yourself."

The thin man looked past Ian at the polished, unmarked front of the Mustang. He stared at it for a moment, trying to keep it in focus, and then turned to look at the back of the Galaxy. He stared at the smashed and twisted metal for a few more seconds then glared accusingly at Ian. "Well, somebody hit me!"

Before Ian could attempt to explain the collision, a Highway Patrol car drove up, followed closely by an officer on a motorcycle. After parking next to the Galaxy, a young patrolman stepped out of the car and started talking to the drunk. The motorcycle cop parked on the other side of the big green sedan and pulled off his helmet. He hung the helmet on a handlebar, swung the kickstand out and ran gloved fingers through his graying hair.

As the young patrolman tried to get the drunk to walk a straight line, the older officer walked over to Ian and started filling out paperwork. Sandy joined them while Ian explained what had happened. As Ian answered his questions, the officer occasionally nodded, or said "uh huh." He wrote everything down including Ian's driver's license and insurance information.

Dewey, the younger patrolman, was cuffing the thin man's hands behind his back while the older Weatherby asked, "Mr. MacAran, how fast were you going?"

"Seventy-five. I had the cruise..."

Weatherby lifted his pen away from his clipboard and cleared his throat. "Excuse me." He looked at Ian. "The limit here is sixty five. How fast did you say you were you going?"

"Sixty-five. The cruise control was set to sixty-five."

"That's what I thought you said."

Sandy gave Weatherby a puzzled look as she watched him write '65 mph'.

A few yards downwind, the younger officer was having some trouble. He had managed to maneuver the drunk into the backseat of the cruiser, but now he was trying to get the man out. "I told you to get the fuck out of the car!"

Sandy, Ian and Weatherby all looked over to see Dewey dragging the Galaxy driver out of the back of the patrol car. Dewey leaned him against the car, but still had to hold onto the drunk's sport coat to keep him from sliding to the ground. The man shook his head as he stared down at the dark, stain covering the front of his pants. "I told you I had to go."

"You told me you could wait!" Dewey caught the drunk as he started falling to one side and pulled him upright. "Just stand here, okay?" The officer looked inside the car. "Damn it!"

The grey-haired cop sighed. "The adventures of law enforcement." He gave back Ian's license and a card with a phone number on it. "You can go now, Mr. MacAran, thanks. Call this number tomorrow after about two and they'll give you all the information you need for your insurance company."

"Thanks." Ian put the cards in his shirt pocket.

"Drive careful." Weatherby turned and walked over to help Dewey.

Sandy and Ian started walking back to his car. "That was exciting. I knew there was something missing in Copenhagen."

"Welcome to America." They got into the convertible and headed toward the freeway. Ian laughed. "I just can't believe we were going seventy-five miles an hour and we got rear-ended!"

"I can't believe that officer just flat out encouraged you to lie."

"I thought he was clearing his throat, you know, fur-ball or something?"

"The technical term would be suborning perjury." Sandy's hair danced furiously in the wind.

Ian's hair was too short to do more than tousle. "I'm sure he was just trying to simplify the paperwork."

"And that would be a rationalization."

"I suppose you could look at it that way." Ian smiled at her but she didn't seem to like the joke.

"Should we file a complaint?"

"No." Sandy looked away self-consciously, "I don't think so, no."

"Fair enough." Ian glanced at the rear view mirror. "What's the easiest way to get to your house?"

"Take the Fourth Street exit."

"Will do." Ian checked the rear view again as the Mustang cruised north at seventy-five.

Three hours later the sun had set, wisps of fog were drifting overhead and Ian and Sandy were coming out of De Vinci's on Fillmore Street. They had dropped Sandy's luggage off at her house and she had changed into a dark purple skirt and black bolero jacket. "What a great restaurant!" She held the door and Ian followed her out onto the sidewalk. "They were nice."

"They were impressed." Ian was still wearing the tan Dockers and white shirt he'd worn to pick her up at the airport. Sandy followed Ian's lead and they started walking toward the parking garage. "Where did you learn to speak Italian?"

"Italy, to begin with. My dad worked for a pharmaceutical company in Milan."

"Is he a doctor?"

"Not a medical doctor. His Ph.D. was in chemistry."

"Sounds romantic, growing up in Italy?"

"I didn't actually get to grow up there. We moved to India when I was eleven. I didn't remember much Italian until I took it in high school in Japan."

Ian raised an eyebrow. "You learned Italian in Japan?"

"Relearned it." She smiled at Ian's puzzled expression. "Do you want the whole itinerary?"

"Sure." Ian nodded. "We've got a few blocks."

"I was born in Manhattan. From there, the Taylor World Tour stopped in Italy, India, Australia, France, England, and finally Japan."

"Finally?"

"Finally. When my parents moved on to Brazil, I ran away from the circus to go to college in New York. Last year my folks moved to Copenhagen."

"Sounds like an adventure." Ian pressed the "Walk" button on the light post and they waited to cross Greenwich Street. "Why all the moving around?"

"Daddy is good at his work. He's a quality control/problem-solving savant. He helps set up production facilities, and then he goes back to supervise the damage control if anything goes wrong. He's always flying somewhere, either to prevent an emergency or to handle one."

"You sound a little un-enthused."

"We didn't see him much."

"Well, at least you learned Italian." Ian looked up and down the street for a break in the traffic, but it was too heavy to cross against the light. "Do you speak any other languages?"

"French, a little Japanese." The light changed and they started across Greenwich Street. "I picked up some

English when we were in Australia, but I still have trouble with it."

Ian chuckled. "I've always wanted to learn English. But I'd rather learn Italian. Do you think you could teach me?"

"Italian? Sure." Sandy nodded. "That would be fun!"

As they reached the other side of the street, Ian stepped up onto the sidewalk and turned toward her "How do you say, 'Would you like to go dancing with me?'"

Sandy said it slowly. "Vorresti accompagnarmi a ballare?"

"Vorresti accompagnarmi a ballare?" Ian pronounced it carefully.

"Si, voluntieri, mi piacerebbe!"

"That's beautiful." Ian was fascinated by her eyes. "What does it mean?"

Sandy grinned, almost imperceptibly. "Yes, I'd really like that."

"Great! Me too. There are a couple of clubs on Union Street."

"Which is that way." Sandy pointed over her shoulder, behind them.

"We could get the car, but..."

"Just as easy to walk."

Ian nodded. "And a lot easier to park." They turned around and headed back toward De Vinci's.

Sandy stopped in front of the restaurant. "God, I'm stuffed, but that smells so good!"

Ian tilted his head up slightly and took a deep breath. "You're so right! Makes you want to go in and have dinner all over again."

Sandy lowered her voice and pretended to talk into a microphone. "Police are investigating the explosion of two people in this Fillmore Street restaurant. They have no suspects but an unofficial source said the fettuccine was 'to die for.'"

Ian laughed. "Film at eleven."

They stepped off the sidewalk to pass a group of teenagers walking the other way. The boys wore bright variations on the tuxedo theme while the girls' formal outfits were each completely unique. Conflicting colognes waged aromatic war in a fragrant no-man's-land behind them.

As Ian and Sandy turned onto Union Street, an old man sitting at the corner bus stop started sneezing. White hair curled out from under his Greek fisherman's cap and spilled onto the collar of his once-expensive black over-coat. He took a tissue out of the plastic grocery bag at his feet and shakily blew his nose.

Ian shook his head. "Sad."

Sandy stepped up onto the sidewalk. "What?"

"Just thinking out loud." Ian glanced over his shoulder at the old man on the bench. "Something about that guy on the bench made me think of the nut that ran into us. I wonder what will happen to him."

"That maniac?" Sandy looked at Ian. "Why?"

"I don't know." They crossed Webster Street. "I feel sorry for him."

"He could have killed somebody. He could have killed us. I'm glad he's off the streets."

"Yeah, me too." Ian looked down at the hairline fractures in the sidewalk. "He looked so bewildered. He'll probably never even know what really happened."

"He'll blame it on the space aliens. Their ship crashed into his car and then disappeared before the police got there."

"Is that what he was running from?"

"Of course, didn't you see them?" Sandy hummed the opening bars of the "Twilight Zone."

A silver limousine came down Webster and turned onto Union Street just as the light turned against it. A young woman in a bright blue formal gown was leaning out the rear window, yelling. She stopped for a moment and said something to the group of high school kids in the car. They all laughed. She took a deep breath and yelled louder. Everyone else on the street turned to look. A young man standing up through the limo's moon-roof was throwing flowers at people on the sidewalk.

Ian caught a carnation and gave it to Sandy. "A gift from the space aliens."

"Why, thank you, Earthman."

There was a short line underneath a sign that said simply "The Dance Club." Ian and Sandy got behind a couple of guys who were whispering hopeful things about two of the women ahead of them. In a few shuffling moments, they were inside the foyer and the noise of the street was drowned out by the thunder of dance music and the buzz of people trying to talk over it. Ian paid the cover charge and they headed for the dance floor.

Four hours later, Ian and Sandy were back in the Mustang. The top was up and the heater was on and they were talking about the songs they'd danced to and their favorite kinds of music. Sandy liked rock and Kathy Mattea. Ian liked Jazz and H2O. By the time he turned onto Gough Street and parked in the yellow zone across from Sandy's house, they had agreed that there really wasn't very much music they didn't like.

Sandy glanced across the street. "That was really fun, thank you."

"Hey, thank you for coming. I had a really great time." Ian turned off the engine. "Can I walk you to your door?"

"That would be nice." Sandy got out of the Mustang and Ian walked around to meet her. They crossed the street together.

"We got all of your bags, right?"

Sandy nodded. "Yeah. Thanks again. It was really nice of you to pick me up."

"It was nice of you to call." Ian followed her up the steps to her door. "I'm afraid to ask what three hours from Copenhagen costs."

"Was it really three hours?"

"Just the first time." He looked up at the stained glass window over the door and smiled.

"You're nice to talk to." Sandy followed his gaze as she took her keys out. "Am I missing something?"

"No." Ian's eyes sparkled. "I was just remembering the first time I walked you to your door."

"That was nice." Sandy slid the key into the lock. "Would you like to come in for a nightcap?"

"Very much."

Sandy opened the door and Ian followed her inside. She led the way through the dining room to the kitchen, where oak cabinets and trim accented the pale blue walls. "What would you like?" Sandy opened the refrigerator.

"I don't know if it's technically a nightcap, but do you have an iced tea?"

Sandy shook her head as she looked in the freezer. "I was thinking of something a little more decadent."

Ian raised both eyebrows. "Decadent?"

Sandy took out a quart of vanilla ice cream. "Can you say root beer float?"

"Not in Italian."

Sandy thought for a moment. "Neither can I. How does it sound in English?"

"Delicious."

Sandy got out two cans of root beer, two tall glasses, and a couple of long spoons. She poured the root beer first, and then spooned several scoops of ice cream into each glass. As the foam rose around the ice cream, she went back to the refrigerator for a bottle of Murphy's Irish Cream.

"Secret ingredient." She poured a little of the thick liquor over each fizzing column, and then handed a glass and a spoon to Ian.

He tried it as Sandy put the Murphy's and the ice cream away. "This is good."

"Thank you." Sandy smiled and picked up her float. "Let's go sit down." She led the way toward the front of the house.

The only light in the dining room came from a row of track lights softly focused on a large blue and gray canvas. Ian paused to admire the painting. A tall, dark tower was wrapped in swirls of fog and spray from the ocean. In the distance, the sky glowed with the faint promise of a rising sun. Ian glanced at the signature in the lower right corner. A tiny, stick-figure horse was running over a small line of letters that Ian couldn't quite read.

"Do you like it?"

"Yeah." Ian turned toward Sandy. "It seems sad, though. A lighthouse without light."

Sandy nodded. "Come on."

The next room was devoted to music and cinema with an entire wall of built-in shelves and cabinets. An extensive collection of video and audio equipment shared the shelves with books, records and hundreds of compact discs. Sandy settled into an armchair and Ian sat next to her on the end of the matching couch. He caught a bit of the foam that was sliding down the outside of his glass, and nodded toward the wall of electronics. "I thought I was gadget happy, but uh... Wow. That's impressive."

"Came with the house." Sandy scooped up a spoonful of foamy ice cream. She licked the spoon and then pointed at the collection with it. "You can play something, if you like."

"Okay." Ian set his half-finished float on the coffee table and walked across to the shelves of CDs.

Sandy watched him flip through the plastic boxes. "They're alphabetical by artist, if you're looking for something specific."

"Here's one." Ian pulled a CD off the shelf and popped the shiny disc out of its box. He studied the eight different audio decks. It seemed like all of them could play CDs. Ian chuckled. "So much for the easy part."

Sandy picked up a remote from the end table and aimed it at the center of the media wall. Several "power" lights came on and one of the CD players whirred open.

"That's a CD player?" Ian studied it suspiciously before dropping the disk on the platter. "I thought it was a coffee machine." He smiled, and held the "select" button down to skip over the first few songs. When he pressed "play", Greedy Aich of H2O started singing You Gotta Dance With Me.

"Is that an invitation?" Sandy set her float down as Ian held out his hand, and Sandy got up to take it. He pulled her close and they danced in the space between the coffee table and the music. After the next song, Sandy looked up and Ian kissed her, softly, barely touching his lips to hers. She rested her head against his shoulder. "This is nice."

They held each other close and swayed gently in time with the music through the rest of the CD. After the last song, Sandy looked up again. Ian smoothed her hair back and kissed her, gently pressing against her. She opened her mouth just enough to tease his tongue with her own. Pulling back a little, Sandy brushed the tip of her nose against his. "I could get to like this." She snuggled against Ian's shoulder again and then yawned. "Excuse me."

Ian grinned. "You wouldn't be a little tired, would you?"

"Oh, of course not!" Sandy shook her head and started to smile, but yawned again. "Excuse me, again. I've only been traveling since yesterday morning."

"Not to mention a night of dancing."

"And a car crash."

"And a car crash." Ian laughed as he looked at his watch. "It is almost midnight."

Sandy pointed at the watch on her wrist. "But it's not even eight in Copenhagen."

Ian smiled. "True, but that's tomorrow morning."

"Oh." Sandy giggled. "Wow. I should get some sleep."

"Yeah." They walked to the front door and Ian opened it. "When can I see you again?"

Sandy thought for a moment. "I'm out of town next weekend, but...oh!" She grinned. "Thursday. I'll see you Thursday."

Ian shook his head. "I can't, I'm working."

"I know." Sandy tried to stifle another yawn. "I had my secretary ask for you. We're going to Cabo San Lucas."

"We are?" Ian raised an eyebrow. "On a Thursday?"

Sandy nodded. "It's a management seminar. They're planning a bunch of presentations and workshops, but I thought I could get away long enough to take you to dinner..." She hesitated. "If that's okay?"

"I'd like that. The schedule shows us down for the whole weekend. Is that right?"

"Uh huh."

Ian smiled approvingly. "Rough life."

"Isn't it?" Sandy put her hand on his arm. "Thank you for a wonderful evening."

"My pleasure." They kissed as if they'd known each other in a previous life. After a few minutes Ian whispered, "Pleasant dreams."

Sandy watched him walk down the steps and cross the street before she closed the door.

Monday, 10:20 am – Captain Hogue's
Office, Narcotics Division, OPD

Barrett Hogue was a large man with smooth skin the color of semisweet chocolate. His thick neck bulged over a white button-down collar barely held together by a thin blue tie. Barrett leaned forward, his arms on his desk and a patient smile on his face. "What, exactly, do you want?"

"All I want, Captain, is for you to keep your people out of my jurisdiction!" L. Whitney Clark was huge. Inches taller, and much, much wider, than Hogue, Clark had pale blotchy skin that reminded Barrett of strawberry yogurt. Clark was wedged into one of the armchairs facing Barrett's desk, his tan overcoat draped across his lap.

"Come on, Leroy, aren't you taking this a little too seriously? We're on the same side!" The phone on his desk rang and he punched the flashing extension button. "Excuse me." Barrett picked up the phone. "Yes?" He leaned back. "Send him in."

Mick Dale stepped into the office wearing blue jeans and a gray "Question Authority!" T-shirt. A white bandage was taped across the bridge of Mick's nose and the skin around his eyes was bruised and swollen.

"Good lord!" Barrett was shocked. "You look awful."

"Thanks." Mick stood at ease next to the empty armchair.

"What happened?"

Mick shrugged. "I broke my nose."

"Really?" Barrett studied L. Whitney for a moment before pressing on. "Mick, you know Captain Clark, Alameda P.D.?"

"Hello, Captain." Mick held out his hand.

Clark shook it, but his dour expression didn't change. "Detective."

Barrett gestured toward the empty chair. "Have a seat, Mick. Captain Clark wanted to know why an Oakland cop was working undercover in Alameda without his authorization." Barrett watched Mick sit down. "Since I couldn't answer his questions, I thought we'd ask you."

"Yes sir." Mick shifted his attention to the man next to him. "Captain Clark, I'm sorry if I inconvenienced you or your men. I should have called your office as soon as I knew I had to go to Alameda."

"Damn right." Clark nodded. "Why didn't you?"

"Well, sir, I was just laying the groundwork with a new source. I didn't expect anything to develop for weeks." Mick shrugged. "Quince was going to introduce me to a supplier at that party. It didn't occur to me that there could be something else going down at the same place at exactly the same time."

"Who's Quince?" Clark looked at Mick until Mick met his gaze, and then looked at Barrett. "And why didn't you identify yourself to the officers on the scene?"

"Quince is a mule. Another guy I've been working on said Quince had connections, but Quince never showed. When your guys showed up I had no idea who was who, and I didn't want to blow my cover." He glanced at Barrett and then back at Clark. "If I can help by testifying...?"

Clark sighed. "At this point I'm not sure how much good that will do. We'll be in touch." He stood up, and nodded at Barrett. "I appreciate your taking the time to see me, Captain." He glanced at Mick. "Detective. Give us a call next time."

"Yes sir." Mick remained seated. "I'll do that."

Barrett stood up and reached across his desk to shake Clark's hand. "Good to see you, Leroy."

"You too, Barrett."

On his way out, Clark left the door open but Barrett's assistant jumped up to pull the door closed.

"God!" Mick leaned forward, massaging his temples.

"You look terrible." Barrett stayed on his feet. "Did they actually break your nose?"

"Yeah." Mick stopped rubbing and just held the sides of his head. "And yeah. Major headache, but I think I'll live." He looked up and nodded toward the door. "L. Whitney sure came a long way to ask the same questions I answered Friday night. What's wrong with his phone?"

"That worthless prick doesn't care about jurisdiction." Barrett sat down, and the big desk chair creaked under the load. "He just wanted to make sure you weren't going to go after his people for beating you up."

"Never trust a man who parts his name on the side."

Barrett studied Mick's face. "Jesus, Mick! You said they roughed you up; you could have told me they busted your nose. You sure you don't want to file a complaint?"

"No. I mean yeah, I'm sure." Mick held up his hand rather than shake his head. "Why make enemies when you can make friends?"

"Your decision." Barrett opened his upper desk drawer. "You want an aspirin or something?"

"No, thanks." Mick shook his head, winced. "My doctor gave me Percocet." He took a bottle out of his pocket and popped the lid off. "You know, aside from the broken nose, things are going pretty well." Mick pushed two of the white tablets to the back of his tongue and swallowed. "I've made some good contacts and collected a lot of information. I'm getting close to some big fish."

"That's good. I've got a limited budget for undercover operations." Barrett closed the drawer. "I realize your expenses are incredibly low but I'll still need something to show for all this groundwork."

"I didn't think Dale Construction would actually make a profit, but it's doing great. I'm going to keep it when this is all over."

"Isn't it owned by the City?"

"Nope. It's my company, completely out of my own pocket. That's why your overhead is so low."

"You realize you're supposed to clear any outside job with the Chief, right?"

"Oh yeah, do you think you could take care of that?"

"Get the paperwork from Kendrick. I'll take it from there."

"Thanks."

"Just make sure the right forms actually get submitted." Barrett leaned forward and rested his elbows on the metal desk. "Tell me about these 'big fish'."

"You ready?" Mick smiled. "I found a way to get Yuri Milanov."

"Milanov?" Barrett leaned back and the chair creaked again. "Really?"

"Yeah, but I'm going to need you to help coordinate with some of the surrounding jurisdictions." Mick rubbed the back of his neck. "Our favorite machinator is expanding his invisible empire."

Barrett looked skeptical. "How are you going to get him to drop his guard?"

"Economics." Mick looked down as he pressed his hands against the sides of his head. "I'm going into competition with him." He glanced up. "Completely separate from Dale Construction."

"Of course." Barrett considered. "I like it. Let me know what you need and I'll make it happen." Barrett looked at Mick for a moment. "I like the way you dealt with Clark. Not as gratifying as punching him in the nose but much better politically."

"Screw 'politically'. Did they really get the wrong house?"

"That's what I heard. None of the people they had warrants for were there." Barrett chuckled. "I also heard that you did real well on the lieutenant's exam. When's your interview?"

"I haven't scheduled one."

"Well, get to it! Bishop is retiring next month and I'd love to get someone I can work with."

"Thanks for the vote of confidence, but I'm thinking about retiring myself."

"Why?" Barrett looked shocked. "What are you forty-five?"

"Forty-eight, and to be honest, I like being a contractor. I'm thinking about switching to construction full time." Mick stood and extended his hand. "I'll give you a call."

"Alright." Barrett shook Mick's hand. "If you have to retire early, Mick, do it as a lieutenant."

"I'll think about it." Mick closed the door, leaving Barrett with a speculative smile on his face.

"Yuri Milanov, eh?" Barrett punched his speaker phone. "Kendrick?"

His assistant, Bob Kendrick answered immediately. "Yes sir?"

"Get Smith for me, will you? And check with the Chief about lunch. Try for one o'clock."

"Right away, Captain."

Tuesday, 10:21 am - Rancho Orozco, Jalisco

24 hours later Mick and Ian were west of Guadalajara descending toward the long straight driveway next to the windsock. Arturo Orozco watched the jet drop lower and lower, like a tan and gold chunk of desert falling from the cloudless sky. His nephew Juan Carlos was supposed to be flying this time. The previous landing had been his brother Carlos' turn and that had also scared the crap out of him. Arturo's fingers tightened on the Hummer's steering wheel as the Citation disappeared below the scruffy trees at the end of the road. He pushed his hat back and leaned forward, straining to see through the glare on the windshield. The fiery Hollywood explosion that Arturo dreaded didn't materialize, but long seconds passed before the Citation reappeared, climbing safely out of the valley. It was headed right at the Hummer.

Arturo scrabbled for the door handle as the jet banked away from the khaki colored 4x4 and lined up with the road. He didn't relax until the plane swept past him. The Citation touched down well beyond the Hummer and the Land Rover next to it. Still moving very fast, the Citation lifted back into the air, floated above the road for a moment and then touched down again halfway down the 'runway'. The engines wound up to a howling roar and the Citation climbed away from the shimmering pavement. Arturo looked at his watch and sighed. He started the Hummer's engine, turned up the air conditioning, and started scanning the satellite radio stations.

In a few minutes the Citation came around again. Arturo watched as it rolled out of a graceful turn lined up perfectly with the runway. The plane flew a straight, stable approach, descended smoothly and touched down right next to the two vehicles. The engines roared to life again, but the thrust reversers directed the blast forward, and the Citation stopped with half of the runway still ahead of it. The jet turned around, taxied to the end of the road and turned around again, ready to take off.

Arturo sighed with relief as he opened the Hummer's door. He froze with one foot out the door when he saw the dark brown Jeep Cherokee rush up behind the jet. The Cherokee had a streamlined red and blue light-bar bolted to its roof and everything that could was flashing or spinning or both. The Jeep swerved off the road to get around the plane then cut back onto the pavement and stopped in front of the Citation, blocking the runway. An officer stepped out from behind the wheel and rested his hands on his gun belt. He smiled up at the flight deck. Another officer stepped out on the other side of the car. He held an AK-47 assault rifle, pointed, for the moment, at the sky.

Earlier, Arturo and Juan Carlos had backed both 4x4s into the chaparral to get them clear of the 'runway', but Arturo couldn't believe the police didn't see them. He pulled his door closed as gently as he could and slipped into the back of the Hummer. He retrieved his M-16 and grabbed the extra clip lying next to it. Looking outside, he searched the horizon for signs of more police cars or helicopters but all he could see were trees and clear blue sky. Arturo glanced back toward the Cherokee. The doors on the right side of the big 4x4 were hidden from the police, even if they did decide to look toward him. Gingerly opening the right rear door, Arturo stepped to the ground and moved around to the back of the Hummer.

Juan Carlos' Land Rover was parked about ten feet behind the Hummer. Arturo could see their cousin Palo behind the wheel. His head was back, his mouth was open, and his gray cowboy hat was tilted forward over his eyes. Palo was snoring. Arturo cursed silently, slipped the extra magazine into his pocket and released the safety on the assault rifle. Taking off his own hat, he risked a quick glimpse around the rear of the Hummer. Both cops were looking at the jet, and either hadn't seen him or didn't care.

On the Citation's flight deck, Ian had stopped going through the engine-shutdown checklist as soon as he saw the Cherokee pull onto the road. He kept the throttles at idle. Sitting next to him in the copilot seat, Juan Carlos yelled back to his father, "Papa! Policia!"

Carlos came forward with Mick right behind him, both men trying to squeeze into the space between the two front seats. They looked out the windscreen at the tall cop leaning against the Cherokee and swore simultaneously. "Shit!"

"We'll take care of them." Carlos studied the Cherokee for a moment and looked at Ian. "I don't think we'll have a problem, but I don't know these guys. As soon as we get the Jeep out of the way, you take off." Carlos tapped Juan Carlos on the shoulder and pointed toward the door.

"Right." Ian took out the before-takeoff checklist. As he tried to methodically check each item, he kept glancing outside at the two cops.

Mick opened the door and Juan Carlos followed his father out of the airplane. Mick closed the door behind them. The bridge of his nose was still covered with a bandage but his eyes weren't as puffy as they'd been the day before. He slid into the copilot seat as Carlos came into view under the left window, walking over to the policeman.

The officer wore neatly pressed dark blue fatigue pants and a light blue shirt with the Mexican flag on his shoulder. His boots were brightly polished alligator skin, and matched his gun belt, which held his gun tipped forward for quick access. Carlos wore white slacks and a light green polo shirt, his gun barely visible in a holster at the small of his back.

Ian and Mick watched the conversation in front of the Citation escalate from smiling pleasantries to a heated shouting match. As the body language intensified, the other Federal Police Officer lowered his AK-47. He looked nervous and he held the rifle tightly with both hands.

Ian looked over toward the other vehicles. Juan Carlos stood halfway between his dad and the Land Rover, holding his gun at his side so the police couldn't see it. Arturo was behind the Hummer, aiming at the officer with the AK-47. Palo was asleep at the wheel of the Land Rover.

Carlos shook his head. It was obvious he was yelling, but all Ian and Mick could hear was the whine of the engines and the rush of conditioned air. The officer pointed at the plane, pointed at Carlos and then at himself. Carlos took a step toward the man, pointing first at the officer, and then sweeping his thumb across his own neck.

The officer glared at Carlos, but he took a step back and for a long moment neither man moved. Then the officer glanced at the ground and nodded his head. He turned and started to walk back to the Cherokee but Carlos stopped him before he could get in.

Carlos pulled his wallet out of the front pocket of his slacks and counted out a handful of bills. He held them out to the cop. The officer hesitated, then took the money and stuffed it into his pants pocket. Both cops got back into the Jeep and the Cherokee backed off the road. The wheels spun in the dirt as they swung around the Citation and then disappeared back down the road toward Guadalajara.

Carlos waved at Mick and Ian as he walked toward the Land Rover. He held his hand up to his ear, as though talking on a phone and Mick gave him a thumbs-up sign. Ian advanced the throttles and the jet accelerated down the ersatz runway. As the wheels retracted and Ian turned the Citation toward America, Mick smiled. "That was interesting."

"Oh, yeah." Ian wasn't smiling.

Mick pulled his cell-phone out of the satchel behind Ian's seat and called Carlos. Ian contacted Center and activated their flight plan to Oakland. As they climbed through 10,000 feet, Ian lowered the nose and set the Citation up for a cruise climb. He took a deep breath and let it out very slowly. "That was way past interesting."

Mick finished his innocent-sounding call to Carlos and turned off the phone. "Carlos said the police won't be a problem. Those two cowboys were on their own and nobody else knows. He also said to thank you again for letting them fly, and for not letting Juan Carlos kill us on that last approach." Mick rolled his eyes toward heaven. "That goes double for me."

"Hey," Ian smiled. "That part was fun. It was when the police showed up that I thought we were in trouble."

Mick laughed. "That was a surprise, all right, but there wasn't anything they could do."

"I don't understand."

Mick shrugged. "If those cops had done anything to interfere with our mission, anything at all, they'd have been fired."

"But they're police officers!"

"So is our partner, Victor." Mick watched wisps of scattered clouds shoot past the window. "But Victor is a much more important cop."

"Oh, really?" Ian smiled. "I can see how being a cop would have its advantages."

"And how! Being a cop is like being everybody's best friend." Mick glanced at Ian. "We were military police. Carlos and I made more money and got away with more shit when we were MPs in Kosovo... We had it made!"

"I thought you were a paratrooper."

Mick nodded. "That was my first tour. I went back with the military police; much safer. That's where I met Carlos."

"And you've been friends ever since?"

"Brothers!" Mick laughed. "I married his sister, remember?"

"Does Clara know what we're doing?"

"Of course!" Mick looked at Ian, puzzled. "How could I keep anything from Clara?" He reached into his pocket for the bottle of Percocet and took two tablets.

Ian leveled off at 31,000 feet. Five miles below the tan and gold Citation, the Sierra Madre Mountains drifted past at 400 miles per hour.

When they passed Avenal, 40 minutes and 190 miles from Oakland, Ian asked Oakland Center for a lower altitude. Mick had gone aft to get ready when they had passed Bakersfield. Now he leaned forward between the two pilot seats. "Everything's set back here. What are the winds like?" Mick had put on a dark green jump suit and a parachute.

Ian handed him a sheet from his notepad. "The winds at San Jose and Livermore are at the top, but the reports are about half an hour old."

Mick did some quick calculations on the back of the notepaper. "Okay. I'll need to jump a quarter mile northwest of the drop zone."

"No problem." The plane had been on autopilot since they crossed into the U.S. Ian typed new instructions into the FMS and the autopilot adjusted to the new destination. He looked at the bruises around the bandage on Mick's nose. "Are you sure your sinuses will be okay?"

Mick took a deep breath in and then out through his nose. "Never underestimate the power of modern pharmaceuticals!"

"Okay." Ian nodded. "Don't open the hatch until I tell you. You won't be able to pull it in until I depressurize and I can't do that until we're lower."

"Same shit, different day."

"Exactly." Ian pointed to the timer on the GPS display. It was counting down through eleven minutes. "Get ready."

Mick headed back and checked to make sure Ian's spare headset was plugged into the seat on the other side of the aisle.

Ten minutes from the drop zone, Ian turned off the autopilot and reduced power on the right engine. He also raised the right wing, as though starting a left turn. The bank to the left balanced the right turn that would have been caused by the unbalanced thrust from the left engine. The jet flew straight, though slightly sideways, with the right wing higher than the left.

As the jet slowed, the computer recalculated, and their time to the drop zone was once again eleven minutes. Ian shut the cabin pressurization off and the pressure inside the plane began dropping. When the cabin pressure gauge indicated the same 13,000 feet as the altimeter, Ian gave Mick a 'thumbs up' signal, and yelled, "Open up!"

Mick rotated the handle on the emergency escape hatch and carefully pulled the panel into the airplane.

Cold air whipped into the cabin and rippled the fabric of his flight-suit. On the other side of the San Joaquin Valley, the Sierra Nevada Mountains were capped with brilliant white snow. Mick leaned the hatch against the front seat on the other side of the plane, next to the cabin door.

Bracing a hand against either side of the opening, Mick carefully poked his head outside. The emergency hatch was almost eight feet in front of the right wing, and by leaning out a little he could see straight down. Spattered over the Diablo Range like textured paint, the scattered clouds that the Weather Service had forecast made scattered shadows on the brown hills.

Ian reduced the power on the left engine to slow the plane even more, and raised the left wing a little to keep the plane on course. The navigation computer registered the change in speed and recalculated their time to the drop zone. Ian turned on the autopilot, took his hands off the controls and watched for a few moments. The plane maintained its wing low attitude as the airspeed stabilized.

The GPS showed that they would be over the drop zone in five minutes. Ian checked his watch against the time-to-checkpoint display and took off his headset. Its cable was too short to reach back to the main cabin, and too awkward to plug in quickly. After glancing over the instruments one last time, Ian slid out of his seat and headed aft.

With its right engine at idle and its left wing lowered to stabilize the plane, the Citation was flying slightly sideways, actually slipping to the left. The right side of the plane was partially shielded from the airstream by the fuselage and Mick could lean out the emergency hatch several inches before he felt the full force of the 130-knot slipstream. To Mick's right, next to the hatch were two cargo sacks, each filled with 75 kilos of cocaine. One rested on the passenger seat and the other in the aisle. Both were strapped into parachute harnesses made of green nylon webbing. In the aft-facing seat to Mick's left was another heavy canvas bag with the remaining 50 kilos. Like the other bags, it had D rings at several reinforced points, but it didn't have a parachute.

Ian slipped his spare headset on and heard a United 757 checking in with Bay Approach. He looked at his watch and tapped Mick on the back. Mick had put on a helmet and a pair of tinted goggles and he had to turn his head to see the two fingers Ian was holding up.

"Two minutes!"

Mick nodded. He leaned back against the smaller cargo sack and clipped it to the bottom of his harness. Ian counted the last five seconds off on his fingers. When he yelled, "Now!" Mick pushed the first green canvas bag out the hatch. He grabbed the second sack from Ian, pushed it through the hatch and then followed it out of the airplane.

Ian looked out the hatch but all he could see was the Citation's wing and the hills and clouds below. He glanced forward. As if turned by ghosts, the two control wheels inched slightly right as the autopilot made a small correction. Ian eased the emergency hatch into place and made sure it was lined up properly, before locking it in place. He glanced around the cabin as he unplugged the extra head-set, and then hurried back to the flight deck. He checked the HSI and altimeter as he slid into the left seat, and then searched the sky for other aircraft. The plane was on course at the assigned altitude, and he didn't see any other planes.

Ian switched headsets and turned off the autopilot. As he rolled the plane back to wings level, he brought the right throttle up until it was even with the left and then brought both engines up to cruise power. The approach controller cleared the United 757 for the approach to Oakland's runway 29 and then called Ian.

"CITATION 229, I SHOW YOU LEFT OF COURSE. TURN RIGHT HEADING 300, EXPECT VECTORS FOR THE ILS."

Ian keyed his mike. "Right 300, 229." He looked back at the empty cabin, and then scanned the instrument panel. He didn't key his mike as he muttered, "Same shit, different day." Ian looked outside and rocked the wings playfully as he turned right. "Excellent!"

Falling away from the little jet at 122 miles per hour, Mick had stabilized himself face down, his legs slightly bent at the knees and his arms out from his sides. He kept himself pointed toward the two cargo sacks just below him. The 75-kilo bags rotated slowly as the group fell toward the ground.

"Shit!" Mick couldn't see the ground. He could see rolling green hills for miles around, but he couldn't see the ground directly below him. A mass of fluffy moisture lay between Mick and his drop zone, and he wouldn't know how close to the ground the cloud was until he broke out below it. Mick clenched his jaw and shouted, "Wombat shit!"

The wind roaring past his ears didn't respond

Mick pulled his ripcord and was jerked upright as the rectangular canopy blossomed above him. The two 75-kilo sacks rocketed away from him, leaving Mick to follow at a much less kinetic 15 miles per hour. He reached down to the reserve chute at his waist and turned off the Automatic Activation Device. Left alone, the A.A.D. would open his reserve chute 750 feet above the selected ground level. Identical devices on the two sacks below him would release their cargo chutes 750 feet above the highest hills around the drop zone. Mick glanced at the two dark specks below him just as they disappeared into the cloud.

"Wombat shit on a stick!" Mick reached back and grabbed the 50-kilo sack. He unhooked the two quick-release connectors and swung the bag around in front of him. It was still attached to his harness, but by a hundred feet of elastic shock cord. Mick lowered the bag a few feet at a time until he ran out of rope.

The duffle bag hanging below him became hazy and an instant later, Mick's sunny afternoon was swallowed by mist. He looked at the altimeter built into his watch. It read 6,400 feet. He make out the duffle bag 100 feet below his army boots, but he couldn't see anything else. The altimeter counted down as Mick watched the mist below his feet. Sixty seconds later, at 5,200 feet, he broke out of the cloud. The terrain below was rolling hills of brown grass dotted with a few scruffy trees. "We're smokin' now!"

Directly below him was a grassy slope to the east of a narrow dirt road. West of the road was a dry stream bed that ran along the bottom of the valley. Mick's truck was nowhere in sight. He searched the area again but didn't see anything familiar. "Wait a minute…" He steered the chute around to look behind him.

There were only a few trees on the hill, a mile or so to the South. One of the duffle bags had landed in the largest of them. The other was just visible beyond the tree, its chute ruffling slightly in the breeze. Mick's red Chevy was parked well off the road, about half way between Mick and the two cargo chutes. Mick turned toward the truck. He knew he couldn't reach the pickup, but he could get closer. He aimed for a level spot a few hundred feet from the road.

When the duffle bag hit the ground, the load on Mick's parachute was reduced by a third and his descent slowed considerably. With his feet together and his knees slightly bent, Mick pulled down on the risers just as his feet touched the ground. He took a step forward to keep his balance but stayed standing.

"Yes!" He released his harness and slipped out of the nylon webbing. "Another perfect landing!"

As it settled to the ground beside him, he pulled the lines together and gathered the chute in. He dropped the awkward mass of cord and canopy in a heap next to the duffle bag. The cloud Mick had fallen through drifted further east and let the mid-afternoon sun into the valley. He shrugged out of the network of nylon straps and dropped the harness on top of the parachute. Mick glanced at his watch and started off toward his truck at a jog.

Fifteen minutes later, the big red Chevy bounced off the uneven dirt road and charged up the smoother hillside. When it reached the pile of parachute and the 50-kilo sack, Mick jumped out and lifted the bag into the bed of the pickup. He shoved the parachute and harness in front of the passenger seat and scrambled back into the truck. All four wheels kicked up dirt and dust as he swung the truck around and drove back toward the other two bags.

The first one was easy. Mick gathered up the cargo chute, tossed it into the cab, and then heaved the 75-kilo canvas sack into the bed of the truck. Looking at the other duffle, Mick sighed. The last bag was hanging fifteen feet off the ground in a gnarled old tree, now half-covered by cargo chute. Mick drove around to get underneath the tree and tried to reach the bag by standing in the bed of the truck. He then moved the truck back a few feet and tried again from the roof of the cab. He was still at least a foot away from even touching it. He looked a little closer at the tree. There were no leaves and, it seemed, very little bark. The tree had been dead for decades.

Mick looked around. Nothing else in the valley was moving. He went back to the cab and dug a steel tow cable out from behind the driver's seat.

The cargo chute had 28 lines that came together in four groups that connected to the risers at the top of the harness. After a few tries, Mick managed to toss an end of the steel cable over the duffle bag, between the sets of risers. He clipped the cable onto itself and pulled it to one side so that the bag wouldn't be caught in the closing noose. Mick jumped down from the cab to the ground, and hooked the other end of the cable to tow ring welded to the bumper of his truck.

Slowly, Mick drove down toward the road, dividing his attention between the slope ahead and the increasing tension behind. As soon as the truck took up all the slack in the tow cable, a riot of cracking wood and tearing fabric erupted from the tree. The upper branches of the tree were breaking away, but not without a fight. Ancient wood gave way to nylon cord even as the sharp branches punctured the parachute canopy. Mick felt the release of tension as the chute came down, carrying a lot of firewood with it. Mick stopped, backed up a few feet, and walked back to inspect the damage.

The cargo chute lay in shreds, with branches of all sizes tangled in the lines. Mick unhooked the cable and freed the duffle, heaving it and its harness into the bed of the truck. He coiled the cable up and stowed it behind the seat. After looking around again, Mick walked back to the cargo chute and picked up some of the lines. They were thoroughly tangled in the heavy branches.

Mick looked at the path of debris that stretched back to the base of the now-lopsided and broken tree. He shrugged, tossed the tangled lines to the ground and turned back toward the truck. A second later, a sharp 'pop' made Mick duck his head and start running before the echo returned from the other side of the valley. He sprinted the few meters to the truck and dove behind it. Digging frantically for the tiny metal zipper pull on the side of his jump-suit, Mick searched the road in both directions, and then scanned the hills for any sign of the sniper. Finding the zipper at last, he pulled his gun out of its holster and waited. The breeze made gentle rustling sounds as it toyed with the ragged strips of parachute.

After a dozen or so interminable seconds, Mick cautiously peered around the rear wheel of the Chevy. He couldn't see anyone anywhere on the hillside. Moving up into a crouch, Mick peeked above the bed of the truck.

Several pops sounded in rapid succession and Mick dropped to the ground, scrambling through the dry weeds to the front of the pick-up. Another loud C-R-A-C-K echoed across the valley. As Mick cautiously peered over the Chevy's hood the ancient tree twisted tortuously to one side and crashed to the ground.

Wednesday, 4:22 pm – Moxie on Skyline Boulevard

Sitting between Jesus and Terri in the front seat of Jesus' 2011 Intrigue, Jamaal listened as the adults discussed marketing strategy. He had Jesus' cell phone in his lap and his job was to screen calls. Jesus was wearing some strong flowery cologne that reminded Jamaal of his grandmother, but Terri smelled nice, like leather and soap. Jamaal waited until she looked outside and then poked the side of her leg. Terri pretended not to notice. Jesus turned left onto Snake Road, and as they wound their way up into the East Bay hills, Terri went on about how her friend was cool and would be a good partner. Jamaal could see her left hand moving toward him.

Jesus shook his head. "I don't need another partner."

"Okay." Terri slipped her left hand onto her knee. "I'm just saying Des is really smart. It would be better to have him working with us rather than competing against us. Make him a regional manager or something."

"Last thing I need is a fucking 'regional manager'!"

Jamaal looked up at Jesus' face to see if he was really getting angry, and Terri tapped Jamaal on the nose with her right hand. Jamaal giggled.

Jesus smiled indulgently. "Settle down, Jamaal, this is business." The eleven year old straightened up a little so he could see over the dashboard.

Jesus turned the Intrigue onto Skyline Boulevard, and they drove south along the ridgeline. The dude in the back seat kept quiet. His name was Hector and lately he had been going wherever Jesus went. Jamaal had tried to talk to Hector a couple of times but the bodyguard wasn't very friendly. The only time Jamaal recalled hearing Hector speak was when he asked for anchovies on a pizza. Jamaal was okay with that; he liked anchovies.

Terri took a pair of fingerless gloves out of her vest pocket and started to put them on. They were black leather, like her vest. Just as she got the first glove on, Jamaal poked her in the ribs. She snapped her wrist and her other glove bopped him on the head. Jamaal grinned up at her as Terri pulled on the second glove.

Jesus followed the twists and undulations of Skyline Boulevard until they reached a small parking lot with a weathered wood sign that read, "Scenic Overlook". Jesus pulled into the lot, parked across two spaces, and left the engine running. Behind the car, commuters raced back and forth on the two-lane road, but no one else stopped to enjoy the view.

The 'overlook' was really just a wide stretch of shoulder with eight faint white lines dividing the pavement into parking spaces. An old stone wall ran along the edge of the lot to keep cars from dropping in on some of Oakland's more expensive houses. On the other side of Skyline Boulevard the rock face rose almost vertically, with more houses at the top of the cliff. The view of Oakland, San Francisco, and the bay between them was spectacular.

They waited.

Eventually, a silver Jaguar pulled off the road and parked next to the maroon Oldsmobile. Jesus opened his door and stepped out. "Wait here, Jamaal. If anybody calls, take a message." Hector got out of the back, and Terri stepped out on her side of the car.

A tall thin man stepped out of the back seat of the Jaguar, and met Jesus halfway between the two sedans. They shook hands. "You're looking good, Jesus."

"Thanks, Yuri. You're looking good yourself."

"Why, thank you." Yuri Milanov had a perfect tan and carefully styled gray hair. "Let's take a look at the view." He nodded toward the wall and they walked over to the edge.

Hector walked along the left side of the Oldsmobile as Jesus and Yuri slipped between the cars. He stopped when they did, never more than a few yards from his boss. A guy in a gray suit and a bright red tie slipped out of the Jaguar's front passenger seat and leaned back against the car. He nodded at Hector and smiled. Hector nodded back. Yuri's driver stayed on the other side of the Jaguar.

The right front fender of the Intrigue was almost touching the rock wall, so Terri walked around the back of the car to join Jesus. By the time she reached the triangular space between the two cars, Jesus and Yuri were involved in what looked like a serious discussion. They didn't seem to be waiting for her, so Terri leaned back against the side of the Olds and watched the cars go by.

Jesus and Yuri laughed, briefly, and Yuri sat down on the stone wall. Sitting down, he was only a little shorter than Jesus. They kept talking. The guy with the red tie walked over to Terri.

"Hi." He was about six feet tall with short dark hair and darkly tanned skin. "My name's Randal."

Terri nodded her head slightly. "Hi."

"I just had to come over here; you look way too cool."

Terri raised an eyebrow. "You're kidding, right?"

"I'm paying you a compliment." Randal leaned against the Olds a few feet from Terri. "Everybody else is stuck in the same boring shit. Suit and tie." He pointed to Hector and Yuri's driver. "Suits and ties." He held up his own red neck piece. "Me too; a bit more classy, you know, but still just a suit and tie. You on the other hand..." Randal raised his eyebrows as he looked at her boots and then followed the line of her chaps up to the curve of her vest. He nodded approvingly. "You look sharp." He glanced at the collar of Terri's white blouse. "I like women who know how to wear leather."

Terri sighed. "It's a shame they don't like you."

"Oh, but they do!" He moved closer and Terri stepped away from the car. Randal caught her wrist. "Let me show you."

"Fuck off!" Terri snapped her hand out of Randal's grip, but he just smiled.

"And you talk dirty, too!" He stepped toward her. "Come on sugar, give us a little hug." Randal grabbed the shoulder of her vest and pulled Terri toward him.

Terri leaned toward Randal as she pivoted on her left foot. With her back to him, she stepped to the side and swung her left arm down, driving her fist into his crotch. Snapping her arm up, she drove her elbow into Randal's chin, and then spun her fist up hammering her knuckles into his face.

Randal dropped to one knee, his left hand clutching the fabric between his legs as his right hand caught the blood gushing from his nose. He looked at his hand. "You bitch!" He reached under his jacket smearing blood on his silk shirt. Terri kicked him, crushing his gun and his fingers between his chest and her boot. Randal fell back on his tail-bone with an audible crack, and his gun clattered to the pavement.

Terri picked up the automatic while Randal tried to rub some feeling into his numb right hand. She stepped back toward the Olds and glanced over toward Jesus and Yuri. Both looked completely surprised.

Hector had his right hand hidden in his suit and was watching Yuri's driver. The driver was trying not to laugh, as he carefully kept his hands in plain view on the roof of the Jaguar. From inside the Olds, Jamaal flashed Terri a big smile and pointed at her. She was obviously very cool.

Terri kept an eye on Randal as she studied his gun. Yuri rose and walked over to her and Jesus followed right behind him. Yuri glanced down at Randal and then smiled at Terri. "Hello." He had an open, disarming smile. He held out his hand "I don't think we've met. I'm Yuri Milanov."

"We haven't met." She shifted the gun to her left hand and shook his hand with her right. "Terri Turner."

"Pleased to meet you, Miss Turner." Yuri glanced at his nephew. "It seems you've met Randal."

Randal looked angry but he sounded surprised. "She fucking attacked me!"

Yuri ignored him. "Miss Turner?"

"Just a misunderstanding." Terri pressed the release on the side of the gun and the clip dropped out. She caught it and tucked it into her vest pocket. She held the gun sideways and slid the action back. The bullet in the chamber sprang up out of the gun and she caught that as well. "He seemed to think that when I said 'fuck off', I meant 'take me home and rape me.'" Terri tossed the empty gun on the ground in front of Randal, and it clattered into his leg. She retrieved the clip from her pocket and handed it, with the bullet, to Yuri. "I think we've cleared that up."

"I see." Yuri slipped the ammunition into his jacket pocket and glanced at Randal. "Is an apology in order?"

"Uh..." Terri looked at Jesus and back up to Yuri. "I'm really sorry we interrupted your meeting?"

Yuri laughed. "Actually, I was thinking my nephew might apologize for his rudeness."

"What?" Randal was being helped to his feet by Yuri's driver, who had already picked up Randal's gun.

Terri smiled and shook her head. "That's okay, Mr. Milanov." She looked at Randal. "No hard feelings."

Randal glared but his uncle nodded. "Very well." Yuri turned to Jesus. "We have an agreement. Delivery as soon as the funds are transferred."

They shook hands as a white and yellow Cessna zoomed over the parking lot. The sound of the engine and the plane's sudden appearance surprised them all.

Everybody looked up and watched the Cessna for a moment as it descended toward Oakland Airport. Hector quickly refocused his attention on Jesus and the people around him.

Travis was trying to help Randal into the front seat of the Jaguar but Randal couldn't stand the pressure on his tailbone.

Yuri turned to Terri. "I like your style, Miss Turner. You've got moxie." He extended his hand and she shook it once more. Yuri smiled as he slipped gracefully into the back seat. The big car edged back, turned away from the scenic view and slipped into the traffic.

Jesus, Terri and Hector returned to the Olds. Jamaal had two messages for Jesus, but first he wanted Terri to explain exactly how she'd laid out the shithead. Hector pulled the rear door closed and leaned forward. "So, what the fuck is moxie?"

Wednesday, 6:23 pm - Mick's Future
Media Room, Alameda

Mick drove the last nail into the 2x6 top-plate, slid his hammer into the metal loop on his belt and stood up on top of the wall. Balanced on the edge of his house, twenty feet above the front yard, Mick could see over every roof in the neighborhood. "This is going to be fucking excellent!" He savored the view for a moment and then jumped down to the new second floor. Mick grinned at Ian. "Starting to look like something, isn't it?"

"Sure is." Ian was wearing a tool belt, shorts, crew socks and tennis shoes. It had been a hot, sunny day, and Ian's T-shirt was draped across a windowsill in what would eventually be Mick and Clara's master bedroom.

Mick's hair was flecked with sawdust and his hands were mottled with dirt and sap from the freshly cut lumber. He was wearing blue jeans and white sneakers. His T-shirt was draped over a box of 16-penny nails and his shoulders were sunburn red. Mick shook some of the dust out of his hair. "I sure appreciate you helping out."

"It was fun." Ian picked up his shirt and used the soft cotton to mop the sweat off his face.

A week and a half earlier, just two days after the first flight to Rancho Orozco, Mick, Ken and six other carpenters had attacked Mick's roof with wrecking bars, Sawsalls and a thesaurus of expletives. They started in at 7:30 Monday morning and Ian's dreams of sleeping in were overwhelmed by staccato bursts of demolition. The crew had tossed, dragged and shoveled the chunks and pieces of roof into a rented dump truck that took three trips to haul away all of the debris.

Ian had tried to sleep in again on Tuesday morning, but a flatbed truck with a defective muffler met the crew at 7:15 with a load of lumber. The construction racket raged until Ian left for Portland late that afternoon. By then the floor joists had been installed on top of the newly-strengthened bearing walls. Half of the crew returned Wednesday to lay the sub floor, and when Ian got home Wednesday night, the top of Mick's house was a flat clean platform ready for walls.

Nothing more was accomplished until a week later, when Ian and Mick returned from a morning flight. Ian had asked why no more work had been done, and Mick had explained that he needed the crew on another job. After they talked about the project for a few minutes, and Ian asked what had to happen next, he offered to help Mick frame a few walls. Five hours later three of the outside walls were standing.

Ian tossed his shirt back on the windowsill and watched a departing orange and yellow 737 climb out over the water. "Maybe I should add a second floor too." He pointed out over the rooftops. "This is a great view!"

Mick looked over at Ian's house. "We could make that happen. I've got a great crew."

"Yeah. Hey, how is Bernie working out?"

"Pretty good. It only took her two days to get my foreman totally pissed off."

"What's his problem?" Ian sounded protective.

"Relax." Mick smiled. "Bernie knows more about reading blueprints than Ken does and that makes him defensive. I think it'll work out okay, though. When I left on Friday, Ken was showing her how to cut plates and do layout. She's smart, and now that he's over the shock, I think Ken is beginning to really like her. She's getting damn good with a Skilsaw."

"She said she's been having a blast."

"Like I said, I've got an excellent crew." Mick pointed at the top of the wall, where he'd been standing. "Wait 'til you see the view from the third floor."

"Oh?" Ian glanced up. "I thought you were only adding a second floor."

"That's all the City would approve." Mick smiled. "I had the architect label my third floor office the 'attic'." He turned around and leaned against the windowsill. "I've got an airplane question for you."

"Shoot."

"I went up to Oakland Tower yesterday, for a tour, and I was watching the controllers. They had all these little blips moving around on different radar screens." Mick whistled, "Man that looks like a tough job! Anyway, I was wondering, without the transponder, all the controller sees is a little blip, right?"

"If they're lucky. Some small planes don't reflect back enough radar to show up on the screen at all."

"Really?"

Ian nodded. "When the radar hits it, the transponder sends back a stronger signal to make sure your plane shows up on the radar screen. Without a transponder, they don't always get enough radar signal bounced back for a small plane to register."

"But if I set my transponder to the code they give me, they see where the plane is and the computer shows my airplane type and number right next to the radar target."

"Exactly. That's the data block."

"And that data block is something the computer remembers, right? It's not coming from the transponder?"

"The transponder just sends a four digit code."

"And each airplane gets a different code, right?"

Ian turned away from the scenery to look at Mick. "Right."

"So far, so good." Mick nodded. "What would happen on the radar screen if two airplanes passed real close to each other, one over the other." Mick held his hands out like two airplanes about to collide. "And just as the two green blips on the screen merged, the planes switched transponder codes?"

"Uh ..." Ian gave Mick a puzzled look as he considered the question. "Each airplane's number and type would switch to the other radar image."

"Okay." Mick switched the position of his hands. "And if one airplane was coming from Phoenix and the other was coming from Mexico..."

"No."

"The empty plane from Phoenix would go through customs and the plane from Mexico wouldn't have to. Right?"

"No."

"Customs would think the loaded plane came from Phoenix and you don't have to go through customs if you're just coming back from Arizona, right?"

Ian shook his head impatiently. "I said, 'No!'"

"I hear you, man, but come on; just entertain the notion for few seconds: A whole plane load, free and clear. We'd be rich!"

"We are rich!"

"Yeah," Mick grinned. "But we're not that rich!"

"How rich do you have to be?" Ian turned back to face Mick. "You've got a wonderful family, a beautiful home, and a successful business. Other than a roof, what more do you need?"

"Hey, I'm doing this for my kids. Do you know what college costs? What it's going to cost in ten or fifteen years?"

"Not millions of dollars."

"Yes, millions of dollars!" Mick nodded emphatically. "Or close to it. And as much as I like construction, I don't want to be sweating deadlines and payroll for the rest of my life!"

"Why not? What's wrong with working for a living?"

"Not a thing, man." Mick pointed at himself. "I like building." He waved his arms at the naked 2x6 framework around them. "I like seeing something good come out of what I do, but I want to do it on my terms. I want to build projects I own a piece of." Turning to look toward the west, Mick glanced back to make sure Ian was listening. "Ian, this isn't just the opportunity of a lifetime! It's fate. It's destiny! How else can you explain our meeting at exactly the right time? One easy trip south and we can work when we want, if we want, or retire in style!"

"You're not listening," Ian shook his head. "I'm not interested. I didn't even want to do the last trip!" Ian paused. "Christ, Mick, I'm still trying to figure out why I went south the first time!"

"It couldn't have been the money?"

"It wasn't." Ian looked at Mick for a moment. "I mean, of course it was the money, but I have to be honest; there was more to it than that. Part of it was just to see if it would work." He looked across the street at his own house. "And it did work. And it was crazy and exhilarating and dangerous and I'm not doing anything like it ever again. I don't need the money and I sure as hell don't need the stress!"

"Is anybody up there?" Clara was calling from the back yard.

Mick walked over to the north wall and leaned out between two of the studs. "Hey beautiful, what's up?"

Clara smiled up at him. "How about dinner, in about an hour?"

"Great!"

"I'm making lasagna. Why don't you ask Ian to join us?"

"I don't know; why don't I?" Mick grinned and Clara blew him a kiss. She walked under him into the house. Mick stepped back into the construction zone and walked back to the bedroom window. "Could we interest you in some New World lasagna?"

"That would be great, thanks." Ian started to put his T-shirt on but stopped and draped it over his shoulder. "I think I'll take a shower first."

Mick sniffed his own armpit. "Yeah, me too. Clara says about an hour." They walked toward the ladder leaning against one side of the soon-to-be stairwell. "Tell you what. I'll do the flying, you stay home and I'll give you half a million just to help me plan it."

"You'll do the flying? You haven't even soloed yet!" Ian stopped at the edge of the stairwell. "Think it through, Mick. You're not talking about three trips around the pattern; Guadalajara is fourteen hundred nautical miles away." Ian shook his head. "No."

"Ian..." Mick put his hand on Ian's shoulder. "Maybe you can say no, but I can't. This is just too good a deal to pass up. Even if you won't help, I've got to go for it. I'll be soloed next week and probably have my license in a month or so. I..."

"Mick, the only planes you can rent from the Club, or any other outfit, won't even lift the weight you jumped with!"

"I know." Mick nodded. "I'm going to buy a twin."

"Christ!" Ian thought for a moment. "Okay, assuming you don't have any problems with the multi-engine rating, who's going to fly the second plane?"

"I, uh..." Mick shrugged. "I don't know yet, but I'll find someone. I found you, didn't I? The point is: I'm going to do it. I've got to do it. And I have a much better chance of making it work if you help me."

"I've got to take a shower." Ian shook his head as he started to turn away.

Mick stopped him. "Come on, man! What can it hurt to talk about it? I'll think up some crazy stuff and you can tell me why it won't work. Completely hypothetical."

"Mick," Ian looked at Mick's eager, confident expression. "When you hit the jackpot two times in a row, you don't hang around to see if lightning is going to strike a third time in the same place. You get the hell out of the casino! You get out before your luck runs out." Ian's tone was apologetic, as though he was ending a romance. "I'm sorry Mick, I'm just not willing to press my luck."

"At least think about it, you know, hypothetically."

"Hypothetically?" Ian started to shake his head again, but ended up laughing. "Christ! Okay, I'll think about it: Hypothetically." Ian started down. "It'll give me a chance to talk you out of it."

"Now you're talking!" Mick noticed that he'd left a dirty handprint on Ian's shoulder. He shrugged and followed him down the ladder.

Thursday, 3:24 pm – Poolside, Magic
Dolphin Hotel, Cabo San Lucas

"I do not know if I can survive three days of this!" Setting his margarita on the little table, Rashad sighed content-edly and leaned back on his chaise lounge. He glanced over at Ian and pretended to eat the paper umbrella that had been floating on top of his drink. Tilting his head back, Rashad coughed, and the umbrella shot out of his mouth. Ian glanced at the brightly colored paper, as it fluttered up and then spiraled down to the table between them. He smiled briefly, and then looked back at the sail boats tacking across the Sea of Cortez. Rashad drank some more of his margarita.

A few feet away, water splashed down the natural looking cracks and fissures of a huge granite boulder and emptied into one end of the swimming pool. The wide concrete patio wrapped around the pool from one side of the waterfall to the other, and the two towers of the hotel rose ten floors above the sculptured concrete rock. The terrace overlooked the sea and was scattered with chaise lounges full of tanned and tanning tourists. There were also dozens of short white tables for drinks and sun-screen. The clear water sparkled in the afternoon sun, and the hotel's logo, a gold dolphin leaping above stylized waves, shimmered on the bottom of the pool.

Rashad leaned over and picked up the little umbrella. "So what is bothering you?"

"What do you mean?"

"I mean, why are you so depressed?"

"I'm not depressed!"

Rashad leaned closer and studied Ian's scalp. "Either something is wrong or you have had brain surgery. You are not the same... Oh! I see the incision. Never mind." Rashad leaned back.

Ian looked at him. "What's with you?"

"What is with you? All the way down we flew on autopilot. You never asked me, 'Where could we land if we lost an engine, Rashad?' or, 'How much fuel to reach our alternate, Rashad?'" He pointed the umbrella at Ian. "You lie there with your margarita melting in the glorious Mexican sun and all you do is stare at the water. You do not even laugh at my death-defying umbrella tricks!" Rashad closed his right hand over the little paper parasol and then opened his fingers. The umbrella was gone. "Obviously something is bothering you." The umbrella reappeared in Rashad's left hand.

Ian looked at Rashad's hands. "That's pretty good. How do you do that?"

"You are changing the subject."

"Deal with it."

"You deal with it. I am only trying to help my very best friend in the western hemisphere."

"I'm sorry." Ian sighed. "I guess I've got a lot on my mind."

"I have been wondering what that could be, but it occurs to me that you were also staring out to sea the last time we enjoyed Ms. Taylor's company. Actually, in Chicago you were staring out at Lake Michigan, but the circumstances were otherwise identical." Rashad considered. "You cannot be worried that she is not equally interested in you; she has been watching you whenever she thought you were not watching her."

Ian smiled. "You don't miss much, do you?"

"It is easy to be observant when one is not being inundated with needless and repetitive navigation problems."

Ian watched Rashad take another drink. "I thought you wanted to be a captain."

"I am a captain."

"In the National Guard."

"Ready to defend my adopted homeland with my very life, if necessary." Rashad took a drink.

"Well," Ian picked up his own margarita but didn't drink any, "If you want to stick with helicopters..."

Rashad swallowed quickly. "Have I mentioned how much I enjoy needless and repetitive navigation problems?"

"Many times. But I get your point." Ian looked at the sky. "We've got a date tonight."

"We do?" Rashad laughed. "I hope you mean yourself and the lady lawyer?"

Ian nodded. "Her name is Sandra."

"She is a delight to the senses, whatever her name. So why do you look so despondent? What in the world is there to worry about?"

"Oh, nothing at all." Ian shook his head. "Except that I have a date on Monday with someone else."

"So?"

"'So?' Don't you think it's dishonest to be seeing two women at once?"

"Only if you don't tell them." The little umbrella disappeared. "Or, only if you get caught." Rashad waved one hand over the other and two little umbrellas appeared. "It depends entirely on your point of view."

"I'm not sure I have a point of view, but I'm not going to lie to anyone." Ian finally took a sip of his warm margarita. "Yuck!" He set the glass down and looked at Rashad. "A month ago, I just wanted to figure out what went wrong with Marcia and me. Now..." Ian shook his head. "Now I'm getting too serious, too fast, with two women at the same time!"

"And you see this as a problem?" Rashad produced a third paper parasol.

Ian noticed that the umbrella from his drink was gone. "Don't you?"

"I see it as a gift from heaven!" Rashad waved at their waitress and she waved back. "Consider the facts: last month you were worried about the past. Today you are worried about the future. By any standard this is a tremendous improvement!" He smiled at Ian. "Of course, if you feel in any way unequal to the challenge, your humble first officer is, as always, willing to help. I could, perhaps, take one of them off your hands?"

"You're a true gentleman." Ian chuckled. "Aren't you getting married!"

Rashad wagged his finger. "Not until I ask her."

"You said you were going to propose when we got back from Chicago."

"My courage is still in Chicago."

"Courage? Aren't you in love?"

"I am in love. Yes I am, but Jocelyn is, uh," Rashad moved one umbrella to his other hand. "I must be honest: she is a formidable woman, as her mother before her. I fear I may be ... unworthy of the challenge."

Ian sighed. "I'm not sure I'm 'worthy' of Bernie or Sandy."

"Bernie!" Rashad dropped an umbrella. "Bernie? I thought you said two women!" Rashad smiled. "Captain, my captain is far more open-minded than I had thought!"

"Her name is Bernadette."

"Oh." Rashad feigned disappointment. "Of course."

A young woman wearing a white halter-top, shorts and sandals walked toward them with several empty glasses on a small tray. "Can I get you anything else?" She picked up Rashad's glass and added it to her collection.

"Two more." Rashad held up two fingers. "And I will try to make him drink his."

The waitress pointed to the melted margarita and looked at Ian. "Are you through?"

Ian nodded. "Yes, thanks."

She placed it on the tray. "They're much better cold."

"I'll drink the next one before it melts, I promise."

"Okay." The waitress smiled and returned to the bar.

Rashad watched her walk away. When she disappeared from view, he turned back to Ian. "So, tell me about this Bernie. Where did you meet? What is he like?"

"She!"

Rashad laughed. "Okay, 'she'. What is she like?"

"She ... she's just amazing. She's smart, and pretty, with long brown hair and the sexiest, most incredible smile." Ian looked at Rashad. "I ought to be happy. I am happy. It just seems like everything is out of control. It doesn't make sense."

"What doesn't make sense?"

"My life!" He shook his head. "My love life, to be exact. If I'm in love with Sandy, why did I sleep with Bernie? And if Bernie was just a casual thing, why can't I get her out of my mind? It just doesn't make any sense."

Rashad smiled. "Does love ever make sense?"

"Of course it does! At least it did." Ian looked out at the boats and seagulls. "I thought it did."

The waitress set two more margaritas on the table between the pilots. Rashad signed the check, tipped her three dollars, and watched her walk back toward the cabana. He drank some of the cold margarita and leaned back on the chaise. "It is a rough life we lead." He took another sip. "So how does this amazing Bernie person compare with Ms. Taylor?"

"Well ... I don't know." Ian thought for a moment. "They're ... different. Sandy has a really sharp sense of humor, but it's kind of dry, you know? Bernie is outrageously funny, I mean, she could be a professional comedian. They're both fun to be with, and I think they're both incredible, and each of them makes it impossible for me to think of anything else when I'm with them."

"Which one do you like best?"

"Uh, Neither. Both. Hell, I can't answer that! I don't have a clue."

"Which one is better in bed?"

"I haven't slept with Sandy."

"But you're in love with her?"

"I think so, I mean; yeah. I'm in love with her."

"You're sure?"

"Sure? I've only known her for a few weeks! I'm crazy, I know that much." Ian hesitated. "I've never fallen in love this fast or this hard before. I'd been sleeping with Marcia for months before I told her I loved her and I wasn't even sure until we moved in together."

"You also love Bernie?"

"I think so."

Rashad nodded thoughtfully. "I am thinking, you cannot marry both of them, at least not in America. Can you?"

"No, I don't think so. Hey!" Ian looked at Rashad. "Who said anything about marriage?"

"Is it not inevitable?"

"Hell, I don't know! You tell me!" Ian shook his head. "It's way too early to be talking about marriage."

"I am glad to hear you say that. I have been thinking the very same thing." Rashad tipped back his glass as Sandy walked in front of him. She was wearing a dark blue bikini and had a white hotel towel draped over one shoulder.

"Hi, Rashad." Sandy stopped next to Ian's chaise. "Mr. MacAran, I presume?"

"Good afternoon, Ms. Taylor." Ian smiled up at her.

The high cut of Sandy's bikini emphasized her long legs. A faint, slightly less-tanned line from a different swimsuit circled her hips. She slipped out of her sandals. "I wanted to swim a few laps before dinner. Can I leave my things here?"

"Of course."

"Thanks." Sandy dropped her towel and room key on top of her sandals. "Be right back." She walked over to the edge of the pool. There was a yellow "No Diving" sign painted on the concrete. Sandy glanced down at the sign and then walked to the corner of the pool and stepped down the ladder into the water.

"What a beautiful woman! She makes me think of Jocelyn." Rashad sighed. "Ms. Taylor is a little thin for my taste, but I can tell you right now who I would choose."

"Yeah, but you haven't met Bernie."

Rashad nodded. "This is true."

They watched Sandy swim. Most of the chaise lounges were occupied, but the only other people in the pool were a boy and a girl playing near the waterfall. Sandy pushed off the wall, and swam away from the "No Diving" sign.

Rashad finished his drink and put the empty glass on the table. "I think I will go call Jocelyn. Maybe she can meet me when we get back Saturday night." He stood and picked up his towel, his key and the book he'd been reading.

"What are you going to do if she asks you first?

"What do you mean?"

"What if Jocelyn asks you to marry her?"

Rashad first looked stunned, and then pretended to be horrified. "What a nasty thing to say to a loyal first officer!"

Ian chuckled as Rashad theatrically stalked off through the crowd of basking bodies. He looked for Sandy, and found her in the middle of the pool, swimming toward him. He stood and walked over to the edge. Just before she reached Ian's feet, Sandy tucked into a racing turn. Her head and shoulders went down and her feet, almost touching her swimsuit, flashed past. When her toes touched the wall Sandy pushed away and twisted back onto her stomach. She kicked her feet up much higher than necessary, splashing Ian with water.

Ian dove in after her, sending waves radiating across the pool. He almost caught her, but Sandy sped up and reached the other side several yards ahead of him. She made another graceful turn, and dove down, surfacing behind Ian. He turned to follow without using the wall as a springboard and fell further behind. Sandy stopped at the edge of the pool where Ian had jumped in, but as he caught up to her, she swam off along the edge, toward the waterfall. Ian swam after her.

The waterfall was actually a huge concrete sculpture, painted to look like ancient granite. Water bubbled out of numerous fissures, and formed a wide sheet that dropped into the pool several feet from the edge. Sandy was waiting behind the curtain of falling water. Ian surfaced next to her and wiped the water off his face with his hands. "You're hard to catch!"

She smiled. "I'm glad you didn't give up."

"Never!" Ian smiled and leaned toward her. Sandy moved closer and they kissed. She put her arms around his neck and Ian lifted her to his eye level. He brushed the tip of his nose playfully against Sandy's, and she pretended to bite him. They kissed again as the falling water sparkled and splashed around them.

Sandy opened her eyes when she heard the laughter. A boy and a girl, both about fourteen years old, were scrunched into a little cave above the water line. The girl was proving the boy to be much more ticklish than he'd been willing to admit. The kids smiled nervously, the boy looking terribly embarrassed. Ian chuckled, the boy looked relieved and the four of them laughed together as Sandy pulled Ian back through the sheet of falling water. The adults climbed out of the pool.

"That was funny!" Sandy wrung some of the water out of her hair as they walked over to Ian's chaise. "They're probably hiding from their parents, we're hiding from my co-workers; I feel like I'm seventeen!"

"Can we make that eighteen?" Ian handed Sandy her towel and picked up his own.

Sandy looked at him for a moment and then nodded. "Oh, at least eighteen." She rubbed the towel over her arms and shoulders and then wrapped it around her waist like a skirt. "We're still on for dinner?" Sandy stepped into her sandals.

"Yes ma'am."

"Great. Meet me in the lobby in an hour?"

"I'll be there."

Sandy glanced around, then stepped closer and kissed Ian on the cheek. "Dress casual."

Three hours later they were savoring cuisine that had been swimming earlier that same day. Ian had taken Sandy's advice and worn slacks, sandals and a polo shirt to dinner. He glanced around at the fishing nets and pieces of boats that decorated the restaurant. "The concierge was right; this place is really good!"

"It's great, but he also said it was a short walk, 'right up the road'!" Sandy was wearing blue jeans, sneakers and a black cotton tunic. "He didn't mention the hills."

"Well, he did say 'up' the road. Besides, we came down as many hills as we climbed, so it should all balance out."

Sandy shook her head, "Only if you're a car."

"Well, he was right about the food. The shrimp are excellent!" Ian reached into a palm leaf basket and pulled out a tortilla. "How is the swordfish?"

"It's perfect. I'll admit - it was definitely worth the walk." Sandy cut off a bite of swordfish with her fork. "Would you like some?"

Ian nodded. "Sure."

Sandy teased him with the morsel, making him lean forward before she slipped it into his mouth.

"Mm." Ian chewed slowly, swallowed. "That is perfect." He was still holding the tortilla. "Can I make you a burrito?"

"Not yet." Sandy poked her fork into another bite of swordfish. "Let me see if I can finish this."

Ian nodded. "Just let me know." He rolled shrimp, rice, lettuce, and cheese into a miniature burrito, and took a big bite out of one end.

The couple at the next table paid for their meal and made their way out onto the pier. Sandy could see them pointing at the boats and talking. She watched them kiss, and then head down the steps toward the beach with their arms around each other.

The waiter brought out two frosty, nearly overflowing glasses. Ian looked at the bright green slush for a moment and then picked it up. "What is this again?"

"It's a Midori margarita." Sandy took a drink as Ian cautiously tried a sip.

"Hey! This is really good!"

Sandy smiled. "You sound surprised."

"Well…" Ian held up his glass. "It looks like a Kryptonite Slurpee."

Sandy laughed. "I like you." She put her glass down and gazed at him intently. "I mean, I really like you a lot."

"I like you too." Ian set his glass down. "Very much."

"I know. I mean…" Sandy glanced down at her plate. When she looked up, she was smiling. "I'm glad."

They finished their margaritas, but Sandy threw in the napkin on the swordfish. Neither one wanted dessert, but both tried an after-dinner mint. After paying for dinner, Ian and Sandy made their way onto the worn timbers of the pier. They paused for a moment to look out at the boats and then headed down the steps toward the beach. The bottom step was broken and Ian held out his hand to help Sandy down.

"Why, thank you, sir." She took his hand, and with dainty exaggeration stepped onto the sand. "Oh, wait a minute." Sandy slipped out of her fair damsel character as she slipped off her sneakers, holding Ian's hand for balance.

"Good idea." Ian took off his sandals, balancing first on one foot and then the other. Sandy held him steady, and their hands remained linked as they walked toward the edge of the sea.

A sheet of frothy water slowed, stopped, and slid back into the ocean. Three sandpipers raced after the retreating foam until they were driven back up the beach by another wave. The birds chased each successive wave, stabbing their beaks into the agitated sand, searching for anything edible.

"Look!" Sandy stopped walking and pointed at one bird that had stopped halfway down the beach. "She's caught something!"

Tiny legs struggled frantically on both sides of the sandpiper's narrow bill. The crab looked much too big for the bird to swallow. Its carapace was like a swollen penny held in a pair of tweezers.

"She's caught it, all right." Ian wiggled his toes in the wet sand. "What's she going to do with it?"

The bird tilted her head back and worked the crab down her throat, bobbing her head up and down as she swallowed. She stood very still for a moment, and then shook her head. She swallowed again, shook her head again, and fell in with the other two sandpipers as they raced a wave back up the beach. The trio stayed with the wave and continued their search for food.

Sandy shook her head. "She can't still be hungry."

Ian chuckled. "There's always room for dessert."

"She should have tried the swordfish."

Sandy and Ian walked hand in hand along the damp line left by the last wave. The craters of their footprints were surrounded by the delicate filigree of sandpiper tracks.

A mile or so further on, the beach narrowed, squeezed into a thin vulnerable strip between the cliffs and the receding ocean. Ian stopped walking. "I can see why the concierge told us to take the road."

"Because he had no sense of adventure?" Sandy pointed at the knee-high stain of flotsam and seaweed that clung to the base of the cliff. "Looks like this is under water at high tide."

"Yeah, but the tide is still going out." Ian glanced at his watch and then at the ocean. "We've got at least three or four hours, according to the waiter."

"Only three hours?" Sandy grinned and let go of his hand. "We'd better hurry!" She ran ahead, toward their hotel.

Ian watched her run. Sandy's hair flowed gracefully behind her, gold and reddish-orange in the setting sun. Her sneakers swung back and forth in her hand and her shadow danced across the cliff face. As the beach curved to the west and disappeared around the base of the cliff, Sandy vanished beyond the curtain of rock. Ian started running after her.

He caught up with her next to a steep-walled gorge where the beach edged up above the high tide mark. The ribbon of fine sand wrapped around the sheer wall into a secluded hollow that had been cut back into the cliff by a small stream. There was high dry sand on one side and a small lagoon on the other.

Racing past her, Ian whirled around, his arms spread wide to catch her. Sandy feinted toward the cliffs and when Ian leaned that way to cut her off, she dodged past him toward the ocean. Ian lunged after her, barely missing her ankle, as Sandy twisted away, laughing. She ran further up the beach. Ian picked himself up and chased after her.

Sandy's laughter echoed off the walls as she ran into the little box-canyon. She stopped, caught between the cliff and the lagoon. Just as Ian caught up with her, Sandy dodged to the side.

Ian twisted toward her, grabbing her arm, but as he started to fall sideways, he let go and tumbled onto his back. Sandy planted her bare foot on his chest.

"Do you yield, brave knight?" She held herself stiff and formal, but her eyes sparkled and she was having trouble hiding her smile.

Ian grabbed her ankle. "Gotcha!"

"Oh?" Sandy wiggled her toes and sand flaked off onto his shirt. She could feel Ian's heartbeat through his chest, and her foot rose and fell with each quick breath. They were both breathing hard from the run down the beach. Sandy raised an eyebrow. "I should think that I have you."

"You do indeed, fair lady." Ian brought up his other hand and started tickling the bottom of Sandy's foot. "I am completely in your power."

Laughing, Sandy tried to pull away. Then she tried to pull Ian's hands off her foot while balancing on the other. "What treachery!" She fell on top of him and tickled him back. Ian stopped tickling her and grabbed her hands.

A wave broke somewhere far away as they looked into each other's eyes. Sandy interlaced her fingers with Ian's and they kissed. Their lips touched, separated, and then brushed together. Ian wrapped his arms around her as the murmur of the ocean whispered around them. Sandy kissed Ian's upper lip but withdrew before he could kiss her back. Sandy turned her head a little, and rubbed the side of her face against his. His cheek was coarse with the beginnings of a beard, and he smelled like peppermint and tequila.

She shifted position to better see his face. "Beautiful."

"That's my line."

"I like the way your eyes sparkle. They're almost a different color every time I see them."

"That's also my line. Except for the different color part." Ian brushed a stray hair back over Sandy's ear. "Remember the first time we flew together?"

"Vegas, yeah?"

"Just after you boarded and I did the 'make yourself at home' speech, I thought you were going to say something, but we just stared at each other. Remember?"

Sandy nodded. "I thought you looked like something out of an old movie."

Ian smiled self-consciously. "Is that good or bad?"

"Good." Sandy kissed him. "Definitely good."

"What were you going to say?"

"Nothing really." Sandy teased his lower lip with her own. "I liked your voice."

"My voice?"

"You sounded confident and professional and terribly sexy." She smiled. "I almost said something silly like, 'You have a really nice voice,' but I couldn't decide if I loved your voice or hated it."

Ian looked puzzled. "Why would you hate...?"

"No rational reason whatsoever. It made me want to trust you and I hate being so irrational." Sandy grinned at him. "You could have been a total jerk."

"I could?" Doubt clouded Ian's expression.

"No." Sandy brushed her fingers against the side of his face and kissed him. "You couldn't."

They necked just above the high-tide line and talked as the orange glow of sunset faded and the sky became cosmic. Sandy recalled an astronomy class in Japan and Ian talked about high school in Alameda. Sandy felt a passion for music much like Ian's passion for flying, though Sandy had never wanted to become a professional musician. Ian admitted that he didn't want to be an airline pilot for the career or whatever prestige still came with the job; he just loved the flying. It was the view and the craft and the peace he felt when he was in the air. Sandy said playing was the same for her and that she'd never wanted to compete to be one of a few artists in an entertainment industry. She would much rather see everyone playing their own music.

Hidden by the cliff behind them, the moon rose in the eastern sky as the stars of the Milky Way passed slowly overhead. The susurrations of the surf edged closer as the tide began reclaiming the beach and soon the waves were washing over the tracks Ian and Sandy had made in the sand.

CHAPTER FIVE

Sunday, 12:25 pm – Clara's Future
Sewing Room, Alameda

D es took a drag from his cigarette and flicked the ash off its tip. The gray flakes scattered across the pale plywood of Mick's second floor. Wearing loafers, gray slacks and a white polo shirt, Des would have looked completely conservative, except for the long black hair that hung loose around his shoulders. Smoke wafted away in the breeze as he spoke. "Where do we get two Catalinas?"

"We don't." Mick was wearing blue jeans and a T-shirt that said, "It takes studs to frame a building!" He smiled. "That's the beauty of it! We only need one PBY and my buddy just bought it."

"But we do need two planes, right?"

"Right, but not two big planes; the second airplane only has to carry a transponder. It can be anything, as long as it can keep up with the Cat, and Catalina's aren't that fast."

Des shook his head. "If it's not the same kind of plane, someone's going to know that something's wrong."

"No one's even going to see the planes when they take off." Mick leaned back against a stud in an unfinished wall and rubbed his shoulder blade against the 2x6. "The pilots take off at night, from uncontrolled airports, one in Mexico and one in the middle of nowhere, say Arizona. They don't contact ATC until they're high up and…"

"What's ATC?"

"Air Traffic Control. Anyway, they don't contact ATC until way after they've taken off and since both planes are using uncontrolled airports, that's the first time they have to talk to anyone. The pilot of the PBY tells the controller that he's in…" Mick stopped scratching his back. "I don't know, a Cessna or something, whatever the other plane is and he gives the controller that Cessna's ID number. Meanwhile the guy in the Cessna says that he's flying a PBY Catalina and gives the controller the PBY's number. After the PBY crosses the border, pretending to be a Cessna, the two planes meet in the middle of nowhere, switch transponder codes and bingo! The controllers have a PBY headed for Oakland and a Cessna or something headed for Los Angeles. Customs wants to see the plane headed for L.A. because they think it came from Mexico. They couldn't care less about the PBY because they think it came from Arizona. They have no idea its carrying two thousand kilos of incredibly fine snow."

Des exhaled another lungful of smoke. "How do the two planes find each other in the dark?"

"I'm not sure yet." Mick shrugged. "We think we can use the ADF, the automatic direction finder, but we're not sure how to hook up a transmitter. My pilot is working on it."

"Sounds crazy." Des shook his head. "Too crazy."

"It's only crazy enough to work." Mick looked out across the houses of Alameda and then closer, at the front porch of Ian's house. "You guys have been moving a lot of product."

"Business is good."

"It must be. You only needed forty keys last week, now you want sixty."

Des smiled. "We're expanding. It's amazing what high quality can do for market share."

"What about Doctor Neault?"

Des took another drag on his cigarette. "What about him?"

"You guys are moving in on his turf, right? Is he going to give you any trouble?"

"Paul may not realize it, but he doesn't have any turf." Des cleared his throat. "Paul is a fucking mental case, and he's becoming totally impossible to work with. But he won't be giving us headaches for much longer."

"Oh yeah? Why not?"

"We're letting him ride, for now, just keeping him happy. He doesn't know we're expanding. He thinks everyone is plodding along, scared of their own shadows, all under his expert guidance."

Mick glanced at a departing airliner and then turned to face Des. "How long are you going to keep expanding?"

"What do you mean?"

"How big do you want to get?"

Des shrugged. "Big, but I think sixty keys a week is about right for now."

"That could be a problem, I don't know how much more importing I'm going to be able to do."

"What the fuck are you talking about?" Suddenly Des looked concerned. "You're not thinking about drying up on us, are you?"

"Not me." Mick shrugged. "But my pilot doesn't want to do any more small stuff. He wants to do a couple of big shipments and then retire."

"So go for it, and then find another pilot." Des considered. "Why are you telling me all this? What does this have to do with me?"

"Most of my money is tied up in real estate. Hell, I could retire right now, but this deal is just too good to pass up. It's a foolproof plan, and the plane can easily carry two thousand kilos. All I need is the cash to get the deal started: Ten million up front, and forty million on delivery."

Des laughed. "All you need is fifty million dollars? I can't..." His eyes narrowed. "Wait; that's only twenty five dollars a gram!"

Mick nodded. "Delivered."

"Same source?"

"Same source, same quality. That's three hundred and fifty, maybe four hundred dollars a gram on the street."

"Son of a..." Des looked out between two boards at the distant towers of San Francisco's financial district.

He nodded to himself. "Tony could solve the radio problem."

"What?"

"Nothing." Des looked back at Mick. "You trust this pilot?"

"Yeah, and he's good. Real good." Mick smiled. "He got me this far."

Des dropped his cigarette and ground the butt into the plywood. "I want to meet him."

"Okay... How 'bout right now? He lives right across the street."

Des looked surprised but nodded. "Let's go."

As they reached the bottom of the ladder, Zachary ran down the hall and wrapped both arms around his dad's legs. "Hey, Zachary!" Mick untangled himself and picked the boy up. "How ya doin'?"

"Fine." Zachary wrapped his arms around his father's neck. "We're gonna see a movie."

"You are? Which one?"

"I wanted to see the movie Ian said I was in, but Mom says I'm too young. I'm not too young, am I?" The boy shook his head and a curl of black hair flopped onto his forehead.

"You're not too young to go to the cooler movies." Mick brushed Zach's hair back into place as Clara came around the corner from the kitchen. Clara smiled. "Oh, there you are!" Zachary turned his head away as Clara kissed Mick on the cheek. "We're going to see Spinning; do you guys want to come along?"

"No thanks." Mick set Zachary down. "We're going over to Ian's."

"Okay. Tell him I said 'hi.'" Clara stepped back to let Xavier and Yolanda squeeze past. The adults followed the kids out into the garage, and Clara opened the side door of their brown minivan. As the three kids piled inside, Clara kissed Mick goodbye. "We'll be back in a few hours."

Mick gave his wife a hug and slipped between the van and his Porsche. "Bye hon." He glanced at Des. "Come on."

Des followed him across the street. Mick stopped at Ian's front door and lowered his voice. "Look, I, uh, I haven't told Ian we need outside money. Just let me introduce you, see what you think, and we'll play it from there, okay?"

"Sure," Des nodded. "Works for me."

Mick rang the bell. A muted three-tone chime could be heard through the heavy oak. They waited. Des glanced back toward Mick's house as Clara turned the mini-van onto the street and headed toward Doolittle Drive. "Are you sure he's home?"

"He said he'd be back from Mexico last night." Mick pointed at the unlit light next to the door. "This light was on all day yesterday." Mick knocked on the door and then rang the doorbell again.

Des took out a cigarette. "Maybe the bulb burned out."

"Maybe." Mick stepped back and looked past the living room window to the fence on the property line. "Maybe he's in the backyard. Come on."

Des followed, unlit cigarette in hand. Mick led the way through the unlocked gate and around to the rear of the house. Ian's back yard was mostly grass, with a concrete patio next to the family room's sliding doors. A metal table with matching patio chairs was at the far corner of the concrete and Sandy was sitting in one of the chairs. She was wearing a short, white terry-cloth robe that barely covered her lap. Her feet rested on another chair, her long legs stretched out across the gap. Sandy modestly adjusted her robe when she noticed Mick and Des.

Before anyone could say anything, Ian came out of the house with two frosty glasses on a tray. "Your daiquiri, milady." He was wearing white tennis shorts. Setting the tray on the table, Ian turned to follow Sandy's gaze. He chuckled. "Morning, Mick."

Mick stepped onto the patio. "Afternoon, Ian."

Ian looked at the sun, and nodded. "So it is."

"Uh, sorry to disturb you." Mick shifted his attention from Sandy to Ian. "I wanted you to meet Des. He's thinking about taking some flying lessons."

"That sounds like fun." Ian remained standing.

"Des Pierrot," Mick nodded toward Des, and then toward Ian. "Ian MacAran."

Ian took a step toward Des and they shook hands. "Nice to meet you, Des."

"Nice to meet you too, Ian." Des nodded toward Sandy. "Afternoon, ma'am."

Sandy smiled politely, "Good afternoon."

"Sandy this is Mick Dale. He's a student of mine."

"Hi, Mick."

"Hi." Mick shrugged. "We knocked but, ah, no one answered."

"Sorry." Ian smiled. "We're not back from Mexico yet."

Mick looked at Sandy. "But..."

"We're space aliens." Sandy nodded matter-of-factly. "We're not really in this dimension at all."

Ian laughed, "Look, Mick, if you like, you can bring Des along on our next flight."

"Yeah, that would be great." Mick looked at Des. "We're flying tomorrow morning, would that work for you?"

"Uh," Des was staring at Sandy's legs. "That would be good."

"Okay." Ian ushered them toward the gate. "So I'll see you guys in the morning, right?"

"See you tomorrow." Mick led the way as he and Des disappeared around the corner of the house.

Ian watched the gate close before returning to Sandy. "I need a big German Shepherd."

Sandy had picked up her drink. "You're away from home too much."

"True. How about an electrified fence?" Ian sat down next to her.

"Much better idea." Sandy tasted her daiquiri. "Oh, this is good!" She took a bigger sip.

"Thanks. Now where were we?"

"You were talking about your car. You said you had an audience at triple A."

"Oh yeah. By the time I finished explaining about that lunatic peeing all over the police car, half the people in the office were gathered around the adjuster's desk! They thought it was hysterical."

Sandy nodded. "I told some of the folks at work we got rear ended going seventy-five. They couldn't believe it."

"My insurance adjuster couldn't believe we got rear ended at sixty-five! She called the Highway Patrol and they read her the report. Turns out the guy wasn't just drunk, he was also high on cocaine and a couple other drugs. The car he was driving was stolen the day before in Tulare."

"Where's that?"

"North of Bakersfield, I think. After she talked to the Highway Patrol, the adjuster looked at me for a second and said, 'We're going to waive the deductible on this one.' The people around her desk actually applauded."

"That's great."

"The car should be ready today." Ian leaned a little closer and lightly brushed his fingers along Sandy's arm. "Are you sure you have to go to work this afternoon?"

Sandy smiled. "I think I could be dissuaded."

"Dissuaded?" Ian raised an eyebrow.

"Yeah, dissuaded." Sandy leaned toward him so that their lips were only inches apart. "You making fun of the way I talk?"

Ian kissed her. "I don't think I've ever 'dissuaded' anybody before."

"I'll bet you haven't!" Sandy kissed him back and, after a few minutes, they walked hand in hand through the house to the bedroom. The daiquiris were left to melt in the sun.

Monday, 5:26 pm – 16th & Mission, San Francisco

The escalator carried Stacia up to the sidewalk above the subway station. As she stepped off the moving stairs, a boy on roller-blades swept past her, his wheels muttering on the imitation cobblestone. Stacia walked around the graffiti emblazoned concrete planters and turned up 16th Street. She was wearing gray slacks and her red-brown ponytail hung down the back of a black blouse. After stuffing her office heels into the dark blue backpack slung over her left shoulder, Stacia had put on her black court shoes for the commute home.

Just past Valencia, a beer truck was double-parked in front of Fong's Liquor Store. The truck's engine rumbled harmony to the noisy hum of the city. The logo on the side read, "Made the American way." Cases of Evian and Dos Equis blocked the sidewalk, forcing Stacia into the street to get around them. She slipped between two parked cars to get back on the sidewalk, but as she crossed the alley in the middle of the block, a black motorcycle roared off the street and stopped in front of her.

"Hi, babe." Terri wasn't wearing a helmet. "Want a lift?"

Stacia started to back away but Terri grabbed her left wrist. "Come on, let's go for a ride."

"Ow!" Stacia tried to pull free. "You're hurting me!"

"And I know you like it, don't you?" Terri grinned. "Admit it."

"Leave me alone, Terri!" Stacia tugged, tilting Terri and the motorcycle toward her. "I like being held, not hurt. There's a difference!"

"Is there?" Terri pulled back to regain her balance. "Let's go over to my place and wrestle with the distinctions."

"Back off, Terri! If you don't leave me alone, I'll call the police!" Stacia pushed into Terri and the bike overbalanced. Terri quickly shifted across the seat so she could put a foot down on the other side of the bike and Stacia snapped her wrist out of Terri's hand. The dark blue backpack slid down from Stacia's shoulder and caught in the crook of her arm. She took a step back and dug her right hand into her pack.

Terri shut off the engine and kicked the bike's stand down. "I do love the way you play hard to get." She swung her leg over, slid off the seat and stepped toward Stacia. "Come here."

The stream of Mace caught Terri on the forehead and splashed across her face onto her chest. She swung an angry roundhouse kick at the little red cylinder in Stacia's hand, but Stacia jerked her hand down and under the path of the black boot.

Terri coughed and tried to wipe the burning fluid from her eyes. "Shit!" She coughed again and shook her head, bending over to hold her face in her hands. Stacia took a step back, holding her hand, and the Mace canister, between them.

Terri straightened up. Her hands were clenched in fists but her voice was icy calm. "That was very naughty." Tears streamed down her face, but she struggled to keep her eyes open. She lowered her head again and then lunged forward, swinging her right hand at the can in Stacia's hand. The second stream of Mace went over

Terri's left shoulder, but Stacia stepped to the side and drove her right foot into Terri's right knee. Terri's leg twisted sideways with an excruciating "pop" and she fell to the sidewalk.

Stacia stepped back and stared down at Terri, curled in a black leather ball around her broken knee. Stacia moved toward Terri, but stopped when Terri glared up at her.

"How could you...?" Terri tried to straighten her leg and screamed. She ground her teeth together. "Christ that hurts!" She took a deep breath and let it out slowly.

"I took your advice. I'm taking a self-defense class." Stacia forced a smile. "How am I doing?"

"Fuck you!" Terri was still holding her knee with both hands.

"I'll call an ambulance for you." Stacia stepped back. "I don't want to see you again; ever." She had started shaking but she held her head up and glared at Terri until Terri lowered her eyes and looked away. "Just leave me alone, Terri." Stacia backed away a few steps before putting the Mace away, trading the red cylinder for her cell phone. She shrugged the backpack up onto her shoulder and pressed 911 'send' as she turned and walked away.

Monday, 7:27 pm – Concert Queue,
Greek Theater, UC Berkeley

A smiling teenager with a ring in her nose took Bernie's tickets, ripped them apart and returned half the pieces. Bernie handed a stub to Ian. Holding hands, Bernie and Ian maneuvered through the crowd toward their seats. All around the sold-out amphitheater there were lines to buy Indigo Girls T-shirts, lines to get hot dogs and beer, and lines to get into the women's restrooms. There was even a line to get into reserved seating. Ian had to fish his ticket stub out of his front pocket so the security guard would let him in. Following Bernie to the middle of the fifth row, Ian noticed there weren't very many men in the audience. "Wow."

"What?" Bernie sat down and Ian sat next to her.

Ian gestured at the college-age crowd around them. "I guess I feel a little outnumbered."

Bernie glanced around at the crowd and nodded. "You are. The Indigo Girls are real popular with women." She reached over and slid her hand into Ian's. "Don't worry, I'll protect you." She grinned at him until he smiled back. "This is gonna be great!"

The couple in front of them was also holding hands as they talked about buying a house. The woman on the right wore a silver and turquoise earring in her left ear. A few inches away, matching jewelry dangled from her girlfriend's right ear. Bernie studied the stage, stretching forward to look into the wings. Beyond the curtains at the side of the stage, people were moving equipment and milling around, hidden from all but the first few rows of seats. Bernie squeezed Ian's hand. "This is gonna be really great!"

Ian returned the caress. "You know, you look like you're waiting for Santa Claus."

"Yeah?" She nodded. "I guess so. I just love these guys. The first time I heard them I couldn't believe it! They were speaking directly to me, to how I felt, to what I was going through. I've got every one of their CDs."

"I know this is a stupid question, but I forgot; who are they?"

"I told you!" She looked at him as though he'd just dropped in from Mars. "The Indigo Girls? Amy Ray and Emily Saliers? We heard them on the radio: "Kid Fears", "Closer to Fine". Don't you remember?" Bernie smiled sheepishly. "I must sound like a total air-head. I guess I should have warned you; I'm a real big fan."

"That's okay. I think it's great!" Ian let go of her hand to put his arm around her. "You've got me jazzed and I've never even heard of these guys before!" Ian hugged her close and they kissed.

A woman in blue jeans and a purple 'pro-choice' shirt walked out onto the stage and for a moment the crowd quieted down. The thousand-odd conversations resumed as soon as people realized she wasn't one of the Indigo Girls. The sound technician ignored the crowd as much as she could, and calmly said, "Check two" several times into each of the two microphones at the front of the stage. She was less than thirty feet from Bernie and Ian.

"They're gonna be right there!" Bernie pointed to the technician and then leaned forward to look offstage again. "God, this is great!"

Ian glanced over his shoulder at the concentric tiers of concrete seats climbing the hill behind them and then looked at the stage, only four rows away. "How did you get these seats?"

"They were a present." Bernie's grin faded for a moment.

Ian had glanced up at the sky and didn't see her suddenly serious expression. Scattered sheets of cloud were drifting across the late afternoon sky. "Nice present."

"Yeah." Bernie's smile had returned. "So, uh, how was Mexico?"

"What?" Ian looked startled. "Oh." He shrugged. "Beach, sun, surf: the usual corporate-pilot nightmare."

She laughed. "I'll bet." Bernie looked directly at Ian. "I thought about this a lot while you were gone."

"The concert?"

"No. Well, that too." Bernie smiled self-consciously. "I meant us."

"I thought about us too. This whole thing happened so fast, it almost doesn't seem real."

"Yeah." The couple in front of them leaned closer together and started kissing. Bernie leaned toward Ian and lowered her voice. "I've never slept with anyone on the first date before."

"I thought this was our first date."

Bernie poked him with her elbow. "You know what I mean."

"I know. Me neither."

"It just seemed like the right thing to do."

"It was that." Ian kissed her.

Bernie brushed her hand against his cheek and they kissed again. Someone behind them was saying that divorce was the last rite of passage to adulthood. Bernie looked down at Ian's left hand. "Have you ever been married?"

"What?"

"Just wondering." Bernie smiled. "We haven't had a chance to talk much."

"That's true." Ian shook his head. "No, I haven't. Have you?"

"God no!" Bernie laughed.

"Does that mean you don't want to be?"

"I wouldn't say that. It's just hard to imagine." Bernie shook her head. "It's strange asking first-date questions after we've already been to bed together."

Ian nodded. "Kind of fun, though."

The girl sitting in front of Bernie turned around just enough to get a glimpse of Ian.

Bernie nodded. "Yeah, I like it."

The technician walked out to say, "check two, and check two" again. The crowd noise rose a few decibels and a lot of people, including Ian, looked at their watches. It was 7:45.

Two women, each carrying an acoustic guitar, walked out onto the stage and the audience started cheering and applauding. Amy and Emily took turns saying how great it was to be back in the Bay Area, and then, as their welcome finally started dying down, they began to play. The amplified music wasn't painfully loud, but the multiple speakers at the front of the stage made it impossible to hear anything else. Ian didn't see any backup musicians, not even a drummer, but the Indigo Girls didn't seem to need them. Everyone in the audience looked completely absorbed in the music, and most of the people around him, including Bernie, were singing along. Ian didn't recognize the song, but by the second verse he was nodding in time with the thousands of fans around him.

The chorus of the second song ended with, "Multiply life by the power of two." Halfway through the song, with everyone except Ian singing that line, there was a sizzling explosion backstage. Sparks preceded a muffled WHUMP, like lightning before thunder, and the floodlights went out. The pounding, amplified passion faded into the still-audible, and still-intense harmony of two acoustic guitars. The Indigos kept playing and, along with everyone else in the theater, looked toward the wings. The curtains that concealed the backstage area couldn't hide the smoke wafting into the air above the stage. The technician appeared at the edge of the stage and signaled to the musicians that everything was okay. She pointed to her watch, held up five fingers, and then brought her hands together as though she was plugging two electrical cords together.

The tech flashed another "okay" sign and disappeared, while Amy asked Emily, "Does she mean five minutes, or five hours?"

Emily shook her head. "Could mean days."

The people close to the stage, who heard the exchange, laughed and a sense of relief spread through the amphitheater. The technician rushed out to the center of the stage and Amy and Emily stopped playing to listen to a brief explanation. The woman had brought a battery-powered megaphone and as she retreated backstage, Amy aimed the megaphone out at the crowd. "We've always wanted to add some fireworks to the show, what do you think?" Most of the crowd laughed and some even applauded. Amy apologized for the delay and explained that power would be restored in a few minutes.

The couple sitting next to Ian was talking about how bright the sparks had been, and hoping no one was hurt. Voices behind Ian were planning a wedding, and the couple in the next row was taking advantage of the break to get caught up on their kissing. The clouds were glowing rose and amber with the imminent sunset. Ian sighed.

Bernie nudged him. "Something wrong?"

"No." Ian shook his head.

"You look sad."

"I'm fine." Ian put his arm around her shoulder. "Just thinking."

"Oh yeah?" Bernie wrapped her arms around him and hugged him tight. "What about?"

"Just stuff, you know, life and all its complications."

"Sounds heavy." Bernie studied his face. "Good complications?"

"Hey, come on." Ian forced a smile. "Let's just enjoy the concert."

"Now you've got me worried." Bernie leaned back in her chair and glanced up at the stage. Amy and Emily were chatting with some people in the front row. "Is it something about us?"

"Sort of..."

"Good or bad?"

"Well..."

"Oh, now you've got to tell me." Bernie stared at Ian expectantly. "Come on. You can't just leave me hanging."

Ian nodded reluctantly. "I, uh, met this woman..."

Bernie tensed. "When?"

"Just a couple weeks ago."

"Before we met!" Bernie pulled her hand away from Ian's. "Oh shit! Why did you sleep with me if there was someone else?"

"I didn't! I mean, there wasn't!"

Bernie smiled a little bit. "So, you didn't sleep with her?"

"No! I mean, I did, but that was after you and I, I mean..."

"After?"

"We were in Mexico."

"I thought you said it was a nightmare!" Bernie looked away and crossed her arms. The girl in front of her glanced back and gave Ian a hostile look. Bernie sighed. "Do you love her?"

"I'm not sure." Ian hesitated. "I think I love you both."

The stage blazed into perfectly illuminated brilliance and Emily leaned closer to her microphone. "Hello?" Everyone in the Greek Theater heard her amplified voice and many responded by yelling, "Hello!" back at the stage. The audience didn't need any amplification.

Next to Ian, Bernie was shaking her head. "How can you be in love with two different people? That doesn't make sense."

"I know."

"You know!" Bernie glared at him. "What do you mean, 'you know'?"

On the stage, Emily strummed a few chords and Amy quipped, "We were away for a while, but we're back now." The crowd applauded.

Ian was trying to explain. "I mean, I know it doesn't make any sense. I..."

Emily's amplified voice interrupted him. "I guess the "Power of Two" was too much for the power company."

Everyone laughed except Bernie, who was glaring at Ian. "You're damn right it doesn't make any sense! How..."

The musicians started over from the beginning of "Power of Two" and the sound drowned out everything else Bernie said. Shaking her head, she gave up and turned her attention back to the stage. Ian kept glancing at her, but Bernie didn't look back. She did seem totally absorbed in the music, but she wasn't singing along.

After "Power of Two", Amy and Emily segued directly into "Land of Canaan." The first time they sang the chorus, Bernie leaned back in her seat. Amy protested, "I'm not your promised land, I'm not your promised one," and Bernie slumped down in her chair and wiped her eyes. The song ended with a plaintive, "I'm lonely tonight!"

and Bernie brushed her hair back with one hand as the crowd applauded.

Ian clapped with everyone else, but his eyes were on Bernie. She just stared at her hands, twisted together in her lap. Ian started to say something but the next song started, and Bernie kept her eyes resolutely on the women on stage.

As Amy Ray sang, "These arms are burning, but they're open wide," Bernie leaned forward and wiped her eyes again. When the line, "Oh, you precious kid," whispered through the crowd, Bernie leaned next to Ian so he could hear her. "I'll be back in a minute." She stood and Ian rose to let her pass.

He could see the tears in her eyes. "Do you want to leave?"

Bernie shook her head. "I'm just going to the bathroom. I'll be right back."

Ian watched Bernie push her way through the people standing in the aisles. He caught a glimpse of her moving along the edge of the reserved seats and then she was gone.

Four or five songs later, about halfway through the concert, the Indigo Girls sang "Kid Fears", the song Ian had heard on the radio. When they reached the second chorus, however, the concert version became something very different. The music stopped and Emily and Amy sang the line "Are you on fire?" acappella. As a single voice, the audience sang back, "Are you on fire?" Still without music, their voices filled with an aching desperate passion, the Girls sang, "From the years?" Almost everyone in the theater responded, echoing the phrase.

The concert continued, with an intimacy and community that Ian could see reflected in the people all around him. People swayed in time with the music and sang along with most of the choruses. At one point, the woman in front of Bernie's still-empty seat turned to hug her girlfriend and glanced back at Ian, her face glowing with the excitement of the concert. She looked away when Ian nodded to her. Shaking his head sadly, Ian rose and slowly made his way out of the reserved-seating section.

He walked past the restrooms and around the perimeter of jubilant fans. He talked to a guard who assured him that security hadn't heard of anyone sick or injured, and that if anything had happened to Bernie, security would know about it. Ian circled back and stood at the edge of the reserved seats, searching the thousands of enchanted fans for some sign of Bernie. He waited.

A dozen songs later, toward the end of the concert, Joan Baez was welcomed onto the stage with a thunderous ovation from the standing crowd. She joined in on two Indigo Girls songs and they joined her in singing "The Night They Drove Old Dixie Down". Finally, they closed the concert with Paul Simon's "American Tune". The trio sang it acappella as the roadies started moving equipment across the darkened stage behind them. They left the stage briefly, only to be drawn back by the continuing applause and the flickering hope of a thousand butane lighters. The audience coaxed the singers back for two encores before the concert was really over.

Half an hour after the singers had gone backstage for good, Ian watched the last few couples and groups of fans file past and make their way out of the Greek Theater. Stars shown through ragged patches between low clouds that reflected the light from the surrounding city. A security guard politely but firmly asked Ian to leave the theater. Outside the theater Ian checked his messages surrounded by the remnants of a good time. He waited half an hour and checked his messages again. He called Bernie's number and left a message. After another hour he made his way home alone.

Tuesday, 11:28 am – Dale Construction's
Jean Street Job-Site, Oakland

The next day Bernie tugged a sticky slice of pepperoni and mushroom pizza away from the cardboard box and folded the gooey wedge in half. The pizza box was on the hood of Ken's pickup, which was parked next to stack of wall studs. Bernie leaned back against the 2x6s, and took a bite of pizza. Tomato sauce oozed out between the crust and cheese and dripped onto her blue denim work shirt. Bernie wiped the sauce off with her hand, hesitated, and then wiped her hand on her jeans.

Ken was ignoring a similar splotch of sauce on his T-shirt. He reached for a second slice. "So how's the new boyfriend?"

Bernie shook her head. "I don't want to talk about it."

"Yesterday you tell me you've got a new flame, and now you don't want to talk about it? What's going on?"

"Nothing." Bernie shrugged and looked away.

Ken reached out and put his hand on her shoulder. "Are you okay?"

"Yeah. I'm fine."

"He didn't hurt you or anything, did he?"

"No. The complications are just a lot harder to handle than I thought."

"But complications are so interesting!"

Bernie shook her head. "When is Mick coming back?"

"Alright, we'll change the subject. He said he'd be back by ten, so we might see him before the end of the day."

"Might?"

"Might not. Mick always makes up for coming in late by leaving early'."

"How can he run a jobsite if he's never here?"

"He hires good people."

"You're so modest."

Ken smiled, "I meant you."

"Oh." Bernie took a bite of her pizza.

A pale green sedan drove up the street and parked illegally next to the office trailer. The Great Seal of the City of Oakland was beginning to peel off the driver's door. Bernie watched a tall man lever himself out of the sedan and walk toward the office. He was carrying a clipboard with a dozen or so official looking forms and several small sheets of red cardstock. She looked at Ken. "Do we have an inspection scheduled today?"

"No." Ken tossed his crust into the box and headed for the trailer.

Bernie hesitated, and then followed him, finishing her pizza as she crossed the street. When she came around the trailer, the guy with the clipboard was tacking a red card onto the frame of the building entrance with a staple gun. He was being polite and professional as Ken careened through the twelve steps of disappointment while reading the top form on the clipboard.

Bernie tried to read the form over Ken's shoulder. "What's up?"

"We've been red-tagged! The city's shutting us down."

"Sorry." The building inspector retrieved his clipboard, removed the top form and handed it to Ken. "Give me a call as soon as you get the changes approved." He pointed to the bottom of the form. "My number is right there."

"Thanks." Ken said, meaning something entirely different than 'thank you'. He pulled a battered cell phone out of his pocket.

"Sorry." The inspector retreated to his car.

Bernie looked from Ken to the red 'Stop Work' tag and back at Ken. "What changes is he talking about?"

"Mick's goddamned penthouse isn't part of the original plans the city approved."

"Shit." Bernie sighed, "Does that mean we're out of a job?"

"No." Ken turned his attention to the phone and pressed '1' to skip the out going message. "Mick! Ken, we got red-tagged again! Call me!"

"He's done this before?"

"Well," Ken thought for a moment. "We did have a job last year that didn't get shut down."

"Terrific." Bernie looked up at the building's naked skeleton. "What now?

"We finish lunch." Ken led the way back to the pizza. "We'll pack up the gear when the rest of the guys get back. Then we find Mick."

Tuesday, 2:29 pm – Espresso Rasputin, UC Berkeley

Three miles north and three hours later Conquistador LLC was facing its own stop work crisis.

Des strode in off the sidewalk and slid onto the bench across the table from Tony and Cindy. "Have you guys heard from Erica?"

"Not since yesterday." Steam rose from Cindy's teacup. They'd chosen a table in the shade, but the sun was climbing and their shade was retreating across the table. Tony had his laptop out and was typing furiously. He muttered under his breath and his cold latte rippled when he hit the keys.

Des took a sip of his coffee. "Any chance she'll change her mind about DKI?"

"I doubt it, Des. I talked to Brian after class yesterday and he said they'd rather dissolve the syndicate than invest in DKI."

"Idiots!" He jerked his cigarettes out of his shirt pocket. "Total fucking idiots!"

"They're just being cautious."

Tony harrumphed. "They're pissing away the chance of a lifetime!"

Cindy leaned back a little and held her tea with both hands. "You said yourself we don't really know anything about this new chip. We don't know how it works; we don't even know if it works."

"That was three days ago." Des lit a cigarette. "Trust me; it works. I went down to Sunnyvale and talked to some of their people. Everybody is freaking ready to explode they're so excited, but management thinks DKI's only problem is cash flow." Des took a drag off his cigarette and smoke burbled out of his mouth as he finished his thought. "They haven't planned anything beyond their next IPO, but after our trip to Mexico, Conquistador can buy controlling interest and if we control it, we can give DKI the management it needs to succeed."

"Our management!" Tony's computer warbled as something furry leaped out at his avatar.

"Damn right." Des took a drag on the cigarette and tried to get Tony's attention. "I talked to your brother. You know Bill is mortgaging his house just to buy as much DKI stock as he can?"

"I told you that last week."

"Right. Did he mention he's seen the thing work? He's convinced DKI will be the next Intel and I think he's right."

"Which means we could own the next Intel!" Tony's computer coughed out a screeching crash and Tony slumped back with a sigh, "Crap."

Cindy leaned over to look at the screen. "Level seven; not too shabby, honey."

Tony shook his head, "Buffalo crap."

"You're going to have the electronics ready by Thursday, right?"

"It's ready now. You're the one who couldn't get everybody together any sooner."

"True." Des crushed his cigarette out on the edge of the table.

Cindy looked into her tea. "You know this thing is really complicated, not to mention illegal."

Tony glanced up from his computer. "Never rule out the illegal."

"But," Cindy looked at Des. "It's still a big risk, right?"

Des shook his head, "I don't think so."

"But you're betting everything you've made over the last three years! That's what, three million dollars?"

"Just over five."

"Five million dollars! And you're willing to risk it on this one deal?" Cindy studied him. "Have you ever wondered how much money you can actually spend in one lifetime?"

Des shrugged. "What does that have to do with anything?"

"Haven't you made enough money with Conquistador?"

"Cindy, this isn't about money. It's about power." Des took another cigarette out of his pack.

"Power?"

"Power!" Tony said as Des lit the cigarette. "The kind of power that defines the course of history. DKI is just the beginning."

Cindy looked worried. "Do you guys have any idea how crazy you sound?"

"I thought you liked crazy." Tony wiggled his eyebrows. It made Cindy smile, but Des was grumpy.

"I don't know what you're bitching about, Cindy. My company and my investments are paying your goddamned way through college!"

"Our company, Desmondo san; our investments." Tony shot Des a puzzled look as he hugged Cindy close and then looked at her. "That means you too, Munchkin."

"I know." Cindy hugged him back "Look, Des, I'm not complaining, I'm just worried about you."

"Me?" Des took a drag off his cigarette. "Don't worry about me, I'm doing great!"

"Yeah, but you keep talking about 'making it', like success is somewhere off in the future. You don't enjoy what you've already accomplished and you certainly don't seem happy."

"Happy?" Des laughed. "I'm on the fast track to nirvana!"

"Then how come you don't smile anymore?" Cindy looked into Des' eyes. "You're becoming obsessed..."

"I'm not fucking obsessed!" Des took another drag and smoke tumbled out of his mouth as he said it again, quietly. "I'm not obsessed."

"Not at all." Tony smiled. He'd started up another game and his attention was quickly shifting to a universe with completely different rules.

Des slid off the bench and stood up. "I'll see you guys Thursday night at nine, right?"

Tony nodded, "Everything will be ready."

"Excellent." Des left Tony and Cindy to ponder the mayhem unfolding on Tony's computer. Des walked around the block to his Ferrari and paused to finish his cigarette. Flicking the still burning butt into the bushes, he didn't notice the silver Jaguar making its way toward the corner he'd just turned.

Yuri glanced outside as the Jaguar turned down Bancroft Way and passed Berkeley's School of Law, but he didn't see Des. Yuri was focused on his passenger. "In theory, of course, I should feel disloyal. I've known Paul Neault since we went to Berkeley together. Of course, he was eccentric even then."

"He's gone way past eccentric, Mr. Milanov." Terri's right leg was stretched out straight with her foot propped up on her backpack. Her knee was locked into a jointed brace designed to keep it together as it healed.

The big car drifted to the curb and stopped next to a frozen yogurt cart parked on the sidewalk. "I have to agree with you." Yuri nodded seriously. "The question is: what do we do?"

"I say we stop working with him."

Yuri nodded thoughtfully as his driver retrieved Terri's crutches from the trunk of the car. A dozen students walked past on the sidewalk as the man opened Terri's door and helped her out of the cool limo. More people passed in front of the Jaguar to cross the street when traffic permitted. The prevailing dress on this hot afternoon was baggy shorts and too-large T-shirts, or, for some, no shirts at all. One young man wore a ring in his nipple with a silver chain that connected the ring to one of his earrings.

Watching the wild variety of people outside the Jaguar, Yuri chuckled. "Berkeley hasn't really changed at all." He handed Terri her backpack and extended his hand. "Take care of that knee, Miss Turner."

"I will." Terri leaned back into the car. Her small pale hand vanished within Yuri's long tanned fingers, but her grip was just as firm as his. "Thanks for the ride, Mr. Milanov."

"It was a pleasure talking with you, Miss Turner." Yuri smiled. "I'll be in touch."

Yuri's driver closed the door as soon as Terri was out of the way. Terri set her backpack down and then glanced at the sedan's mirrored windows. The Jaguar eased away from the curb and merged smoothly into the flow of traffic.

The mid-afternoon sun was rapidly heating Terri's leather jacket. She shifted her weight to get a crutch under each arm, winced, and quickly stepped back off her right leg. "Goddamn you, Stacia!" Terri took a deep breath and started awkwardly crutching across the sidewalk toward the administration building. A few of the students coming out of Sproul Hall glanced at her sympathetically as they passed. Others walked around her to ascend the steps and disappear inside. As she teetered back and forth on the crutches, Terri's technique improved a little, but by the time she reached the bottom of the stairs, she was exhausted. A sign pointing toward the handicapped ramp caught her eye and she was considering changing course when someone tapped her on the shoulder.

"Excuse me?"

Terri turned around to see a young woman in blue jeans and a Budget Lumber T-shirt. "Yeah?"

Bernie had seen the Jaguar pull away from the curb, and she'd noticed the backpack, forgotten on the sidewalk. She offered Terri the pack. "You left this by the curb."

"Hey, thanks." Terri grabbed one of the shoulder straps.

"No problem." Bernie smiled.

Terri smiled back. "Thanks again." Terri swung the pack onto one shoulder and started cautiously up the stairs.

"Take care." Bernie's backpack was the same round-top/square-bottom shape, but in gray and forest green instead of black. A large screw-top plastic tube stuck out of the top and wobbled from side to side as Bernie walked back to the sidewalk. She continued down Bancroft for a few more blocks before turning south on Ellsworth. Her apartment was in an old building in the middle of the block that had survived a dozen major earthquakes as its residents evolved from freshmen to retiring professors. Bernie stopped in the recently renovated lobby and jiggled a key into her mail box. When she finally managed to get the little door open, Bernie extracted her mail and shoved it into her backpack.

Apartment 401 was at the end of a dimly lit hallway, but the dark walnut-stained door opened onto a bright, spacious studio. Skylights between the long sloping rafters let warm, natural light into the two-story space. The only walls under the 18-foot ceiling enclosed the bathroom, and held up part of the bedroom, a loft nestled in the southeast corner. A post supported the northwest corner of the loft and anchored one end of the long counter that ran beneath it. Cabinets above the counter faced into the kitchen below the loft and oak stairs spiraled from the main floor up to the studio's sleeping area.

Bernie locked the deadbolt, set her keys on the tiny desk by the door, and dropped her backpack between the desk and her drafting table. The big table looked like an ancient derrick with stainless steel rigging and it dominated the southwest corner of the studio. Bernie had built it out of 2x4s and a sheet of furniture-grade plywood. The smooth work surface was suspended by thin cables and could be adjusted to any angle. Around the table and throughout the studio, there were drawings and models of all sorts of buildings. They shared the walls with paintings that ranged from city-scapes to traditional and not-so-traditional nudes.

The little red light on her answering machine flashed three times and then paused before repeating the pattern. Bernie pressed, "play".

Beep

"Hi, this is Ian. I got your message when I got home last night. I'm glad you're okay, but you didn't say why you left." He hesitated. "Please give me a call."

"God!" Bernie shook her head and glanced through her mail.

Beep

"Hi, this is Ian. Give me a call, or, uh, I'll try again later."

Bernie threw a frilly mail-order catalog and the rest of the junk mail into the trash can next to her desk. "Leave me alone!" One of the circulars fluttered to the side and landed on the floor. Bernie picked it up and pushed it down on top of the other trash.

Beep

"Hey! This is Mick! Call me!" *Click*

Bernie glared at the machine. "You can go fuck yourself too!" She pressed, "Clear" and the machine reset itself. Bernie walked across the hardwood floor to the kitchen. She looked through the refrigerator and most of the cupboards before taking a chocolate chip cookie out of a glass jar on the counter. She took a root beer out of the fridge and ate the cookie as she walked around the counter, through the dining area and onto the Persian rug that defined her living room. She turned the stereo on, selected "radio", and adjusted the volume. A mellow saxophone solo filled the apartment.

Moving to her drafting table, Bernie slid the shipping tube out of her backpack and unscrewed the top. Inside was a set of construction drawings. She smoothed sheet number three onto the plywood and tacked the corners down with short strips of masking tape. The title block at the bottom read: People's Park Homeless Shelter / B.J. Selleca. Bernie popped open the can of soda and picked up a mechanical pencil. Holding the pencil in the middle she twirled it like a miniature baton and the tiny rods of graphite inside it clicked against the sides. After a few minutes, she set the pencil down and took a sip of soda.

As the afternoon wore on, the bright rectangles under the skylights crept off the floor and up the kitchen counter toward the loft. Bernie picked up one pencil and then another, setting each down in turn after spinning it or just holding it above the drawing, as though she was about to carve the last detail in a printing plate. When she wasn't spinning a pencil, she played with an eraser, absently turning it over and over in her hand. Hours passed without a single change to the plan.

The sky-lit rectangles reached the paintings above Bernie's bed and began to fade through ruddy shades of sunset orange. When she could no longer see the finer lines on her drawing, Bernie stepped away from her project and walked over to the light switches by the door. With the flick of a switch the studio brightened under halogen floodlights that bounced their warmth off the walls and ceiling. Bernie rubbed her eyes and crossed over to an ancient oak table under the dining room skylight. Eight elaborately carved high-backed chairs stood ready for formal dinner guests, but the table was covered with piles of drawings and blueprints. Bernie sorted through the stacks of drawings for a few minutes and then stopped. She stared at the pile for a moment, and then looked up at the ceiling. She muttered, "What did I want...?"

The radio answered with the nasal twang of a local jewelry salesman doing his own commercial. Bernie walked over and switched the stereo to the CD player. She hit "play" without looking to see what was inside and the Indigo Girls started singing "One, Two, Three."

"Oh, God!" Bernie hit the stereo's off button and the system's status lights winked out. Stepping around the coffee table, she slumped onto the couch, and rubbed her face with her hands. She rubbed her eyes, blinked a few times, and took a deep breath. She let it out slowly. After a few more breaths, she leaned back, resting her head on the back of the couch. Looking at the ceiling, Bernie sighed. "This is not working."

She straightened up, grabbed the remote and turned on the TV. An energetic man in a three-piece suit came into focus walking across a small stage. He looked incurably happy as he smiled out at a small studio audience. Dynamically colored signs on either side of the stage reminded everyone that he was Chuck Williamson.

His voice was strong and confident and terribly cheerful. "Be positive! Invest your positive energy into your life! Take charge! Positive action can lead to..."

"I am taking charge." Bernie changed the channel.

An intricately detailed blue and gray spaceship moved across the screen. The camera zoomed in through one of the ship's elliptical windows to focus on two furry creatures looking out at the passing stars. Like big otters with thick ocher fur, they spoke in long fluid syllables as they turned and shuffled on all fours down the low-ceilinged corridor. The camera followed the aliens and as each otter spoke, an English translation appeared at the bottom of the screen.

"Ur Capella will meet you at Caans. We can trust her, but be careful around her husbands."

"How many are there?"

"Three. Chohan might be sympathetic but we have no information on the other two. They could be allies, or..."

"Or they could be Uchili." The second otter nodded to the first. "I'll be careful."

As soon as Bernie set the remote on the arm of the couch, the science fiction was replaced by a montage of luxurious terrestrial locations designed to sell luxurious and expensive diamond jewelry. A deep voice urged husbands to "Show her you'd propose to her all over again." Bernie snatched up the remote and changed the channel.

Channel two didn't come in very well, four and five were starting game shows, and channel seven was covering a golf tournament. Bernie kept switching stations until she was back to channel nine and Chuck Williamson. She sighed. "Well, Chuck. It's either you or "Furballs in Space." She pressed the remote again and was back on 20 watching an infomercial.

"I have got to get cable." She shook her head as she pressed 9 and enter. "You win, Chuck. If only because PBS doesn't have commercials." Standing, Bernie stretched, then carried the remote into the kitchen.

"You have the power to change the things you need to change." Chuck Williamson smiled as the audience applauded. "You have the strength to accept the things you cannot change." He was genuinely charming and the audience obviously loved him. "And you have the wisdom to know the difference." They applauded again.

Bernie took two boxes of Chinese food and a container of Parmesan cheese out of the refrigerator. She forked some rice and some broccoli chicken onto a plate and set the plate in the microwave. After twisting the timer, Bernie put the boxes back in the fridge and got out another root beer. Two minutes later, Bernie pulled the steaming food out of the cool oven and sprinkled a thin layer of Parmesan over the whole plate. She carried the plate, the Parmesan, and the root beer to the couch and as Chuck Williamson outlined the path to personal success, Bernie ate dinner.

"Strange things will happen when you start to be positive. Your friends, your co-workers, even your loved ones may think something is wrong with you. They may get upset. They may try their best to help you get back to being your good old, familiar old, self." He smiled. "Whether you like it or not." The audience laughed.

"I ran into a friend of mine at a party just a few weeks ago. I hadn't seen this guy since high school and as we tried to catch up on each other's lives, he told me a story that illustrates this beautifully. Diego had gone to college, fallen in love, been hired by a big company to head their computer department, and moved in with his girlfriend. They were planning on getting married, but then he got this crazy idea. He wanted to write a screenplay." Chuck stopped pacing for a moment. "His friends wanted him to be realistic. His coworkers just laughed. His girlfriend tried to be supportive, but it was obvious she didn't really believe in him.

"My friend kept working on it, though." Chuck started pacing again. "He wrote when he could. He wrote at night and on the weekends. His fiancé didn't like it. Not only was he spending time away from her, he was changing. He was becoming goal-oriented, more sure of himself. Not bad things to be, but very different from the man she thought she knew.

"They fought. He quit writing to spend more time with her but he didn't stop believing in his screenplay. He could already see the movie in his mind. Eventually they broke up." Chuck smiled and rested his hand on the podium at the center of the stage. "She called him up recently. She said she'd seen his name in Newsweek and asked if he would like to get together for drinks. The article had been about the recent trend toward paying screenwriters as much as movie stars. Diego was mentioned because he'd just been paid three million dollars for his screenplay, "Fair Game". The screen showed an impressed and enthusiastic audience. "Perhaps you've heard of it?" Everyone laughed.

"My point is this: as you wrestle with change, the people you know and love will have to wrestle with it as well. Some people will be more understanding than others, but remember: the people laughing at you now because you have the courage to dream are the same people who will be asking you for a favor, or a loan, or a job when your dream becomes reality." Chuck Williamson smiled out at the audience. "And it will become reality."

Bernie got up and carried everything back into the kitchen. She rinsed the plate in the sink, put the Parmesan in the fridge and leaned back against the counter. Page three was still taped to her table. She glanced from that to a few of the pictures on the walls and then at the television.

"Don't let anyone else or anything else keep you from doing what you want to do. You have the power, you have the strength, and you have the wisdom! Use them to change your life! You can do it!"

"Okay." Bernie nodded resolutely. "It's crazy, but I'll do it." The remote was on the counter where she'd left it. She touched the mute button, picked up the kitchen phone and dialed Ian's number. After listening to his answering machine, Bernie left a message: "Hi, Ian. This is Bernie. Look, I'm sorry about last night. I'll be home the rest of the evening if you want to talk. Thanks. Bye." Bernie hung up the phone and then looked across the room at her own answering machine. She turned off the TV and started adding details to her homeless shelter.

Wednesday, 10:30 am - OHI Legal, 33rd
Floor, Osmund Bldg. San Francisco

Sandy's new phone rested in the middle of the floor, lit up
by the mid-morning sun. The cord to the phone's handset
swung in and out of the direct sunlight as she paced back
and forth from wall to opposite wall. She was wearing a
pale blue suit with a gray silk blouse and gray low-heeled
shoes. When a large bottomed man in gray coveralls
started backing into the office, Sandy grabbed the phone
base and stepped back to give the movers more room. She
gestured for the men to put her desk against the western
wall as she spoke into the handset. "Are you sure about
that, Tam?" She shook her head as the old mahogany desk
settled into the new cream-colored carpet. As the men
straightened up, she pointed at the desk. "You've got it
backwards." The movers looked at the desk, glanced at
each other, and then turned it around so the drawers
weren't trapped against the wall.

"Not you, Tam. The movers had my desk turned the
wrong way." Sandy mouthed a silent thank you. The men
shrugged at each other and closed the door on their way
out. She leaned back against her grandfather's desk and
looked out her new window at the neighboring high rises.
"Well, it isn't as plush as your office, Tam, but it'll do for
now and guess what? I finally got a window!" She set the
base of the phone on her desk. "Yeah! I can see the ocean!
Listen, you've got to take a closer look at the latest appraisal
... no, that's three weeks old. Get the current assessment
from Gwen and check their out-of-state holdings. Then

call me back, okay?" Sandy leaned back against her desk. "Well, my "gorgeous" assistant is out on maternity leave, Tam, but I'll tell the temp you're interested. His name is Jeff." Sandy smiled as she hung up the phone.

Her view of the ocean was really just a sliver framed by the buildings on either side of the street but Sandy could see a few sail boats and as she watched a ferry powered past on its way to Sausalito. Still smiling, Sandy dialed Ian's number, but the anticipation faded when she got his voice mail. Sandy sighed, disappointed, and waited through the outgoing message. "Hi, Ian. This is Sandy. I got your message. I guess we're playing phone tag. I hope everything's all right, you sounded really serious." She hesitated. "I'm sorry I'm busy this weekend. I'd really like to see you and I hate to have to wait until Tuesday. I'll try you tonight at your hotel in Denver. I miss you. Bye." As soon as she hung up, the intercom light flashed. Sandy pressed the speaker button. "Yes?"

"Someone to see you, Ms. Taylor, but she doesn't have an appointment."

"Who is it?"

"I, uh... I'll ask."

Sandy shook her head. "That's okay, Jeff. Donna said she'd stop by with some notes on Croydon Mechanical. Send her in."

"Right away, Ms. Taylor."

Sandy switched off the intercom and turned toward the opening door just as Bernie Selleca stepped into the office.

CHAPTER SIX

Thursday, 1:31 pm – Floating At Anchor, Clearlake

The following afternoon, Bernie and Ian had packed a picnic and flown the Catalina north to have lunch on the water. The big seaplane was pointed into the breeze and she rose and fell with the gentle swells that crossed and re-crossed the lake. With the afternoon sun beating down and reflecting off the water's surface, Ian had opened all the PBY's windows and hatches to keep the inside of the black plane cool. The far-off burr of an outboard motor mingled with the sound of water lapping at the hull and the laughter inside the plane.

"What do you mean you're not ticklish!"

Ian shook his head, laughing. "No, actually I'm..." He managed to stop laughing but he couldn't stop grinning. "I'm not ticklish at all."

"Then why are you laughing?" Bernie traced her finger along his thigh to the smooth skin just inside his knee. She moved her finger in tiny teasing circles until Ian twisted away.

"Purest coincidence." Ian shifted position to get his feet under the blankets that they had pushed down to the foot of the berth. Bernie started wiggling her fingers across his stomach, and he grabbed her hand. He pushed her away just enough to turn her around, and then pulled her close again. Kissing her shoulder, Ian wrapped his arms around her.

Bernie snuggled into him. "I like this."

Ian kissed the back of her neck. "Me too."

They were in the cone-shaped compartment at the very back of the PBY where the tail tapered to just a few feet in diameter. The V-shaped bed barely gave their feet any room, but there was plenty of room for their shoulders. In the middle of the teak-trimmed headboard at the top of the "V" was a short hatch in the bulkhead that opened into the seaplane's main cabin.

Bernie rubbed her leg back against Ian's. "I still feel like a complete jerk."

"You're not a jerk."

"I shouldn't have left the concert like that."

"Hey," Ian kissed her again. "Stop worrying about it."

"But..." As she shook her head, her hair tickled his chin. "I shouldn't have just left."

"I told you; it's okay." Ian brushed her hair aside. "It's my fault, really. I'm the one who dumped the whole situation on you."

"It wasn't just that. I can handle sharing you." Bernie hesitated. "At least, I think I can." She took a deep breath. "I know I can. But at the concert everything seemed to be crashing in all at once."

Ian brushed his hand across her hair again and then rested his hand on her arm.

Bernie covered his hand with hers. "We used to go to concerts a lot, especially the Indigo Girls. It was like; they were our group, our songs." She sighed. "We were supposed to go together on Monday."

"I thought you broke up?"

"We did. Four months ago. The concert tickets were a kind of peace offering, I guess. I wasn't even going to go, but..." Bernie shrugged.

"I'm sorry."

Bernie rolled around to face him. "It's not your fault."

"I know. I just..."

"I'm the one who invited you to the concert. I should have..." Bernie shook her head and made herself smile. "I guess we're having too much fun. Why else would I be trying to ruin such a great day?"

Ian started to say something but Bernie stopped him. "Look, I'm happy. Right here. Right now." She kissed him. "I'd rather be with you when I can than never see you at all; even if there is someone else." She moved her head back and studied his face for a moment. "I would have hated you if you hadn't told me about that."

"I didn't want to hide anything from you."

"Good." Bernie snuggled up close to him again.

Ian stroked her back and his fingers brushed across the rough circle of skin below her ribs. "You said your brother shot you by mistake when he was aiming for your dad?"

"Yeah. I was fourteen. T.J. was thirteen. Dad was in my bed and T.J. shot him."

"And he hit you instead of your dad?"

"Oh, he hit Dad too. He hit me, Dad, my fish tank, our neighbor's Winnebago." Bernie chuckled. "Those two bullets went out the open window. Old man O'Keefe didn't notice the holes in his RV for a month." Bernie shifted her position a little. "One bullet went through the floor, right past my mom's head and into the fridge. Totally destroyed the icemaker. And of course, all my fish died."

"Wow." Ian shook his head. "What about your dad?"

"Him too. The coroner found five bullets in his body."

"Jeez! What kind of gun fires that many bullets?"

"It was our dad's Colt 45." Bernie sighed. "It was like a dream, it didn't hurt at all. T.J. wrapped a sheet around me to stop the bleeding and Mom went totally hysterical. I held the sheet tight while T.J. called 911 and Mom just kept crying. She kept saying it was all her fault and that she should have done something sooner, but by the time we heard the cops outside, she was totally calm. It was eerie. Then..." Bernie paused. "Then she picked up the gun and carefully wiped off T.J.'s fingerprints. She was the one holding the gun when the cops came in, and she told them that she had shot her husband because he was raping her little girl. Which, of course, he was."

"God. That must have been terrible. Did they believe her?"

"Oh yeah." Bernie nodded. "They arrested her of course, but they were real polite about it. After they read her that Miranda stuff, they let my mom sit with me until the ambulance arrived. When it was all over, Mom just said that T.J. might have frightened a jury, but that she was someone they could identify with."

"Did they?"

"Oh yeah: they totally acquitted her." Bernie propped herself up on one elbow. "Pretty crazy, huh?"

"Pretty scary."

Bernie laughed. "I guess it was at the time, but not anymore. That was a long time ago." She noticed Ian's worried expression. "Hey! Don't look so gloomy!" Bernie glanced through the open hatch into the sunny aft cabin and then grinned at Ian. "Still want to go swimming?"

"Definitely." Ian kissed her. "Are you going to let me get my suit on this time?"

"Maybe." She gave him an appraising look. "It's not my fault you have a cute butt."

After Bernie and Ian swam in the lake, they showered in the PBY's tiny bathroom and had lunch in the elegantly appointed galley. When Bernie reminded him that they both had to get back to the city, Ian pulled up the anchor. He showed Bernie how to start the seaplane's modified engines, startling several fishermen with the cough and roar of the big Pratt and Whitney radials, and they taxied out into the middle of the lake. Bernie turned the PBY into the wind. She listened carefully as Ian checked each item on the before-takeoff checklist. With Ian's hand on her own, Bernie advanced the throttles, and the plane accelerated across the lake. He talked her through each phase of the takeoff, and when Bernie pulled back on the wheel, the seaplane rose gracefully off the water.

Thursday, 7:32 pm – Equinox Bar,
Hyatt Regency, San Francisco

Six hours later Sandy seemed to be watching the neighboring office buildings inch past the rotating restaurant but she wasn't really focused on the view. She drank the last of her water, leaving a haphazard column of ice in the glass. The cubes clattered against the sides when she set the glass back on the table. The plates and silverware had been cleared away, and except for a few crumbs from the French bread, there was no evidence of their dinner. Bernie returned from the restroom and slid into the opposite seat. She was wearing a black leather vest over a burgundy blouse and new jeans. Bernie smiled at Sandy and then glanced out the window at the streets and buildings of San Francisco's financial district. "I really like this place."

"I've missed it." Sandy was wearing the blue blouse and gray wool suit she had worn to work.

"Me too." Bernie looked out the window for a moment longer and then turned her full attention to Sandy. She rested her elbows on the table. "I wish I'd known."

"What?"

"That you broke up with him."

"You should have returned my calls."

"I'm sorry." Bernie shrugged. "I was mad."

Sandy studied her for a moment. "Does that mean you're not mad now?"

"I guess." Bernie hooked a finger through the braided silver chain around her neck. "No, I'm not mad anymore."

She glanced down at the necklace and then up at Sandy. "So what happened?"

"Why?" Sandy lifted an eyebrow. "I mean, I'm really glad to see you. But, well, I'm surprised. Last time we talked, I couldn't even say Jean Claude's name. Why the sudden interest?"

"It's not that sudden." Bernie let go of her chain. "I've been thinking about you a lot. A lot of stuff has been going on and I, uh," She looked down at the table. "I just wanted to see you."

"I'm glad." Sandy smiled when Bernie briefly looked up at her. "What kind of 'stuff'?"

"Just stuff. Life, you know?" Bernie nervously toyed with the thin paper wrapper that had covered her straw. "Stuff. Besides, I asked you first."

"Asked me what?"

Bernie flattened the paper out on the table. "What happened to Jean Claude?"

"He asked me to marry him."

"Really?" Bernie wadded the strip of paper into a little ball. "Isn't that what you wanted?"

"Marriage? Yes. To Jean Claude?" Sandy shook her head. "No. Not someone I've only known a month."

"Did you tell him you wanted more time?"

"That wasn't the point. I already knew it wasn't going to work out."

"That bad?"

Sandy nodded. "He said a lot of mean things after I finally convinced him I didn't want to marry him, but I think he was just hurt."

Bernie nodded. "I said a lot of mean things too."

Sandy reached across the table and touched the back of Bernie's hand. "It's okay."

Bernie looked up and smiled sheepishly. "I'm sorry I got so mad."

"You had a right to be angry." Sandy smiled reassuringly. "You know, I was afraid I'd never see you again."

Bernie turned her palm up and squeezed Sandy's hand. The waiter walked past and smiled indulgently at the two women. They didn't notice. After a while the ice in Sandy's glass settled with a muted splash and Bernie blinked. "So, uh, are you seeing anyone now?"

Sandy hesitated, and then nodded.

"Is it serious?"

"Well..." Sandy took a deep breath. "I think so."

"That's great!" Bernie squeezed Sandy's hand again. "Tell me all about him."

Sandy looked surprised and relaxed her grip. "Are you sure you want to know?"

"Everything!"

"You've certainly changed a lot in the last five months." Sandy shook her head slowly. "What's going on here?"

"What?"

"You don't talk to me; don't return my calls or e-mail, nothing for five months. Then you show up at the office yesterday and ask me out to dinner. I can tell something is bugging you, but you don't say five words all through dinner. Now, all of a sudden you want to take a deposition." Sandy paused. "Am I missing something?"

"No."

"So what's going on?"

"It's, uh…" Bernie pretended to be unconcerned. "Jeez, counselor, you don't have to tell me about him if you don't want to."

"I'm sorry. I do want to." Sandy hesitated. "I think. But how do you know it's a guy?"

Bernie chuckled confidently. "You wouldn't leave me for another girl!"

"I didn't leave you!" Sandy pulled her hand away. "You said you never wanted to see me again!"

"Because you slept with Jean Claude!" Bernie glared at Sandy for an instant but her expression quickly softened. "I'm sorry."

"It's okay. Jean Claude was a big mistake." Sandy reached out and they held hands again. "You sure you want to talk about this?"

Bernie nodded. "I tried to tell you about Jean Claude."

Before Sandy could reply, the waiter returned with her American Express card.

"Hey, that's not fair." Bernie objected. "I invited you out."

Sandy signed the credit slip. "Too late." The waiter left two mints on the table and took the paperwork away.

"Okay, you can pay for dinner, but you've got to let me pay for the movie."

"Movie?" Sandy put the card and the receipt in her purse.

Bernie tried to look innocent. "Would you like to see a movie this evening?"

"Well..." Sandy considered. "Okay, sure."

"Super!" Bernie smiled. "Fair Game is opening today at the Shattuck. It's getting great reviews. We could see that and maybe get some ice cream at Bouillebay's?"

"That would be fun. You'll absolutely love Fair Game." Sandy lowered her voice. "Kim Kelly is really hot!"

"You sound like you've already seen it."

Sandy nodded. "Ian took me. That was our first date."

Bernie looked disappointed. "Do you want to see something else?"

"No! Fair Game is really good. I could see it a dozen times and still love it!"

"Wait a minute." Bernie frowned. "How did you see Fair Game if tonight is the first night?"

"Ian knows the guy who wrote it. We went to the sneak preview at the Kabuki."

"That's rude." Bernie pretended to be offended. "You sure you don't mind seeing it again?"

"I'd love to see it again." Sandy smiled. "I'd see it again just for the soundtrack. Did you know there are two Indigo Girls songs in it?"

"No way! Really? Which ones? Are they new?"

"No, not new, but good. They used "Three Hits" and "Welcome Me"."

"Cool!" Bernie nodded. "That's really cool!"

"Did you go to the concert?"

Bernie lowered her head. "I never did thank you for the tickets."

"That's okay. How was it?"

"Well, I went, but," Bernie shrugged. "I couldn't stay. I kept thinking about us."

"Oh, hon." Sandy squeezed Bernie's hand. "You should have called me."

"I couldn't call you, not then. What could I have said?" Bernie forced a smile. "I know it sounds silly, but I just felt, I don't know, rotten. Everything was okay, you know? Not ideal, maybe, but okay. I met this guy and we started going out. I was really feeling better about myself. But I screwed it up. We went to the concert and all I could think about was you. All those feelings came flooding back; everything you and I ever did together was right there all around me!" She shook her head. "The more I listened, the more I thought about us. The more I thought about us, the worse I felt."

Sandy's eyes had widened and her mouth was slightly open. She just stared at Bernie.

Bernie shifted in her chair. "What?"

Sandy blinked. "You're dating a man?"

"I've dated men before."

Sandy thought for a moment. "I guess I knew that." She sounded uncertain. "You were so down on Jean Claude, I just..."

"That was Jean Claude."

Sandy took a deep breath. "Wow. So, uh, what's he like?"

"He's cool. He's funny, charming, smart and he's brilliant in bed. I'm not giving up women or anything stupid like that, but we're having a lot of fun!" Bernie smiled. "So what's your guy like?"

"Ian's nice." Sandy slid her chair back. "I like him. You ready to go?"

"Sure." Bernie stood. "And?"

"What?" Sandy picked up her purse and they walked together toward the elevators.

"That's it? He's," Bernie paused for effect, "'nice'?"

"What do you want me to say?"

"Is he funny?"

"Yes."

"Is he charming?"

"He can be."

"Is he brilliant in bed?"

Sandy glanced around. There was no one else in the elevator lobby.

Bernie pressed the elevator call button and they waited. "Well, is he?"

"Yeah." Sandy smiled. "I really like him a lot."

Bernie adjusted the collar of her blouse and tried to sound unconcerned. "Do you love him?"

"I don't know, maybe." Sandy laughed. "Give me a break, we only met a few weeks ago! I told him I didn't want to rush into anything."

Bernie nodded. "What did he say?"

"I think he feels the same way. He said we should just take things a step at a time." Sandy looked thoughtful. "You know, I've never met a guy like Ian before."

"What do you mean?"

"He's just really nice." Sandy laughed. "Almost too nice. We got rear-ended on the freeway and he was nice to the guy that hit us."

"Why?"

"Well, the guy was a real basket case and Ian felt sorry for him. Jean Claude would have sued everyone involved, including the guy's mother for having him."

"Even you."

Sandy considered, "You're right, he would have found a way to sue me too." They both laughed.

"So what happened?"

"We were driving up 101 from the airport, he insisted on picking me up."

"Nice."

"We're going seventy-five miles an hour, when this drunk rear-ended us!"

"Rear ended you?"

"Can you believe it? We're ten miles over the limit and we get hit by this ugly green Land Yacht going about a hundred and twenty. No one was hurt, but Ian's new car got dented. Even though the guy tried to drive away, Ian was still worried about him."

"He sounds nice." Bernie studied their reflections in the mirrors on the elevator doors. "It also sounds like you love him a little more than "maybe"."

"Yeah." Sandy grinned. "I do."

"Then why take things slow?"

"I don't know." Sandy pressed the glowing elevator call button. "I want to get to know him better before we start making any long term plans. Assuming he wants to get more serious. I don't know. I get the feeling that there's more going on with Ian than he's willing to share."

"Does he love you?"

"I think so. I hope so."

"But you're not going steady or engaged or anything, right?"

"Well," Sandy shook her head. "No. Why?"

"Then you're still free, right?" The elevator doors slid open and Bernie stepped into the car.

"Comparatively." Sandy followed her. "That depends on what you mean by "free.""

"Or on what I had in mind?" Bernie pressed 'Lobby,' "Going down?"

Sandy smiled as the mirrored doors slid shut. "You haven't changed at all."

Thursday, 8:33 pm - Asteroid Belt,
Sector 51, Martian Federation

Tony advanced the throttles and the roar of the rocket's engines thundered through the speakers. A vast field of asteroids lay directly ahead of the little survey ship, filling the forward video and stretching to the stars on both the right and left screens. Maneuvering the ship with a small black joystick, Tony accelerated toward the tumbling rocks. At the edge of the field, a small boulder spun toward Tony's fighter, passing seamlessly from screen to screen as it tumbled across his path. Tony pulled back on the stick and slowed the ship down as it entered the asteroid field.

Suddenly, two wildly decorated fighters shot past, one on each side. Shaped like shark's teeth, and bristling with weapons, the fighters turned to attack. Tony smiled. "Let the games begin!" Charging toward the sharks at full power, Tony launched two missiles and fired a flash from his lasers. As Tony's ship swept past them, the aliens fired back and swung around to chase after him. Missiles and laser blasts shattered the surrounding asteroids in loud, brilliant explosions.

Tony circled around a big asteroid and caught one of the fighters head on. He fired a single missile and rocketed away from the explosion. Multicolored pieces of twisted wreckage drifted off in all directions.

"Excellent!" Mick was standing behind Tony watching the screens over his left shoulder. He glanced past Tony at Ian. "Is this game totally excellent or what.?"

Tony blasted away from the second fighter at full power, but as he reached the edge of the asteroids, he shut off his engines. "Check this out." As the ship coasted out of the asteroid field, Tony used his attitude thrusters to turn it around. The jets coughed and the stars revolved around them. Tony tweaked the thrusters again and the asteroid miner stopped turning. As the ship drifted backwards, the alien fighter blasted toward them in the center of the front screen. When the purple stripes on the alien ship's nose came into focus, Tony fired two missiles. The fighter fired its lasers, and destroyed one of the missiles, but the second missile hit its mark. The alien vanished in a bright, theatrical explosion.

"Excuse me." The voice came from the same speakers as the roar of the rockets, and sounded exactly like Darth Vader. "There's someone at the front door."

"On screen, quarter size." The windows of the spaceship were three large video monitors in a half circle around Tony's keyboard. A black-and-white picture of Des Pierrot appeared in the lower left corner of the center screen, covering some of the colorful debris from the fighter. Des was smoking a cigarette by the front door. He turned and blew smoke at the security camera.

"You jerk." Tony glanced back at Mick and Ian. "He's always late." Tony turned back to the computer. "Open front door. Audio on."

Darth Vader answered. "Front door open. Audio on."

Tony raised his voice. "It's about time, Des! Lose the cigarette and come on in. We're in the basement."

They watched Des walk through the opening door. The door closed automatically behind him.

"Front door closed."

Tony looked over his shoulder at Ian as he tapped the computer under the left screen. "This old PC controls almost everything in the house: doors, windows, lights, climate, you name it. It's voice-activated, watch: standby."

"By your command." The picture of the front door disappeared.

"That shuts off the voice and video links and puts the Smart-House program back on automatic. You can access it from anywhere in the house, just by talking to one of the intercoms. We synthesized the voice from an interview James Earl Jones did on PBS."

"This whole setup is pretty amazing Tony. Hey! Look out!" Ian pointed at something spinning toward them on the center screen. A jagged chunk of metal with charred purple stripes smashed through the windshield of the ship. The grating crash and the rush of escaping air were followed by silence.

"Ouch." Tony shook his head. "God, I hate it when that happens."

Mick looked from Ian to Tony. "What happened?"

"I forgot to get out of the way." Tony brushed his brown hair back with the fingers of both hands. "That fighter was coming toward us when we blew it up, and Asteroid Pirate doesn't let you forget about debris. The pieces kept coming and we got nailed by a chunk."

Ian whistled. "Talk about reaching back from the grave." Mick and Tony laughed.

The long rectangular basement was divided into equal halves by a flight of carpeted stairs. To the right of the stairs there was a pool table, some chairs and a bar against the far wall. The other half of the room, where Ian and Mick were standing next to Tony, held an enormous U-shaped workbench and the elaborate computer setup. Opposite the stairs, between the workbench and the pool table, sliding glass doors opened out onto a large deck overlooking the Bay.

Treads underneath the carpet creaked as Des came down the stairs. "Greetings, gentlemen." He walked over to the workbench. "I've got..." He paused to look closely at Mick. "Holy shit, what happened to you? You get arrested again?"

"No." Mick shrugged, with difficulty. His left arm was covered with a cast that went from his wrist to his shoulder. There were tiny scratches all over the left side of his face and stitches crisscrossed a long cut on his chin. "I ran under a truck."

"What?"

Mick nodded his head, carefully. "This fucking semi pulls out into the street, right in front of me, right? Then he stops. He just stops! I'd have made it under the fucking trailer if he'd kept going! But the asshole sees me, too late, and he stops. I went right into the landing gear."

Des studied the damage to Mick's face. "Landing gear?"

"You know, those dinky little wheels they park the trailer on?"

"Only you, Mick." Des studied the puffiness under Mick's eyes. "You're okay though, right?"

"Yeah, but my Porsche is totaled. I'll tell ya, man; this month has been a mother-fucker! So far I've busted my nose, my arm, three ribs and two teeth. My truck is in the shop with a broken axle and my Porsche... fuck!" Mick shook his head sadly. "My Porsche is fucking history!"

"What happened to your truck?"

"Broken axle, didn't I tell you? It got loaded with too much plywood. The Chevy dealer loaned me a Cadillac until the truck gets fixed." Mick shook his head sadly. "What a month."

"Hell, look on the bright side." Des pointed to Mick's nose. "Your nose is looking better."

"Thanks. So are your ears." Mick smiled sarcastically. "What happened to your hair?"

"Like it?" Des' hair was cut short and neatly combed. "This is the corporate takeover look. I figure if I'm going to swim with the sharks, I'd better look like one." Des looked at the assortment of electronics on the workbench. "Is everything ready?"

Tony nodded. "It's been ready all week."

"But does it work?"

Tony looked offended. "Of course it works."

"Well, let's go. Time is money."

Tony said, "Only if you invest it right."

"Hey, what are you worried about?" Des turned to Ian. "Tony is the only millionaire I know who still lives with his parents."

"I'm not living with my parents." Tony grinned. "They moved out."

"Really?" Des looked surprised. "I thought your dad loved this place."

Tony nodded. "He did, but my folks gave us the house when Cindy moved in."

Mick whistled. "Nice parents!"

"I suppose." Tony shrugged. "I think they just wanted a change. Besides, Dad said it would be easier to move than to learn how to operate the system."

"It's a nice system." Ian was looking at the three wide, flat cases under the video screens. "You said one PC controls the house. What do the other two computers do?"

"The one in the middle produces devastating real-time graphics, which you need for a game like Asteroid Pirate or even a decent Flight Simulator." Tony pressed a few keys and the screens once again became windows, this time looking out of an airplane at other airplanes at a medium-sized airport. A Lear jet taxied across their field of view, the exhaust shimmering behind the engines.

"Jesus!" Ian leaned a little closer. "The detail is ... It looks real!"

"That's our video enhancement of the new release of Flight Simulator."

Mick pointed to the computer underneath the right video monitor. "What does this one do?"

Tony chuckled. "That's last year's box. It keeps the monitor at the right height."

Des had picked up a flat gray box slightly larger than a paperback novel. One end was black plastic and had a long liquid crystal display and a rotary switch. Next to the display, the switch had positions labeled "off", "on" and "altitude". Below the LCD was a row of four smaller knobs, each lined up with a single number on the display. Des read them aloud. "Zero, one, two, three: is this the transponder?"

"The very latest commercially available mode-alpha model." Tony pointed to a tiny black box attached to the gray one by a short cable. "Now, this little marvel of modern technology isn't commercially available. In fact, this controller and its twin are the only two in the world. When they're airborne, the two controllers will communicate with each other by radio and the transponders will actually transmit their four digit codes to air traffic control. For this demonstration, however, the controllers are connected through the computer." Tony handed Des the little black box so that he was holding a component in each hand.

Tony picked up the other transponder and controller pair. "These two units are the same as the two Des is holding, except that the controller I've got is the master; it controls the other one. And this is how it works." Tony turned his transponder around so that Ian and Mick could see the code on its LCD. "This transponder is set to 4567. Every time the radar sweeps across it, the transponder replies with 4567 and the Air Traffic Control computer displays the aircraft type and number on the screen." Tony pointed to the unit Des was holding. "The slave is set for 0123, I've got 4567. All I have to do is press one button..." Tony pointed to a small button on the side of his black box. "The master transmits its frequency to the slave controller and interrogates the slave for the slave's code. That sets up the standby frequency for each transponder as the other transponder's active frequency. The master then waits until just after a radar sweep to signal the slave to change frequencies." Tony pressed the button. "For this demo, the computer is simulating the radar signal." A second later, the 4-digit identifier displayed on each unit's LCD switched to the other's code.

The transponder Des was holding switched to 4567, and Tony's changed to 0123. Tony smiled proudly. "The specific numbers don't matter; whatever numbers ATC assigns to the two airplanes are fine. The master and slave controllers will exchange whatever codes the transponders are set to when the button is pressed." Tony changed his transponder to read 7777 and pushed the little button again. Des' transponder switched to 7777, and Tony's became 4567.

Des smiled. "Jackpot!"

Ian shook his head and laughed. "I don't think so, Des. 7777 is the military code for target drones."

"Target ...?"

"Those are the remote-controlled planes they practice shooting down with air-to-air missiles."

"Ouch!" Tony dialed in a new code. "I really hate it when that happens. " He pressed the master button and changed the codes again. "The two airplanes can meet at an intersection, or over a VOR, anywhere really. As long as they're close enough for their targets to merge on the radar, ideally one over the other, they'll be able to change identities and destinations without anybody noticing a thing."

"Perfect!" Des set his component pair back on the table. "Let's..."

Beep

Mick looked at Ian.

Beep

Ian held up his hands and shook his head.

Des pulled his phone out of his vest pocket. "Hello?" As he listened, his smile disappeared. "I'm right in the middle of something, Paul. How 'bout later, ten-thirty or... okay. Okay! I'll be right over." Des folded up the phone and shoved it back into his pocket. "Fucking Christ!" He shook his head. "I gotta go, guys. Tony, you're a genius. Mick, have you got a minute?"

"Yeah, sure. I'll walk up with you."

Des turned and headed for the stairs.

Mick started after him, but glanced back. "See you guys later."

Tony watched the two disappear and then looked at Ian. "Jeez. Was it something I said?"

Ian laughed. "Don't look at me. I took a shower last week."

Tony chuckled. "I've known Des since we were freshmen, and he's always rushing somewhere. I don't think he ever sleeps." Tony set the transponder/controller assembly on the table next to its twin. "You want a soda?"

"Sure." Ian followed Tony to the bar at the other end of the room. There was a metal-and-plastic hand on the bar, its fingers splayed in a frozen wave. Tony went behind the bar while Ian sat on a leather-covered bar stool and studied the hand. "This looks like a suit of armor for Thing."

Tony reached into the short refrigerator below the counter. "Thing?" He set two cans of 7-Up on the oak surface.

Ian popped his 7-Up open. "Thing. You know, the hand in The Addams Family?"

"Oh yeah. I liked that movie." He pointed at the hand. "This was an engineering project that doubled as an assignment for my art class."

"Does it move?"

"It used to. It's fully articulated and completely programmable. At least it was until the chip overheated. I didn't allow for enough cooling." Tony sipped his 7-Up. "Now it's just art."

"I like it. Did you allow for enough cooling in the code changers?"

"Even if we put them in the sun on the glare shield they'll be fine, though they would mess with your compass something fierce."

"You seem to know airplanes. Do you fly?"

"My fiancé does." Tony shook his head. "It's all she talks about. Cindy's not even thinking about grad school anymore. All she talks about is becoming an airline pilot. She keeps bugging me about taking lessons, but there's always something else I'd rather do with the time. Besides, sometimes she scares the crap out of me!"

"Really?"

"Oh, not on purpose, and she's totally safe, I know she is, but sometimes... Like this one time we were coming in to land and she was all focused on putting the wheels right on those lines just after the runway numbers, right?"

"The touch down zone."

"Yeah, I guess. So I'm looking outside and thinking it'll be cool to hit the restroom when we get to the flight club, but she's a little higher than she wanted to be so when it looks like she'll have to land further down the runway than she wants she says, 'We're not going to make it.'" Tony rolled his eyes toward the ceiling, "I thought we were going to crash! Freakin' wet my fur, man!"

Ian couldn't help but laugh. "Wet your fur?"

"Drenched." Tony sighed and took a sip of his 7-Up. "So what do you think? Will this shell-game scheme work?"

"I don't know." Ian considered. "I don't think a controller would be happy with two planes crossing the same intersection at the same time. There are all kinds of things that can slow an airplane down. Maybe..." Ian thought for a moment and then set his 7-Up on the bar. He held up his hands, flat, one above but a little behind the other. "If the planes are already on the same airway, but one is moving faster than the other, catching up to it..." he brought his top hand forward, directly over the lower hand. "If the planes could change codes and indicated altitudes just as the slower plane sped up and the faster plane slowed down..." He moved his bottom hand ahead again. "To the controller, it would just look like a faster airplane had passed over a slower one a few thousand feet below it."

"Perfect." Tony smiled. "It wouldn't matter where the planes met, as long as the pilots know when to trade codes."

"It could work." Ian picked up his 7-Up. "You still need to find the planes, and at least one plane has to have an over-flight permit. You also need the pilots."

"Aren't you and Mick going to fly the planes?"

"Me and Mick?" Ian shook his head. "Mick is just a student, and I think I've had enough misadventure for one lifetime. I'm just trying to keep Mick from spending the rest of his life in jail."

"Oh yeah." Tony chuckled. "Hell, I wasn't even thinking about jail."

"Mick isn't thinking about jail either." Ian sighed. "A minor detail."

Tony nodded. "You want to play some pool?"

"Sure." Ian stood and they carried their drinks over to the pool table. There was a mirror behind the bar and Ian glanced over Tony's shoulder at his own reflection. Ian pointed at the mirror. "You know, neither one of those guys looks like a drug smuggler to me."

Tony turned to look their reflection and laughed. "Makes 'em perfect for the job, then, doesn't it?"

Thursday 9:34 pm – Lobby, Shattuck
Theaters, Berkeley

With pen and pocket calendar in hand, Sandy stood next to the popcorn maker. As the noisy machine kept the theater lobby filled with the aroma of genuine butter flavor, she wrote, "Follow-up on Penalty clause" next to a March 30th note that said "Dinner with Harris." She used neat, efficient letters very different from the vibrant entry she'd made for the afternoon of the 31st, still five days away. Under the business-like notes for that Tuesday morning, Sandy had scripted I-A-N in big happy letters. She'd even added a wildly smiling exclamation mark next to his name. Below that she'd written "Dinner & Hamlet / 7:00". Her note for the coming weekend, however, was tragically subdued: "Ian in Coeur d'Alene." She'd drawn a little frowning teardrop next to the line between Saturday and Sunday.

Thursday the 26th was packed with AM appointments. Little checks marked the ones Sandy had actually taken care of before meeting Bernie for dinner. Her only entry for the evening was a capital "B", with a big question mark next to it.

"Hi there!"

Sandy jumped. She hadn't seen Bernie come out of the rest room. "Hello yourself."

Bernie started humming Welcome Me.

Sandy tucked her day-planner into her purse. "I thought you'd like this movie."

Bernie nodded and sang a line out loud, "...devil prophets still hold my hand." She swayed gracefully from side to side and led Sandy toward the exit.

The entrance to the movie theater was actually in the center of the building; a large outer lobby connected the cinemas to the sidewalk along Shattuck Avenue. An art gallery, a music store, and a restaurant shared the lobby with a Freaky Rainbow ice cream parlor. Bernie and Sandy stopped to look at a movie poster for Fair Game. The poster showed an almost-naked woman leaning back into the bite of a tall, shadowy figure. Sandy glanced at Bernie. "She was hot, wasn't she?"

"Incandescent!" Bernie nodded her head, enthralled. "I'm going to marry her."

Sandy laughed. "What about your new boyfriend?"

"Who?" Bernie pretended to look puzzled and they both laughed. "I, uh... I was wondering if you'd like to drop by for a bit? I've got a painting I'd really like you to see."

"Another in your series on the rebirth of modern architecture?"

"Not exactly." Bernie stepped back and then led the way toward the doors that opened onto the sidewalk. "I think you'll like it, though. It's definitely your style."

Sandy followed Bernie out of the lobby but glanced back at the ice cream parlor. "Didn't you want to get some ice cream?"

"Uh..." Bernie shook her head. "Not yet. I've got some Dreyer's and root beer at my place, though."

Sandy glanced down the street toward the subway entrance. "I don't know..."

"Come on, it'll only take a minute." Bernie smiled enthusiastically. "I've still got some Baileys, and I'd really like to get your opinion of this painting."

"You want me to come look at a painting?" Sandy looked skeptical, but amused.

Bernie nodded. "I really think you'll like it."

"Are you trying to seduce me?"

"Maybe." Bernie took a few steps toward her apartment but quickly returned when Sandy failed to follow. "Are you non-seducible?"

Sandy shook her head uncertainly. "A lot has happened since we were together. I can't just..."

"You can't what? Be yourself? Have some fun?"

"Be unfaithful."

"Fair enough." Bernie nodded, as though giving in. "Tell you what: I promise not to come between you and Ian, okay? I just want to spend a little time with you, show you a painting. Would it kill you to take a look at one painting?"

"No." Sandy considered. "Are you still on Ellsworth?"

"Of course!" Bernie started walking. "I'm not moving 'til I get my doctorate."

Sandy fell into step next to her. "How's that going?"

"Good." Bernie smiled. "Incredibly good! My graduate project might actually get built."

"The low-income housing design?"

"It won the competition! I get the grant either way, but one of the judges is a developer. He thinks he can get the city to actually build it."

"That's fantastic!"

"I hope so. I mean, I hope it works out." They walked the few remaining blocks to Bernie's building in companionable quiet.

Sandy glanced at the mailboxes while Bernie unlocked the front door. "You've got some mail."

"I'll pick it up later."

Sandy followed Bernie up the stairs to the top floor. "Does that jerk in 403 still play disco 'til dawn?"

"No, Bruce moved out two months ago." Bernie unlocked the door and opened it for Sandy.

Sandy walked into the studio. "The place looks really nice."

"I don't think I've changed anything." Bernie directed Sandy toward the drafting table. The adjustable work surface was tipped almost vertical to act as an easel for an elegantly framed painting.

Sandy took a few steps toward the painting and stopped. "You uh..." She took another step closer and self-consciously brushed her hair back. "You made me look..."

"Perfect."

"I was going to say content or maybe serene."

"That too." Bernie was standing to one side, a little behind Sandy. "I only paint what I see."

Sandy pointed to the dark green collar locked around 'her' neck. "I don't remember wearing that."

"Artistic license." Bernie rested her hand on the shoulder of Sandy's gray jacket, much as the gloved hand in the painting rested on the naked shoulder next to the collar. "Would you like some Bailey's?"

Sandy nodded slowly, and Bernie left her alone with the portrait. In the painting, the person behind Sandy was lost in shadow. Only the black leather glove and a wisp of brown hair were visible. Soft sensuous light brightened the smooth skin between Sandy's breasts and highlighted the curve of her neck. After a few moments, she reached out to touch the leather-gloved hand in the painting. She didn't notice the music when Bernie turned on the stereo

"What do you think?"

Sandy pulled her hand back and stepped to the side. Bernie handed her a short tumbler full of ice and Irish Cream. "I'm sorry, but it looks like I'm out of Dreyer's."

"Don't worry. This is fine." Sandy was still focused on the canvas. She took a sip of Bailey's and shivered. "It's amazing."

"I started it just before you met Jean Claude. I guess I finished it about a month ago. Do you like it?"

"Yes. Very much!" Sandy found it hard to look away from the painting. "It's almost as if there's more than paint there. It's beautiful."

"I only paint what I see."

"You said that before."

"It's true; you are." Soft music whispered from the corners of the room. Bernie leaned against the drafting table. "What did you think of Fair Game the second time around?"

"It was good." Sandy forced herself to turn and look at Bernie. "I noticed a lot of details that I didn't see before, but I still feel like it was too plausible."

"Plausible?"

"Well, yeah. It was too realistic. There was a clear-cut, logical explanation for everything, you know? Too much science fiction, not enough fantasy."

"I thought you liked science fiction."

"I do, but not in a vampire movie. I just would have liked a little more magic, that's all."

Bernie smiled. "More romance?"

"Well..." Sandy looked at the painting.

"Did you like the part where Kim Kelly was looking out her bedroom window?"

"Yeah. She looked just like a fairy tale princess."

Bernie stepped back and set her glass on the desk, next to the drafting table. "Remember the moon over the valley?"

Sandy stared at the gloved hand on 'her' shoulder. "I liked the way the moon was reflected in Kim's eyes."

"Remember how the mist flowed out, through the gates of the castle and down toward the city?"

"What mist?" Sandy drank some more Irish Cream.

Bernie took the glass from Sandy's hand and whispered. "Do you want to get seduced, or not?"

"What about your boyfriend?"

"We haven't been going out that long."

"What does that have to do with anything? Do you love him?"

Bernie didn't answer.

"Well?"

"So I love him. We have something of an understanding, you know. He sees other people. This isn't any different from what he's been doing. What's important right now is that I love you." Bernie met Sandy's reproachful look with frustrated anger. "Okay, so I'm a greedy, manipulative bitch and I want you both. Is that so terrible?"

"It isn't practical."

Bernie started to shake her head, but then accusingly pointed her finger at Sandy. "You're not helping here."

"Of course I'm not helping. I told you: I think I'm really serious about Ian."

"And I respect that, but you were serious about me when you started seeing Jean-Claude!"

"And that drove you nuts!"

"Exactly! You didn't have a problem with it. You were okay seeing us both. You're the one who said it wasn't cheating if you weren't seeing another woman."

Sandy glared at her. "You're the one who left!"

"And how stupid was that?" Bernie glared back.

They glared at each other for a moment longer, then smiled self-consciously and then they both laughed.

"Okay, stupid is no longer part of the plan." Bernie moved closer. "But I do have this carefully laid out, dare I say cunning plan and I'm not going to let it go to waste."

"Carefully laid out? You don't even have any Dreyer's."

"You're going to have to cooperate."

"Oh, am I?"

"You are. Now before we got sidetracked, I was talking about the mist and you were giving into your better instincts."

Sandy looked from Bernie to the painting. She took a deep breath. "I liked the mist a lot." She smiled. "I thought the mist was an absolutely brilliant touch."

"Thank you." Bernie stepped closer. "The mist swirled around the mortal princess and pressed against her." Bernie kissed Sandy softly on the lips, and then her neck. "As the vampire took shape, she pulled the warm body close." Bernie drew Sandy closer and lightly edged her teeth across Sandy's collarbone. She exhaled slowly, her breath burning Sandy's skin.

Sandy shivered. "You sure know how to curl a girl's toes!"

They kissed as Bernie trailed the fingers of one hand down Sandy's spine from the collar of her blue blouse to the top of her gray skirt. Sandy leaned her head back and Bernie kissed her throat.

"Mm." Sandy combed her fingers through Bernie's hair and pulled her head up to kiss her. "Let's go upstairs."

Bernie's eyes followed her up the winding treads as the stereo played a steady, insistent beat. They reached the top of the stairs separately, but their eyes held each other. Sandy pushed off her shoes as Bernie unzipped and struggled to pull off one of her boots. Sandy moved to help her and they unzipped and removed Bernie's second boot together. The boot fell to the floor as Bernie caught Sandy's arm and pulled her close. Their mouths almost touched. They hesitated and then pressed together. The sweet liquor on their breath mixed exotically with the fragrances of soap, perfume and arousal that swirled around them. Hands moved, cautiously at first, over bodies at once familiar and unexplored. Bernie unfastened Sandy's skirt, and the gray wool rustled to the floor.

Bernie's eyes followed the long, lightly tanned legs up to the thin line of black lace visible under Sandy's blouse. "Wow." Bernie shrugged off her black leather vest and tossed it toward the closet as Sandy started unbuttoning Bernie's blouse. Bernie started on Sandy's buttons and soon burgundy cotton and blue silk were slipping to the floor together. Sandy's black lace brassiere matched her panties and seemed to offer rather than support her breasts, barely covering her nipples.

Sandy unbuttoned Bernie's jeans and pushed the dark blue denim down to her knees. Bernie's cotton panties were bright sky blue. Sandy pushed Bernie's jeans down to the floor, and kissed her stomach just below the teal-green Speedo bra. "You make the most surprising color combinations look so sexy."

"Why, thank you." Bernie stepped out of her jeans.

Bernie tilted Sandy's head up and looked into her eyes. Heart was playing on the radio downstairs. Bernie listened to the second verse, and then sang the chorus to Sandy.

"'I want your world to turn, just for me. I want your fire to burn just for me.'" Bernie touched a finger to Sandy's lips.

"'Like the moon affects the tide and the sea,'" Bernie smiled, watching Sandy kiss her finger and then open her mouth to suck on it. "'I want your world to turn just for me.'" Bernie moved onto the big bed and Sandy followed, as though led by the finger in her mouth.

Bernie repeated the refrain once more. "'Just for me.'" She slid her other hand across Sandy's chin, then down her throat. They lay on the bed still joined, mouth to finger. Bernie whispered, "'Just for me.'" She ran the tip of one finger along the line of Sandy's shoulder where it curved up to join her neck. She brushed Sandy's hair back.

Sandy let go of Bernie's finger and tugged on Bernie's ear with her teeth. "You smell hot."

Bernie shivered as Sandy traced the edge of her jaw with the tip of her tongue.

"You taste hot too." Sandy kissed Bernie's neck, but then drew back a little. She studied Bernie across the inches of rumpled comforter that separated them. "Remember Too Familiar?"

Bernie's eyes opened wide. "Yeah."

Slowly, Sandy moved her hand across the fabric as she whispered. "'Purring seductively, she slid her hand across the bed, feeling the warmth before her fingers even touched the smooth, fiery skin.'" Sandy brushed her hand across Bernie's thigh.

"'Hands stroked gently at first, then with subtle insistence. Imperceptibly, their breath quickened. She felt dizzy, uncertain, and yet more sure of herself than ever before.'" Sandy infused each caress with the same compelling passion that imbued her voice.

"'Feeling those hands upon her, she wanted to close her eyes, lean into the familiar caress. Her back arched, thrusting her breasts into the palm of that waiting hand. Silently, she begged, 'touch me, feel me, know me, with your fingers, your mouth, your touch.'" Sandy slipped her hand under Bernie's bra and gently pushed it up, over her breasts.

"'Her hand swept up to touch her face, trace her mouth. She seized her fingers and stared at that small deft hand that knew her so intimately. She tasted a fingertip. Suddenly ravenous, she licked at the palm and sucked the fingers into her mouth.'" Sandy slowly savored the shape of Bernie's finger, the knuckle against the roof of her mouth, the sensitive tip against the back of her tongue. She held Bernie's wrist with one hand. With the other she reached down to push off Bernie's panties. Bernie lifted her hips off the bed and helped Sandy slide the thin blue cotton down her legs.

"'It was as if a floodgate had been opened.'" Sandy slid her hand across Bernie's thigh and teased her fingers through the curls above Bernie's sex.

"'She couldn't get the intoxicating scent out of her nostrils, nor the taste from her mouth.'" Sandy pressed her fingers firmly against Bernie's mound and easily slipped a finger inside her.

"'Needing more, she drew closer to the soft source of the fire. So hot.'" Sandy kissed her way down to Bernie's chest. "'So close.'" She teased her tongue across Bernie's nipple and Bernie moaned.

"'When contact was finally made, it was electric, a shock that burned the pleasure deep inside her. It tugged and burned along the length of her body until it settled into a fiery ache between her slim thighs.'" Bernie moaned again, and Sandy briefly pressed her lips against the soft skin.

"'Her fingers danced above the tawny skin, barely skimming the surface, electrically charged.'"

Bernie curled her fingers through Sandy's hair and pressed Sandy's mouth against her breast. Sandy tugged on the hardening nipple with her lips and Bernie moaned. Bernie's voice was rough. "Harder."

Sandy gently bit Bernie's nipple as she inserted a second finger. Sandy's hand seemed pale next to the tanned skin of Bernie's thighs. As she moved in and out, Sandy added another finger and brushed her thumb across Bernie's clitoris.

"Oh!" Bernie lightly ran her nails down and up Sandy's back. Sandy squeezed a fourth finger in with the others and Bernie cried out, clenching her fist around Sandy's hair.

"Hey!" Sandy tensed. "Careful."

"Sorry." Bernie relaxed her grip. "That just feels so good."

"Yes it does." Sandy turned her wrist and slipped the rest of her hand into Bernie, whose whole body stiffened. Sandy kissed Bernie's chest and stomach as she held her hand still. As Bernie relaxed, Sandy pushed her hand a little bit further and then pulled back. She worked her fist and forearm slowly, gently, in smooth irresistible strokes. She said, "'They touched, kissed, kneaded each other's bodies almost to the point of pain, until finally her legs opened wider.'"

Bernie shifted her hips to comply.

Sandy whispered. "'The steamy wetness was compelling, irresistible. She reached out to touch her just once with the tip of her pointy tongue.'"

Bernie arched her back and Sandy slowed the pace. "Squeeze me." Bernie's eyes narrowed in concentration. Sandy twisted her hand. "Harder." Bernie closed her eyes and Sandy rocked her hand against the increased resistance. Sandy shifted her position to look at the folds of Bernie's sex tugging at her forearm, Sandy's hand and wrist buried inside. Bernie growled and Sandy added that to the story. "'The throaty gasp of desire spurred her on. Gently she touched, then licked again.'" Sandy's mouth was just inches from Bernie. She exhaled, teasing the tufts of brown hair with her breath. "'She knew so well where to hold, where to hover; when to caress and when to wait,'" Sandy stopped moving. "'Just wait, until the woman she loved arched into her waiting mouth.'"

Sandy was teasing, no longer matching her actions to her words. Bernie arched her back but Sandy kept herself just out of reach. "'A mouth as warm...'" Sandy moved closer, "'As wet...'"

Bernie raised her hips again, trying to press herself against Sandy's lips, but Sandy raised her head. "'As demanding as the sweet flower it was coaxing into submission.'"

"Please..." Bernie implored her.

Sandy slowly twisted her wrist, and pressed the base of her thumb up. Bernie cried out, and when Sandy finally kissed her, Bernie arched up off the covers. Sandy held her steady, and rode the hurricane as Bernie tore at the comforter with one hand, and pressed Sandy's head closer with the other.

The storm passed, and Bernie's breathing began slowing to just above normal. Sandy gently withdrew her hand, and moved up to lie next to Bernie.

A dozen minutes later Bernie was still staring at a point somewhere between the ceiling and Halley's Comet. She took a deep breath and managed to say, "Wow!" She sounded content, euphoric. More minutes later she chuckled, "I thought I was seducing you!"

"You were." Sandy slipped her arm under Bernie's neck.

"Why do you always have to take over?"

Sandy looked embarrassed. "I don't always."

Bernie turned her head to look into Sandy's eyes. "God, it's good to see you again."

"It's good to see you too." Sandy smiled and snuggled up next to her.

Thursday, 10:35 pm – Paul Neault's House, Berkeley Hills

Barely visible at the top of the private drive, the outline of three castellated roofs was silhouetted against the stars. The garage formed one side of the courtyard and was mirrored by a guest house on the other. The main house formed the longer side of the courtyard and was connected to the outbuildings on either side by curving glassed-in galleries. Des parked by the southernmost of the four garage doors and stepped out onto the cobblestone driveway. Other than the stars, the only light came from the second floor windows above the garage. Des walked around to the side door and knocked on the heavy oak. He leaned back to glance up at the second floor and took out a cigarette. Des started to light up, but the door opened, spilling light into the surrounding yard. Des flicked the match away in a bright arc that sputtered out in the wet grass.

"Nice of you to join us." Terri pivoted on her good leg and headed back up the flight of stairs just inside the door. "Come on up." Terri's not-so-good leg was still Velcroed into the brace that held her knee together. She held onto the oak railing that ran along the wall and took each carpeted step with her left leg first. She then carefully shifted her weight to her right leg before tackling the next step.

After locking the door, Des followed her up the stairs. "Terri, what the hell is going on?"

Terri limped around the elegantly carved railing at the top of the stairs. "Damage control." The upper floor of the carriage house was a single large room with a high vaulted ceiling. The exposed rafters seemed to rest on dozens of floor-to-ceiling bookshelves lining the walls. Terri's crutches were leaning against a black leather couch next to the railing. She tucked one under each arm and moved carefully toward the other end of the room.

Des walked along next to her, staying clear of the swing of her crutches. "What happened to you?"

Terri's destination was a black leather chair facing Paul Neault's huge oak desk. Carefully lowering herself into the armchair, Terri stretched her injured leg out in front of her. "I fell in love."

"What kind of truck was Cupid driving?"

Terri pretended to chuckle. "Very funny."

Next to Paul's desk was a cardboard box half full of Pain As Pleasure, by Dr. Paul Neault. The doctor himself, looking older and thinner than his dust-jacket picture, was leaning back with a phone pressed to his ear. He was smiling. "You're embarrassing me..." Paul nodded at Des and pointed to a second armchair. "It's selling very well, thank you." Paul's hair was black with a hint of gray at the temples. His brown eyes watched Des and Terri from under perfectly trimmed eyebrows.

Des stayed on his feet and glanced over at Terri. "What 'damage' are we trying to control?"

"Hang on a minute." Terri nodded toward Paul.

"Thank you again, John. Good bye." Paul leaned forward to hang up the phone, and looked at Des. "Personnel records show Michael Dale is on 'administrative leave' from the Oakland Police Department, but he's actually working undercover."

"Mick is a cop?" Des shook his head. "Bullshit."

"I'm afraid not." There was a single blue file folder on the desk. Paul pushed it toward Des, leaned back, and folded his hands together in his lap.

"I checked him out." Des picked up the folder. "You checked him out." He slid the unlit cigarette behind his ear and opened the folder. A picture of Mick in a police uniform was paper-clipped on top of a short stack of papers. Des shook his head. "This is not fucking possible!"

"It's totally fucking possible." Terri looked at Des. "Face it: Mick is a goddamned cop!"

"Sonofabitch!" Des tossed the folder back onto the desk. "Why didn't you tell us?"

"I am telling you."

"Now?" Des sounded sarcastic. "Now is just a little too late, don't you think?" He glanced at Terri who nodded her agreement.

"Intelligence is as much an art as a science, Desmond. I found out. I'm telling you." Paul opened the folder and turned it toward Des. "Mick's real name, the name on his employment records, is Vale. If you look closely, you'll notice that he's wearing a Los Angeles Police Department uniform. Given that our own Captain Hogue was previously with the LAPD, and that Hogue heads the Drug Task Force in Oakland, it's probable that Hogue hired Mick out of LA to be an undercover resource. As far as I can tell, Mick has been on 'administrative leave' since his first day on the job. Nobody in the police department, well, nobody I've talked to, knows anything about Vale."

"This is bullshit!" Des pulled the cigarette from behind his ear and pointed it at Paul. "If nobody knows he's a cop then how did you find out about him?"

"One of my patients is on the Oakland City Council. He's disturbed by what he perceives to be fascist forces at work within the police department and the Council." Paul's voice was calm and professional as he glanced at Terri and back at Des. "He's also worried about the YMCA. Technically, the Councilman is paranoid schizophrenic, so of course I don't take much of what he says seriously. To give him something pro-active to obsess about I suggested he hire a private detective. The friend I recommended discovered much more than I had expected." Paul waved his hand, palm up, toward the file on the desk.

Des looked from Paul to Terri and back to Paul. "Shit!"

"Well put." Paul leaned forward and rested his arms on the desk. "Obviously we're shutting down; immediately. Don't sell anything, buy anything, say anything or do anything. All I've been able to find out about Vale is that he's been with the police for at least ten years. I've got some financial and personal history but I don't know what he knows or who he's talked to. We can't afford to do any more business with anyone until we find out how badly we've been compromised."

"What about the twenty keys from Yuri?" Des shook his head again. "I've got orders for that shit. My people need..."

Paul held up his hand. "We have no choice. I'll explain the situation to Yuri. Your people," he glanced at Terri, "and your people as well, will have to wait."

Terri glared at him. "How long?"

Paul shrugged. "Until it's safe."

Des repeated Terri's question. "How long?"

Paul shrugged. "Until we find out exactly what our esteemed police department has discovered."

"Until..." Terri raised an eyebrow. "How do we do that?"

"Well, we need to know what Officer Vale knows." Paul tapped the file folder and smiled. "He may not be a patient, but there are all sorts of ways of gathering information."

Friday, 12:36 am – Intermission,
Bernie's Loft, Berkeley

Bernie had her head propped up on two pillows and her arm curled protectively around Sandy's shoulders. "Are you guys still not talking?"

"Oh, we're talking." Sandy sighed. "We're just not saying anything."

"Talking is a start."

"I guess." Sandy shook her head. "They're still in Copenhagen. Daddy sent a ticket and asked me to visit for my birthday. No apology, no explanation, just the ticket and a note that said, 'Come see us if you can get away.'"

"Did you go?"

"Yeah." Sandy traced the edge of Bernie's jaw with her finger.

Bernie twisted her head a little and kissed Sandy's finger. "Does that mean your parents have un-disowned you?"

"They seem to think so. Daddy said he loved me no matter what, but I'll bet that only applies if the 'what' is history." Sandy brushed her cheek against Bernie's hair. "You don't feel like history to me. Mom just pretended nothing ever happened. Of course, they won't talk to me about it but they talk to everyone else! Two days after I got there, Aunt Sofia called from Australia to congratulate me! She was ever so saccharine sweet and sanctimonious just because Mother told her I was dating a man!" Sandy made her voice sound old and scratchy. "'Don't worry, dear, many successful women have gone through a homosexual phase.'"

"What did you say?"

"I said I didn't think she knew enough about success, women, or sex to have an opinion."

"Good answer! What did she say?"

"I don't know; I hung up on her."

"Right on!" Bernie hugged Sandy tight against her. "What did your mother say?"

"Nothing." Sandy snuggled up close and sighed contentedly. "I've missed this."

Bernie nodded. "Me too."

A little bit later, a departing airliner flashed across the skylight over the bed. Sandy was almost asleep, her arms around Bernie and her head resting on Bernie's shoulder. The plane reached the edge of the Plexiglas and slipped behind the wood trim next to the exposed rafter. Bernie's gaze followed the trim strip along the beam to the living room wall and studied the crack in the joint compound between the wall and the ceiling. Sandy stirred and Bernie turned her attention to the tousled blond hair that partially hid Sandy's face.

Bernie brushed the hair back and Sandy smiled. "Hi."

"Hi yourself."

Sandy pressed a little closer. "You look worried."

"Not worried." Bernie shook her head. "I was just thinking about something you said."

"Something good, I hope."

"I don't know." Bernie studied Sandy's face. "It was a long time ago."

Sandy smiled supportively. "What did I say?"

"You said you couldn't sleep with anyone you didn't love."

"That's true."

"So, does that mean?" Bernie looked over at the fissure between the wall and the ceiling.

"Yes." Sandy pushed herself up so she could see Bernie clearly, and waited for Bernie to look back. Sandy nodded when Bernie met her gaze. "It means I love you." Sandy chuckled. "I never stopped loving you, silly. How could I?" She snuggled up close. "I'll always love you, no matter what."

Bernie hugged her tight. "I love you too."

When Sandy tilted her head back to look at Bernie, she noticed a mischievous glint in her lover's eye. "What?"

Bernie grinned as she pushed Sandy over onto her back. "Your turn!"

Sandy lay back against her pillow. "And you said I was the one who always took control."

"Shut up." Bernie kissed her, softly at first, but with steadily mounting intensity. When she finally let Sandy go, both women were breathing in short, ragged gasps.

Sandy stroked Bernie's shoulder. "Tell me about the mist."

CHAPTER SEVEN

Saturday, 9:37 am – Some Assembly Required

Ian was on his knees in the dining room surrounded by particleboard, packing paper and little bags of assorted fasteners. When the doorbell rang, he called out, "Come in!"

"Ian MacAran?"

Ian looked up at the huge official-looking man. "Can I help you?"

"Are you Ian MacAran?"

"Yes?" Ian let the instruction sheet slip to the floor as he got up and stepped carefully through the bits and pieces.

"Barrett Hogue, Mr. MacAran. Oakland Police." Hogue pulled his jacket back to reveal the badge clipped to his vest pocket. "I'd like to ask you a few questions."

"Okay," Ian smiled politely, "What about?"

Barrett surveyed the furniture parts in the dining room as he closed the door behind him. "Did you just move in?"

"No."

"What are you building?"

"It's a china hutch."

"I see. That'll go real well with your pool table." Hogue walked toward a row of framed photos leaning against the living room wall. Planes from both World Wars were crowded in with airliners and modern military aircraft. "I'm looking for Michael Dale. Do you know where I can find him?"

"Not off-hand." Ian closed the door. "Why? Is something wrong?"

"It's a police matter."

"Is he in some kind of trouble?"

"I really can't say at this time." Hogue picked up a picture of a boxy, menacing, green and brown aircraft. "Tough looking plane; what is it?"

"That's an A-10 tank killer. They call it the Warthog."

"I like it." Hogue set the picture down. "Do you know where Mick might be?"

"One of his job sites, maybe? He works a lot of Saturdays. I'm assuming you tried his house?"

Hogue nodded. "His wife hasn't seen him since Thursday evening."

"Really? Clara called looking for him Friday night, but she didn't say he hadn't been home."

"You're Mick's flight instructor, is that correct?"

"Yeah. We're scheduled to fly tomorrow morning."

"When?"

"Uh, nine o'clock."

"Where?"

"Oakland Aero. It's on the North Field, at Oakland Airport."

"Is Mick any good?"

"Uh," Ian hesitated. "How do you mean?"

"Is he a good pilot?"

"Well, he's a good student." Ian smiled. "He soloed after ten hours. That's very good."

"'Soloed' means he can fly by himself?"

"Exactly."

Hogue nodded. "Could he be flying now?"

"He would have called me."

"So he wouldn't be able to rent a plane without your approval?"

"Well, he's supposed to call me but I suppose he could have forgotten to call."

"And could he have flown a plane down to Los Angeles or someplace like that?"

"Not legally." Ian shook his head. "He's only signed off for Oakland and Hayward."

Hogue nodded. "What about illegally?"

"What do you mean?"

"Would he be able to navigate from here to LA on his own?"

"With a little luck, maybe." Ian considered. "He's about ready for his long cross-country, but I wouldn't let him fly to L.A."

"Could you check and see if he's flying today?"

"Sure." Ian nodded. "I'll call the club."

"That would be a big help." Hogue smiled.

"The, uh, phone's in the kitchen." Ian took a step back. "Do you want something to drink? Water? Tea? Root Beer?"

"No thanks, I'm fine."

"I'll only be a minute." Ian turned and headed for the phone.

Hogue followed Ian as far as the family room. While Ian waited for the speed-dialer to connect him, Hogue stopped to examine the rows of CDs over the fireplace. "You've got a lot of bootleg Beatles."

"Yeah. I, uh... excuse me. Hi Doug, this is Ian." Ian watched Hogue sort through the contraband Beatles CDs. "I'm doing great, Doug, thanks. Could you check the schedule and see if Mick Dale is flying today?"

Hogue slid out one of the Beatles CDs and read the back of the case.

"Yeah?" Ian listened to the phone while the police officer swapped the first CD for a second. "That's strange. ... No, I'll talk to him. It won't happen again. ... Sorry, Doug."

Hogue looked at Ian expectantly.

Ian shook his head as he hung up the phone. "That's really weird. Mick had a 172 booked for nine o'clock this morning, but he never showed up. He's usually there an hour early to preflight."

"How big is a 172?"

"Single engine, four seats. He can't take anyone with him, though; he's just a student."

"Hm." Hogue reached into his vest pocket, the one without the gold badge, and pulled out a plain white business card. "Can you think of anywhere Mick might have gone just to get away for a while?"

"To get away? No." Ian took the business card and glanced at the CD in Hogue's other hand. "It might help if you told me what this is all about."

Hogue pointed to the card Ian was now holding. "Please give us a call if you think of anything."

"Sure thing."

"I haven't seen this one before." Hogue held up the Sessions CD. "It looks like a great compilation. Is it any good?"

Ian smiled. "It's very good."

"You've got a hell of a collection here, Mr. MacAran."

"Call me Ian, please."

"Ian." Hogue flipped the CD over as he turned toward the entryway. "Do you have the twenty-two minute version of "Helter-Skelter"?"

"Not yet. I've been trying to find a copy but, uh, no one seems to have it." Ian followed Hogue to the door.

"I've got it on cassette, but I haven't been able to find a CD." Hogue paused in the entryway and handed Ian the Sessions CD. "Thanks for your time, Ian. Can I ask you one more question?"

"Sure."

"Why aren't you nervous?"

Ian hesitated. "I beg your pardon?"

"Well, I didn't think you seemed nervous when I was asking about Mick Dale, but you weren't curious or put out either. Most of the people I talk to, especially the ones who aren't sure why I'm asking them questions, get really nervous about talking to the police, especially a cop my size. As far as I can tell, you'd rather talk to a cop about illegal CDs than about the whereabouts of one of your students."

"I like to talk about the Beatles because I like the Beatles. Since I don't know where Mick is, there's not a lot

I can say about his 'whereabouts'." Ian considered, "We don't have an engine fire to deal with, is there something else I should be nervous about?"

"I don't care about bootleg music; I've got some of this stuff at home." Hogue leaned a little closer. "What I do care about right now is Mick Dale." He pulled out a pen and took back the card Ian had been holding. He wrote a number on the back of the card. "This is my cell number. If you think of something, anything, and I don't care if it's two in the morning; call me." He put the business card back in Ian's hand and opened the door. "Any help you can give us will be greatly appreciated." Hogue nodded politely, turned and headed down the walkway.

Ian looked at the card as he closed the door. It read: Captain Barrett Hogue, Narcotics Division, Oakland Police Department. Ian rested his forehead against the hard oak and took a deep breath. He let it out slowly as he looked out through the spyglass and watched Hogue squeeze into the front passenger seat of an unmarked car. Ian waited for the car to turn around and drive away before he headed over to Mick and Clara's house.

Sunday, 1:38 pm – Wallaby Grove, UC Berkeley

Des slid a pack of Pall Mall Reds out of his vest pocket and leaned back against the railing. Strawberry Creek burbled under the wooden footbridge as shadows from the trees shifted back and forth with the breeze. Des tapped the pack of cigarettes against the palm of his hand. "What about the pilot?"

Paul stared at the red package in Des' hand. "MacAran is not a factor, and I would appreciate it if you wouldn't smoke."

"We're outside, Doc. Relax." Des tore off the cellophane wrapper and tossed it over his shoulder. Des was wearing a white shirt with a tan vest. His jeans had an artistic slash across one knee, but his hiking boots were new. "What did you find out about Ian?"

"He was a crossing guard in fourth grade and he's had a few speeding tickets." Paul was wearing a pale gray suit with a white shirt. The white streaks in his burgundy tie echoed the white hairs beginning to gray his temples. A falling leaf stuck to Paul's lapel until he carefully picked it off and let it drop. "MacAran has been flying for sixteen years, twelve professionally, and he voted in the last election."

Des nodded. "What about his finances?"

Paul shrugged. "He pays his bills. He has money in the bank and a new car."

"How much money?"

Paul shook his head. "What difference does it make?"

"I'm just curious. You dig up the most amazing information." Des peeled open the top of the cigarette pack. "A crossing guard in fourth grade? How many computers did you have to hack through to dig that up?"

"Just one. The records for all the schools in Illinois, at least for that time period, are archived on one system." Paul smiled. "His financial report was harder to pin down, but his bottom line is a total of six thousand dollars in two accounts. I couldn't find any direct sign of the cash he got from Mick, but two casinos in Las Vegas filed 10-99Gs on him for a total of $28,000."

"10-99Gs?" Des shook a cigarette out of the pack.

"It's an IRS form. He probably bought casino chips a hundred or so at a time and then cashed out all at once. The casino cashiers would assume he won it, even if he didn't say so, and they'd file a 10-99G with the IRS." Paul smiled paternally. "I think it's quite clever. He has to pay tax on the money, but he doesn't have to explain where he got it. It's now legitimate income. Some of it went to pay off credit cards and some went to the IRS as estimated tax. MacAran will probably have a lot more 'winnings' to declare as time goes on. Mick paid him almost two million. That will take some time to legitimize if he only 'wins' $28,000 at a time."

"So where's the rest of the money?"

"I don't know. I would expect it to be hidden in his house, but that's obviously not information my industrious hackers can access." Paul noticed a fly on his sleeve and waved it away. "In any event, MacAran is not important. Just stay away from him."

"Why?" Des watched the fly circle around and land on Paul's shoulder. "He could be useful."

Paul shook his head. "He is far more likely to prove dangerous."

"Bullshit!" Des pushed the pack into his vest pocket and pointed the unlit cigarette at Paul. "You just said he's clean. He's a pilot, not a cop. Mick wouldn't have told the cops about us or about Ian because he wanted to keep the money. That means the cops don't know about us and MacAran will only know what I want him to know. What's the problem? He's not a risk, he's an opportunity!"

"As Mick was an opportunity? What if MacAran is another undercover cop?"

"Not possible." Des shook his head. "Mick wouldn't have worked with him if he was a cop and Mick would have known."

Paul sighed. "Must I spell it out for you? Mick swore he didn't tell anyone about us and, given the circumstances, I'm inclined to believe him. He planned on keeping their money and arresting Yuri Milanov to cover his tracks. Mick was keeping two entirely separate sets of contacts and books, and he didn't tell his superiors or anyone else about MacAran, or about the flights to Mexico."

"Then there's no reason..."

Paul held up his hand and Des fell silent. "We cannot infer that just because Mick didn't tell anyone, it necessarily follows that no one suspected him. Mick was doing a lot of things that he wasn't telling his superiors about, but he wasn't working for fools. That kind of behavior rarely goes unnoticed. We don't know whether or not anyone was watching Mick, but if someone was, they would have placed MacAran under surveillance as soon as he flew Mick to Mexico. I'm trying to recruit someone who'll be able to absolutely confirm that Mick was not under investigation, but until he shares a little more information we can't be sure of MacAran. Any of several agencies might be watching him even as we speak, and you, my foolish friend, could quite easily become the focus of their investigation."

"Nobody is watching MacAran!"

Paul took a step toward Des. "Leave MacAran alone." He stared at Des until Des looked away. Paul nodded, a brief triumphant smile on his lips. "Is that clear?"

"Yeah, yeah. Whatever you say. I'm..." Des stopped abruptly and looked toward someone approaching from the south bank of the stream. Paul turned toward the short, plump, gray-haired woman who stopped a few meters away. She studied Paul with a friendly, albeit puzzled, expression on her face.

Des reached into his vest pocket for a book of matches.

The woman looked down at the wooden deck and then met Paul's patient gaze. She smiled shyly. "I don't mean to intrude, but I just had to ask. You are Doctor Paul Neault, aren't you?"

Paul nodded politely. "I am."

"I knew it!" Smiling triumphantly, she glanced back at a tall gray-haired man waiting on the bank, and then stepped closer. "Rolf was sure you'd be taller, but no worries. We're here for your lecture, Dr. Neault: "The Psychology of Sado/Masochistic Behavior". I must say we loved your book. It's saved our marriage." She reached into her very large handbag and pulled out a copy of <u>Pain As Pleasure</u>. "Well, I don't think our marriage actually needed saving, but your book certainly has spiced things up!" She held it out to Paul with both hands. "Could you autograph our copy?"

"Of course." Paul chuckled. "To whom shall I make it out?" He took the book from her and opened it to the inside cover.

She handed him a pen. "Mistress Victoria and her obedient servant rolf, with a small 'r'."

Paul started writing. Des lit his cigarette and tossed the spent match over the railing. It landed in the stream and floated back toward them, disappearing under the bridge. Paul shook his head disapprovingly, but Des ignored him and took a deep drag on the cigarette. Tilting his head back, Des blew a smoky halo into the branches overhead. He smiled sarcastically at Paul's back.

Paul finished the dedication with a calligraphic flourish and returned the book to Mistress Victoria. "Here you are. I hope you enjoy the lecture."

"Oh, I'm sure we will! Thank you again, Dr. Neault."

"My pleasure." Paul watched her retrace her steps back to her companion. The couple then headed up toward Dwinelle Hall arm in arm. Paul looked contemptuously at the wisp of smoke rising from Des' cigarette. "Did you have to light that damned thing?"

"Yes." Des took a deep drag and smoke spilled out of his mouth when he said, "Deal with it."

"You have an appointment with Yuri's nephew Tuesday evening. You may pick up the money at four o'clock. Please be on time." Paul nodded curtly, crossed to the south bank and walked up the path toward Dwinelle Hall.

Des blew smoke at the retreating professor.

Monday, 6:39 pm – Strawberries at Bernie's, Berkeley

Late afternoon sun angled through the skylights and cast tall thin rectangles across the paintings above Bernie's bed. One picture showed a woman and a horse. The gray stallion's head was lowered and the woman's forehead rested against the blaze of white above the horse's eyes. The other canvas showed a city at night. Bright stars surrounded a thin crescent of moon that seemed to float on the city-lit clouds. Both paintings, like most others in Bernie's apartment, were signed with quick fluid strokes that might have been the letters B and J, but looked more like a running stallion.

Throughout the loft, canvases from the beautiful to the bizarre hung next to framed blueprints and scale models of buildings and sailboats. In one corner, a cardboard shopping mall hung next to a wooden clipper ship under full sail. The architectural drawings were all signed "B. J. Selleca" in neat block letters. The signatures on the paintings varied. Some had "Bernadette" or "Bernie" neatly scripted in the lower right corner, but most were signed with some form of the running stallion.

Downstairs, Ian pointed at the stallion glyph on a cityscape above the breakfast bar. "That was your painting!"

Bernie was on the other side of the bar washing their dinner dishes. She glanced up to see where Ian was pointing. "It still is."

"Not this one! Another one I saw..." Ian hesitated, "... last month."

"Really? Which one?" She reached into the sink and pulled out a plate.

"A ... uh ... lighthouse."

"The one with the bats?"

"I don't remember any bats." Ian silently cursed himself. He'd seen the painting at Sandy's.

Bernie didn't notice Ian's consternation. "There was a long thin jetty with waves washing over the path, right?"

"Uh, I guess so." Ian watched her scrub off bits of soapy lasagna.

"Nobody sees them until I point them out. They ended up looking like a big swirl of cloud because they were so tiny. I tried to highlight some groups of bats to evoke larger bat shapes, but I think it was too subtle an effect to work." Bernie rinsed the plate and set it in the drainer next to the sink.

"Do you remember every painting you've ever done?"

"I haven't done that many." Bernie pulled a second plate from the soapy water and scrubbed it clean. "Just what you see here and, I don't know, maybe a dozen more."

"I would have thought you'd have sold more than a dozen."

"Oh, I don't sell them." Bernie rinsed off the plate and set it in the drainer with the other dishes.

"But they're really good." Ian looked puzzled. "You don't sell any at all?"

"Nope. I don't see my paintings as products." Bernie dried her hands on a dishtowel and tossed the towel on the counter. "Architecture is commercial enough.

Painting is more personal, more me. I can give something I've painted to someone I know, but it would feel weird to sell something like that. Every painting is like a piece of myself, you know?"

Ian nodded. "So, uh, how do you know Sandra Taylor?"

"I gave her 'Homecoming' after my first summer at OHI."

Homecoming?"

"The bats live in the abandoned lighthouse and it's morning so they're flying home." As Bernie watched Ian, an amused expression flitted briefly across her face. "Sandra was really nice. I think she hung it in her dining room. Would you like some dessert?"

"Uh..." Ian started to nod, but then shook his head. "No, thanks, I'm stuffed. I didn't know you worked for OHI."

"Didn't I point out Medford Plaza the first time we went flying?" Bernie left the kitchen and walked around the spiral stairs to join him.

"Oh yeah. You called it Osmund ... something, right?"

"Harris and Ikaki. They were the founders." Bernie slipped onto the bar stool next to his.

"I guess I didn't connect the initials with the names." Ian cleared his throat. "Isn't OHI an engineering company?"

"Among other things. Twenty years ago, Joel Ikaki's son became an architect. When Joel Junior joined the firm, he started what has become a widely-respected architecture department." Bernie pointed behind Ian to a drawing of a 48-story high-rise. "We were the principal contractor on Medford."

Ian turned to look at the intricate drawing. "You make it sound like you still work there."

"Hm." Bernie nodded. "You're right. I know I don't work there anymore, but I still feel ... loyal, you know? Joel Junior asked me to come back permanently in the fall, but I couldn't do it."

"Why not? Wouldn't that be the perfect place to start your career?"

"If I still wanted to be an architect, yeah." Bernie shook her head. "I've thought about it a lot, especially after Joel's offer, but I just can't see myself working in an office for the next forty years."

"I thought you liked the business."

"I do but I love the actual construction side. It's a little weird, but it's a lot of fun!" Bernie made a fist, as if she was holding a hammer. "Construction is like building models, except that when you're done people actually move into the space you've created. I like that aspect the best. And I've been learning so much! Ken knows almost everything about carpentry and construction and he's totally cool about explaining anything I don't understand. I've actually been thinking about staying in construction after I get my degree."

"Would you keep working with Mick?"

"God no!" Bernie looked horrified. "He's way too flaky and totally unreliable. Did I tell you the Jean Street job got shut down last week because Mick went ahead with some design changes without getting the new plans approved?"

"No."

"On the plans we've been using, the building has a penthouse, but those aren't the approved plans. The penthouse apartment was added on later and the inspector who caught that 'minor little detail' red-tagged us; now nobody can even go on the site." Bernie sighed. "Ken was about to show me how to do the roof, but now that has to wait until Mick gets all the paperwork cleared up."

"Is it complicated to get changes approved?"

"Not if you know what you're doing! Mick said he didn't have time, but I don't know why; he's never at the job! What the hell does he do all day?" Bernie sighed. "At least Ken and I are still working. We get to work on Mick's house this week, but Mick doesn't think there's enough work for more than the two of us. The rest of the crew is out of work until Mick can get the city to okay the new plans for Jean Street."

"They're out of a job, just like that?"

"Welcome to the construction industry. I still think we could use some of the guys on Mick's house, you know, just to get the job done faster, but Mick didn't want anyone else working on his house. Ken and I were talking about getting rid of Mick and taking over the Jean Street job, if only to get the guys back to work, but Ken doesn't have a contractor's license. I was thinking of quitting all together, but I can handle a little bullshit. It is great experience. I'm learning a lot and I really like working with Ken."

"I met Ken at Mick's. He seemed like a nice guy."

"He is." Bernie nodded. "He lives a couple blocks from here so we've been car pooling, but he never lets me chip in for gas."

Ian turned toward Bernie and his foot knocked over some paintings below the breakfast bar. Three fell face up on the hardwood floor. Bernie moved to pick them up, but Ian was closer, and he grabbed the one on top before she could reach it.

A dark-haired woman stood in profile, with her head tilted back, and her hands loosely tied behind her. She wore only thigh-high boots and a silver chain that connected her nipples. Someone was standing just outside the frame of the picture, reaching in to lift the center of the chain with one finger.

Ian glanced at Bernie and back at the painting in his hand. "I like this." He looked closer. "Hey! She's got earrings in her nipples!"

Bernie laughed. "That would make them nipple rings."

Ian studied the picture. "Ouch!"

"Oh, but look at her face. See how she's smiling? It's supposed to be just like having your ears pierced. See?" Bernie tugged on the hoop in her ear. "Once they heal, it doesn't hurt at all." She nodded at the painting. "Do you like them?"

"Uh," Ian leaned the painting against the wall and picked up the next canvas. "Yeah, I do."

"Me too."

"Really?" Ian raised an eyebrow. "I don't recall any rings."

"I mean I like the idea." Bernie crossed her arms across her chest. "I've thought about it, but I don't think I'd ever go through with it."

"Why not?"

"Hey, just because something looks sexy doesn't mean I'd actually want to do it. It's a fantasy, like the rest of these paintings."

"All of them?" He showed the painting he was holding to Bernie. A woman was kneeling on a bed wearing nothing but a black silk blindfold. She held her hands behind her back. Her mouth was open, and a shadowy figure was holding a bright red cherry just above her tongue. Ian glanced at Bernie. "Is this just a fantasy too?"

"Oh, I don't know. That doesn't look too fantastic." Bernie smiled nervously. "Do you like it?"

"Yeah." Ian nodded. "I like it a lot." He leaned toward her and they kissed.

Bernie voice was almost a whisper. "Would you like to try it?"

"I would." Ian glanced back at the painting. "Do you have a scarf?"

"I think I can dig something up. Come on." She took the painting from him and set it on the floor. Bernie grinned, kissed him playfully and led him up the spiral stairs. "You know it's strange." Bernie opened a drawer under the bed and pulled out a long black scarf. "You can be around some people for years and never really know them, and then you meet someone you feel like you've known all your life."

"I know what you mean." Ian reached for the scarf, but Bernie pulled it away.

"Have you ever done this before?"

"Uh … " Ian shook his head. "No, but there's a first time for everything."

"There certainly is." Bernie nodded. "Turn around."

Ian laughed. "Yes, ma'am." His voice was teasing.

"I like the sound of that. Take off your shoes." Bernie doubled the scarf as Ian kicked off his shoes. "Socks too." Bernie moved behind him and covered his eyes, tying the loose ends of the scarf behind his head. "Hold your arms straight out to the sides." Ian held his arms out. Bernie smiled. "Very good."

Bernie started unbuttoning his shirt. "This is a game, a role-playing game, and part of the fun comes from playing your role to the very best of your ability. It's kind of like improvisation. With me so far?"

"Yes, ma'am."

"I'm going to give you a code word, a safe word. You can say stop, or please, or no, or anything you like and I may or may not." She smiled mischievously. "Probably not. If you say red, that's the safe word: red. If you say red, I'll stop." Bernie slid her hands under his shirt and across his nipples. "Your challenge is to play your part no matter what happens. You're only to say "red" if we go too far and you can't stay in character." She kissed his chest. "Understand?"

Ian nodded. "Yes, ma'am."

Bernie unfastened the last button. "Are you my slave?"

"Yes, ma'am." His voice was almost serious.

"Do you exist only to please me?"

"Yes, ma'am."

"Lower your arms." Bernie pushed the shirt off Ian's shoulders and down his arms. Once she got the cuffs past his hands, she let the shirt fall to the floor. "Put your hands behind your neck."

Ian did as he was told.

Bernie brushed her hands across his stomach and up to his chest. "Forgetting something?" She pinched Ian's nipple.

Ian jumped, but he kept his hands behind his neck. "What?"

"And we were off to such a good start." Bernie pinched his other nipple.

"Ma'am?"

Bernie released him. "That's better." She slid her hands down to his hips and then around and across the fly of his slacks. "Your pants have gotten a little too tight, haven't they?"

"Yes, ma'am."

She unbuckled his belt and slid the braided brown leather out of the belt loops. She doubled the belt in her hand and ran it across Ian's chest. "The challenge for me is to get you as close as possible to saying "red" without actually pushing you over that line." Bernie stepped behind him and playfully slapped his bottom before tossing the belt on the floor. She trailed her fingers across his shoulders as she walked around him. "Are you willing to do anything I ask?"

Ian turned his head toward the sound of her voice. "Yes, ma'am."

Bernie slid her hand down his side and across his stomach. Her voice was reassuring. "It is okay to say "red", you know. It doesn't mean we'll stop forever, just for now."

"Yes, ma'am."

Bernie knelt in front of him and slowly unzipped his slacks. She kissed his stomach and pushed his slacks and underwear down further. With her cheek, she pushed his cock to one side and kissed his thigh. She repeated the gesture to kiss his other thigh, then stroked his legs as she pushed his slacks down to his ankles. "You look so good." She kissed the base of his shaft and then used her tongue to draw a line to its tip."

Ian reached down to comb his fingers through her hair.

"Hey!" Bernie roughly pushed his hand away and stood up. "Where did I tell you to put your hands?"

Ian smiled and put his hands back behind his neck.

"You look amused. Are you laughing at me?"

"No, ma'am." Ian shook his head, a trace of a smile at the corners of his mouth.

"At the situation?"

"No, ma'am." Ian struggled to look respectful, but he couldn't get the smile off his face.

Bernie grabbed his cock, and pressed her nails into the soft skin. "Are you having trouble taking this seriously?"

The rough grip helped Ian concentrate and he managed to look sufficiently chastened. "No, ma'am."

Bernie nodded. "I think you need some help keeping your hands to yourself."

"No, ma'am."

She squeezed him harder. "Are you disagreeing with me?"

Ian winced. "No, ma'am, not at all."

"Come here." Bernie guided him toward the bed, letting him use his hands to get onto it. "Stretch out on your back." She reached into the open drawer and pulled out four scarves, each identical to the one covering Ian's eyes. Bernie made Ian move to the center of the bed and stretch his hands and feet toward the corners. The cleats that gave the bed its nautical air proved to be more than decorative, as Bernie looped the scarves around them and quickly tied Ian down. She stepped back to admire him. Ian's pale skin contrasted electrically with the dark blue comforter. "You look absolutely delicious."

Slowly climbing up on the bed, Bernie settled between Ian's knees. She watched the rise and fall of his chest, then bent down to kiss him softly. Stretching out on top of him, Bernie kissed and gently bit each of his nipples. She moved down, kissing his stomach before she took him into her mouth. Ian moaned softly, but held still.

Barely moving, Bernie held him there. When she finally released him, she slid back slowly, her lips closing to kiss him before she broke the contact completely. "You taste as good as you look." She leaned forward squeezing his cock between the silk of her blouse and the soft skin of his abdomen. She kissed his neck, his chin, his lips, then stopped when Ian tried to increase the pressure.

Bernie pushed Ian's blindfold up. He blinked, surprised. She gazed into his eyes for a moment and then smiled mischievously. "I'll be right back."

Ian watched her move off the bed, listened to her walk downstairs. Cupboards opened and closed, ice cubes clanged against metal and then the stereo started playing something soft and instrumental. When Bernie returned, she set a metal mixing bowl on the headboard just out of Ian's view. She climbed back onto the bed. "Hi there."

"Hi..."

Bernie smiled. "Having fun so far?"

Ian nodded.

Bernie raised an eyebrow.

"Yes, ma'am."

"Very good." Bernie carefully unfastened the top button of her blouse. She worked her way down to the last button before slipping one arm out of the blue silk. Sliding the blouse off her other arm, she trailed the soft fabric across Ian's chest. She tossed it toward her closet, but the blouse landed on the edge of the bed. Reaching back, Bernie unfastened her bra and then crossed her arms to hold the cups in place. She slid the shoulder straps off her arms and slowly lowered her hands. She drew the white lace across Ian's chest before tossing the bra over the side of the bed.

"Now listen carefully." Bernie unzipped her jeans. "If I ask if you like what we're doing," she pushed her jeans down over her hips. "And you do like it," she had to raise herself up and lean to the side to get the denim past her ankles. "You will answer, 'Only if it pleases you.'" Tossing the jeans behind her, Bernie settled back onto Ian's chest. She was still wearing her thong bikini panties, and she slid down, pressing the small triangle of blue cotton against him.

Ian tried to thrust forward, just a little, to increase the pressure.

Bernie rocked away from him. "If I ask you if you like what we're doing, and you don't like it, you will answer, 'Not unless it pleases you.' Do you understand?"

Ian nodded. "Only if it pleases you."

Bernie smiled. "I do like the way that sounds!" She moved down a little and leaned forward to kiss him. Her nipples brushed across Ian's chest as she slid the blindfold back over his eyes. Ian arched his back to press himself against her and Bernie immediately lifted herself up off him.

"Looks like we're going to have to cool you down." Bernie reached into the bowl on the headboard.

Ian could hear ice shifting, and then a few drops of cold water dripped onto his chest.

Bernie kissed him, her tongue pressing his lips apart. She pulled back just enough to whisper, "Open your mouth." After another kiss, she breathed, "Wider." Bernie traced the circle of his lips with her finger. "Stick out your tongue."

A drop of cold water splashed into Ian's mouth. Bernie moved closer and touched the tip of his tongue with something much rougher than her finger, and not quite ice cold. She pushed it partway into his mouth, and the coarse round object pushed Ian's teeth even further apart.

Her face was right next to his, her cheek brushing against the blindfold. "Bite."

Ian obeyed and his mouth was flooded with cool strawberry juice.

Pressing herself against him, Bernie licked some juice off Ian's chin and whispered, "Chew." She watched his jaw move as she reached down and moved the blue triangle to the side. Inching back, Bernie began to ease herself onto Ian's cock. She stopped. "Swallow."

Ian swallowed and Bernie bit into the other half of the strawberry. Juice dripped onto Ian's chest.

Lifting herself off him, Bernie moved to one side, and pushed off her panties. She felt him shiver as she got back on top of him. She kissed his chin, his neck, and then teased his mouth open with her tongue to feed him the last bit of strawberry. "Don't move." Ian held the fruit still in his mouth as Bernie rocked back, impaling herself.

"Oh yeah!" Bernie raised up and broke their connection. She whispered. "Eat it."

Ian did as he was told.

Bernie reached back and guided him back inside her. "You are so hot!" She slid down his length and then rose up as if to let him go. Ian arched his back to maintain contact. Bernie grinned and her voice was teasing. "Too hot."

Bernie grabbed an ice cube out of the mixing bowl. Turning the rest of the way round, she straddled Ian's chest and slid her ankles under his arms. She traced the length of his shaft with the edge of the melting ice as she lowered herself to his mouth. "Make me come."

Ian pressed his tongue against her and Bernie licked off the cool water. She brushed her teeth across the head of his cock. "Harder." She moaned, "Oh yeah." Taking him into her mouth, Bernie held the ice next to her lips and slowly backed away. The ice cooled his skin as she slid off him, and then her lips and tongue returned the heat. Ian pressed harder, using lips and tongue as forcefully as he dared. Bernie ground herself against his chin and growled, "Harder!"

Bernie rose up, and the last bit of the ice cube slipped through her fingers. It melted immediately on Ian's stomach. With her hands on his hips and her knees squeezing his chest, Bernie stiffened, shuddered, and then collapsed on top of him.

She had pulled away from him, but Ian raised his head to kiss her again. Bernie shivered and rolled off him. "Wow." Breathing in short ragged gasps, she turned around and Ian smiled. The blindfold had ridden up a little and Ian could just see under the edge. Bernie smiled back and tugged the blindfold back in place. She kissed him; he tasted like strawberries and sex. Bernie held her lips to his as she crawled on top of him, and reached back to guide him into her. She sank back, covering him completely. "God, I love the way you feel!"

Ian nodded. "You feel damn good yourself."

Bernie moved up, almost releasing him, and hesitated. "Do I sense a less than obedient attitude?"

"Not, uh..." Ian cleared his throat. "Not unless it pleases you."

"Very good." She eased herself back down his length until she held him completely. "You are an extraordinary slave and you shall be rewarded." Bernie began slowly moving up and down, her hands massaging his chest and nipples. In moments, Ian was arching his back and driving himself into her.

When Ian let go of the sheets he had clenched in his fists, Bernie pushed his blindfold off. She smiled. "That was very good. You have definitely earned your freedom."

Ian blinked.

"You are no longer my slave, and I am no longer your mistress." Bernie stroked his cheek. "You did really well. I liked that."

"Me too. It was..." Ian struggled to think of the right words. "Different."

Bernie looked slightly worried. "Good different?"

"Oh, yeah!" He shifted his arms as much as he could with his hands still tied to the headboard. "Very good."

Bernie smiled and squeezed him tight. The pressure seemed to push him out of her, and she frowned, disappointed. She slid to his side, keeping her body pressed close to his. "You look really good like that, you know. Are you comfy?"

Ian smiled. "Only if it pleases you."

Bernie grinned happily. "You sure learn fast."

"Thank you ma'am." A serious look crossed his face. "You seem to have a lot of experience at this sort of thing."

"Some." Bernie pulled her hand back across his chest. "Actually, I just read a lot. The whole 'only if it pleases you' routine comes from a book called The Claiming of Sleeping Beauty." Bernie rubbed the palm of her hand across his nipple. "You can borrow it if you like."

"Mm." Ian tugged at the scarves around his wrists. "Maybe later, I'm a little tied up right now."

"Cute." Bernie tickled his stomach and Ian tensed. She stopped for a moment, admiring his reaction. "I just love the way you move." She started tickling him again. Ian tried not to react but he was soon shaking the bed almost as violently as they had moments earlier.

"Stop, please." Ian gasped between fits of laughter.

"Okay." Bernie stopped, but kept her hand poised above his stomach. She grinned. "I'll bet you'd tell me anything I wanted to know right now, wouldn't you?"

Ian had a huge smile on his face. "Yes, ma'am."

"So tell me about this other woman of yours."

Ian looked startled.

"What's she like?" Bernie teased her fingers across his stomach and Ian laughed nervously.

"Actually," Ian hesitated, "This is a little weird, but I think you know her. I mean; I know you know…"

"What do you like most about her?"

"I, uh… "

"Is she very loud?"

"What?" Ian looked stunned.

"You know, vocal. Does she cry out when you make her come?"

"Red, okay? Red!" Ian shook his head angrily. "Could you untie these please?" He pulled harder on the scarves, and one of the knots started to come apart.

"I'm sorry." Bernie hurriedly untied the scarf and freed his hand. "I'm sorry." She reached across him and unknotted the scarf on his other wrist. "I had no right to do that." She moved down to untie his ankles.

"Goddamn right you didn't!" Ian flexed his hands and fingers.

"I can't believe I said that." Bernie glanced up at Ian, but looked away when she saw his expression. She started untying his right ankle. "I'm really sorry."

"Me too." Ian shook his head in frustration. "Goddamn it! I didn't want to hurt you, or anybody else! I didn't plan on meeting two women at the same time and I sure as hell didn't mean to get serious with both of you, it just..." Ian sighed, his anger rapidly fading to frustration. "I just let it happen. That's my fault and I'm sorry, but I honestly didn't know what to do. I told you as soon as I realized what was going on, and our relationship went from perfect to past tense in a chord change. You left me hanging at the concert, you wouldn't return my calls, and then the next day everything was back to perfect! Better even!

"You said we could work out the details as we went along and that you were totally okay with this, but now it seems like everything isn't okay. You've got every right to be angry or indifferent or whatever the hell you want, but could you please pick one and stick with it?"

Bernie silently nodded her head. A tear trailed down her cheek.

"Hey. I'm sorry." Ian reached down to touch Bernie's shoulder. "Come here." He pulled her up next to him and tried to give her a hug. Bernie hesitated but then let him hug her close.

"I'm sorry." Bernie pressed her head against his chest.

"Don't be. This is my fault. I'm the one who got us into this mess."

"Don't take all the credit. I shouldn't have asked about her. Not like that." Bernie turned her head to look at him. "I took advantage of the situation, and that was wrong. A scene is supposed to have a clear beginning, middle and end, and you're not supposed to let the real world muck it up. I just couldn't help it. I wanted to know how important we..." She took a breath and then shook her head as she let it out. "I just wanted to know about her. It's crazy. I don't mind that you're seeing her, I really don't. I'm really not the possessive type!" She sounded defiant, but then her voice got quiet. "I just want to know where I stand."

"But that's not what you asked about."

"I was getting there! I just wanted to know how it was different, you know, with her." Bernie studied him for a moment. "How would you feel if I was seeing another man?"

"I'd go crazy!"

"You'd be jealous?"

"Terribly."

Bernie ignored the tear starting to trail down her cheek. "You know, it's not fair to be jealous if you don't expect anyone else to be."

"But I do expect you to be. I mean, I can't believe you're not plotting to kill me!" Ian leaned back to look her in the eye. "I'm serious. I wouldn't blame you if you strangled me in my sleep."

Bernie wiped the tear away. "Then why did you let me tie you up?"

"I, uh..." Ian smiled. "I liked that."

"Me too." Bernie looked directly at him. "Does that mean you trust me?"

"I guess so." Ian met her gaze and nodded. "Yes, I do."

"You can, you know."

"I know."

Bernie rested her chin on his chest and studied him for a moment. "Do you love her?"

Ian smiled. "I love you."

"I love you too, but..." Bernie looked startled. "Is that the first time I've said that out loud?"

"To me? I think so."

"I do love you Ian, I really do."

"I'm glad. I love you too."

She took a breath, "Do you love her?"

Ian hesitated, then nodded reluctantly. "Yes."

"You seem ashamed to admit it."

"No! I'm not. I just don't want to hurt anyone."

"Good." Bernie looked relieved.

"Good?"

"It wouldn't be fair if you didn't love her."

"What do you mean, 'it wouldn't be fair?'" Ian looked confused. "How is it fair now?"

"Well, if you feel so bad about it, you could stop seeing her." She paused. "Or me."

"I..." Ian shook his head, glancing around the loft as though the right words were hidden within her paintings. "I could stop seeing you because I met her first, or I could break up with her because you and I slept together first, but I can't base a decision like that on some kind of first-come-first-serve luck of the draw."

"No pun intended."

"No? Oh god." Ian smiled. "You're terrible, you know that?"

Bernie giggled. "You said it."

"I know, I know. Look, I can't stand the thought of losing you. I love you." Ian sighed.

"But you love her too."

Ian slowly nodded his head. "I'm sorry."

"Hey, that's okay. I'm on your side." Bernie brushed her fingers along the side of his face. "How does she feel?"

"What do you mean?"

"Does she love you?"

Ian shook his head.

"She doesn't?" Bernie looked surprised.

"I'm not sure." Ian paused. "I don't know."

"I do." Bernie smiled. "She does."

"How would you know?"

Bernie snuggled up close to him. "Because she'd be crazy not to."

"There's a lot of craziness going around." Ian tried to curl around her and then started laughing.

"What?"

"Could you untie my foot?"

Tuesday, 7:40 am – The Dawn of a Bright New Day

The next morning Bernie bounded down the stairs and blasted through the lobby barely breaking stride long enough to shove the entry door open. As the door started to ease shut, she reached the sidewalk, turned and ran back through the door and into the lobby. Impatiently jogging in place at the bottom of the stairs, Bernie's blue and gold Berkeley shorts and T-shirt shifted with each step. When Ian rounded the corner and started down the last flight of stairs, Bernie grinned. "I was afraid I'd lost you!"

"Hey, come on! You had a head start." As Ian reached the ground floor, Bernie threw her arms around his neck, jumped up, and wrapped her legs around his waist.

"I had a really good time last night." She playfully kissed the tip of his nose. "I can't wait until Saturday. When are you going to pick me up?"

"I'll call you as soon as I get back, probably about noon." Ian shifted their weight a bit to keep his balance. "Do you really run every morning?"

"Four point four miles." She kissed him again and hopped down to the floor.

"Why four point four?" Ian followed her out of the building.

"Twice around campus." Bernie started jogging in place. "I would have been done by now, but you are such a distraction. You better get a lot of sleep on Friday!" She stood still long enough to kiss him and then jogged away.

Ian watched her run to the corner. She looked back and waved, Ian waved back, and then she jogged out of sight. "Sleep? Friday? I'm seeing Sandy on Friday." Ian's smile suddenly faded and he started walking toward his car. "That's gonna be a fun conversation."

The thick blanket of fog that had rolled in the night before was fraying into wispy chunks and the trees along Ellsworth cast mottled shadows on the sidewalk. Ian watched the flash and flicker of sunlight and his overcast expression began to clear. Two blocks from Bernie's apartment the storm clouds returned when he saw the parking citation tucked under the Mustang's left wiper. He pulled the green envelope off his car and read down the pre-printed list of citable offenses. A check mark had been scrawled across the box for "parking in a red zone."

"Aw, come on!" Ian walked around to the back of the car to look at the curb. He didn't notice the beige sedan across the street or the man in the dark suit who stepped out of it. Ian checked the ticket again. "I'm barely a foot into the red!" He'd been talking to himself, but the dark-suited man behind him responded.

"That still puts you in the red zone."

Ian turned around. The man had curly hair almost as dark as the brown leather wallet he took out of his jacket pocket. He barely flipped the wallet open long enough for Ian to see his badge. "I'm Detective Moisin. Is this your car?"

"Yeah, but give me a break! We're talking inches here." As Ian pointed at the blurred edge of the fading red paint, he noticed another man walking toward them from the sidewalk.

Moisin pointed at the other man, who wore a similar, slightly larger suit. "This is my partner, Detective Nagant and you must be Ian MacAran, am I right?"

"Yeah..." Ian nodded, trying to watch both men as Nagant stepped off the curb.

Moisin smiled. "Mr. MacAran, please face the car and put your hands on the roof."

Ian didn't move. "Why?"

Nagant grabbed Ian by the shoulders and spun him toward the Mustang. Ian thrust his hands out as he fell against the car and the parking ticket fluttered to the pavement. Nagant kicked Ian's feet apart as he said, "Spread your legs." Starting at the back of Ian's neck, Nagant methodically worked his hands over most of Ian's body. He handed Ian's phone, keys, wallet and money clip to Moisin.

Out of the corner of his eye, Ian saw his wallet disappear into Moisin's jacket pocket. "Hey! What the hell are you doing?"

Nagant pulled Ian's right arm back and slipped a handcuff around his wrist. "I'm handcuffing you." He pulled Ian's left arm back and Ian fell against the trunk of his car.

"Why?" Ian arched his back to keep his face off the red paint. "Why are you arresting me?"

Nagant cuffed Ian's other wrist. "Did we say you were under arrest?" He grabbed Ian's elbow and pulled him upright.

Ian stumbled, but stayed on his feet. "Dammit, what the hell is going on?"

Moisin bent down to pick up the parking ticket. "Let's just say this li'l ol' citation is probably the least of your problems right now."

They walked Ian across the street to the beige sedan and Nagant opened the rear door. "Watch your head." He pressed Ian's head down as he shoved him into the back seat.

"Sonofabitch!" Ian glared at the two men as Nagant slipped into the front passenger seat. "Will somebody please tell me what this is about?"

Moisin slid behind the wheel. "You want to get some breakfast before we drop him off?"

Nagant shook his head. "Nah. Let's get rid of him."

As Moisin drove the five miles to the police station, the partners traded stories about the horrors of prison life and joked about a man who'd been raped by another suspect in a holding cell. They ignored Ian completely.

When the trio reached Barrett Hogue's office, Ian's hands were still cuffed behind his back. Hogue's secretary gave Ian a cursory glance before nodding to Moisin. "Captain's expecting you."

"Thanks, Bob." Moisin led the way and Nagant shoved Ian in after him.

"Morning, Captain."

"Detective." Hogue nodded to each of his men, as he stood and extended his hand toward Ian. "Thank you for stopping by, Mr. MacAran."

"You make it sound like I had a choice." Ian turned sideways to show Barrett the handcuffs, and noticed that the detectives behind him were reflected in a mirror on the back of the door.

Barrett glared at Moisin and Nagant impatiently. "Dammit, I only asked you to pick him up!"

"Sorry, Captain." Nagant pulled his keys out of his pocket and stepped behind Ian. The detective sounded apologetic, but his reflection was smiling. He took off the handcuffs and gave his captain a thumbs-up that he thought Ian couldn't see.

Still acting outraged, Hogue shook his head disapprovingly as Moisin set Ian's belongings on the captain's desk. "That will be all, Detectives."

Moisin stood the parking ticket on edge between Ian's phone and wallet. "Yes, sir." He followed Nagant out.

"My apologies, Mr. MacAran." Hogue extended his hand again as the door snicked shut. "Even the best of us get carried away sometimes. I'm really sorry about the handcuffs."

"So am I." Ian stopped rubbing his wrist long enough to shake Hogue's hand. He glanced at his watch. "I need to make a phone call."

Hogue smiled. "You're not under arrest, Mr. MacAran. I just need to ask you a few questions."

Ian picked up his cellular. "I still need to make that call." He punched in five numbers, glanced up at Hogue and hit the wrong sixth digit. "Damn!" Ian pressed disconnect, and punched in the right numbers.

Hogue watched patiently as Ian waited for the call to go through, then pointed to a chair. "Why don't you have a seat?"

Ian shook his head as he spoke into the phone. "Ace? Ian. You're going to have to get another pilot for Pittsburgh."

Hogue's chair creaked as he sat down. He leaned back and listened.

"Well, no. I'm not positive I can't make it." Ian looked at Hogue. "How long is this going to take?"

Hogue shrugged. "That depends."

"Terrific." Ian rolled his eyes at the ceiling and spoke into the phone. "I'm sorry, Ace, I don't know how long I'll be, but Rashad is ready for a left seat checkout. ... What? ... I'm at the Oakland Police Station. ... Well, I don't know why. I'll give you all the details as soon as I find out myself." Ian met Hogue's patient stare and picked up his wallet. Glancing at some of the pictures on the wall, Ian slid the wallet into his back pocket. "Ace, I've got a better idea. Why don't you ride with Rashad and sign him off? ... You'll be impressed. ... No, I'll be free tomorrow." Ian glanced at Hogue, who hesitated before nodding his agreement. "Thanks, Ace." He closed the phone and slipped it into his shirt pocket.

Ian looked angrily at Hogue. "All right, Captain, why am I here?"

"Please, have a seat." Hogue waved toward the chairs facing the desk. "I just want to ask you a few questions."

"Did you lose my address?" Ian stayed on his feet.

"No. As a matter of fact, those two detectives spent much of the night waiting for you to get home. You were apparently otherwise engaged."

"Yeah, well, I wish I could say I was sorry I missed you, but I still haven't heard from Mick, I still don't know where he is and I still don't know where you can get the 22 minute version of "Helter Skelter" on CD."

Hogue shifted his weight forward and rested his arms on his desk. "You seem awfully sure of yourself."

"Sure of myself? Captain, I'm terrified. I'm afraid I may not be asleep and that this isn't just some Kafka-esque nightmare that'll be over as soon as I wake up." Ian glanced around the office. Numerous pictures of Hogue at various stages in his career stared out at him. Ian looked at the Captain. "Now. Why did you have your thugs drag me down here?"

"They're not thugs, but you're entitled to your opinion. You're here because I need to know everything you know about Michael Dale."

Ian picked up his keys. "We had this conversation last week, remember?"

"I remember a similar conversation. You were very polite and very cooperative. You weren't angry that I interrupted your construction project, and you weren't the least bit nervous that a cop was asking questions about you and your neighbor." Hogue stood up. "That's not normal."

"Maybe not, but it's civilized." Ian slipped his keys into his pocket. "Look, I'm sorry I don't fit your neat little psychoanalytical profile. Would you rather I just told you to 'fuck off?'"

"MacAran," Hogue angrily pointed his finger at Ian. "I know you're hiding something. If it has anything to do with Mick Dale, I need to know what it is."

Ian pointed back at Hogue. "Talk to Mick."

"Mick is dead."

"What?" For a moment, Ian stared at Hogue in shock, but then a knowing smile replaced his startled expression. "Bullshit."

Hogue seemed unprepared for that response. "I beg your pardon?"

"I said bullshit. It means I don't believe you. First the "bad" cops pick me up and try to get me off balance, then you come to the rescue pretending to be the "good" cop. That didn't get whatever results you expected, so now you're telling me my friend is dead. You think I would betray whatever state secrets Mick might have trusted me with just because you say he's dead? It really doesn't matter because I don't have any secrets! I don't know why you've staged this little production, but I'm not auditioning until I see a script."

"Fair enough." Hogue bent forward and took a large manila envelope out of his top desk drawer. Closing the drawer he tossed the envelope in front of Ian. "Try this."

Ian looked at the envelope for a moment before cautiously picking it up. He looked inside, glanced at Hogue and pulled out a dozen color photos. The top picture showed a white Cadillac in an otherwise empty parking lot. The driver's door and the trunk were open. Ian turned that picture up to look at the one underneath it.

"Oh my God." Ian flipped through a few more pictures, and then dropped them all on the desk. Backing away from the scattered bloody photographs he slumped into one of the chairs facing the desk.

Hogue left the pictures where they'd fallen. "Late Sunday night, some kids noticed that the keys had been left in Mick's rental. They decided to go for a drive. After a while, they stopped to see if there was anything valuable in the trunk." Hogue pointed to a photo of Mick's naked body, bent double and awkwardly crammed in next to the spare tire. "When they saw that, they panicked. One of them called 911."

The white walls of the trunk were smeared with blood, as was the plaster cast that covered Mick's left arm. Crusty handprints streaked the inside of the lid where he had tried to force his way out.

Hogue pointed to a close up of the open trunk. "From the marks, it's obvious he tried to get out, but he was probably very weak. The coroner estimates that he was in there eight or nine hours before he died early Sunday morning."

"My God." Ian stared at the picture. "How could this... who could... what happened to him?"

"At first we thought he'd bled to death, but actually, technically, he died of shock. They peeled off his skin a strip at a time. The coroner said she'd never seen anything like it. There's a distinct pattern to each group of cuts, the same design. Strips about 5 millimeters across and 50 centimeters long were cut in groups of three." Hogue showed Ian a close-up of Mick's arm. "The first attempts were rough. The depth of the cuts varies and some of the long strips tore away when they were twisted to the side. At the top of the later designs, the cuts spread out and the strips get wider." Hogue pointed to another photo. "On his right arm and on the right side of his chest, what we think were the last two designs, they braided the strips of his skin together like rope."

"How could anyone...?" Ian turned his head away from the picture and then looked up at Hogue. "Who did this? Why would anyone want to hurt Mick?"

"I don't know. The kids found the car at the marina, but it could have been driven there from almost anywhere. We're getting as much information from the kids and the car as we can, and we're canvassing the marina for anyone who may have seen something useful." Hogue shifted his weight a little. "The only other lead we have at the moment is you."

"Me? Why me?"

"Because I know you're not telling me everything you know. I know that..." Hogue leaned back to reach into the open desk drawer, "because I read Mick's logbook." He opened the short wide book to the second page. "What were you and Mick doing in Guadalajara on March 5th," Hogue turned the page, "and again on March 17th?"

Ian didn't say anything.

"You know what really puzzles me? Except for his solo flights, these are the only two entries written by Mick himself. Why is it that you signed his logbook for all the other flights you went on, except these?" Hogue pointed to several "dual instruction" entries with Ian's signature, instructor number, and the expiration date of his certificate. "When he flew by himself, of course, you didn't sign his book, but I'm sure Mick didn't fly a Citation jet to

Mexico by himself." Hogue looked at Ian expectantly. "Did he?"

"No." Ian shook his head. "But there's not much point in logging multi-engine turbine time before you have a pilot certificate. Besides, Mick only flew for a few minutes each trip."

"Then why did he log the whole trip, Oakland to Guadalajara?"

"He probably thought it would look cool." Ian sighed. "Does it matter now?"

"Where did you go in Guadalajara?"

"I went to Shaggy's."

"Shaggy's Pizza?" Hogue raised an eyebrow. "In Mexico?"

"At the airport."

"Okay, and where did Mick go?"

"I don't know." Ian shrugged.

"He didn't log the trip back. Why not?"

"Mick didn't come back with me."

"Then how did he get back?"

"He said something about a Cinco de Mayo celebration and that he'd be driving back."

"Both times?"

"He told me not to worry about it. I didn't worry about it."

"So, who did he meet in Mexico?"

"I don't know, but let me ask you something. You're in charge of Narcotics. Wouldn't Mick's murder be a homicide investigation?"

"They're working on it, but this is also a Narcotics matter." Hogue considered him for a moment. "Mick was working undercover for me. He was a police officer."

"What? How could Mick be a cop? We…" Ian scanned the office as though the answer might be in one of the pictures on the walls. In one photo, a much-younger Hogue stood proudly next to an LAPD patrol car, wearing a patrolman's uniform. Another picture showed an older Hogue and what looked like his family: a wife, kids, a Doberman.

"Oh God!" Horrified, Ian looked at Hogue. "I didn't even think: Have you told Clara?"

"She identified the body."

"Oh, Christ! How is she? Is she all right?"

"How could she be all right?" Hogue shook his head. "She's coping. School's out so she took the kids to stay with her family in Guadalajara. I took them to the airport yesterday after… wait a minute!" Hogue pointed an accusatory finger at Ian. "That's where you landed, isn't it?"

"Guadalajara, yeah."

"Not Guadalajara, after that. Clara's family owns all that land just outside the city. What was it…?" Hogue glanced up at the ceiling, trying to remember. "Something Cattle and something-or-other. Orozco! Carlos Orozco!" Hogue stared triumphantly into Ian's eyes. "You refueled at Guadalajara, picked up the cocaine at the ranch and used your overflight permit to bring it back to Oakland."

Ian didn't blink. "What cocaine?"

"The cocaine Mick was using to smoke out…" Hogue cut himself off. "You know damn well what cocaine!"

"Captain, when I got back to Oakland, I was met by two Customs agents and a dog who went through every compartment of the airplane. They didn't find anything, cocaine or otherwise."

"Dammit, MacAran, I know you were living off your credit cards until you flew Mick to Mexico. Now you have a new car, and all your past-due bills have been paid up. Where did all that money come from?"

"Las Vegas. I figured out how to win at blackjack."

"Blackjack?"

"I count cards."

"Bullshit." Hogue glared at him but Ian just shrugged. Hogue shook his head and sighed. "Bullshit." He stepped over to the wall and pointed to a photo hanging between a commendation for bravery and a diploma from Southern California State University. It was a picture of a corner liquor store with a spray-painted mural covering the side of the old building. In the mural, black and brown families were linked collar to collar by a powdery white chain, and above their heads, "Keeping us in chains!" had been sprayed in the same bright white. Below the children's necks, big block letters begged, "Boycott Cocaine!"

"MacAran, I'm not naive. I realize there's an unholy amount of money in all this. Christ! We busted a kid last week with two hundred thousand dollars in his trunk! How can I tell a teenager with that much money that he'd be better off with a part-time job at Burger King?" Hogue looked back at the photo. "What would the FAA think about your flights to Mexico?"

"I told you, I go through customs every time I get back."

"There's more to it than that, and I'm going to find out what it is." Hogue studied Ian's confident expression. "What about your license?"

"What about it?"

"I'm sure the FAA wouldn't want you flying until we can assure them that you're not involved in any illegal activity."

"So much for due process. I thought you were investigating a murder. What does harassing me have to do with finding the bastards that killed Mick?" Ian glared at Hogue for a moment, and then his anger faded to disgust. His voice was quiet, disappointed. "You don't have a clue, do you?"

"Don't I?"

"Your detectives dragged me down here in handcuffs talking tough about how much trouble I was in, but they were careful not to tell me I was under arrest. They didn't read me my rights or any of that technical stuff they'd have been so brutally careful to do if you actually thought I had anything to do with this. You're fishing. What was I supposed to do, get all flustered and confess?"

Hogue shook his head uneasily. "I do owe you an apology there, MacAran. You weren't supposed to be handcuffed."

"You didn't have to go through all this theatrical bullshit, Captain. I'd still have been happy to tell you everything I know. I just don't have the information you need. Mick was my student and my friend. Obviously not a close friend; he didn't tell me he was a cop!"

"MacAran, everybody makes mistakes. If you've just stumbled into this thing and you're trying to find a way out, I can help."

Ian glanced from the captain's eyes to the bloody photos on the desk.

Hogue also looked down at the pictures of Mick and sighed. "Right now I just want to find Mick's killer. I don't care about anything else. If you know anything that can help me find the people who did this, tell me. I guarantee I can get you immunity from prosecution on anything short of murder."

Ian considered Hogue's offer just long enough for the Captain to smile and nod knowingly.

"If," Ian emphasized, "and I mean *if* I knew anything, which I don't, and if I'd done anything I'd want immunity for, which I haven't," Ian pointed at the photos, "could you protect me from the bastards that did this to Mick?"

Hogue didn't answer.

"I'd be in a lot of trouble, wouldn't I?"

"I'm afraid so."

"Right." Ian glanced at his watch. "You said Mick was working undercover. Would the people he was investigating have killed him if they found out he was a cop?"

"That's a definite possibility."

"Who knew that Mick was a cop?"

"We're checking into that."

"Good. Any more questions?"

Hogue reached for his intercom. "I'll have someone take you back to your car."

Ian started toward the door. "I'll walk."

Hogue watched him leave before moving back to the working side of his desk. "Who else knew that Mick was a cop?" The big chair creaked as Hogue sat down. "Damn good question, MacAran."

Ian actually took a cab back to his car, and he only glanced over his shoulder through the rear window twice. When he started his car the radio rocked to life in the middle of "Whole Lotta Love." Ian jabbed at the power button and silenced Led Zeppelin. His hand was shaking. "Calm down, MacAran." He took a deep breath, and let it out slowly. "Don't panic." Ian turned the radio back on, found an all-news station and looked at his hand. His fingers were still shaking. Ian made a fist, straightened his fingers and the tremors disappeared. He shifted the car into reverse, backed into the red zone and then pulled out into the street. Instead of heading for the freeway home, Ian drove down Shattuck into Oakland. He stopped in front of Weaver's Guns.

A buzzer sounded when Ian walked into the gun shop, and buzzed again as the door swung back through the infrared beam. A middle-aged man looked up from his stool behind the counter. He had a jelly donut in one hand and there were flakes of sugar on his upper lip. A Styrofoam cup of coffee seemed to float above the dozens of different handguns displayed in the long glass counter, and the wall behind the clerk was covered with racks of rifles and shotguns. The clerk swallowed. "Morning."

"Hi." Ian glanced at the guns below the steaming coffee. "I'd like to buy a gun."

"Well, you've come to the right place." The clerk stood up. "What kind of gun would you like?"

"I'm not sure. Something reliable." Ian glanced over the man's shoulder at a row of assault rifles. "What would you recommend for self defense?"

"Hm. I'm no expert, at least not on guns. I sell real estate, but my brother-in-law had a heart attack, so I'm helping watch the store for him and my sister. I can show you the gun he usually recommends for most people."

"That would be great. Thanks."

The real estate agent unlocked the back of the display case and slid open one of the doors. Pushing aside an old western-style revolver, he took a large black automatic from the front of the case. He grabbed a large square of green felt from the back counter and spread it on the glass before lowering the gun to the counter-top. "This is a," The clerk read the tag tied to the trigger guard and then set the gun on the felt. "Glock 9mm. It holds 13 bullets."

Ian picked it up. "It's heavy." He raised the gun and pointed it toward the back of the store. The sights drifted across a dark blue vest that hung below a "LAW ENFORCEMENT ONLY" sign. Ian chuckled. "Fishing vests for police officers?"

The clerk glanced at the rack below the sign and nodded. "They're bullet proof."

"Oh." Ian set the Glock on the soft felt. "What kind of bullets does this use?"

"It's a 9mm. You can use either hollow point or jacketed. My brother-in-law says the right round will stop a charging elephant."

"A gun this size?"

"That's what he says."

"That's okay." Ian nodded. "I'm only worried about charging burglars."

The real estate agent chuckled as he took a card out of his shirt pocket. "Do you live in an apartment?"

"Uh, no." Ian reached for his wallet. "House."

"Do you own it?"

Ian took out his Visa card. "Me and the bank."

"Hm." The agent slid his business card back behind his ballpoint pens.

Ian set the credit card next to the Glock. "I'll take it. What kind of shells did your brother-in-law say would stop elephants?"

"Uh; the best bullets for stopping power are Law Grabbers, but you have to be a cop to buy those. I can sell you some great hollow points."

"Okay, I'll take a box."

The real estate agent picked up Ian's credit card. "You know there's a waiting period, right?"

"I need something as soon as possible, like today."

"Sorry. In California you have to wait 10 days between the purchase and receipt of any handgun. It's called a cooling off period."

"Only in California?"

"It varies from state to state. Hell, in Nevada you just walk in, buy what you want and walk out. No muss, no fuss.

I used to deal blackjack and I remember one time a friend of mine bought a shotgun on her coffee break." He chuckled. "Scared the shit out of the pit-boss."

"I'll bet." Ian pointed at the rifles on the wall behind the clerk. "Can I buy one of those?"

"Sure, but this isn't Nevada. You'd still have to wait. Do you want to stay with the Glock?"

Ian nodded reluctantly. "Yeah."

"Great. I just need you to fill out a few forms."

The agent stepped over to the cash register and returned with a short stack of paper. "This one's for the state. This one is for the Federal government, and this is for, uh..." He turned the form right side up so he could read it. "Oh, never mind. That's just an old one of these." He pushed the newer federal form toward Ian and tossed the old one in the trash. "Do you need a pen?"

"Please." Ian took the "Bob's Real Estate" pen and started printing and signing.

Tuesday, 4:41 pm – Security Gate,
Cyclotron Road, Berkeley

When Tony heard the Ferrari approaching, he picked up his pack and stepped back from the edge of the sidewalk. The black Spyder roared toward the security checkpoint, screeched through a tight bootlegger turn and stopped inches from the curb facing back down the hill.

"Excellent timing, Des-man!" Tony stepped off the curb, swung open the door and carefully slipped into the passenger seat. "Thanks for making like a taxi."

"You said it was an emergency." Des flicked his cigarette butt out into the street. "What's the problem?"

Tony wedged his pack between his feet and closed the door. "If we play this right, nothing. In fact..." He reached for his seatbelt as Des accelerated through the intersection. The light turned green behind them. "Everything is freaking fantastic! They've found the grail. That is, they've invented it. They've invented the holy fucking grail!"

"Who?"

"Which going-to-be-the-next-Intel freaking company have I been talking about for the last three weeks? DKI! They've got a new chip, the T-minus. They actually named it after one of their physicists, somebody obscure, but everyone's calling it the T-minus, and this thing totally kicks ass! It's a quantum leap beyond parallel processing. We're talking the definitive computer architecture for the next century; hell, the next millennium! It's all new technology so everything about the T-minus chip is patented and that means zero competition for at least 7 years!"

"Patents only give you the right to sue, Tony. If this thing's any good, it'll be copied." Des shook his head. "Besides, I thought they were months away from making an announcement. Last time you talked to your brother, he said they were having major problems. Does it even work?"

"No, Des, I want to spend everything I own buying DKI because the defective chips will make great designer jewelry. Of course it fucking works! Rob's seen it, and my brother knows his stuff. I'm telling you, this chip is going to totally redefine the video gaming industry!"

"Do you ever think about anything but games?"

"No. Well, there's also sex. You gotta understand, Des, games are competition and competition is life! Look, in addition to games, this thing will revolutionize everything that has anything to do with computers and anybody who buys in now will get filthy rich, which is why you're going to be on board but that's not what I'm into. This chip is going to create a simulation gaming revolution that I'd give my left testicle to be part of. DKI is the place to be, and with or without you guys, I'm going to be there!"

"Okay, okay." Des stopped behind a line of cars waiting for the light at College Avenue. "We'll do it but at the right time. This morning the stock was down another quarter, and..."

"Now, Des. Right now! DKI rallied about three hours ago, and closed up four and half."

"What happened?"

"A report in the Journal listed DKI as a long shot with enormous potential. They cited "reliable sources" talking about a "breakthrough product". If they know about the T-minus Chip, we may already be too late. Goddammit, we've got to move now!"

Des glanced sideways at Tony. "What are you on?"

"What do you mean?"

"I've never seen you like this."

"You've never seen anything like this fucking chip. It's absolutely freaking fantastic. The games I'm gonna be able to create with this..."

"How much faster can this T-minus Chip be? I thought we were already pushing the limits of processor speed."

"It's not just faster, Des. It's instantaneous."

"Bullshit!"

"Virtually instantaneous."

"How many seconds in 'virtually'?"

"Less than," Tony snapped his fingers. "Did you catch the announcement last month about particles that move in negative time?"

Des considered. "No."

"I guess it wouldn't have been in the financial section." Tony chuckled. "Okay. Take notes, 'cause this will definitely be on the test. About a year ago, a team at Stanford started studying an anomaly that kept turning up in specific kinds of accelerator experiments. Up 'til then, no one could explain why they were getting exactly the same kind of erroneous readings, nanoseconds before the collision took place. What they were getting was fringe traces of the collision before it actually happened. About six months ago, a physicist named Braen Anwir was able to reproduce the effect without using an accelerator. He immediately took a sabbatical or something and went to work for DKI."

Des shifted gears. "Are you saying they put a particle accelerator on a chip?"

"No, Des, the effect was discovered while they were using an accelerator. It turns out that generating the t-minus signal doesn't require anything like an accelerator."

"You keep saying t-minus. What is that?"

"Time, Des. Negative time."

"Right." Des shook his head skeptically. "When do we beam up?"

"Hey! Some science fiction is actually about the science!"

"Not the crap you've been watching."

"Fuck you!" Tony crossed his arms and stared out the window.

"Okay, I'm sorry." Des rolled his eyes. "How does this thing work?"

"The T-minus Chip uses a matrix of standard and t-minus transistors to create a virtually instantaneous processor, regardless of how complicated the task is."

"What's a t-minus transistor?"

"That's a very closely guarded secret."

"You can tell me."

Tony hesitated, "I don't know."

"Okay, what's the clock speed?"

"Clock speed doesn't mean anything with this processor. If you want to use clock speed as a reference, you could say that it has the equivalent of a clock speed in the giga-hertz range."

"Come on! Giga-hertz? That's crazy." Des glanced suspiciously at Tony. "You are on something."

"Open your brain, Des, every new discovery since fire has sounded crazy. This thing works. Rob says it's toasted every benchmark they could think of. The T-minus Chip isn't the next generation, Des, it's a completely new technology and it's our ticket to anywhere we want to go. Are you with me or not?"

"Well..." Des considered. "What did Brian say?"

"He won't do it. Not even if Erica goes along, which she won't. I spent all afternoon trying to talk some sense of adventure into her, but she's flat-out not interested."

"Why not? Is this a sure thing or isn't it?"

"Absolutely. But Erica says she's happy where she is and she doesn't want to risk losing what she calls her 'financial independence'."

"Figures. That means we can't do anything without dissolving Conquistador."

"Exactly, but if we cash out Conquistador, we each get a little under four million. That'll get me influence," Tony's expression changed and he shook his head angrily, "but not much direct input into the company. Why did Brian and Erica have to go soft now? Together, the four of us could have put someone on the Board of Directors."

"I didn't think you cared so much about power and money."

"You really don't listen do you? It's not the money, Des, it's never been the money! I want to be on the team! I want to be part of this technology! Think about what this kind of processing power can do! Virtual reality that's literally, I mean totally and completely, indistinguishable from the real world. I'm talking three-dimensional, 360-degree simulation, totally involving all your senses." Tony looked up at the sky before staring intently at Des. "The games I can make for the T-minus will fucking blow people away! A year from now it'll be just me and Bill Gates, man!"

"Hey, I'm not out of this yet." Des considered. "What if we rolled over the eight million we have into eighty million?"

"How?"

"Shell-game."

"That crazy Mexican drug thing?"

Des nodded as he slowed down for a stop sign. "How much of DKI could we buy with eighty million dollars?"

"Eighty? Not quite half, but that would still give us effective control of..." Tony thought about it. "Jesus! How long will Shell-game take?"

"Total turnaround, four, maybe five days, but think about it; we'd own half of DKI."

Tony shook his head. "Actually, eighty million would only buy about a third of it. Less if the stock keeps going up, but that's more than we'd have even if Erica did have balls to go for it." Tony nodded his head decisively as Des pulled into his driveway. "Let's do it!"

Des turned off the engine. "We won't be able to cash out Conquistador overnight. But we can borrow against the stock, can't we?"

"Definitely. I'll check with Dad. I'm sure he knows some people who can help."

"Good. We've got one pilot, but we need someone for the second plane." Des paused. "In fact, we need a second plane. Could Cindy...?"

"I'll ask her." Tony unbuckled his seatbelt. "I bet she'll be thrilled."

"Great. Call me as soon as you've talked to her and we'll work out the details."

Tony opened the door and stepped out onto the driveway. "You got it, Des-man." He grabbed his backpack, closed the door and rushed toward his house. As he ran, the house sensed the tiny remote on his key chain and the front door opened automatically.

Two hours later, Des' cell phone rang as he shot off Highway 880 onto the Hegenberger exit. He slowed to 70 mph, and slipped his half-finished CafFiend into the drink holder. He slipped the phone out of his pocket, but quickly dropped it in his lap. He needed both hands as he downshifted twice and screeched to a stop behind a Friendly Cab. Des retrieved the cellular. "Yeah?"

"Des, I got it!"

"Tony?"

"No, Attila the Hun." There was a whining, rumbling hum in the background. "Actually, I'm going to get it. Nothing's signed yet but that won't be a problem. Bottom line: we're solvent! We've got the money!"

"Excellent!" The light changed and Des followed the cab toward Oakland airport. "Where are you? You sound like you're in a blender."

"I'm on BART, man. I'm meeting Tobin in Walnut Creek."

"Who's Tobin?"

"Dad's lawyer."

"Oh, yeah. Why are you meeting him?"

"Because his firm is loaning us 7.4 million against our half of Conquistador."

"But it's worth more than eight!"

"Of course it is, Des, but he's not buying us out, the stock is just collateral. He's a friend and all, but he's not going to loan us full value." Tony paused. "7.4 is enough, isn't it?"

"Yeah, it'll have to be. What about Cindy?"

"She was all gloom and doom at first, but I told her that if she didn't do it, somebody else would. So we talked about it for a while and I reminded her how much we both liked "Mission: Impossible". Now she's totally excited about it. When do we go?"

"When can you get the cash?"

"I'm on my way. Figure... 7:30, maybe 8:00."

"Tonight? He is giving you cash, isn't he?"

"But of course! Like I said, I'm on my way right now."

"And he has no problem with that?"

"Don't worry about Tobin, he's my Dad's attorney. I hinted that we're worried about an insider trading charge and that we're trying to be discreet. He won't ask questions."

"Then we're on for tomorrow morning. Plan on ten o'clock at Cindy's airplane club. Can she get a plane on such short notice?"

"Usually. I'll call you if there's a problem. Have you ever been to her club before?"

"No."

"It's kind of hidden behind ... shit! I gotta go. I'll call you later with directions. Bye."

"Later." Des slipped the phone into his pocket and zipped across Bay Farm Island at about 60 mph. He pulled up in front of Ian's house humming the theme from Mission Impossible, but he stopped humming when he glanced across the street. The skeleton of Mick's unfinished second floor stood out against the traces of fog drifting toward the East Bay hills. All along the rest of the block, trash cans and recycling bins waited for the next morning's pickup, but the sidewalk in front of Mick's house was empty.

Des checked his hair in the rearview mirror and then stepped out of the car. He tossed his shades on the passenger seat and adjusted his shirt as he walked up Ian's driveway and around the garage to the front door.

Inside, Ian was putting detergent in the dishwasher. When the doorbell rang, he yelled, "Come on in, it's open." He latched the door to the dishwasher and twisted the timer to START. Water surged as Ian walked around the breakfast

bar and into the family room. "I'm all set. How was ... oh."
He stopped next to the pool table. "Hi, Des."

"Hey, Ian. How's it going?" Des closed the front door.

"It's going okay, but I am on my way out." Ian looked
at his watch. "What's up?"

"We are." Des flashed a friendly smile. "Everything's
set for tomorrow morning; ten o'clock. I even talked to
Carlos. He wants to talk to you before we go south, but
I'm sure..."

"I told you I'm not interested."

"How can you not be interested? This is your plan!
You're the pilot, the mastermind; you have to be
interested."

"No." Ian shook his head. "I don't."

"Come on, Ian, don't fuck with me. Carlos won't
deliver if you're not the pilot."

"Why not? Doesn't he trust you?" Ian studied Des suspiciously. "Where is Mick, Des? Why isn't he with you?"

"He's just, uh..." Des shifted his gaze down to Ian's
chest and then back up to his eyes.

"He's just dead. But you knew that, didn't you?" Ian
moved toward Des. "You wouldn't be here trying to take
over unless you knew he was dead."

Des stayed where he was, on the brass trim strip
between the entry tiles and the family room carpet.
"Look, things have gotten a little bit complicated, Ian, but
that doesn't affect your end of this."

"I don't have an 'end of this.'" Ian stopped next to the
fireplace and noticed the long row of Beatles CDs. He
whispered, "Shit."

"What?"

Ian's hands balled into fists. "How did you find out Mick was a cop?"

Des held up his hands. "Don't leap to any conclusions. I didn't have anything to do with that."

"But you know what happened, right?"

"What's your point, Ian? I know Mick was a cop and I know he's dead, but I didn't kill him. I'm sorry he's dead, but life goes on, and so does business." Des looked directly into Ian's eyes. "This is business, serious business, Ian, and I'm a very serious business man."

"Don't flatter yourself, Des." Ian looked disgusted. "You're just a punk thuggy drug dealer."

"Yeah? Well you're a mule, Ian. My mule!" Des pointed his finger at Ian's chest, but quickly softened his angry expression into a tense smile. "Ian, you've got to realize that you're in way too deep to have any choice in this. Just carry what I tell you, where I tell you, and everything will be all right. All right?"

Ian raised an eyebrow. "What's a mule? A smuggler?"

"Yeah." Des nodded. "A carrier: a mule."

Ian considered that for a moment, and then shook his head. "Not anymore." Ian stepped past Des and opened the front door. "Go fuck yourself, Des."

"Ian, listen to me." Des followed Ian back into the entryway, but reached ahead and pushed the door shut. "You don't have a choice, because I don't have a choice. We're both stuck in the same high stakes game with some very serious people. These guys play for keeps and there is absolutely no middle ground. You're either an asset or a liability. And if you're a liability..." He hesitated.

"Yes?"

"Do I have to spell it out?"

Ian spoke very softly. "Are you threatening me, Des?"

"Come on, Ian. Be reasonable. Neither one of us wants to end up like Mick, but look at the positives: you can make more money in one day than most people see in a lifetime." Des paused dramatically. "You can also get yourself killed." He snapped his fingers. "Just like that."

Ian grabbed the front of Des' shirt and shoved him against the door. "It does look like you think you're threatening me!"

"Hey!"

"What happened to Mick, Des? Did he become a liability? To you? To somebody else? Who killed him?" Ian was seething. "Who killed Mick you motherless fuck? Did you help them peel off his skin one strip at a time and leave him to bleed to death in the trunk of that goddamned car?"

Des struggled until Ian pulled him back and slammed him into the door. "I want an answer, Des. Did you kill Mick?"

The frame shuddered as Ian shoved him into the door again. Des winced. "No!"

"Then who did?"

"I don't know!"

"You're lying." Ian slammed Des into the door even harder. "Now, I want to know who killed Mick."

Des jumped when the doorbell rang. "Paul Neault! It was Paul."

They stared at each other for a heartbeat, and then Ian called out, "Just a minute!" He slid Des to one side to look through the tiny hole in the door. Muttering, "Saved by the bell," Ian pulled Des away from the door. Des braced himself for another hammering but Ian just glared at him. "Stay away from me, Des. You understand?"

"Yeah." Des smiled, trying to shrug off Ian's anger. "Whatever you say."

Ian stared at him until the smile faded and Des looked away. Ian loosened his grip on Des' shirt. "Now I'm going to open this door, Des, and you're going to politely and graciously get the fuck out of my life! Got it?"

Des nodded and Ian shoved him to the side. Des hastily straightened his shirt as Ian opened the door.

Standing outside, on the concrete porch, Sandy was wearing a knee-length red skirt with an off-white blouse. She looked concerned. "Is everything all right?" She leaned forward to kiss Ian, but then noticed Des standing to one side of the door. "Oh. Hi, Des."

Des nodded to her. In the kitchen, a saucepan was gently knocking against the side of the dishwasher.

"Everything's fine, come on in." Ian motioned Sandy inside. "Des was just leaving."

"Bye, Des." Sandy waved as Des stepped outside.

Ian shut the door before Des could say anything.

Des stood on the porch and finished straightening his shirt. "Asshole!" He glared at the closed door for a moment before stalking back to his car. Fishing his keys out of his pocket, he opened the trunk and pulled a small leather case out of the cramped space next to the spare tire. Glancing at Ian's front door, Des slammed the trunk lid closed.

Setting the case on the passenger seat, Des slipped behind the wheel. He looked up the street and then adjusted the rearview mirror as he checked behind the Ferrari. Glancing furtively at Ian's door, he reached inside his shirt and pulled out a silver cylinder that hung on a thin chain around his neck. Des shook the cylinder a few strokes and then unscrewed the top. A miniature spoon attached to the top slid out with a dose of fine white powder. Des snorted the coke into his left nostril and then repeated the ritual on the right side. Tucking the tube back into his shirt Des leaned back and sniffed a few times to get all the coke into his system.

"Fucking asshole!" Des glared at Ian's front door as he opened the leather case. Inside was a nickel-plated Colt .45. Des pulled out the gun and a magazine of hollow point shells. He sniffed again as he pushed the magazine into the .45, and angrily slid the action back to chamber a round.

Des jumped when something moved in the Ferrari's right side mirror. He shoved the gun under the lid of the case and held it out of view as he watched Ian's garage door slide up. Ian's Mustang pulled out of the garage and turned toward Doolittle Drive. Des waited until the car disappeared around the corner before flipping the .45 over so it nestled into its padded compartment. Closing the leather case, he reached for his cell phone and hammered out a Berkeley number. While he waited for the connection, Des angrily pushed in the Ferrari's cigarette lighter and dug out a cigarette. "Come on Ross, pick up the phone you fucking... Ross?" Des listened. "Yeah, it's me. Listen, I need you and Gil to meet me in Alameda. You remember where Mick Dale's house is, on Russell? Yeah, I'm parked across the street."

Des closed the phone and shoved it back into his pocket. When the lighter popped up, he glared at it for a moment before lighting his cigarette and taking a deep drag. He settled back into the driver's seat and drummed his fingers on the gun case. Smoke swirled from his nose as he stared at Ian's house.

Tuesday, 10:42 pm – Trash Night,
Russell Street, Alameda

Des and his Ferrari were gone by the time Ian and Sandy returned. The garage door started up when Ian keyed the remote, but he drove past his driveway to let Sandy out at her car. Then he backed the Mustang up the drive and into the garage.

Retrieving her briefcase from her trunk, Sandy glanced across the street. The only other car she could see was a black Pontiac GTO parked between the trash containers a few driveways past Mick's house. The muscle car's engine was running, and wisps of vapor trailed from the exhaust pipe, fading away as they drifted toward San Jose. Sandy grabbed a canvas tote bag, closed the trunk and met Ian at the driveway. "You look thoughtful."

Ian pointed at the house across the street. "I was just noticing the way the stars shine through the framing." Mick's addition stood bleak and skeletal against the night sky. "Ken got a lot done today. They didn't even have the ceiling joists up yesterday."

"It looks spooky." Sandy shivered. "See that black car across the street?"

"Yeah?"

"There aren't any lights on inside, but the engine is running and I'm pretty sure someone is sitting behind the wheel. Who could they be waiting for at this time of night?"

Ian looked. "It's probably the police."

"A stakeout?"

Ian nodded.

"Who do you think they're after?"

"Me." Ian reached for the canvas bag in Sandy's hand. A fold of white terry cloth was visible at the top of the bag. "Don't you like my towels?"

"It's a robe, silly." Sandy let him take it from her.

"But I like the way you look in my shirts."

"It's too cold in the morning for just a shirt."

He leaned toward her. "I'll turn up the heat."

"I'll wear whatever you like." Sandy kissed him, but her expression was more concerned than passionate. "Why would the police be watching you?"

Ian turned his head to glance at the GTO. "Do you want the long version or the short version?"

"I've got all night."

"Let's go inside where it's warm." Ian led the way through the garage and into the house. He set Sandy's bag just inside his bedroom door and continued down the hall. "I'm going to get a beer. Would you like something?"

"No, thanks." Sandy set her briefcase next to her bag. "Wait, do you have any more root beer?"

Ian was already halfway down the hall. "I'll check." When he got to the kitchen, Ian took both drinks out of the fridge and set the soda on the counter. Twisting the cap off his Henry's, Ian downed a third of it in several big gulps. When Sandy joined him, he set his beer down and opened the soda. "Would you like a glass?"

"No, thank you."

Ian handed her the can and she took a sip. "So tell me."

"What?"

"Why would the police want to stake you out?"

"Right, the police." Ian raised his bottle again, but lowered it before it touched his lips. "Do you remember Mick?"

"The pushy guy from across the street?"

"Yeah. I thought he was just a contractor, slightly crazy maybe, but basically a normal guy." Ian hesitated, trying to figure out where to start. "I don't think I've ever been so clueless about somebody! First I thought he was okay, then he told me he was a drug dealer, but it turns out that Mick was actually an undercover cop. I found that out this morning when the police dragged me in for a chat. I got handcuffed but not arrested because somebody killed Mick and the police think I know who did it."

"My God! He's dead?"

Ian nodded.

"And the police think you know ... do you?" Sandy held up her hand to keep Ian from answering. "Wait. First things first: who's your lawyer?"

"I don't have one."

"Well, you do now."

"Thanks, but I don't think I need..."

"Hon, if the police think you're involved in the murder of an undercover cop, you need a lawyer." Sandy looked at him carefully. "Now, do you know who killed Mick?"

"I'm not sure. I don't really know enough about what Mick was doing, or who was involved."

"But you think the police are watching you?"

"Maybe. Hell, I don't know. That car across the street is probably just a couple of kids making out." Ian shrugged. "Listen, there's something else we need to talk about."

"You're not going to drop this just when it's getting interesting, are you?" Sandy looked disappointed. "Why would the police think you knew something about Mick's death?"

"They have his logbook." Ian hesitated. "I flew Mick to Mexico a couple times and he recorded both trips in his logbook. They know I'm involved in the investigation he was working on."

"Really? What kind of investigation?"

"The part I know about is drug smuggling."

"You definitely need a lawyer! I need something to write on" Sandy pulled a magnetized pad off the fridge. It had "We Need" printed across the top and a pen attached to it by a short string. Sandy popped the cap off the pen. "Okay, the first thing we have to do is get..."

Ian interrupted her. "Sandy, listen, I appreciate the offer, but there's something else we really need to talk about first." He studied her face. "I don't know how to say this, but, uh..."

Sandy waited expectantly.

"I love you, Sandy, I really do."

She smiled. "I think you said that very well."

"That's not what I meant! I mean yes, I love you. I do. But..." Ian shook his head in frustration. "That's not what I need to tell you."

"Okay." Sandy waited.

"Maybe this isn't the right way to handle this, but I've been trying to tell you this all week, and either the timing isn't right, or our schedules don't mesh, or..." Ian sighed. "Or I just lose my nerve. I never wanted to do anything to hurt you, I swear. The longer I wait, the more despicable I feel."

"This sounds pretty serious." Sandy smiled reassuringly. "It's okay. I don't care what's going on with the police. That doesn't matter. Whatever happens, I'm on your side." She took his hand and squeezed. "I believe in you."

"This isn't about that!"

"Whatever it is..."

"I've been seeing someone else."

"What?" She dropped his hand. "You mean seeing as in sleeping with? That seeing?"

"I'm sorry."

"You're sorry? What, was it some kind of accident and you just couldn't help yourself? You fell into somebody else's bed and you couldn't get up?"

"Look, I didn't mean for this to go on for so long. I just..."

"No? How long did you intend ... oh forget it!" Sandy turned and stormed out of the kitchen. After retrieving her bags from the master bedroom, she turned to find Ian blocking the door.

"Sandy, that's not what I meant."

"Let me give you some free advice. One: get a lawyer. And two: if you're going to break up with someone, don't invite them to spend the night!" Sandy pushed past him and slammed the front door on her way out.

Ian caught up with her as she was opening the trunk of her car. "Will you please wait a minute? I don't want to break up with you!"

"You just did!" Sandy threw her bags into the trunk and tried to slam the trunk closed, but the lid bounced off the corner of her briefcase. She shoved the case to one side and slammed the lid down again. "You said you hadn't meant for this to go on so long."

"I meant lying! I didn't mean for the deception to go on for so long. I didn't mean to deceive you at all."

"So you don't want to break up?"

"No!" Ian reached out to put his hand on her shoulder. "I love you."

Sandy shrugged away from his hand. "And you're seeing someone else?"

"I, uh..." Ian's hand sunk to his side. "I didn't mean for this to get so complicated either."

Across the street in the GTO, someone lit a cigarette and Sandy glared at the glowing red ember. "Right. Let's deal with one crisis at a time, shall we?" She stepped past her car and started walking towards the Pontiac.

"Sandy!" Ian rushed after her.

When they got about halfway to the GTO, the Pontiac's driver shifted into reverse and started backing away from them. Sandy ran after the big muscle car but it turned around in a two-car driveway and quietly sped away. "So much for the direct approach." Sandy stopped running and shook her head as Ian caught up with her.

"What were you going to do if you caught them?"

"Ask them for ID."

"Why?"

"To find out if they were cops and, if so, what they were doing here." Sandy considered. "I don't think cops would have just driven off like that. Besides, the kid driving certainly didn't look like a cop. You were probably right: just some kids making out."

"With the engine running?"

"It's cold!"

Ian nodded. "Would you like to come inside and talk?"

Sandy looked at him for a moment. "All right." They started back. "Look, Ian, I don't know that I have any right to be mad at you. I mean, I'm upset, but..."

"I understand. I'd be angry too."

"That's just it. I haven't exactly been faithful either."

Ian stopped walking.

Sandy turned to face him. "I've been sleeping with someone else, too."

Ian glared at her. "Why didn't you tell me?"

Sandy glared right back. "Why didn't you tell me?"

"I just did!"

"Well, so did I! You were out of town and I, oh, God!" Sandy's flash of anger was short-lived. "How could this happen?"

"I've been asking myself the same question. It was just before you and I went to Cabo." Ian rubbed his temples. "I met Bernie at Mick's house."

"Bernie?"

"Yeah. Mick was having a barbecue. I was on call so I took her flying and we, uh...".

"Bernie Selleca?"

"Yeah, how did you…?" Ian remembered the painting. "Oh shit."

"You're Bernie's new boyfriend?" Before Ian could answer, Sandy started angrily toward her car. "That bitch! That fucking bitch!" She whirled back toward Ian. "I told her all about you! I told her how we met, what we talked about, how much I liked you... that little bitch! She knew that we were both talking about you and she didn't say a word, not a goddamned word!"

"Was Bernie the one your parents didn't approve of?"

"They met her once! They never gave her a chance." Sandy stared at Ian for a long moment, her expression flashing through anger, fear and confusion to settle on amusement. "This is totally weird."

"So are you two back together, then?"

"No! I mean it was just… I thought…" Sandy threw her hands up, exasperated. "I have no idea." Her hands dropped to her sides for a second but then she crossed her arms. "You said you met Bernie before we went to Cabo?"

"Yeah."

"But I didn't talk to her about you until after we got back. Where did you meet her?"

"At a party at Mick's house." Ian pointed across the street.

"How long has she known Mick?"

"She met him that day. She was applying for a job."

"She must have followed you from my house. Oh, God! That means she was following me! What the hell is she thinking?" Sandy considered. "Is she trying to prove something? Is she trying to break us up?"

"You think she was stalking you?"

"Not stalking like 'creepy' stalking, but yeah. I can't believe she'd be so duplicitous. Bernie can be hotheaded and clever and crazy but she'd never hurt anyone. This is too bizarre." Sandy took a deep breath and let it out slowly. "I don't know why she'd... What the hell does she think she's doing?"

"And what are we going to do about it?"

"Well, she definitely needs to be punished."

"Punished?"

"We can't just let her get away with this!" Sandy said defensively.

"Maybe we should try to figure out what it is she's trying to get away with."

"Agreed." Sandy shivered. "Could we figure that out somewhere warmer?"

As they walked back toward Ian's house, the engines of a departing 737 roared overhead. The navigation lights winked and sparkled across the clear night sky. As the plane turned west, the lights faded, lost among the more distant stars of the Milky Way.

CHAPTER EIGHT

Wednesday, 1:43 am – Doctor Neault's
Residence, Berkeley Hills

Three hours later the stars above Paul Neault's house were slipping behind the incoming fog. All at once the vague shapes and shadows of the classic-revival estate flashed into blinding clarity as floodlights illuminated the buildings and grounds. The three men at Paul's ornate front door were caught in the halogen crossfire. Randal reached for his gun as he jerked his head around and searched the brightly lit courtyard for signs of danger, but nothing sinister lurked on the carefully trimmed lawn. Beyond the grass, the long silver Jaguar was alone, parked at an angle across the faux cobblestones. Randal looked uncertainly from Yuri to Travis, his hand still inside his jacket.

Standing on the porch between his nephew and his driver, Yuri sighed, "At ease, Randal."

Randal straightened his tie before lowering his arm.

Travis shifted the heavy case he was carrying to his left hand and rang the doorbell again. Someone glanced out through the Palladian window and a chain rattled on the other side of the door. The door opened just enough for Paul to look out. "What on earth are you doing here, Yuri?"

"It's a pleasure to see you too, Paul." Yuri smiled sardonically. "Where's Desmond?"

"He said he'd already called you. Didn't you talk to him?" Paul opened the door a little wider, but didn't step out of the way. "He's been in an accident."

"That's what he said." Yuri pushed the door open, forcing Paul back, and stepped into the foyer. Randal and Travis followed Yuri through the entryway and into the only room with lights on. Paul hurriedly closed the front door, locked one of the dead bolts and followed the trio into the tastefully appointed sitting room.

Randal smiled and pointed at Paul's feet. "Nice shoes."

Paul was wearing red silk pajamas, a long red robe and fuzzy red slippers. He ignored Randal, focusing his irritation on Yuri. "It's two o'clock in the morning, Yuri. Why are you here?"

Yuri slid back the sleeve of his wool coat to check his watch. "It's only 1:45, Paul, and I'm here because Desmond didn't meet me as agreed."

"I'm dreadfully sorry for the inconvenience, Yuri, but as I said, and as Des told you on the phone, he was involved in an accident. It couldn't be helped. He will be able to meet with you tomorrow."

Yuri shook his head slightly. "I think not." In the center of the room, an antique coffee table held a silver tray with a bottle of cognac and a single glass. The bottle and the glass were both half empty. Yuri put his palms together as if in prayer and looked at Travis. Nodding toward the coffee table, Yuri opened his hands like a book, and then let them fall gracefully to his sides. Travis nodded and shoved the silver tray toward the far end of the table. The decanter toppled onto the glass, shattering it. Pieces of the glass held the decanter at an odd angle as a pool of cognac sloshed around the silver tray like the moat of a fallen castle.

"Dammit, Travis!" Paul rushed to rescue the cognac, as Travis set the suitcase down and opened it so that Paul could see the neat plastic bags of cocaine inside.

"Leave that for now, Paul. Just try to concentrate on the business at hand." Yuri waved a long-fingered hand at the cocaine in the suitcase. "Twenty kilos, per our agreement."

"For God's sake, Yuri, this is my home! I don't want that here!"

Yuri shrugged. "I realize you like to play a less active role in your business than I do, Paul, but it's still your business. It remains, therefore, your responsibility."

"I'm perfectly aware of my responsibilities, Yuri. I can assure you that Des will meet you tomorrow, whenever and wherever you..."

"No. I will no longer conduct business with Desmond. I don't know if your favorite student is out of the country or simply out of his mind, but I doubt that he's been in any kind of accident."

"What are you saying?"

"I'm saying that no accident involving Desmond or his car has been reported. I suspect that he isn't being completely candid with you, but Desmond is your problem and you may take care of him however you wish. As for this," Yuri pointed to the case on the coffee table, "you ordered twenty kilos. Twenty kilos has been delivered. I expect payment as we agreed."

"But Yuri," Paul looked horrified. "You can't leave that here."

"Can't I?" Yuri raised an eyebrow. "Given the questionable reliability of your associates, it would be foolish to leave it anywhere else. I certainly don't want your merchandise in my car."

"But Des has your money."

"No," Yuri shook his head. "Desmond has your money."

"Yuri, I don't know what's going on, but I'm sure we can figure this out." Paul nervously glanced at the spilled cognac, and then gestured toward a bar against the far wall. "Would you like a drink?"

"No, Paul. I would not like a drink. I would like my money." Yuri considered the shorter man for a moment. "But I'm a reasonable man. You have until tomorrow."

Paul put his hands on his hips, exasperated. "Dammit, Yuri, what the hell has gotten into you? I honestly don't understand your attitude."

Yuri's obsidian eyes narrowed briefly, but there was no discernable expression. Travis shifted his weight forward onto the balls of his feet and Randal reached into his jacket as he took a step closer to Paul.

"We've known each other a long time, Paul, and I've enjoyed your friendship. You've been..." Yuri smiled, "Entertaining." The perfect teeth disappeared. "But this is business. As I wish to have no further misunderstandings,

I will put this as clearly and concisely as possible. An important part of our relationship has been information. You have in the past provided me with timely information on the activities of the police departments with whom you consult. This has helped my associates and myself maintain a low profile, while expanding our operation throughout the region. And yet, as we speak, police officers from multiple jurisdictions are interrogating my associates in an attempt to find the killer of an undercover detective named Michael Vale. A detective you not only failed to warn me about, but subsequently killed without consulting me. That was foolish. His death will cause problems for us for some time to come."

"Yuri, I can assure you..."

"You can assure me of nothing! You've taken action, dangerously stupid action, as though you play the only decision-making role in this enterprise. You've insulated yourself from your responsibilities so effectively that you haven't a clue as to what your people are actually doing. Did you know your people have been distributing more product than you buy from me, at prices substantially below our target? Do you realize that this has started a price war that threatens to de-stabilize the entire area? Do you know where your former subordinates were getting all this surplus cocaine?"

"Yuri, I don't..."

"Of course you don't. Until you killed him, it was coming from Detective Vale."

"I'm aware of that, Yuri. I was taking steps to ensure..."

"Your first step should have been to let me know what you'd discovered. Your second step would have been to do exactly as I instructed which certainly would not have included murdering a police officer!" Yuri stepped toward Paul, who didn't realize that he was standing between Yuri and the front door. "To be quite honest, Paul, I'm only leaving the twenty kilos with you because I don't have a choice. Until I know what Des is doing, and to whom he has spoken, I don't wish to travel with anything unusual in my car. Randal will return tomorrow evening for my money." Yuri looked to Randal. "Can you be here at eight o'clock?"

"Uh, sure." Randal nodded. "Wednesday at eight. Or would that be Thursday?"

Yuri closed his eyes. "Randal, what day is this?"

"Well it's Wednesday morning, but you could also say it's Tuesday night, 'cause it's only..."

Yuri sighed. "Randal will be here Thursday evening at eight o'clock." He glanced past Paul toward the hall. "Now, if you'll excuse us?"

Paul stepped aside to let the trio pass, and then followed them down the hall. Randal flashed a sarcastic grin before pulling the door shut behind them. Tight-lipped, Paul methodically shot each of the dead bolts home and then angrily walked back to his sitting room. He shook his head at the spilled cognac and the bright white packets of cocaine. "Yuri, my psychopathic old friend, after all these years you still don't realize who controls whom." Paul set the cognac decanter upright and picked up the stopper. "But where in the world could you get such accurate information?"

Wednesday, 7:44 am – All Fool's Day

The pulsating jets from the shower massage splashed off Ian's back as he lathered Sandy's neck and shoulders. The soapy sponge left a bubbly mosaic of tanned skin and mottled foam. Sandy pressed her forearms against the peach tiles and lowered her head. "That feels so good." Ian tossed the sponge into a corner and started rubbing her neck with his fingers.

"Oh yeah!" Sandy arched into his fingers. "God, that feels good."

"You certainly do. What time did you say you had to go to work?"

"Well, technically..." Sandy raised her head. "What was that?"

Ian heard the doorbell when it rang again. "I guess someone's at the door." He tried to keep rubbing Sandy's back, but she turned to face him.

"What if it's Bernie?"

"Why would it be Bernie?"

"You said she was working across the street."

"Christ!" Ian started to panic, but then he noticed the wry smile and realized she was teasing him. "You're enjoying this aren't you?"

"Well..." Sandy shrugged. "It is April 1st."

"God!" Ian rinsed his hands. "You're beginning to scare me, you know that?"

Sandy grinned. "I love you, too."

The doorbell rang again as Ian opened the shower door and stepped out onto the peach bathmat.

Sandy raised an eyebrow. "You'd better see what she wants."

"It's not Bernie!"

"Of course not." Sandy stepped to the other end of the big tub and unhooked the Shower Massage. "She wouldn't want to pop over just to say hi, or ask about your other girlfriend." She started to rinse her back but then aimed the spray toward Ian. The water splashed out across the clear glass door and flowed in a rippling sheet into the tub. She grinned at him through the shimmering barrier. "If you make it back before the hot water runs out, I'll make it worth your while."

"Deal." Ian blew her a kiss as he took his robe off its hook. "It's an in-line heater; it'll never run out."

"Really?" Sandy looked at the temperature selector.

"Just don't turn it too hot. The max temperature got set a little higher than it should be."

Sandy bent down to rinse her legs. "I'll be careful."

Ian closed the bathroom door behind him, and hurried out of the master bedroom. The doorbell rang again as Ian rounded the corner into the entryway. He hesitated, about to turn the dead bolt, and glanced through the spyglass. "Des? What the hell do you want?"

Ian turned the bolt and dropped his hand to the doorknob, but it started turning just as he grabbed it. The door was shoved open, hitting Ian in the shoulder and pushing him back. He held onto the knob as he stepped back. "Goddamn it, Des!"

The man forcing the door open was several inches taller than Ian and almost a foot taller than Des. Wearing a red and gold 49ers jacket, the intruder looked like a linebacker. He'd been standing next to Des, out of view, and as Des followed him inside, the big man pushed Ian away from the door.

"Hey!" Ian knocked the hand off his chest. "Get the hell out of my house!"

Following Des, a heavyset kid in a black leather jacket and a thin guy in a brown sport coat stepped inside. Ian looked at the four of them. "Des what the hell is going on?

The thin guy closed the door. Des smiled. "First things first, Ian: where's Sandy?"

Ian glared at him. "Get out of my house before I call the police!"

Des turned to the 49er. "Find her, Ross." The big guy nodded and headed toward the kitchen.

Ian yelled down the hallway, "Sandy! Call the police!"

The kid in the leather jacket moved toward Ian. He was also bigger than Des, about Ian's height, but much stockier. Ian tried to fend him off, but the kid swept Ian's arm to the side with one hand and punched him in the stomach with the other. Ian bent forward around the fist in his mid-section. Looking at the floor, Ian could see the kid's black engineer boots. Looking higher, Ian noticed the blued metal revolver tucked behind the kid's "SMEGHEADS!" belt buckle.

Ian tried to yell, "Call the police!" again, but it came out as a whisper. As the kid pulled his fist back for another shot, Ian straightened up enough to jab at the acne-pocked face with the fingers of his left hand. Ian's ring and middle fingers poked into the kid's eyes.

"Fuck!" The wrestler covered his eyes with his hands and Ian grabbed the revolver. Still rubbing his eyes with his left hand, the kid swung frantically at Ian with his right. He had a big silver ring on his middle finger and it glinted as the kid's fist swept inches from Ian's face.

Des put his hand on the wrestler's shoulder. "That's enough, Lenny. I don't want..."

Lenny swung his arm back to get the hand off his shoulder and smacked Des in the face. The silver ring cut a triangular gash in Des' cheek.

"Goddamned right that's enough! Everybody freeze!" Ian pointed the revolver at Des.

Everybody froze, except for Ross, the guy in the 49er jacket, who had gone through the kitchen and ended up in the family room, behind Ian. Ross tried to grab the gun, and succeeded in jerking Ian's arm back before he pulled the trigger, punching a hole through the ceiling above the entryway. With the gunshot still ringing in their ears, Ross stepped back and Lenny caught Ian with a glancing blow across his right cheek. The blow knocked Ian back onto the floor. Blood welled up where Lenny's ring had broken the skin.

Ian started to raise the gun again, but froze. The thin guy who had come in behind Lenny had an ugly, boxy-looking sub-machine gun pointed at Ian's face. The thin guy spoke very quietly. "Put the gun down."

Ian set the revolver down on the carpet.

"Very good." Des picked the gun up. His leather jacket looked much too big for him. "Where's Sandy?"

Ian shook his head. "What do you think you're doing, Des?"

"What the hell do you think I'm doing, asshole? I'm making sure you fly to Mexico." Des glanced at Ross, who was still standing behind Ian. "Well, don't just fucking stand there, Ross. Find her!"

Ross lumbered down the hall and glanced in Ian's office before trying the master bedroom. Des turned his attention back to Ian. "As I tried to explain yesterday, Ian, you're dealing with some very serious people." Des wiped some of the blood off his cheek and looked at the wrestler. "Jesus, Lenny! We're gonna have to get you de-clawed!"

"Huh?" Lenny had been smiling at the cut on Ian's face. He turned and saw a mirror-image cut into Des' cheek. "Oh, shit, Mr. Pierrot! I'm sorry, I ..."

"Its okay, Lenny. Don't worry..."

The scream carried loud and clear down the hall from the master bedroom. It was a deep, masculine howl of pain that segued into a staccato burst of four letter words. The expletives ended with a crash and a dull porcelain thud. A door slammed at the end of the hall and Sandy barreled out of the bedroom and started running down the hall. She stopped when she saw the gun pointed at Ian.

"Morning, Sandy." Des beckoned her forward. "Glad you could join us. Lenny, see what's keeping Ross, will you?"

"Right." Lenny headed down the hall and Sandy flattened against the wall to let him pass. She watched him warily, her right hand balled into a fist. There was blood across her knuckles.

Ross stumbled into the hall just as Lenny reached the door to the master bedroom. Lenny caught him as he overbalanced and started to fall forward. "Jesus, dude! What happened?"

"God-damn bitch!" Ross' face and hands were almost as red as his 49er jacket, and he was soaking wet. He wiped some of the blood off his mouth. "She scalded me!"

Des rolled his eyes toward heaven. "Is he okay, Lenny?"

"I guess." Lenny leaned closer to examine the cut on Ross' lip, and nodded. "Yeah. She busted his lip pretty good, but he'll live."

Sandy glanced down at her hand and wiped Ross' blood off with the sleeve of her robe.

Steam rose off the red and gold jacket as Ross glared at Sandy. "Bitch."

Des glanced at his watch. "We're running behind schedule here people. We need to head for the airport." He looked at Ian. "Carlos will be calling in about 20 minutes to confirm your itinerary, Ian, so you'd better get dressed while I tell you what you're going to tell him."

"It won't work, Des. There's paper work that has to be filed…"

"Don't bullshit me Ian! You've just lost your god-damned nerve! This is your fucking plan and you will fucking make it work! If you don't fly to Mexico, I'll make damn sure you don't fly anywhere, ever again."

Des pointed Lenny's gun at Sandy's temple and smiled cheerfully. "Right after we kill your sweetheart."

Across the street, Ken was in what would become the second floor hallway, studying the plans for Mick's third floor "attic". Bernie was in the new master bedroom staring through the 2x6 framing at Ian's front door. She considered the row of cars across the street and the white and pale green Econoline van in his driveway. She glanced back at Ken. "You didn't hear anything?"

Ken looked up from the plans. "What?"

"Are you sure you didn't hear anything?"

"Just now?"

"No; when I asked you a minute ago!"

Ken shook his head patiently. "I told you a minute ago, I didn't hear anything."

"Well I did." Bernie unbuckled her tool belt and let it fall behind her. Hammer, nail bags and assorted hand tools dropped to the plywood sub floor. "I'm going over there."

"Why? What's going on?"

"I don't know. Twenty minutes ago that van was parked down the street, but it just moved into Ian's driveway." Bernie pointed to the line of cars in front of Ian's house. "What's weird is the GTO belongs to a jerk named Gil Kranz. He fronts a grunge band called the Smegheads. They call themselves a cover band but it's just a cover for dealing drugs."

"And you know these guys?"

"I used to date the jerk's ex-girlfriend."

Ken walked over to the wall and surveyed the row of cars. "Looks like a party."

"I'm sure I heard a gunshot." Bernie crossed the room and slipped through the framework into the hallway. "I'll be right back, Ken. I just want to find out what's going on."

"Hang on. You didn't say anything about gunshots." Ken started to unbuckle his own tool belt. "I'll come with you."

"Thanks, but uh... This could be really awkward if I'm just, you know, imagining something... Could you wait here? Call the police, I guess; if anything weird happens but ..."

"Anything weird? Your not-exactly-ex girlfriend and your brand-new boyfriend are partying with the Smegheads and you think you heard a gunshot. Weird? We could sell tickets!"

"Ken, please?"

"Okay." Ken shrugged as Bernie disappeared down the stairs. Heavy nylon suspenders that wrapped over his muscular shoulders held his tools up whether the belt was buckled or not. He left it unbuckled and pulled out his cell phone. As Bernie walked purposefully across the street, Ken dialed 911. He waited through the automated messages as he watched Bernie walk up to the van parked in Ian's driveway.

The former phone company workhorse still bore the company colors, though the Pacific Bell name and logo had been painted over. The pale green paint was chipped and rusty in places, and the right rear corner of the old Econoline was crumpled in. Sitting in the van's right front seat, Nancy Benson had a cellular phone in her lap and a walkie-talkie balanced across the knees of her jeans. The windows were down and the FM radio was playing something too faint to recognize. Nancy nervously reached toward the volume knob, but pulled her hand back without touching anything. She glanced up and down the street, glanced in the passenger side mirror and then looked at the dashboard clock. She pressed the status button on the phone, making sure it was on standby, and then checked the volume on the walkie-talkie. Nancy sniffed and wiped her nose absently. "What is taking you bastards so long?" She picked up the walkie-talkie and held it to her ear.

When Bernie appeared at the driver's side window and said, "Hi, Nancy. What's going on?" Nancy threw the walkie-talkie at the floor and jerked her head around.

"Bernie, what...?" Nancy's pale complexion turned bright red and an embarrassed tear started down her left cheek. She angrily wiped her eyes as she bent forward to retrieve the radio. "What do you want?"

"I could say I saw the van and I thought I'd come say 'hi,' but did you hear a gunshot?"

Nancy straightened up and nodded. "No." More tears flowed as she juggled the walkie-talkie in one hand and two of its four batteries in the other. Nancy looked at the radio and the batteries and then looked helplessly at Bernie.

"Chill out, Nancy. It'll be alright." Bernie cleared her throat and tried to look supportive. "You'll need the cover plate to hold the batteries in."

"Right." Nancy nodded, tucked the batteries next to the phone and bent forward again. Bernie waited until Nancy found the gray plastic square and one of the other batteries.

"So, what are you guys doing here?"

"We're uh," Nancy froze. "We're not doing anything."

"Do you guys know Ian?"

"Who?" She looked helplessly at the empty space where the missing fourth battery should have gone. "Look, I don't know what's going on, Bernie, honest. I'm just supposed to wait here and let Gil know if anyone comes near the house but now..." she glanced at Bernie and then bent forward to look for the missing battery.

Behind the van Ian's garage door started going up and Bernie turned toward the sound.

Gil Stern, the thin guy in the brown sport coat ducked under the opening door. "Hey!" He walked toward Bernie. "What the fuck are you doing here?"

"Hi, Gil." Bernie took a step back, "I just wanted to talk to Ian."

"The pilot? He's busy. Piss off."

"Come on Gil. I just want to say hi."

Gil backhanded Bernie across the face, took a step forward and shoved her away from the van. "I said 'Piss Off!'"

Bernie stumbled, but came up with her fists raised like a boxer. Gil had pulled a chrome-plated automatic out of his belt and had it leveled at Bernie's bleeding nose. He glanced at Nancy. "Hey Babe! Looks like we're gonna hit the trifecta: kidnapping, smuggling and homo-cide. All in one day!"

Nancy buried her head in her lap.

Bernie had opened her hands. "I'm leaving, okay; I'm leaving." She backed away toward the street. Gil slid the gun back into his belt as he watched her cross the sidewalk.

Somebody called from inside the garage. "You got a problem Gil?"

"Nothing I can't handle." Gil shouted back as he walked around to the back of the van and opened the rear doors.

Bernie touched her nose, winced, and looked down at the blood on her hand. "Asshole." She sniffed cautiously as she wiped her hand on her cutoffs. Looking up she saw Ken in Mick's front yard painfully limping toward her. She hurried the rest of the way across the street and they met at the edge of the sidewalk. Ken balanced on his right foot, keeping his left foot completely off the ground. Bernie glanced from his foot to his angry expression. "What happened to you?"

"Later. Are you okay? You're bleeding."

Bernie sniffed and wiped her nose with her hand. "It's stopped. I'll be fine."

Ken glared across the street. "I'm gonna kill that bastard!"

"He's got a gun."

"And I'm gonna make him eat it." He started toward the van but stumbled. "Jesus, that hurts!" He managed to stay upright while getting his weight back on his good foot.

Bernie grabbed his arm and helped him balance. "We've got to call the police."

"They're on the way."

"You called 'em already?"

Ken smiled, "Right after you asked me not to."

"Good call. What did you do to your foot?"

"I just sprained my ankle: no big deal." Ken lowered his foot to the sidewalk and forced an embarrassed smile as he glanced over his shoulder at Mick's second floor. "I've jumped off lots higher shit than that, but there was some kind of Tonka bulldozer thing in the flower bed."

"You jumped off the second floor?" Bernie looked at the dirt under the living room window, and then up at the spaces between the studs of the second floor. "Thanks for leaping to my rescue. Next time use the stairs."

"Bernie, that bastard hit you!" Ken looked across the street. "Why did he hit you?"

"He still blames me for Julie."

"His ex-girlfriend?"

"Okay, so they weren't actually broken up at the time." Bernie looked down the street. "Where are the cops? You called the cops, right?"

"Yeah. What the hell is going on over there?"

"Gil said something about kidnapping."

"Jesus."

"Look, we should get inside. We need to call the cops again and we need to take care of that ankle."

"It'll be fine."

"Right." Bernie steered Ken toward Mick's front door.

Ken tried to walk normally, but had to stop after a few steps. Bernie slipped under his arm to help him balance.

Across the street the van's doors slammed shut and the engine grumbled to life. Ken and Bernie both turned to see what was happening. Gil glared at them from behind the wheel as he swung the van into the street and headed toward Harbor Bay Drive. Nancy was walking toward Gil's GTO. Ken looked down the street hoping for sirens and red lights but once the van turned the corner the only movement was Ian's Mustang rolling out of his garage. Ian was in the right seat and Ross was driving. Lenny was wedged into the back seat. Des was getting into his Ferrari. He wrenched the Spyder into a tight U-turn and roared off toward Harbor Bay Drive. Ross followed him with Ian and Lenny and the GTO finished a three-point turn to join the convoy.

"What the hell is going on?" Bernie looked at the scene for a second then turned to Ken. "I need your truck."

Ken dug into the front pocket of his jeans. "Are you going to follow them?"

"I don't know what else to do."

"Wait for the police?" Ken handed her his keys.

"Call the police and tell 'em what's happened." She headed for Ken's truck. "I'll call you!"

"Be careful!" Ken shouted.

He watched her back down the driveway, over Mick's mailbox and halfway into the street. The wheels spun a bit as Bernie floored the gas pedal and then she was roaring after the kidnappers.

"I said be careful." Ken dialed 911.

Wednesday, 9:45 am - 180 Miles Southeast of Alameda

Ninety five hundred feet above the San Joaquin Valley, the pale yellow Mooney cruised southeast at two miles per minute. The sleek single engine plane was perfectly centered on Victor 107, a low altitude airway connecting the Bay Area with Los Angeles. Cindy leaned over to look directly at the magnetic compass. While she was adjusting the gyrocompass to match, Tony leaned toward his fiancé and gave her a kiss.

"Hey!" Cindy straightened up. "Don't distract the pilot."

"You started it." Tony smiled.

It had been clear all the way from Oakland, but to the east, past Bakersfield, cumulus clouds were beginning to build up over the Sierras. Tony pointed past Cindy to the clouds on the other side of the valley. "Is that stuff going to be a problem?"

"Shouldn't be." Cindy shook her head. "We won't be turning east until after Mojave. There're pilot reports over the desert for a little turbulence, but no clouds."

Tony glanced at the airsickness bags on the bottom of the map box. "So, uh, how much is a 'little' turbulence?"

Cindy smiled sympathetically. "You'll be fine."

Sitting on top of the sick-sacks was a little gray box pretending to be the Mooney's transponder. A yellow reply light flashed on the face of the box each time it answered a sweep of ATC radar. Next to the gray box, the black controller box was poised to change the transponder's code. Wires led from the gray box across the copilot's yoke to the rectangular cavity where the Mooney's original transponder had been. Tony had pulled the Mooney's legally certified transponder out of the avionics rack to get at the antennae and power leads.

Sounding brusque and official, the Oakland Center controller warned them of another airplane approaching from their right. "MOONEY 812, TRAFFIC AT 2 O'CLOCK, NORTHBOUND. ALTITUDE UNKNOWN."

Cindy pressed her microphone button as she looked past Tony, searching the area ahead of their right wing. "812, negative contact." She released the button on her yoke and asked Tony, "Do you see it?"

"Not yet." Tony studied the seemingly-empty sky. "That couldn't be him, could it?"

"It shouldn't be, but if your portable NDB isn't working, he could have gotten off course." Cindy kept scanning the sky for other airplanes. "And if the altitude encoder in Ian's little black box isn't working, Oakland Center wouldn't show an altitude for him."

"Your faith in my electronic wizardry is underwhelming." Tony turned around to check the Non-Directional Beacon sitting in the back seat. The wires were connected properly, and the power light was on. "He should be able to fly right to us."

"MOONEY 812, TRAFFIC MOVING FROM 4 TO 5 O'CLOCK IS NO LONGER A FACTOR. ADDITIONAL TRAFFIC IS A PBY CATALINA, 6 O'CLOCK AND 1 MILE. ALTITUDE INDICATES 7,500. HE'LL BE PASSING BELOW YOU."

"812, roger." Cindy released the mike button. "Forgive me, oh Wizard. How could I ever have doubted you?"

"CATALINA 92 WHISKEY, TRAFFIC AT 12 O'CLOCK IS A MOONEY AT 9,500."

"92 Whiskey, traffic in sight."

There was a brief pause and then Cindy and Tony heard Ian's voice through the other radio. It almost sounded like he was whispering. "Red, this is Black: are we on for lunch?"

Cindy turned the transmit switch from #1 to #2 and adjusted the volume. The second radio was set to 122.75, the standard plane-to-plane frequency. Cindy keyed her mike. "Black, this is Red. Affirmative. Lunch would be great. We're ready when you are." She enriched the mixture and poised her right hand over the side-by-side throttle and propeller controls, ready to apply full power.

"Roger. I'll let you know if everything checks out."

Tony watched the code on the transponder. The numbers in the little LCD windows still read 4220, the numbers they'd been assigned in Oakland. A moment later the code changed to 3214, the code Ian had been assigned. Tony nodded to Cindy and said, "Go!" Cindy pushed the throttle and propeller controls forward and the Mooney surged ahead.

Two thousand feet below the accelerating Mooney, Ian set Tony's other black box, the master controller, back on the shelf below the radio stack and reached up to reduce the Catalina's engines to 55% power. The Catalina slowed down as Ian pulled back on the yoke to maintain 7,500 feet. He watched the Mooney move ahead, slipping from the clear hatch over his seat to the angled windscreen above the instrument panel. Ian glanced at Ross. "So far, so good."

Ross nodded nervously. He looked like he'd been strapped into an electric chair and was waiting for someone to throw the switch.

Ian keyed his mike. "You're clear, Red."

"Roger."

Ian glanced at Ross as he switched back to his #1 radio. "Now we see if the altitude feature worked." Ian pushed the throttles forward and pulled the nose up. The big seaplane started climbing. As they passed through 8,000, Ian could see that the Mooney was descending through the same altitude as it pulled further and further ahead of him. Ian called ATC. "Center, Catalina 1292 Whiskey. Is that Mooney still behind me?"

"AFFIRMATIVE 92 WHISKEY. TRAFFIC IS TWO MILES BEHIND YOU NOW, INDICATING 9,500."

Ian pointed to the Catalina's altimeter, which hadn't quite reached 8,600. "Perfect! It's telling them we're already at 9,500." Ian keyed his microphone. "92 Whiskey, roger, request cancel flight following."

"92 WHISKEY SQUAWK 1200, FREQUENCY CHANGE APPROVED, G'DAY."

"92 Whiskey, G'day." Ian left his transponder on the Mooney's assigned frequency, 4220, and switched to his #2 radio. "Red, did you get that?"

"Roger, Black. Good luck." Cindy released her mike button and glanced over at Tony. "Are we squawking 1200?"

Tony nodded as he finished dialing 1200 into the gray box in the Mooney's map compartment. "So, how does it feel to be flying a PBY Catalina?"

Cindy smiled. "You're a genius."

"True." Tony grinned, very pleased with himself. "Worked perfectly, didn't it?"

Cindy nodded. "That's what I love about you."

"My perfection?"

"Your humility."

"Touché!" Tony laughed. "Tell me, is that all you love about me?" He leaned toward her.

"Well..." Cindy glanced toward him and Tony tried to kiss her. "Hey!" Cindy turned her head and the headsets clicked together. "Didn't I tell you not to distract the pilot?"

Oakland center interrupted. "MOONEY 812. I'M NOT ABLE TO COORDINATE A HAND OFF TO L.A. CENTER RIGHT NOW. SQUAWK 1200, FREQUENCY CHANGE APPROVED. SUGGEST YOU MONITOR L.A. CENTER ON 124.15."

Cindy keyed her mike, but Tony held up his hand and she released the button. "Shouldn't I answer that?"

Tony pointed to the gray box, already set to 1200. "We canceled flight following when they thought we were Ian."

They listened for a few more seconds and then Ian answered in a passably high falsetto, "812, roger."

Tony laughed. "I never realized before what a sexy voice you have." He studied her for a moment. "Let's get married."

"We are getting married." Cindy smiled.

"I mean right now."

Amused, Cindy shook her head as she dialed 124.15 into the # 2 radio and switched frequencies.

"I'm serious." Tony glanced at his watch. "We're supposed to be hanging around for five or six hours in Phoenix, right? Why not stop in Vegas? We could get lunch, get married; get a room?"

"You're crazy!"

"About you! Marry me?"

"My parents would kill us!"

"So would mine, but only if we tell them. It'll be our secret."

"Des won't like it."

Tony laughed. "Honey, nothing we do is going to keep his head from exploding."

"Did you notice how stressed out he was this morning?"

Tony nodded, "Even more than usual, and that's saying something."

"Ian seemed pretty edgy too." Cindy reached over to adjust the throttle.

"Ian's the one actually crossing the border, so he's got a right to be on edge."

"Yeah, but I thought he was mostly upset with Des. What do think that's about?"

Tony thought for a moment, and then shrugged, "No clue. Des wants a call every two hours; we'll call him from our hotel. Beyond that I'm not tripping." He leaned over so his head was almost in Cindy's lap and looked up into her eyes. "Marry me! Today!"

"I love you!" Cindy bent forward and kissed his forehead. "I'll call flight-watch and see what the weather is like in Las Vegas. Now that ATC isn't following Ian, we can go back to being a Mooney, right?"

"Right, but we should wait until we're in another control zone before we contact ATC again."

"You mean sector."

"Okay, sector."

"Right." Just before Cindy changed frequencies, they heard Ian calling L.A. Center on 124.15. Cindy took her hand away from the radio and they listened.

"L.A. Center, Catalina 92 Whiskey."

"CATALINA 92 WHISKEY, CENTER."

"92 Whiskey is 5 miles south of Avenal on Victor 137, Request IFR clearance direct to Calexico at Flight Level 210."

"ROGER, 92 WHISKEY, CLEARANCE ON REQUEST. UH, 92 WHISKEY, YOU DID SAY YOU'RE A CATALINA? A PBY?"

"92 Whiskey, affirmative."

"ROGER, 92 WHISKEY, I DIDN'T THINK A CAT COULD REACH 21,000."

"92 Whiskey has turbo-chargers."

"UNDERSTOOD, 92 WHISKEY. WE'RE WORKING ON YOUR CLEARANCE."

"Why's he going so high?" Cindy glanced at Tony. "I don't know what the service ceiling on those turbo charged radials is, but I know the plane isn't pressurized. They'll have to use oxygen above 12,500."

"Is that a problem?"

"Not really, just a hassle." Cindy pointed to an outlet next to Tony's headphone jack. "This plane is set up for oxygen, but I don't like dealing with all the tubing. Besides, my throat always gets dried out."

"I know how we can solve that problem."

"I'll bet you do." Cindy changed frequencies and called Flight-watch. She didn't hear L.A. Center call 92 Whiskey with a clearance to 21,000.

A few miles behind the Mooney, Ian read back the clearance as he advanced the mixture, propeller and throttle controls. With the increase in power, the Catalina started climbing even before he pulled back on the yoke. Ian glanced over at Ross. "Are you still feeling queasy?"

"I'm fine!" Ross nervously looked out the side window since the Catalina's nose blocked his view of the terrain ahead. "What's going on? Where's Calexico? We're supposed to be going to Guadalajara, right?"

"Des didn't give me time to file direct so we have to go through customs at the border."

"Why do we have to go higher?" Ross' fingertips were buried in the foam of the co-pilot seat cushion. His knuckles were white against his scalded-red skin.

Ian nodded to their left at the billowing columns of cloud over the Sierras. "I just thought you'd rather go over those storms than through them."

Ross nodded and his eyes widened as he looked past Ian at the wall of thunderclouds. The sky ahead was clear and blue, but Ross couldn't take his gaze off the weather over the Mountains.

The Vertical Speed Indicator showed a climb rate of 500 feet per minute. As they passed through 12,000 feet, Ian looked at Ross and nodded toward the right side window. "Can you see any other airplanes out there?" During the preflight, Lenny and Ross had quickly tired of watching every move Ian made. While they were bemoaning the wet-bar's lack of beer, Ian had managed to thread a clear plastic tube in between the microphone and headphone cables of his headset. Now, when Ross turned his head to look out the right window, Ian tucked the end of the tube into his mouth.

The linebacker shook his head. "I don't see anything."

"Good." When Ross looked back, Ian pointed to the magnetic compass. "Looks like the DG is off a bit." Ian used his right hand to adjust the Directional Gyro. Ross attentively watched Ian's fingers twist the gyrocompass a few degrees off and then back to match the magnetic compass. Ian repeated the adjustment several times. Behind his seat, where Ross couldn't see, Ian adjusted the knob on a short green cylinder labeled "Oxygen." An identical cylinder was strapped to the back of Ross' seat in a similar backpack-like sling, but its mask was still attached to the tube coiled around the top of the bottle.

The Catalina kept climbing.

As they passed through 17,000 feet, Ian glanced at his watch and then over at Ross. The big guy had relaxed his death grip on the seat cushion and he sat with his hands in his lap. Ian smiled. "How are you feeling, Ross?"

Ross shrugged his shoulders. "Fine."

Ian glanced back into the galley. "How's your buddy doing?"

Ross leaned into the aisle between the two seats and yelled, "How you doing, Lenny?"

Ian hastily turned down the intercom volume and shook his head to clear the ringing in his ears. He hadn't given Lenny a headset, so he didn't hear Lenny's response. Ross leaned back, flashed Ian an "okay" and started to say something Ian couldn't hear. Ian turned the volume back up.

"...keep asking how we're doing. We're doing great!" Ross smiled amicably. "Why are you so fucking worried?"

Ian was carefully holding onto the oxygen tube with his teeth. It made him sound like Humphrey Bogart. "I just want to make sure you guys aren't getting hypoxia."

The altimeter wound through 18,000 feet.

"What's hypo...?" Ross smiled. "What is that?"

"Hypoxia is also called altitude sickness. It's caused by a lack of oxygen." Ian pointed to the altimeter. "We're climbing pretty high. The air pressure at this altitude is less than half of what it is at sea level. That means that even when your lungs are full, you still get less than half the oxygen you would on the ground. Do you smoke?"

Ross thought about the question for a moment and then shook his head. "No. Why?"

"Just asking." Ian shrugged. "The carbon monoxide from cigarettes cuts down your blood's ability to carry oxygen. You get hypoxia at a much lower altitude if you smoke." Ian blinked his eyes rapidly and took a few breaths through his nose. "It's a delicate balance. Too much oxygen can be almost as bad as too little."

"Why?"

"It can make you dizzy, nauseous."

Ross nodded amicably. "I feel fine."

"That's good, Ross." Ian opened his mouth a little as he inhaled, mixing some of the thin cabin air with the oxygen coming from the tube between his teeth. "Hypoxia can sneak up on you. The first symptom, for most people, is a sense of complete well being, but you're feeling okay, right?"

Ross nodded enthusiastically. "Oh yeah."

Ian smiled. "I notice you don't seem too worried about being in an airplane."

"Nah." Ross shrugged. "I'm cool."

"Good. You were pretty freaked when we took off, but I'm glad you're feeling okay now. Another symptom of hypoxia is that your fingernails turn blue." Ian held up his hand so Ross could see it. Ian's cuticles were pink.

Ross held up his own hand and Ian noticed the bluish purple under his nails. "Wow, your nails are really blue! That's okay, though, as long as you're feeling all right."

Ross and Ian both smiled as Ross stared at his fingertips.

The Catalina was struggling to climb a hundred feet per minute when Ian leveled off at 21,000. He switched on the autopilot and studied Ross for a moment. "Can you see okay?" Ian waved his hand at Ross and the linebacker turned his head toward the moving fingers. "How about your peripheral vision?" Ian moved his hand next to Ross' shoulder. "Can you still see my hand?"

Ross nodded slowly.

"Jesus!" Ian shook his head. "Why are you still awake?"

Ross looked puzzled. "Huh?"

"When I did the high altitude class I was out cold before the chamber reached 19,000!" Ian glanced back into the galley. Lenny was slumped forward drooling onto the dinning table. Ian looked at Ross. "Hypoxia does affect different people in different ways, but at 21,000 feet, you should at least lose your peripheral vision. Then, just before you pass out, everything should fade to black."

Ross shook his head deliberately. "I feel great!"

"Maybe you have to have brain cells before they can be affected by lack of oxygen." Ian considered. "Let's try putting a little more load on your metabolism. Your body doesn't need as much oxygen when you're not worried or doing something physical. You should probably move around a little."

"Okay." Ross smiled. His hands remained folded comfortably in his lap.

Ian glanced back into the galley again. "Oh my god! What's wrong with Lenny?"

Ross leaned way over into the aisle and looked back. "He's asleep." It took him a moment to straighten back up.

"Are you sure?" Ian shook his head. "I think he may be dead. You'd better go check on him!"

"Dead?" Ross tried to get up, but the seatbelt held him in place. "Lenny? How could he be dead? What did you do to him?" Ian leaned over to release the belt, but then Ross got his arm caught in the shoulder harness. Halfway into the aisle, Ross tugged his arm out of the nylon noose and stumbled down the stairs to the galley. At the bottom, Ross fell to his knees as though he'd found another step, and then toppled forward onto the carpeted deck.

The tube in Ian's mouth made his grin a bit lopsided. "Finally!" He took a deep breath of pure oxygen, and unfastened his seatbelt. "Now for the hard part." Making sure he didn't dislodge the oxygen tube attached to his headset, Ian carefully leaned over toward the copilot's seat. He lifted the oxygen rig off the back of the right seat and placed it in his lap. Trading his headset for a thin elastic strap that held two small plastic pipes just under his nostrils, Ian opened the valve on the copilot's oxygen cylinder. He sniffed, pulled the other oxygen tube out of his mouth and sniffed again. Satisfied that the second unit was working, Ian turned off the valve on the first cylinder and stood up between the two seats. He slung the backpack-like holder over his shoulders, and adjusted the pipes under his nose.

Ian rested his hand on the instrument console as he scanned the instruments. Outside, the sky was a darker shade of blue than it had seemed during preflight, but

Ian's cuticles glowed the same oxygen-rich pink they'd been at sea level. The autopilot would keep the Catalina on course and at the right altitude until the big seaplane ran out of fuel. Ian nodded resolutely and turned away from the instruments.

Moving aft, Ian was careful not to step on Ross. He pressed two fingers against the thick neck and searched until he found a pulse. He then checked Lenny, searching first for a pulse, and then for the revolver they'd fought for earlier. Searching through the unconscious man's pockets with the table in the way was awkward, but Ian eventually found the gun in Lenny's jacket. He slipped it into his own jacket pocket and then checked to make sure Lenny wasn't carrying anything else. Ross didn't have a gun, but there was a mean looking commando knife in his belt. Ian set the knife on the counter on the left side of the aisle, and turned to look forward.

The yokes turned a few degrees to the left, as if ghosts were flying the plane. The autopilot was holding the Catalina on course at 21,000 feet. It was 15 degrees below zero outside, and even with the cabin heat on full, the aluminum skinned Catalina didn't feel much warmer inside. Ian blew on his hands to warm them. "This is insane!"

Ian opened the locker above the galley table. Emergency survival supplies shared the space with parachutes, blankets and a case of oil. Letting the door spring closed, Ian looked aft into the main cabin and thought out loud. "The only other rope I've got is anchor line and that's way too stiff." He shook his head. "Necessity is definitely a mother."

Ian pulled out one of the parachutes and set it on the table next to Lenny's head. Using Ross' commando knife, Ian quickly separated a handful of lines from the parachute harness and canopy. It took only a few minutes to tie Lenny's hands behind his back, and a few more to bind his feet to the post that supported the table. Ian raised Lenny's head and slid the remains of the parachute under his face.

It took less than a minute for Ian to realize he couldn't get Ross off the floor, let alone slide him in next to Lenny. He used the remaining cord to hog-tie the big man's wrists to his ankles and left him face down on the carpet.

Ian straightened up and surveyed the galley. Looking at the two former hijackers, he chuckled. "Piece of cake." He nodded, very pleased with himself. "Clever MacAran. Damn clever." He'd left Ross' knife on the counter next to the sink and when he reached for it, he noticed the purple hue of his own cuticles. He chuckled again. "This is really not a good sign."

Reaching around to the cylinder on his back, Ian opened the valve another full turn. He stepped past Ross' knee as he pressed the oxygen cannula against his nose and took a deep breath. He blinked to clear his head, and reached back to open the valve all the way. The last of the cylinder's oxygen trickled out.

The first step up to the flight deck was easy. The second step wasn't where he thought it should be and Ian ended up on his knees between the two pilot seats. His peripheral vision was gone and he had to turn his head to see the headset, resting on the left seat. Grabbing the microphone boom, Ian clamped the oxygen tube between his teeth and then fumbled with the sling on the back of the chair. By the time he reached the valve on the cylinder, his vision had gone completely black.

A little oxygen seeped through his clenched teeth, and then much more flowed through the plastic tube when Ian relaxed his bite. His vision began to clear with the first deep breath. Still holding onto the pilot's seat for support, Ian scanned the instruments. The autopilot still held the plane on course at 21,000; right where they were supposed to be. Ian took several more breaths and then struggled up into the pilot's seat. He looked outside, rubbed his eyes, and then searched the horizon for any other planes.

"Stay on the flight deck, MacAran." Ian muttered around the tube in his mouth as he slipped the headset over his ears. "Just stay on the goddamned flight deck!" He pushed the tube a little further into his mouth and keyed the microphone. "L.A. Center, Catalina 1292 Whiskey."

"1292 WHISKEY, I'VE BEEN TRYING TO CALL YOU, SIR. YOU'RE LEAVING MY SECTOR, CONTACT CENTER NOW ON 135.5."

"92 Whiskey, roger. My apologies. Is this radio any better?"

"92 WHISKEY, AFFIRMATIVE. NO PROBLEM, SIR. HAVE A GOOD FLIGHT."

"92 Whiskey, thanks." Ian changed frequencies. When the new controller answered, Ian changed his destination to Las Vegas and requested a lower altitude. Cleared to

11,000, Ian reduced the power and set the autopilot to that altitude. The Catalina began a smooth descent. Ian retrieved his kneeboard from the glare screen and connected the Velcro straps behind his knee. Clipped above the L.A. sectional chart was a scrap of paper with the number Carlos had given him that morning. Ian reached into his jacket pocket for his phone but brought out Lenny's gun. He set the gun on the kneeboard and reached again for his phone. Moving one earphone back behind his ear, Ian dialed the number in Mexico. Someone answered on the first ring.

"Hi, this is Ian MacAran. Is Carlos available?"

"Momento."

Ian reduced the power a little more to speed up the descent, and scanned the horizon.

"Ian? This is Clara."

"Clara!" Ian hesitated. "How are you holding up?"

"We'll be okay. Everything happened so fast we didn't get a chance to say goodbye."

"I'm, uh, I'm really sorry about Mick."

"Me too, but I'm glad you're coming down. We've got a lot to talk about."

"I can't come down, Clara, at least not today. That's why I'm calling. I couldn't say anything when I was talking to Carlos earlier because Des had a gun in my ear."

"I don't understand."

"Des has flipped out, Clara. He's got everything he owns riding on this one deal and it's making him crazy. When I told him I wouldn't fly for him, he went nuts. This morning, he stormed into my house with a bunch of thugs and kidnapped my girlfriend. He says he'll kill her if I don't do what he says."

"But if you do what he says, he'll let her go?"

"Maybe, but it's not that simple. Did Mick tell you about shell-game?"

"Of course."

"Well, it won't work, at least not without some details that Des wouldn't give me time to arrange. There's paperwork that takes a few days to get processed. I told Des we needed more time to get it set up, even if I was willing to fly for him, but he wouldn't believe me. I've only got until tomorrow afternoon to find another way to make him let Sandy go. I was hoping Carlos, Arturo and a few of the guys could help. I certainly can't go to the police."

"Why not?"

"Des said he had "influential friends". I think someone inside told him, or the people he works for, that Mick was a cop. I think that's why they killed him. Clara, if I talk to the wrong cop, Sandy and I are both history."

For a moment, the static on the line seemed louder. "Are you saying Des killed my husband?"

"I don't know anything for sure, Clara. Des denied it. He said that somebody named Paul killed Mick, but Des is the one who kidnapped Sandy. Right now, I don't trust anything that little bastard says."

"Des works for a college professor named Paul Neault. I met Paul once. He seemed like a nice man." Clara paused. When she continued, she sounded far away. "Des was a friend, Ian. We trusted him. I can't believe he'd want to hurt Mick."

"Until this morning I'd have agreed with you, Clara, but the last thing he said before I took off was that I'd never be able to find all the pieces of Sandy's body if I didn't make this goddamned deal work, and I can not make it work!"

"We'll do what we can, Ian. Carlos is in Mexico City, but he expected to be back before you got here. Can he reach you on your cell phone?"

"Yeah."

"I'll ask him to call you as soon as I hear from him."

"Thanks, Clara. Like I said, I'm really sorry about Mick. If there's anything ..."

"Mick really liked you, Ian. He never planned for you to get into any trouble." Clara paused. "It bothered him that he couldn't tell you he was a cop. He thought of you as a younger brother."

"Really?" Ian was surprised. "I'm really sorry."

"Me too. I don't know when I'll be coming back to the States, Ian. The house in Alameda will be sold as soon as Ken finishes the remodeling. You'll have to come visit us after we've settled our affairs."

"I will, Clara. Thanks."

"We'll take care of Mr. Pierrot, Ian. You just take care of yourself. I'll have Carlos call you when he gets back."

"Goodbye, Clara." Ian folded the phone and slipped it back into his jacket pocket. As the Catalina descended, Ian divided his attention between watching for other planes and plotting a course for Las Vegas. Dropping through 14,000 feet, Ian heard a muffled thud behind him. He turned to look back into the galley.

Struggling to roll over, Ross pounded his knee into the table. "Ow!" He looked up and saw Ian looking back at him. "You motherfucker! Let me go!" A much louder thump was followed by a series of expletives and then, "Lenny! Goddamn it, why didn't you wake me up?"

"I don't know." Lenny's speech was slurred and groggy. "What happened?"

"The sonofabitch turned off the fucking air or something." Ross raised his voice even further. "And if he doesn't cut us loose right fucking now, I'm gonna kill him!" Ross was struggling furiously against the parachute cords, but despite his efforts, he didn't look any less secure.

Ian turned back to scan the horizon as he shouted over his shoulder. "You were right about the air, Ross. This isn't a pressurized airplane so we need to use bottled oxygen at higher altitudes. No pressurization also means I can open a door any time I want, so if you want to stay on board and stay alive, Ross, stop trying to piss me off."

"I'm gonna do more than piss you off, asshole! I'm gonna rip off your head and shit down your fucking neck if you don't untie us right fucking now!"

"Obviously keeping you two aboard was a mistake." Ian switched off the auto-pilot, pushed the throttles forward and pulled back on the wheel. The seaplane surged through level flight and started climbing, pushing everyone aboard toward the aluminum bilges. "We'll just climb back up to twenty thousand, Ross. I'll drop you guys off as soon as you fall asleep. You won't feel a thing." Ian turned to look Ross in the eye. "Of course, you'll probably wake up on the way down, but that won't last too long." Ian shrugged and turned back to the controls.

"Wait!" Lenny screamed, "We're cool! We're cool!"

"I'm sorry, Lenny, but I've got too much to deal with right now, and your buddy isn't cooperating."

"We're okay. We're cool. Honest, man. We don't want any trouble. Ross just has a big mouth, man. Tell him you're sorry Ross!"

"Fuck you, Lenny, no way I'm..."

"Ross, you motherless fucking shit, I'm gonna kill you. I swear to almighty God I'm gonna break every bone in your skank-ass body if you don't do exactly what the nice pilot says. Now tell him you're fucking sorry!"

"Okay, okay. Chill out, Lenny. Jesus." Ross looked at Ian. "We won't give you any trouble, Mr. MacAran."

Ian nodded. "Good plan, Ross." Ian eased the throttles back and the thrum of the twin radials faded into the background.

After a few minutes of silence Lenny said, "Hey, could you untie me? Please?"

Ross said, "Hey! Watch it!"

"Come on, I said 'please!'" Lenny raised his voice and yelled, "Untie me, you fucking bitch!"

Ian glanced back into the galley. "I've never been called a..." In a panic, he ripped Lenny's gun out from under the Las Vegas chart and swung it toward the galley. He'd grabbed the gun at an awkward angle and couldn't get his finger through the trigger guard. An instant later, he realized that it wasn't Ross or Lenny who was stepping up to the cockpit and he stopped fumbling with the gun.

Bernie yawned and pointed back at the thugs in the galley. "How'd you do that?"

Ian just stared at her.

"Seriously, how'd you manage to tie them up?" Bernie picked up the copilot's oxygen cylinder, slid the green tank into the canvas holder on the back of the right seat and sat down. Ian stared at her as she buckled her harness. Bernie smiled self-consciously. "What?"

"CATALINA 1292 WHISKEY, LOS ANGELES CENTER."

"Uh," Ian cleared his throat and then keyed the mike. "Center, 92 Whiskey."

"92 WHISKEY, SAY ALTITUDE AND INTENTIONS."

"92 Whiskey is descending through," Ian looked at the altimeter, "13,600 for 11,000, request cancel IFR. We'll be VFR to Las Vegas." Ian set the revolver in his lap, on top of the L.A. sectional chart.

"92 WHISKEY SQUAWK 1200, FREQUENCY CHANGE APPROVED. FOR FLIGHT FOLLOWING SUGGEST L.A. CENTER ON 132.85."

"132.85, 92 Whiskey, roger." Ian glanced at Bernie and then looked outside the plane. He eased the nose down and started a left turn. "Bernie, are you feeling all right?"

"Yeah."

"No headache or nausea or anything like that?"

"Nope." Bernie shook her head. "Why?"

"We were at 21,000 feet for about fifteen minutes. That's what knocked out the two stooges." Ian studied her closely. "There isn't much oxygen at 21,000."

"I feel fine, really." Bernie stifled a yawn. "I didn't realize this plane would go that high."

"The miracles of turbo-charging. Lean over here." Ian pulled the oxygen tube away from his headset and held it out to her. "Breathe in."

Bernie leaned toward him and puffed on the clear plastic tube. Her eyes opened wide. "Wow!" She straightened up and looked out the front window. "A second ago, everything was kind of fuzzy but now, Christ! I can see all the way to Reno! Those clouds are fantastic!"

"Reno is that way." Ian pointed behind them and to the left. "I used the bathroom just before takeoff so you must have stowed away in the crew quarters. "How'd you get in there?"

"You left the door open when you guys went back to Des' car."

"Okay. That explains how you got here." Ian looked at her suspiciously. "Why are you here?"

Bernie explained how she'd watched from across the street and then followed Des to Hayward Airport. "I couldn't just stand by and do nothing so I came along."

"And Ken called the police?"

"Yeah, but they didn't get there in time. What can I do to help?"

"Who?"

Bernie looked confused. "What do you mean?"

"Help who? Who are you trying to help? Me? Sandy?" Ian hooked his thumb toward the galley. "The two stooges? Who?"

"You, of course. I came to help you."

"To do what, exactly?"

Bernie met his intense gaze with irritated concern. "What's wrong with you?"

"What isn't wrong? My girlfriend," He gave Bernie a sarcastic look. "Excuse me, *our* girlfriend has been kidnapped by a lunatic who swears he'll kill her if I don't bring him a plane load of cocaine that I can't get into the country because Cindy's goddamned Mooney is the plane that will be going through Customs and it isn't on the overflight permit!"

"Who's Cindy?"

"Tony's fiancé."

"Who's Tony?"

"The computer genius who made this shit." Ian tapped the gray box on the console between the seats.

"What does that...?"

"Not the point!" Ian glared at her for a moment before continuing. "Des, that's the lunatic, may or may not have killed Mick but he sure as hell had something to do with it, and I think he's crazy enough to kill Sandy if I don't do exactly what he wants. The problem is, I can't do what he wants because this goddamned plan of Mick's can't possibly work without the three day notice Des wouldn't let me give the FAA."

"Des killed...?"

"I can't go to the police because they'd either put me in jail or get Sandy killed. Probably both. I'd gladly go to prison if it would get Sandy out of this mess, but that wouldn't help."

"Prison? What the hell is going on, Ian?"

"I just told you!"

"But if Des kidnapped Sandy, and he killed Mick, and he's threatening to kill Sandy if you don't smuggle drugs for him, why would you be going to prison?"

"Because I already did it twice."

"Oh my god."

"Yeah. I'm a drug smuggler." Ian hesitated. "Wow. I've never said that out loud before: 'drug smuggler.' Who'd have thought?"

"Certainly not me." Bernie looked at Ian as if she was seeing him for the very first time.

"Right." Ian checked their heading against the auto-pilot bug. "Okay that's my baggage. Let's talk about yours. We've got a few minutes. What are you trying to do with me and Sandy?"

Bernie rolled her eyes at the ceiling. "I told you I could handle that."

"No, you told me you could handle my seeing some-one else. You didn't mention that Sandy was the one who gave you the concert tickets or that the two of you had been lovers for two years!"

"I didn't know she was the other person you were seeing."

"You sure as hell knew I was the guy you were seeing when Sandy told you all about me at the Hyatt. That was

Thursday, right? The same day you and I flew to Clearlake!"

"Thursday night was after Clearlake." Bernie said.

"But you'd already seen Sandy at her office the day before. You already knew who I was seeing when you were asking me to tell you about the 'other woman.' After two years I'm sure you know a lot more about her than I do!"

"But I didn't know how you felt about her."

"You could have asked me!"

"I did. And I told you why I was asking about Sandy; I wanted to know where I stood."

"Where you stood was that I loved you, and I trusted you. Didn't I tell you I loved you?"

"I told you I loved you too!"

"So what about Sandy?"

Bernie shifted in her seat, first turning toward Ian, but then looking out the front windscreen. With the engines throttled back for the descent, they could hear Ross snicker, "Jesus, Lenny, sounds like a fucking soap opera, don't it?"

Ian exploded. "I swear to God, Ross, if you don't shut up you're going skydiving without a parachute!" He glared at Ross and the Smeghead lowered his eyes to the floor. Ian looked at Bernie, and took a deep breath. "Getting a job with Mick wasn't a coincidence, was it?"

Bernie hesitated.

"Was it?"

"What difference does it make?"

"Right now I think being completely honest makes all the difference in the world. How did you find Mick?"

"I followed you from Sandy's house, after the movie. I saw you and Mick talking and I saw his phone number on the side of his truck."

"So you were stalking her?"

"I wasn't 'stalking' her! That sounds so ugly. I just didn't know what else to do."

"So that whole scene at the concert... why all the drama?"

"I told you: it caught me off guard."

"But you knew I was seeing someone and you knew exactly who it was! We wouldn't even have met if you hadn't planned it! What could possibly catch you off guard?"

"I forgot how much I missed her."

Ian considered. "You said you loved me, was that just another part of your cunning plan?"

"No!" Bernie shook her head. There was a tear at the corner of her eye, but she glared at Ian. "I don't have a cunning plan. I mean, well, I didn't plan on caring about you, you jerk, but I do. And I wouldn't have said I loved you if I didn't mean it."

"So you meant it?'

"I still mean it!" Bernie said angrily. Then she whispered. "I love you."

Even with the headsets, Ian couldn't hear her last three words over the hum of the engines but he knew what she'd said. "You said it wasn't possible to love two people at once."

"I didn't think it was! What about you? You said you loved me; don't you love Sandy too?" Bernie glared at Ian for a moment and then, before he realized what she was doing; she snatched the revolver off his lap. Ian caught a glimpse of bullet down the short barrel as Bernie swung the gun past his face and pointed it down the aisle. "Freeze, asshole!"

Ross froze. He'd gotten his hands free and had been cutting through the cords around his ankles when Bernie had noticed what he was up to.

Keeping her eyes on Ross, Bernie asked Ian, "Can I shoot him?"

"What?" Ian was staring down the aisle at the knife in Ross' hand, the knife Ian had left on the counter.

Bernie was sighting down the short barrel at the bridge of Ross' nose. "Can I shoot this sonofabitch without hurting the plane? I might not hit him with all six bullets."

Before Ian answered, Ross slowly set the knife on the floor and raised his hands. Ian glanced at Bernie. "It would be better if you didn't miss, but if you have to shoot him, go right ahead."

Ross interlaced his fingers on top of his head and tried to look harmless. Bernie lowered her arm to her lap, but made sure the gun still pointed at the center of the big man's chest. She glanced at Ian, "Now what?"

Wednesday, 12:46 pm - Douglas & Sons Sporting Goods, Las Vegas

"Mrs. Wilson, I didn't take any pictures because there wasn't anything to take pictures of. Your husband..." Orson Douglas shook his head philosophically as she talked over him. A tall, broad shouldered man with curly red hair and a dark red beard, Orson nodded his head occasionally as he listened to his client rant. His deep baritone voice revealed only a hint of his impatience. "Mrs. Wilson, if you'll just..." He was sitting in a padded, ergonomic chair in the manager's office of Douglas and Sons Sporting Goods. Orson was the youngest of the four sons.

Three steps up from the sales floor at the end of the last gun counter, the office afforded an excellent view of the front half of the store. Standing at the handgun counter was a blond guy in a white shirt. On the other side of the counter, Vince, the store manager, was showing him a pair of handcuffs. Guns, holsters and extra magazines were piled on the counter between the two men, along with a dozen boxes of ammunition. Vince looked pleased with the transaction, but the customer looked agitated, intermittently glancing at his watch and the door while they talked.

Orson stood up to get a better view of the nervous customer. "I'm sorry, Mrs. Wilson. I thought you'd be delighted that your husband isn't having an affair." Orson moved the phone away from his ear to protect his hearing. On the counter next to the guns and ammo, Vince had spread out the forms that needed to be filled out to purchase the firearms. The customer glanced at his watch again.

Orson cautiously moved the receiver back to his ear. "Mrs. Wilson? Listen, I appreciate your business, but there just isn't anything else I can do for you. In my opinion, my professional opinion, your husband has been entirely faithful. His business trips are purely business and when he says he's going to his model railroad club, that's where he goes. Save your money, Mrs. Wilson. Aside from Belgian steam locomotives, Lucius only has eyes for you." Orson smiled. "Yes ma'am, my pleasure. Goodbye." He hung up the phone and muttered, "Poor Lucius," as he stepped down to the sales floor.

There was a slight edge of impatience in Vince's voice, "As I've already explained, Mr. MacAran, it's not a state law, it's a federal law. It's called the Brady Bill. You can't buy a handgun without waiting three days. If anyone told you anything else, they were mistaken. I'm sorry."

The customer nodded, glanced at his watch again, and then looked out through the front door of the store. "What about a rifle?"

"Sir?"

"Can I buy a rifle or a shotgun or something and take it home today?"

Vince hesitated, so Orson stepped over to help.

"Perhaps I can be of assistance?" Orson extended his hand. "I'm Orson Douglas, the owner."

"Ian MacAran."

They shook hands cordially. Orson looked down at the assortment of weapons on the counter. "Looks like you're getting ready for something big." He noticed the cut on Ian's cheek and the swelling around it. "That looks painful."

"It's not that bad. Look, I just want to make sure my house is safe." Ian glanced at the guns, holsters, ammunition and accessories. "It's a big house."

Orson nodded skeptically. "And you want something right away?"

"Is that possible?"

"Well, it's possible. In fact, if you just want to defend your home, you're probably better off with a shotgun anyway. Do you have much experience with handguns?"

Ian shook his head. "Not really."

"Then I'd definitely recommend a shotgun. That's something you can take home today, as long as your paperwork checks out. You fill out a form, we wait about twenty minutes for the results of your background check, and you're all set."

"Okay, can we get that started first? You could help me pick out the gun while the paperwork gets approved."

"My thought exactly." Orson glanced at the stack of forms Vince had left on the counter and pushed the top one toward Ian. "Just fill in all the information on the first page."

"Right." While Ian filled out the form Orson passed the handguns to Vince who began placing them back on the shelves below the counter. Orson gathered up the ammunition, pausing for a moment to watch Ian fill in all the appropriate blanks. The Citizen pilots' watch on Ian's wrist marked the seconds with quartz precision. Orson also noted the pens and Ray Ban sunglasses neatly lined up in the pocket of Ian's uniform shirt. Orson put the ammo away, but left the handcuffs on the counter. There were two pairs, each in its own cardboard box. He held up a shoulder holster for a small revolver. "Is this for a gun you already have?"

"What?" Ian glanced up from the form. "Oh yeah. It is."

Orson nodded. "And do you have that gun with you now?"

"Yeah, uh, no. It's across the street, in the plane." Ian finished signing his name and turned the clipboard toward Orson. "This only takes twenty minutes?"

"Usually." Orson looked over the information Ian had put down. "In your case, though, there may not be much of a hurry. You live in California?"

"Is that a problem?"

"Not a problem. We just need to send any guns you buy in Nevada to a licensed dealer in California. You can pick them up there."

"But I need something today."

"Why?"

"Uh," Ian glanced uncertainly from Orson to Vince and then back to Orson. "It's a little complicated."

Orson nodded and then handed the clipboard to the manager. "Run this through for me, will you, Vince?"

"Sure." Vince walked down to the other end of the counter and started typing Ian's information into a terminal next to the cash register.

"So," Orson reached into his vest pocket and pulled out a business card. "You've got a plane parked across the street. At Signature?"

Ian shook his head. "We're parked at Eagle."

"That would've been my second guess. What kind of plane is it?"

"PBY Catalina."

"Is that some kind of business jet?"

Ian shook his head. "World War II seaplane."

"Really? Are you the owner or the pilot?"

"Both."

"Both." Orson tapped the holster on the counter with the business card in his hand. "So you're visiting from California with a medium sized revolver that you forgot the holster for, but you want to buy more guns, which you need in a hurry." Orson set the card on the glass next to the cuffs. "What are the handcuffs for?"

Ian sighed, exasperated. "You wouldn't believe me."

"Maybe not, but I've seen more than a little weird in my life. Try me." Orson picked up the card and handed it to Ian. The card was blue gray, with "Orson Raymond Douglas - Private Investigator" printed across the center. "You know, we sell more handcuffs to adventurous couples than we do to cops, and I don't usually ask embarrassing questions, but you don't seem like the handcuffed-to-the-bedposts type."

Ian glanced at his watch and then looked again at Orson's card.

"Are you planning to kill somebody?"

"Of course not!" Ian looked appalled.

"Well, that's reassuring." Orson nodded. "Are you planning something illegal?"

Ian set Orson's card on the counter. "No, but I am running out of time." He turned to leave.

"Mr. MacAran, please." Orson took a step toward the door, stopping when Ian stopped. "Tell me what this is all about. Please. Not just to satisfy my curiosity, but because I really might be able to help you." Orson waited for Ian to turn back toward the counter before he continued. "I'm a Private Investigator, not a cop. I used to be a cop and I've got a lot of experience, but if you hire me, I'll be working for you and nobody else. That means I keep your business completely confidential. My instincts tell me you really should hire me, but even if I can't help you, I'll still keep anything you tell me in the strictest confidence."

"I appreciate the offer, Mr. Douglas, but I don't see how you can help."

"Come on, Mr. MacAran. Where do you go from here? I can help you. I don't know what you're up against, but I'm willing to help you and I'm dying to hear the rest of this story. Satisfy my curiosity, Mr. MacAran, please? I'll do anything I can to help and I just might die a happy man."

Ian shook his head resignedly and glanced at his watch. "I've, uh..." He hesitated, and then met Orson's open, friendly gaze. "I've gotten a friend into a lot of trouble and I have to get her out of it."

Forty minutes later, Ian was leading Orson through the Eagle Aviation Terminal. Orson carried two large hard-shell cases and Ian had a third heavy case slung over his shoulder. Orson hesitated even after the automatic doors sensed their approach and slid open. He looked around, but there were no metal detectors for them to carry the heavy cases through. Across the tarmac, a bright orange Southwest 737 turned off the runway, exhaust from its engines shimmering across the pavement. Orson hurried to catch up with Ian, who was walking toward the only black plane on the ramp.

92 Whiskey was also the only propeller driven plane on the ramp. It looked completely out of place surrounded by business jets ranging in size from 8 place Citations to an Airbus configured to carry the entire Pirates baseball team. Bernie was sitting on the settee under the open gun blister and when she saw Ian approaching, she impatiently beckoned him to hurry up. Ian quickened his pace, but the long case made it impossible to actually run. He searched for signs of trouble as he dropped the case and hurried up the ladder into the Catalina. "What's wrong?"

"Nothing's wrong." Bernie snapped. She kept the revolver pointed forward toward Lenny and Ross as she grabbed Ian's right hand and brought it up to the gun. "Shoot Lenny first. He's been whining about going to the bathroom since you left, and I think he may have gotten his hands free again." Bernie wrapped Ian's fingers around the .38, ducked under his arm and disappeared into the bathroom.

"Wow." Orson paused on the ladder's second rung and stared at the Catalina's teak-trimmed interior. "The outside says World War II, but the inside says luxury yacht." He set one of his cases on the port settee and stepped down to retrieve the other two.

By the time Bernie emerged from the bathroom, Ian had given the revolver to Orson in exchange for an odd looking shotgun that said Ludovick on the high-impact plastic stock. Bernie looked from the shotgun to Orson and then at Ian. "Looks like you brought back more than some extra firepower." She pointed to Ian's shotgun. "What is that thing?"

"Ludovick Close Assault Weapon," Orson was opening a second case. "It's the state of the art in shotguns."

"Why a shotgun?"

Ian lowered his voice. "I told Orson I'd never fired a gun before. He said it's hard to miss with one of these."

Orson nodded. "You also have more options with a shotgun. This will fire standard twelve gauge shells, but it also fires smoke, tear gas and incendiary grenades."

"Incendiary grenades?" Bernie looked from Orson to Ian and back. "Is Rambo coming with us?"

"Bernie," Ian kept the Ludovick pointed at Lenny and Ross. "This is Orson Douglas. Orson, this is Bernie Selleca. Orson owns the gun store, but he's also a private investigator. He pretty much insisted I hire him to help us."

"Hi Orson." Bernie studied him for a moment. "Have you had much experience with this sort of thing?"

"I've had a lot of experiences, Miss Selleca, though nothing exactly like this."

"Welcome to the party." Bernie looked at Ian. "Where's my gun?"

"We brought you one of these," Ian hefted the shotgun, "or you can stick with the .38."

"Hey!" Lenny pointed down the aisle at Bernie. "That's my goddamned revolver!"

"I'm keeping the gun, Lenny, but I'll give you back the bullets, if you don't shut up." Bernie softened her tone and smiled at Ian. "I told you he got his hands free."

Ian nodded. "We'll take care of that right now. Orson?"

"Two pairs of handcuffs coming up. But first," Orson slipped the .38 Ian had given him into its new holster and offered the rig to Bernie. "Have you ever worn a shoulder holster before?"

"No." Bernie slipped past Ian so she could reach the gun.

"I can show you how it's supposed to fit, or you can just slide the holster onto your belt." Orson glanced at Ian. "I'd recommend the shoulder holster. It's a lot easier to conceal." He was down on one knee between the two open cases. Assorted odd-looking boxes and some lightweight headsets filled one case while the other held an assortment of cameras, microphones and other paraphernalia.

"Thanks." Bernie looked at the straps attached to the holster for a moment and then slipped her arms through the loops as though she was putting on a shirt. "Like this?"

Orson nodded approvingly. "Exactly like that."

Bernie pointed to the open cases. "Are we really going to need all that stuff?"

"I hope not." Orson smiled. "But Sun Tzu did say, 'Those who face the unprepared with preparation are victorious'."

"I thought that was the Boy Scout motto."

"Be prepared?" Orson chuckled as he dug out the handcuffs, but then his expression grew serious. "You know, we can get away with holding onto these guys for a day or so, but eventually we either have to turn them in to the police or let them go."

Bernie glanced at Ian. "We could kill them."

"Don't tempt me." Ian looked like he was considering Bernie's suggestion.

Orson looked from Bernie to Ian. "Seriously."

"I am serious." Bernie nodded emphatically. "You spend thirty minutes listening to these two bitch and whine and try to out stupid each other and you'll feel the same way."

Ian shook his head. "We can't turn them over to the police until we know who Des' friends on the force are, and we certainly can't let them go. They'd tell Des I didn't go to Mexico. I have no idea what he'd do if he found out we're not following his plan."

"This is the guy who killed your undercover friend?"

"I think so, yeah."

Orson handed Ian a bullet resistant vest. "Is he using?"

"Drugs? I don't know. Why?"

"Dealers who use drugs are a lot less predictable." Orson handed Bernie a vest. "Does this guy have too much energy; does he talk really fast?"

"I guess so," Ian nodded, "Sometimes."

"Does he seem anxious or jumpy?"

"He was kidnapping my girlfriend, Orson; he 'seemed' deranged!"

"Okay, but before today, did he have a runny nose or maybe a lot of nose bleeds?"

"He said it was allergies."

"He's probably using."

"That's probably not good." Bernie shrugged into her vest and looked at Ian. "So, what's our plan?"

"My original plan was to get the stooges back there to tell me where Des took Sandy. Then I was going to get her out of wherever that turned out to be." Ian looked from Bernie to Orson to the pair in the back of the plane. Ross sneered back at them. "I thought they'd be a lot easier to work with." Ian said, "I'm open to suggestions."

"It's not a bad plan." Orson looked at their prisoners. "I'm sure these guys know something about where your girl is. Get us airborne." He shrugged philosophically. "I'll see what I can do."

Bernie was also looking at Ross and Lenny. "And what do we do with them when we get back? If we let them go they're gonna warn Des and if we keep them with us we're going to spend all our energy making sure they don't escape. If we can't kill them can we at least drug them or something?"

"Farallons!"

Bernie and Orson both said, "What?"

Ian smiled, "I know the perfect place to store these guys."

Four miles to the north, Cindy and Tony were at the Shotgun Wedding Chapel of the Stars. Elvis was singing "Love Me Tender." When Cindy had begun her approach into Las Vegas she'd chosen the general aviation field north of the city. Landing at the big international airport didn't even occur to her. While Ian had approached McCarran from the southwest, Cindy had come into North Las Vegas Airport from the north. With radio handoffs from different approach controllers to different towers at different airports, they'd managed to arrive in Las Vegas at exactly the same time without hearing or seeing each other. By the time the big black seaplane flew up the Strip and turned West toward San Francisco, Cindy and Tony were inside exchanging their vows with Frank Sinatra and a six foot tall Liza Minnelli as witnesses.

Wednesday, 5:47 pm – 4500 feet
over Big Daddy's Surf Shack

In the hour and a half it took the Catalina to get back to the Golden Gate Orson had taken Lenny to the back of the plane and left Ross with Bernie in the main salon. Every once in a while he'd come up and ask Ross a few questions and then return to Lenny. Ross was little help, but Lenny described the entire planning session with Des and the Smegheads down to what each of them had for breakfast when they went to the Grababite Café.

As the seaplane crossed over Stinson Beach and Big Daddy's Surf Shack, Orson headed up to the flight deck and leaned between the front seats. "As of this morning they were planning to take Sandra to an apartment in Berkeley. I've got the address. They're not even trying to conceal their identities and that worries me. It could mean they're not planning on the victims being alive to testify once the ransom is delivered, but in this case I think Des is counting on you not being able to go to the police. Des said as much to these guys this morning, but that doesn't mean he's not planning to kill the Smegheads along with you and Sandy once he gets what he wants."

"You think he'd do that?"

"I've never met the guy, so I'm assuming the worst. If I'm wrong I can handle being pleasantly surprised."

"Yeah." Ian nodded as he banked left and looked out the window. "We're about ten minutes out."

"We'll get 'em ready." Orson headed aft.

Nine minutes later, just as Ian reached up and pulled the throttles back, Bernie slid into the right seat and buckled up. The thrum of the engines eased with the reduction in power. Ian checked the gauges as he recited the abbreviated-landing checklist. "Gas, fullest tanks. Undercarriage..." He pressed two fingers under the wheel-shaped lever to make sure it was all the way up, pointed to the amber gear-up lights, and said, "Up. Mixture, rich. Props, full. Seatbelts..." Ian tugged on his own belt and shoulder harness and then glanced at Bernie's, before looking back into the galley. "Make sure your seatbelts are fastened tight! This will be rough."

The radar altimeter showed only thirteen feet when the stall horn warned that the airflow over the wing was starting to get more turbulent. To keep the wing flying and producing lift, Ian needed to lower the nose, but Ian raised the nose even higher, using the rudder to keep the PBY headed into the wind. The stall horn's uncertain stutter became a steady panicked wail. All Bernie could see through the windscreen was sky. She glanced at Ian nervously and then looked out the side window.

With a crash that shook the whole airplane, the Catalina's belly sliced into the first wave. Successive crests hammered against the seaplane as it cut into the salty water. The PBY slowed, the nose dropped and the plane began pitching with the swells.

"Whew." Bernie started unbuckling her harness. "That wasn't that rough."

The wind was blowing white streaks off the tops of the waves, and Ian had to add power to keep the seaplane taxiing into the wind. "Wait 'til you see the takeoff."

"What happened to reassuring the passengers?"

"You're part of the crew."

"Oh." Bernie headed back to help Orson. She passed through the empty galley and stopped next to the restroom between the galley and the aft cabin. She grinned. "Looks like you guys have been having fun."

Orson shook his head. "They're really not my type." He was sitting under the port blister pointing a Beretta at the two Smegheads. Lenny and Ross were sitting on the couch under the Plexiglas dome on the starboard side of the cabin. Both had their fingers interlaced on top of their heads, and both were naked. Clear plastic garbage bags in each man's lap held their clothes, shoes and the dark blue towels that Bernie had last seen in the bathroom.

Orson unbuckled his seatbelt and got out of Bernie's way. Motioning to the two on the opposite settee, Orson said, "You can unbuckle your seatbelts, gentlemen." They hesitated until Orson leveled the gun at Ross and added, "Now."

Bernie moved to the port side of the cabin and unlatched the hatch across from the Smegheads. Resting her knee on the port settee, Bernie rotated the interlocking panels up and out of the way. Cool, wet, salty air whipped into the lounge. Bernie glanced at the shivering former-hijackers, and smiled at Orson. "Did you really have to strip search them?"

"I didn't want them to freeze to death." Orson pointed the Beretta out at the blue-green water. A hundred meters distant, much of the rocky shore was in shadow. "The water is cold and it'll be dark soon. If they're going to survive the night, they'll need dry clothes."

Bernie nodded and then looked closer at the gun Orson was holding. "What's that?"

"Beretta 9 millimeter."

"But what's that thing in front, under the barrel?"

"Oh." Orson turned the gun sideways and held it so Bernie could see it better. "It's a laser sight." He thumbed a tiny switch and a tiny red light lit up on the front of the gun. Orson pointed the gun at Ross and a red dot appeared in the center of his forehead. "It shows you where the bullet is going to go."

"Hey! Point that somewhere the fuck else, will you?"

"Sure thing." Orson flicked off the laser and pointed the Beretta at Ross' knees.

Bernie looked at Lenny and Ross. "Ian was telling me that the fishing boats dump a lot of blood and guts in the water as they clean their catch on the way back through the Golden Gate. That's why there's so many sharks between the Farallons and Marin County. I wouldn't even dream of trying to swim to shore. To a shark, you guys would probably look like a couple of albino seals." Bernie pointed out the hatch at the island. "We'll tell the Coast Guard you're out here as soon as we make sure Sandy's safe, so just sit tight and try to stay warm. Got it?"

Lenny nodded, but Ross glared at her. "Fuck you!"

"Right." Orson slipped the Beretta into the shoulder holster under his vest and snapped the leather safety strap over the hammer. "Time for you to go." He grabbed Lenny's elbow and tugged him toward the open hatch. Lenny grabbed the plastic bag as it slid toward his knees and Orson levered Lenny's other arm behind his back. Lenny started to struggle, but his balance was all wrong and Orson easily flipped him out into the water.

Ross lunged at Orson, but Orson saw him coming and deftly stepped to the side. Ross wound up hanging out the hatch with one foot on the couch. Orson grabbed his ankle and flipped him out into the cold water.

Bernie grabbed the garbage bag Ross had dropped and waited for the linebacker to surface. "Hey moron, you forgot your clothes!"

Ross paddled back toward the seaplane and Bernie heaved the bag out. Ross retrieved his bobbing belongings and glared at Orson and Bernie. Orson pointed to a point past Ross and squinted. "Is that a shark?"

Ross whirled around and started frantically swimming after Lenny.

"Assholes. We should have let them freeze." Bernie rotated the Plexiglas blister closed and latched it shut. "I'll tell Ian we're ready."

"Right." Orson followed her forward as far as the galley and then buckled himself into a seat at the galley table. The PBY nosed over another swell. The deck leveled for a moment as the plane went over the top and then the tail rose like the flukes of a whale. As the plane dove into the trough, Orson gingerly pressed a hand to his stomach and exhaled slowly.

On the flight deck, Bernie flashed Ian a thumbs-up. "They're out of here!"

"Good job." Ian waited for her to buckle the seat belt and shoulder harness before advancing the throttles to fifty percent power. He pushed the left lever a little further forward than the right and used the extra power from the left engine to turn the Catalina to the right, parallel with the waves. As the plane turned crosswind, the vertical sta-bilizer began to act like a big sail and the plane started to weathervane back into the wind. Ian advanced both throt-tles, but kept the right a little bit short of full takeoff power. With the power difference between the two engines coun-tering the plane's tendency to weathervane into the wind, Ian could use the rudder and ailerons to keep the wings level. The Catalina stopped rolling as Ian guided her to the top of a swell, and the plane smoothly rode along the crest of a single wave. The floats below each wing hung high above the troughs on either side of the plane.

It took much longer for the turbo-charged engines to wrest the Catalina from the water than it had taken the ocean to pull the plane from the sky, but the PBY contin-ued to gather speed as Ian kept it balanced on top of the wave. Inevitably the wings took up the full weight of the seaplane and the ocean dropped away from the Catalina's dripping belly.

Ian brought the right engine's power up to match the left, and then banked left, into the wind. He continued the left turn until they were headed back toward the small rocky island, 30 miles west of San Francisco. Looking out the window, Ian shook his head and muttered, "Come on, you bastards."

"What's wrong?" Bernie looked worriedly at the instruments.

"I don't see them. Dammit! I didn't even think to ask if they could swim. Wait ... there they are. Lenny is pulling his shorts on and Ross is flipping us off." Ian smiled, relieved. "Same to you, Ross." Ian returned the gesture and turned south toward Half Moon Bay.

Bernie looked past Ian toward Ocean Beach and the City beyond. "Isn't the airport over there?"

"I want to come in from the south so we don't fly over Oakland."

"Right." The setting sun was reflecting back at them from windows all over the city. Brightest were the big office buildings of the financial district. "Remember our first flight?"

"Yeah?" Ian glanced at Bernie and then followed her gaze. "I do. Was that only four weeks ago?"

"Three and a half." Bernie looked at Ian. "You don't regret that, do you?"

"What do you mean?"

"You know, wish we'd never met?"

"God! If I could relive the last month I'd do everything smarter and I wouldn't do any of the stupid at all. I really wish the circumstances had been completely different and it would certainly make things simpler, but no," Ian held out his hand. "I don't wish we hadn't met."

Bernie wrapped her fingers around his. "Me neither."

Ian pressed the microphone switch with his left thumb and asked Bay Approach for a transition around SFO to Hayward Airport. When the controller gave him a transponder code and cleared him into the Class Bravo airspace, Ian let go of Bernie's hand to dial in the frequency.

Wednesday, 7:48 pm – Parking Lot,
Shaggy Dragon Pizza, Berkeley

"Freakin' ouch already!" Ken Hamilton carefully lifted his left foot through the minivan's open window and tried resting his ankle on the open door. He'd given up trying to get comfortable and was just trying to find the least uncomfortable position for his foot. He grimaced as his ankle tapped against the side mirror. He took a deep breath, let it out slowly and leaned back in the driver's seat. Then he tried turning sideways.

"Fuck it." Ken straightened up and adjusted the rear-view mirror so he could see the entrance to the apartment building across the street. He had backed into a space across from a travel agency that shared the Haste Street mini mall with a 24 hour grocery, a flower shop, and the world renowned Shaggy Dragon Pizza Parlor. Halogen streetlights lit up the front of each business and created oases of illumination along the sidewalk between the parking lot and the street.

Behind him, Ken heard a screech of tires, a duet of angry car horns and then the mousy whine of a small car accelerating for all it was worth. He watched in horror as a Shaggy Dragon Pizza car sped into the lot, stopped in front of him, and then surged backwards into the space next to him. The little Geo stopped less than an inch from Ken's open door. The teenaged delivery driver glanced across the roof at Ken as she slammed her door shut. "What's wrong with your foot?"

Ken smiled halfheartedly. "I think it's broken."

"Bummer." The kid shrugged and started across the parking lot toward Shaggy's just as a big white Lincoln Towncar swung in off the street. The kid froze, and the Lincoln jerked to a stop inches from the bright red nylon of her Shaggy Dragon windbreaker. Eyes as wide open as they could get, the pizza kid stood between the headlights staring at the Towncar's hood ornament like a paralyzed deer.

Ken glanced at the brunette driving the Lincoln, and then looked closer. "Bernie?"

Bernie waved at Ken, as though she'd heard his startled question, and gestured at the pizza kid to get out of the way. The kid blinked, Bernie honked her horn and the kid ran off toward the pizza parlor. Bernie swung the big car around a light pole and stopped with a wheel in each of four parking places. By the time Ken got his foot off the window sill and levered himself out of the minivan, Bernie, Ian and Orson had gotten out of the Lincoln and covered the distance between them. Ian and Ken nodded greetings.

Bernie noticed Ken's hobbling gait and hurried to his side. "I thought you said your foot was okay?"

"My foot's great, it's the ankle that's fucked up."

"Liar." Bernie ducked under Ken's arm and helped him balance. "Twenty minutes ago you said your ankle was fine. Which is it?"

"Twenty minutes ago it was fine. Now it hurts. I'll live." He looked up at Orson and held out his hand. "My name's Ken."

"Orson Douglas." Orson was a foot and a half taller, but Ken had the stronger grip.

"Are you a cop?"

"Private investigator. You?"

"Carpenter, uh, just a friend." Ken squeezed Bernie's shoulder. "Where's my truck?"

"It's still at Oakland. We had to hide Ian's plane at Hayward. The tank is a loaner. Where'd you get the minivan?"

"It's my mom's." Ken seemed embarrassed. "You had to hide an airplane?"

"This all sounds crazy, doesn't it?" Ian tiredly rubbed his eyes. "We need Des to think I'm still in Mexico. All he'd have to do is call Oakland Tower and they'd tell him the Catalina was parked at Air Charter. That would blow any chance we have of surprising him."

"And we should get somewhere less public for the same reason." Orson led the group over to the Towncar and they sorted themselves inside. Ken stretched out in the big backseat with his foot on Bernie's lap and Ian took the wheel. Orson went back to retrieve something out of the trunk. When he maneuvered himself into the passenger seat Ken was explaining that he hadn't seen Sandy or anyone else.

"I got here about forty minutes ago. I haven't seen any of the cars we saw this morning. I poked around the building a little, but I didn't knock on any doors. 4K is on the fourth floor. It sounded empty." Ken looked at Bernie. "Why would anyone want to kidnap your friend?"

There was an awkward silence during which Orson handed Ken some oblong white pills and a bottle of water. After Ken swallowed the pain meds, Ian outlined his particular version of the smuggler's blues.

Ken listened, nodding his head occasionally. When Ian finished Ken took a deep breath and said, "Wow."

"Yeah." Ian looked at Orson. "Any suggestions?"

"Sun Tzu would say 'Those who know when to fight and when not to fight are victorious,'" Orson nodded toward Shaggy's. "Let's get some pizza."

Twenty-five minutes later, Orson was standing outside apartment 4K wearing a too small, bright red windbreaker and a Shaggy Dragon baseball cap. Glancing toward the stairwell at the end of the hall, he whispered, "Here we go." into the microphone on the thin wire dangling from his ear. He knocked on the door then slid his hand into the borrowed pizza bag. In a cheerful, friendly voice he yelled, "Pizza!" and listened for a response. After almost a minute, Orson slid his hand out of the bag long enough to knock again. "Hey! Your pizza's here! Anybody home?" In a much softer voice, he whispered, "I don't hear anything at all."

Orson looked down the hall in both directions before lowering his right hand and letting the pizza bag drop to the floor. He pulled his hand clear of the insulated carrier and pointed his Beretta at the ceiling. With his other hand he cautiously tried the door. "The door's locked, but I think a credit card might work. It's an old lock."

Orson tucked the Beretta into its holster. He dug his billfold out of his vest and pulled out a blue and white credit card. Shoving the billfold back in its pocket, Orson glanced over his left shoulder at the stairwell. They'd propped the door open with a wad of Shaggy Dragon napkins, and Ian and Bernie were standing just out of sight, on the landing.

"Like I said: here we go." Orson slid the card between the door and the frame and worked it down toward the doorknob. It caught on the bolt. Orson jimmied the card back and forth until he managed to push the bolt back into the door. As the door snicked open, he yelled, "Pizza man!" and picked up the Shaggy Dragon bag.

When Orson flipped the wall switch inside the door, Ian could see a strip of dingy white wall above a slice of pale green couch. The receiver in Ian's ear crackled as Orson disappeared into the apartment. Ian pushed the earpiece in tighter and switched the short Ludovick shotgun to his other hand. He reached for the volume on the pager-sized radio in his shirt pocket and turned the volume up to full.

Bernie nudged him impatiently. "What's he doing?"

"He's going inside."

"Okay." Bernie was leaning over Ian's shoulder so she could also see the door to apartment 4F. She was holding her .38 with both hands, the snub-nosed barrel carefully pointed at the cracked plaster ceiling.

Ian shifted impatiently and checked to make sure the shotgun's safety was off. "What's taking him so long?"

Bernie glanced at the receiver in Ian's ear. "Can you hear anything?"

"Not since he went inside." He spoke directly into the transceiver. "Orson? Orson, can you hear me? Ken, can you hear anything from Orson?" Ian shook his head. "Just static. I'm not getting anything from either of them."

"Then how do we know Orson's okay?"

"We don't." Ian stood up and moved into the doorway. "Let's go."

After crossing the hall with the muzzle of the Ludovick pointed at 4K's open door, Ian hesitated next to the door before leaning into the doorway just long enough to glance inside. Bernie stayed right next to him, her gun still pointed at the ceiling. When he turned to her, Ian looked puzzled. "There's nobody in there."

"What?" She followed him into the apartment.

To the right of the door, the little living room was littered with taco wrappers, soft drink cans, and sections of the San Francisco Chronicle. The comic pages lay open across an arm of the dirty green sofa. The coffee table held an open pizza box with a single piece of desiccated pepperoni.

Orson's pizza bag was on a counter wedged between a small refrigerator and an even smaller stove. There was a smoky odor, too acrid to be the burnt sludge in the bottom of the Mr. Coffee. Just as Ian started toward the short hallway opposite the front door, Orson stepped out of the apartment's only bedroom. He looked irritated. Ian started to raise the Ludovick, but lowered the shotgun as soon as he realized who it was.

Orson pointed to the little beige speaker in his ear. "You guys hear anything on this?"

Ian shook his head. "Not after you went inside."

"Damn it!" Orson pulled the ear bud out of his ear and left it hanging from the transceiver in his pocket. He pointed past Bernie at the still open door. "You'd better close that - wait!" He held up his hand and Bernie froze, her fingers a few inches from the dusty surface. "Don't touch anything with your hands. This is a crime scene and we don't..."

"Sandy!" Ian had noticed that Orson's fingers were covered with blood. He pushed past Orson and rushed into the bedroom.

"Ian, she's not here." Orson flashed an 'okay' to Bernie, who was closing the door with her elbow, and turned to follow Ian.

Two young men shared the room's single bed. Both lay on their backs, one atop the other. The one on top had bullet holes in his chest and neck. The other twenty-something stared at the ceiling with wide-open eyes that didn't move when Ian lurched to a stop inside the doorway. Orson was right behind him. When Ian reached for the doorjamb to steady himself, Orson grabbed Ian's wrist.

"Careful. You don't want to confuse things by leaving your fingerprints on anything." He held Ian with his left hand. He had used his right hand to see if either of the students had a pulse.

Ian stared at the bodies on the bed for a moment, then bent forward as though he was going to be sick. He shook his head sadly as he straightened up. "Why would anyone...?"

"I don't know. It doesn't look like they fought back. I'd say they haven't been dead more than a few hours."

"They wouldn't be dead at all if it wasn't for me." Ian pulled free of Orson's steadying grasp. "If I hadn't flown with Mick, he'd still be alive, Sandy wouldn't be in trouble and these kids... Holy shit!"

"You don't know that. This could be entirely unrelated." Orson pulled a handkerchief out of his vest and started wiping the blood off his fingers. "Even if you did push the first domino, you didn't pull the trigger here. Someone else did this."

"It's still my fault."

"You can look at it that way if you want to." Orson tilted his head philosophically. "Sometimes 'disorder arises from order, cowardice from courage, weakness from strength.'"

"What?" Ian stared at the bodies. "Whatever that means, it doesn't do them any good."

"True." Orson nodded. "What I'm trying to say is that you can't change what's already happened. You should focus on what you need to do next."

"What I need to do is find Sandy!"

"Exactly."

"Right." Ian looked at the bodies on the bed. "We should call the police, let them know."

"Definitely, but not from here. We'll call them from a pay phone and then fill them in after we've found Sandy." Orson glanced at his watch. "Meanwhile..."

Loud agitated knocking interrupted him. Orson and Ian both stepped back into the hall as Bernie looked through the spyglass in the front door. She quickly pulled the door open and Ken stumbled into the apartment.

"Des..." Ken gasped as he pushed the door closed. He took a breath as he stared at Ian. "Is your phone on? I tried to call from the car, but I couldn't get through."

Ian shook his head. "I didn't want it ringing in the middle of all this."

"Terrific!" Ken pulled a transceiver with its little beige earpiece out of his pocket. "You've got your phone turned off and this high-tech piece of shit quit working about two minutes after y'all went upstairs." He tossed the radio at Orson, who caught it easily.

"Sorry about that. They all probably need new batteries." Orson shoved the little radio into a vest pocket. "You said something about Des?"

Ken nodded emphatically, still out of breath. "He stopped at the mini-mart across the street, but he's gotta be on his way up here. I don't know how long..."

There was a knock at the door.

Moving toward the door, Ian whispered to Ken, "Was he alone?"

Ken nodded.

Bernie was looking out the spyglass, but she stepped aside when Ian nudged her shoulder. Ian turned to Orson and whispered. "He had a gun under his jacket this morning." Ian pointed to his left armpit and Orson nodded.

On the other side of the door, Des knocked more impatiently. "Come on guys, I brought dinner!"

Ian handed the Ludovick to Ken and grabbed the doorknob. He paused to set his feet and then yanked the door open.

Des "knocked" through thin air as the door flew away from him. His other arm was wrapped around a bucket of Grizzly's Chicken, and he didn't even realize the door was open until after Ian had punched him in the nose. Des started to reach for his gun, but Ian grabbed that hand and jerked Des into the apartment. The chicken bucket bounced between Bernie and Ken as Des stumbled past. Shifting his weight Orson stuck out his foot, and Des tripped sideways onto the threadbare carpet. Orson dropped to one knee right beside him.

"Just relax." Orson pushed Des onto his back and reached under the leather jacket for the gun. Des tried to stop him, and then tried to reach for the gun himself, but he was much too slow. Orson pointed the heavy automatic at the bridge of Des' nose and Des stopped struggling. Orson nodded. "Much better."

Bernie pushed the front door closed with the barrel of her revolver. Des glanced at Bernie, Ian and Ken before glaring at Orson. "Who the fuck are you?"

"Fair question." Orson patted Des down, looking for other weapons. "My name is Orson Douglas. I'm a private investigator. Mr. MacAran has hired me to help find Sandra Taylor, the woman you kidnapped this morning." Orson paused. "Where is she?"

"She's not here?"

"Nope."

"Where'd everybody go?" Des looked genuinely surprised.

Ian planted a foot next to Des' ribcage and bent down next to Orson. "That's not funny, Des." Ian grabbed the leather lapels of Des' jacket and hoisted him to his feet. "Where's Sandy?"

"Last time I saw her, she was right here!" Des wiped his nose and looked at the blood. "Jesus. I was bringing 'em some dinner, you know?"

"This is your last chance, Des." Ian pushed him backwards, down the short hall. While Des was still off balance, Ian jerked him around the corner into the bedroom and threw him on the bed.

"You fucking jackass! I'm..." Des quickly realized he was lying on something more than tangled bedclothes. He screamed as he scrambled off the bed, and retreated to the far corner of the little room. Des looked thoroughly terrified for a moment, but he recovered quickly. He took a step sideways, towards the window, as his expression shifted from horror to rage. "You didn't have to kill them!"

Ian glanced back. Orson had followed him down the hall and was standing in the doorway holding Des' gun. Ian reached out for the gun. Orson hesitated, but handed it to him, and Ian pointed the gun at Des. "Where's Sandy?"

"I don't know! She was here when I left this afternoon. Ask Gil or Nancy." Des edged closer to the window. "Where's Gil? Did you kill them too?"

As he crossed the room toward Des, Ian raised the .45 and slid the action back to chamber a round. The cartridge that was already in the chamber was ejected out of the gun. It arced across the room and landed on the top teenager's chest.

"That was dramatic." Des sneered. "You don't know much about guns, do you?"

"I'm learning." Ian shoved the gun into Des' stomach. "I pull the trigger and it goes bang, right?"

"Ian. Please." Des already had his back against the wall. "Sandy was here when I left a couple hours ago. Joey and Butch were gonna stay with her 'til I got back." Des glanced at their bodies. "Jesus Christ! Nobody was going to hurt her, Ian. Gil and Nancy even stopped at the store to get some contact lens stuff for her."

"So where are they now?"

Des threw up his hands. "I don't know!" His hands were shaking.

"It's hard to believe you're the same macho little shit who threatened to cut Sandy into pieces." Ian raised the .45 and lined the sights up with Des' left eye. "But this is the same gun."

"Ian, please?" Des nervously glanced from Ian's eyes to his index finger, already squeezing the trigger. "Please! We can find her. Gil and Nancy were here, and they must know something. I can call them, or, uh, I can take you to them. Please don't shoot me!"

"You just told me you didn't know where they were."

"I can find them! I'm sure I can. Please?"

Ian stared down the sights into Des' left eye.

Orson broke the short silence. "Who do Gil and Nancy work for?"

Des tried to look at Orson, but he couldn't keep his focus from snapping back to the wrong end of his own gun. Bernie was standing in the doorway behind him and

Ken was watching from the hall. Des licked his upper lip. "They work for me."

"These guys work for you too?" Orson pointed his Beretta at the bed.

"Yeah."

"All four in the same band – the Smegheads?"

"No that was all Gil. Joey and Butch weren't into thrash-metal."

"Right." Orson nodded. "Des, do the math. You left four people here with Miss Taylor. Two of those people are dead. The other two are gone and so is your hostage. I'm betting Gil either killed your friends here, or helped someone else do it before he left with Miss Taylor. Could Gil and Nancy be striking out on their own?"

"Gil and Nancy couldn't handle a lemonade stand on their own."

"Then they must be working with somebody else."

"Dammit Des!" Ian had let the gun drop a little but he brought it back in line with Des' eye. "You said you were working for dangerous people and that Paul was the one who killed Mick. How does Paul fit into this?"

"He doesn't know anything about this."

"But you work for him, right?"

"We're more like partners."

"Partners." Ian nodded. "But Paul doesn't know you kidnapped Sandy?"

"No."

"So, do Gil and Nancy work for Paul?"

"I already told you: they work for me."

Orson's voice was calm and friendly, "You're the only person we can be sure they're not working for, Des. Come on. You must have some idea who else Gil and Nancy could be working with."

Des shook his head. "The only other person I know Gil was tight with was Terri, but Terri wouldn't, uh..." Des still had his hands up. They were still shaking. "Oh, Christ! Terri could have told Paul! If he knew what was going down... Christ!" Des started to lower his arms. "It all makes sense. Gil knows Terri! God DAMN it! They must have... That bastard sold me out! When I..."

Des raised his hands again when Ian poked him with the gun. "If Paul has Sandy, where would they be?"

"His house. He lives on Keeler, in Berkeley. I can give you the address."

"That doesn't make any sense, Des." Orson raised a hand to indicate the apartment around them. "You went to the trouble of finding an anonymous place to hide Miss Taylor; why wouldn't he?"

"This is Joey's place." Des glared at Orson as though Orson's questions were the only reason Ian was pointing a gun at him. "If Paul has her, she's at his house."

"How can you be so sure?"

"Because Paul is a twisted mother-fucker with a jail cell in his basement. He calls it his dungeon."

"Terrific." Orson glanced at Ian and then back at Des. "You told Ian you had friends on the police force. Who?"

Ian glanced back at Orson. "Does it matter who else is involved with these guys?"

"If we know who's dirty, we can go to someone who isn't. This whole thing would be a lot easier if we could get some help from the police."

Ian looked back at Des. "Well?"

Des raised his hands a little higher and shrugged. "Paul is the one with the connections. He does psych evaluations, you know. He knows half the cops in the East Bay."

"Okay;" Ian raised an eyebrow. "So which one told Paul that Mick was a cop?"

"No idea." Des looked nervously from Ian to Orson.

Orson nodded. "Looks like we're on our own."

"Right, and Paul is our only lead." Ian studied Des for a moment. "You want to live?"

Des nodded.

"You've been inside Paul's house? You know how to get into the basement?"

"Yeah?" Des shrugged.

"Okay. You help us with Paul, help us rescue Sandy and I'll let you go."

"What's in it for me?"

Bernie answered before Ian could. "How about your life?"

Ian lowered the gun to Des' stomach. "You don't have a clue how much trouble you're in, do you, Des? I'm not talking about the kidnapping and accessory to murder charges that could probably put you away for life. I'm talking about..."

"I didn't kill anybody."

"Kidnapping is a felony." Ian indicated the bodies on the bed, "Whoever killed your friends made you an accessory to murder because they were killed during your commission of a felony." Ian glanced at Orson for confirmation. "Isn't that right?"

"Not exactly." Orson shook his head. "With kidnapping the charge would be murder one."

Ian nodded. "Even better."

Des looked puzzled. "You really didn't shoot them?"

"No, but I've been thinking about shooting you all day." Ian raised the .45 and flexed his fingers on the grip. "You're still alive because killing you wouldn't help Sandy. Turning you over to the police won't help her either. Of course, it won't do you much good at all. You'll never live long enough to stand trial."

"Fuck you! My lawyer will kick your..."

"Fuck me?" Ian poked him with the gun. "Do you remember Carlos, Des? Carlos thinks you killed his brother-in-law. If you're arrested, you'll be dead long before you make it to trial. If you're not arrested you'll be having a very unpleasant talk with Mick's in-laws within the week. Your only chance to make it out of this alive is to get as far from here as fast as you can. I'm thinking China, but wherever you run, you're going to need money. If you help us, I'll give you half the money on the PBY."

"That's my money."

"Used to be. This also used to be your gun." Ian poked him again. "Here's the deal: you help us get Sandy out of this mess, I'll give you half of that money and a head start before we tell the police who's responsible for all this. If anything happens to Sandy," Ian twisted the .45 into Des' stomach, "Carlos will be extraditing you in pieces. Understood?"

Des nodded grudgingly. "Yeah."

"Will you help us?"

Des looked down at the gun. Ian hesitated, but stepped back and lowered the .45.

"Okay." Des nodded reluctantly. "I'll help you."

CHAPTER NINE

**Thursday, 12:49 am – Doctor Neault's
Estate, Berkeley Hills**

Paul jerked his robe onto one arm and then jammed his fist through the other sleeve. "Patience, you invertebrate prick!" The red silk slipped smoothly over his arms, but the collar got caught on one of the straps crossing over his shoulders. He stopped halfway down the narrow stairs and impatiently lifted his arms higher to slide the silk over the black leather.

The doorbell rang again.

"I'm coming!" Wrapping the floor length robe around himself, Paul tied the sash and hurried through the door at the bottom of the stairs. The curving, glassed in walkway that connected the garage to the main house was well lit by the floodlights outside. Paul could easily see Des through the floor-to-ceiling windows. Waiting at the front door, Des was screwing the cap back onto a silver cylinder he then tucked inside his shirt. He glanced toward the garage, but Paul knew he couldn't see in. All anyone could see in the gallery windows was a reflection of the courtyard.

Paul noted the mini-van parked on the cobblestones before glancing down. As he walked through the sitting room at the front of the house, the red robe swirled around his boots, completely covering his leather chaps. Pausing at the front door, Paul took a deep breath in through his nose and exhaled through his mouth. He repeated the calming exercise as he unlocked the door. By the time he opened it, he was smiling. "Des! Please come in. I'm so glad to see you!"

"I'm glad to see you too, Paul." Des mimicked Paul's effusive tone. "It's been almost, what, two whole days now?"

"You're right, of course." Paul's smile briefly turned patronizing. "It only seemed so much longer because I was so worried about you. Is your car alright?"

"Totalled."

"Pity. At least you're still walking, but," He pointed to the cut on Des' cheek, almost touching it. "Why didn't they put any stitches in that? You did go to the hospital didn't you?"

Des brushed Paul's hand away. "I didn't want to waste time in the waiting room."

"It should make an interesting scar." Paul glanced past Des into the courtyard. "Pity about your car. That little van is quite a step down from your Spyder."

"It's a loaner. It runs."

"Of course. Well, we certainly have some catching up to do, don't we?" Paul motioned Des inside and gestured down the hall. "I was about to have a drink. Why don't you join me?"

"Okay."

Paul dead-bolted the door and headed past the sitting room toward the kitchen. "I'm drinking Chivas. What can I get you?"

Des followed as far as the main staircase. "Beer would be nice, but I need to use your bathroom first."

"Go right ahead."

"Thanks." Des opened the door under the stairs, and watched Paul continue down the hall. When Paul turned into the kitchen, Des rushed to the front door and unbolted it. He ducked back into the bathroom long enough to flush the unused toilet and caught up with Paul in the kitchen. The professor was pouring scotch into a tumbler full of ice. A can of beer sat next to a frosty mug on the counter.

Des popped open the can and took a sip. "Sorry about dropping by so late, Professor."

"Quite all right, Des. My insomnia has been a bit worse than usual the past few days."

"Insomnia?" Des glanced down. The toe of a black leather boot was peeking out from beneath Paul's robe. "You might try taking your boots off."

"Well, as it happens, this evening I'm entertaining a guest." He allowed himself a self-satisfied smile. "She's a little tied up at the moment."

"Just one?"

Paul echoed Des' sarcastic tone. "It's a weeknight." He opened the freezer and put the Chivas away. "Yuri wasn't able to reschedule, so he dropped the shipment off yesterday morning. You do have his money with you?"

Des took a sip of his beer. "It's in the van."

"Good. His nephew will pick it up this evening. Meanwhile, why don't you..."

A loud ringing interrupted them, but Paul didn't seem alarmed. "Stupid raccoons." The ringing continued as he took another sip of his drink. "That's one of the perimeter alarms. Probably the one next to the garage. I had salmon for dinner and the little beggars can smell the bones in the trash. They can't get to it, of course, but every time they try to open the gate, it triggers the alarm. This will only take a moment." Paul set his glass on the counter and walked past the refrigerator. He opened the door to the basement and consulted the home security panel at the top of the stairs. "I thought I locked the front door." He switched the system off and the ringing stopped. "Wait here. I'll be..."

"You'll be staying right where you are." Des pulled out his .45, Des spoke into the microphone pinned inside his jacket. "We're in the kitchen. There's nobody else here except..."

Paul whirled around and started toward Des. "You treacherous bastard!"

"Me?" Des leveled the gun at Paul's gut. "You're the son-of-a-bitch who keeps fucking with my team! Where is she?"

Paul had stopped advancing when he saw the gun. "Where is who?"

"Your guest, Sandra Taylor." Des walked past Paul to unlock the back door. "Is she downstairs?"

Feigning confusion, Paul held out his hands and took a step toward Des. "Come on, Des. What are you talking about?"

Des flipped open the deadbolt, but when he reached for the doorknob, Paul lunged for the .45 and pulled him off balance. Des tried to hold onto the gun, but Paul kicked him in the crotch with the toe of his boot. Des crumpled to his knees. Paul wrested the gun from Des' fingers, pulled back and swung the .45 like a hammer. The butt of the gun slammed into the side of Des' head and he toppled to the floor.

Paul slid the action back enough to make sure there was a cartridge chambered, thumbed off the safety and checked that the hammer was cocked as he turned toward the back door. He waited for Orson to push the door open and step inside before taking aim and pulling the trigger. The hammer sprung forward with a loud click.

"Damn!" Paul jacked the action back and released it. The unspent cartridge arced out of the gun and clattered into the kitchen sink as a new cartridge was chambered. Paul pulled the trigger again and the gun responded with the same anemic click.

Orson leveled his Beretta at the professor and closed the door. "Put the gun on the counter, put your hands in the air and take a step back."

Paul hesitated, staring at the black automatic pointed at his face.

Orson hefted the Beretta. "This one has a firing pin."

Paul nodded and set the .45 on the counter next to the toaster oven. "What do you want?"

"I want you to put your hands up and take a step back."

Paul glared at him, but did as he was told.

"Very good." Orson glanced at Des and pulled a handful of paper towels from a roll on the counter. "Now Professor, I'm looking for Sandra Taylor, and I want you to tell me where she is."

"Who?" Paul looked away from Orson as Ian and Bernie came in from the hall. Both wore lightweight headsets like Orson's, but Bernie was wearing cutoffs and an old T-shirt and Ian still had his uniform shirt on. Neither looked like a cop. "Who are you people?"

"Oh my God!" Bernie rushed to Des' side. "What happened? Are you all right?"

Des was struggling to get up on his hands and knees. There was blood all over the side of his head, and he was spreading bloody hand-prints across the kitchen tiles. Bernie tucked her revolver back in its holster and helped Des sit up. He leaned back against the cabinets and grinned lopsidedly. "Hi."

Ian nodded to Orson. "There's nobody else on the first floor. Did you see anything?"

"No." Orson had folded the paper towels into a neat, square bandage which he handed to Bernie. "Keep him upright and apply just enough pressure to keep the towels in place."

Bernie carefully pressed the towels against the side of Des' head.

Ian walked over to Paul. "Where is she?"

"Gentlemen," Paul nodded toward Bernie as he cleared his throat. "And lady, I don't mean to be uncooperative, but I honestly don't know what you're talking about. Is this some kind of raid? You're obviously not police officers. Federal agents?" Paul's hands were still raised above his shoulders, pulling the hem of his robe a few inches off the floor.

Ian glanced at the leather boots beneath the red silk. He raised the shotgun in Paul's direction, but then switched hands and handed the Ludovick to Orson. He stepped over to Paul. "Where is Sandra Taylor?"

"As I said, I don't..."

"Goddamn it!" Ian grabbed the front of Paul's robe. "Where is..." Ian hesitated as though there was something wrong with the red silk. "Put your hands down." Paul complied and Ian pushed the robe off and down to Paul's elbows. Beneath the robe, Paul was wearing a harness of black leather straps that crisscrossed through the white hair on his chest. White hair also formed a fuzzy "V" between his chaps and his studded leather jockstrap.

Paul's face turned as red as the robe as he angrily shrugged the silk back onto his shoulders and tied it closed.

"Ian." Bernie pointed toward the door next to the refrigerator. "Des says the cell is through there, in the basement."

"Right." Ian turned toward the door, but hesitated, looking at the blood pooled on the floor. "Is he gonna be okay?"

Bernie hesitated, "I don't know."

Des pushed her away and managed to stand up. "Don't worry about me. I'll be fine." He leaned back a little too far and Bernie grabbed him to keep him from falling over.

"Who's worried?" Orson handed the shotgun back to Ian before folding up another improvised bandage to replace the one Des had dropped on the floor. "Just hold this against your head so you don't bleed to death."

Des took the towels and cautiously pressed them against the side of his head.

Orson motioned for Paul to follow Ian. "Let's go, Leatherman." Paul tied his sash in a more secure double knot as Ian gave Orson a questioning look. Orson explained. "It'll be easier to keep an eye on him if we take him with us."

"Okay." Ian opened the basement door and flicked on the light switch.

Orson moved his microphone up closer to his mouth. "Ken, are you still with us?"

Ken answered immediately. "You bet, go ahead."

"Any signs of police or nosy neighbors?"

"Nothing yet, but I'll let you know."

"Thanks." Orson motioned Paul down the basement stairs after Ian.

The only furniture in the oak-paneled space was a row of four-drawer file cabinets and a long rack of wine bottles. The floor was carpeted with the same burgundy-red shag as the stairs from the kitchen. The basement seemed much smaller than the house above it. As Ian searched for a jail cell, Orson studied the carpet just past the last step.

"I don't see anything but sheet-rock." Ian raised the Ludovick toward Paul. "You said you had a guest; you said she was tied up. Where?"

"Gentlemen, please." Paul glanced from the shotgun leveled at his stomach to the Beretta Orson was pointing at his head. "Isn't it possible you have the wrong house? Check your warrant. There must be an address on it."

Ian looked uncertainly from Paul to Orson. "There's no cell down here, and if Des was wrong about the cell, maybe ..."

"I don't think he was wrong." Orson pointed at the floor. "Look at the carpet."

The burgundy shag hadn't been vacuumed recently, but the piles still stood up fluffy and undisturbed at the edges of the stairs. A curving track of matted shag curved off from the bottom of the stairs toward the wine rack, but there was also a track that curved the other way, as though someone regularly walked through the basement wall.

Ian nodded to Paul. "Open it."

"Open what? I honestly don't know what you're talking about."

Orson rapped the sheet-rock with his knuckles in several places across the wall. There was a hollow sound a third of the way across. He reached up and felt along the oak trim that ran along the ceiling, then bent down to tap against the wall near the floor. "This house is way too big to have such a small basement."

Paul sighed. "It doesn't have a basement. This is a wine cellar."

"Of course." Orson reached up and pressed the trim strip where one section of wood butted into the next. He pushed and a section of the wall swung inward. Ian and Orson looked into the passage, their eyes trying to adjust to the darkness.

Seizing the moment, Paul took a quick step toward Ian and shoved the shotgun toward Orson. He grabbed the short stock and fumbled for the trigger as the barrel briefly pressed into Orson's back.

Twisting his body away from Paul and Orson, Ian jerked the shotgun up toward the ceiling. Orson turned to see Paul awkwardly swing his fist at Ian. Paul's arm swung high as Ian ducked down and drove the butt of the shotgun into Paul's stomach.

"Oof!" Paul dropped to one knee. "Goddamn you!" His face was bright red. "You have no right to invade my home like this!"

"How would you prefer us to invade your home?" Orson nodded to Ian. "Thanks."

Ian pointed through the secret door. "Is she here?"

Orson found a light switch, just inside the door and flipped it on. "Hello!" The walls had been painted to look like rough stones and one wall was covered with whips, cuffs and assorted leather accessories. Orson whistled. "Looks like the Sheriff of Nottingham's leather-sex phase."

Ian pushed past Orson into the elaborately decorated dungeon. "Sandy?"

Orson stepped back, grabbed Paul by the harness and jerked him to his feet. "Let's go, Sheriff." Pushing Paul ahead of him, Orson followed Ian into the other half of the basement.

In the corner opposite the door stood a large cage made of black metal bars. It was about the size of a pool table, and barely tall enough for someone to stand inside it. The door stood open and the cell was empty.

"Dammit!" Ian searched the room again as though he might have missed something, but there was nothing else. He looked at Orson. "She's not here."

"You may be right." Orson studied the walls. "But where there's one secret passage, there could be more."

"That's logical." Ian raised the shotgun, pointing it at Paul's face, and took a step closer to the professor. "Last chance, Professor. Where is she?"

Paul didn't move, didn't breath. His expression hardened as he met Ian's angry stare. "I'm truly sorry, but I can't help you."

"You think I'm bluffing?"

"Not at all. I just don't know anything about a Sandra Taylor."

"Ian." Orson kept his attention focused on Paul. "Why don't we lock up the Sheriff here while we search the house? That'll give him a chance to jog his memory, and if we can't find her, we can come back and have another chat."

Paul smiled diplomatically. "That sounds fair to me."

"I'll bet it does." Ian pushed Paul over to the cell. "Orson, do you still have those cuffs?"

"Yeah, but why?" Orson glanced back at the secret door to the dungeon. "Oh, yeah: there would have to be other exits only the Sheriff here knows about." He pulled a set of handcuffs from the outside pocket of his vest.

"Gentlemen, please!" Paul struggled as his hands were pushed through separate spaces between the bars of the heavy steel door. "This is entirely unnecessary. Where could I possibly go?"

Orson stepped over and cuffed Paul's wrists together. "Nowhere." He flicked the light switch off as he followed Ian upstairs.

In the kitchen, Des was leaning against the counter holding the paper towels against the side of his head. Bernie was peering intently into his eyes. Ian moved next to Bernie. "We left Neault downstairs."

"I heard." She pointed to her headset. "Do his eyes look dilated to you?"

Ian studied each of Des' eyes and then leaned back to compare them. "I'm not sure, but his pupils are the same size and that's supposed to be a good sign. How do you feel, Des?"

Des blinked. "Lousy."

"I'll bet. Look, Sandy wasn't downstairs. Where else could Paul lock someone up?"

"Hell, I don't know. Guest house, maybe." Des pointed past the dining room. "Through the gallery."

"Right." Ian started toward the dining room.

Bernie stopped Orson before he could follow. "Can you stay with Des? I really want to make sure Sandy is all right."

Orson hesitated, then nodded. "I'll wait here."

"Thanks." Bernie rushed off after Ian. "Hey, wait up!"

Ian flipped on the lights in the living room and paused to let Bernie catch up. They took turns turning on lights as they made their way through the house. Moving into the covered hallway that led to the next building, they could hear Des talking to Orson through their headsets. He was speaking very slowly and slurring some of his words.

"You know shumthing? I's jutht thinking, you know? The office over the carriage house is where Paul spends most of his time. Maybe sheeth up there."

"Can you show me where that is?"

"Sure. It's uh, across from the guest house. You go through that door there, through the sitting room and into the gallery/walkway thing. Then you go up the stairs and, uh... Oh fuck it. I'll show you; come on."

"Ian, we're going to check out the other side of the house."

"Okay, Orson. Understood." Ian flipped another light switch, illuminating a small lounge with a fireplace and a pair of high-backed chairs. Stairs led up to the second floor and a door opened into a small guest suite.

Bernie glanced through the door before starting up the stairs. "I'll meet you back here."

"Right." Ian was checking the suite's walk-in closet when Orson called them.

"Oh, God! She's, uh... Ian, Bernie; she's over here." Orson sounded shaken. "Miss Taylor, you're gonna be okay.

I'm here to help you. We'll get you loose in just a second. Des, give me a hand here. Des? Oh, Christ, I lost Des. Ken?"

"Yeah?"

"Call an ambulance!"

"With what?"

"Don't you have Ian's phone?"

"No. I gave it back to Ian."

"Shit! Somebody call an ambulance!"

"I'm doing it now." Ian jerked his phone out of his pocket and flipped it open. He dialed 911 by pressing the emergency button, but he spoke into the microphone attached to his headset. "Orson, where are you?"

"We're upstairs in the attic, Ian, over the garage."

"Is Sandy all right?"

"I, uh... Jesus! I'm sure she'll be okay, Ian, but we really need an ambulance up here."

Ian ran through the foyer past the front door with Bernie right behind him. Ian turned and started up the stairs to the second floor, but Bernie kept going straight into the sitting room and toward the other side of the house.

"Ian! The garage is over here!" Beyond the sitting room was another curving gallery that connected the main building to the two-story carriage house.

"You're gonna be okay, Miss Taylor." Orson lowered his voice. "Where is that goddamned key?"

Ian caught up with Bernie in the middle of the curving gallery. She was crouched over Des, who was sprawled out on the beige carpet; face down in a puddle of vomit.

"Des? Wake up! You stupid shit. You can't go to sleep now, Des. Des!"

Ian pressed the phone to his ear. "Hello?" He pressed the emergency button, listened, and then pressed 9-1-1 on the keypad. "Hello? Hello! God Dammit!" Ian turned and threw the cellular back down the hall. It slammed into a marble statuette, breaking into several pieces. With a quick glance at Des and Bernie Ian rushed past them down the hall. A door at the end of the gallery led to the garage, but the attic stairs were hidden behind the door from the gallery, and it took Ian a frantic moment to find the way up. Once he found the stairs, he charged up the burgundy shag two steps at a time.

"Sandy?" Turning the corner at the top of the stairs, Ian froze. A white painter's tarp covered the floor a few feet in front of him. It was splattered with blood, as were the boots and bare legs of the woman bent over the tarp-covered desk. Her feet were cuffed to opposite legs of the desk while her wrists were handcuffed to a chain that stretched her arms across to the other end of the polished surface. Orson had unlocked one of the handcuffs and was hurrying to unlock the other. Blood oozed from the cuts on the arm Orson had released. Thin strips of skin had been peeled up from elbow to shoulder and then braided down to a line of tiny sutures that held the ends in place. The blood around the most recent strip of bizarre artwork was still bright red. The other braids down her right arm, back and legs had crusted over and the blood between the strips of skin was almost black.

Orson unlocked her other wrist. "I'll have your feet loose in just a second."

Her mouth was covered by a leather strap that locked in place behind her head, but while Orson bent down to unlock her ankles, she stretched to the side and slid open the middle desk drawer. Pulling out a pair of scissors, she straightened up, slid a blade under the strap next to her cheek and quickly cut through the thin leather. She pulled the strap off her face and threw it and its attached rubber gag across the room.

Orson released one ankle and moved to unlock the other. "Almost done, Miss Taylor."

"Who the fuck is 'Miss Taylor'?" The stocky, black-haired woman glared down at Orson. "And who the hell are you?"

"I ..." Orson turned the key as he looked questioningly at Ian.

The ankle cuff sprung open as Ian shook his head. "This isn't Sandy."

"Goddamn right!" The woman jerked her ankle away from Orson's hand and put her feet together. Except for the tears in her eyes, her expression was pure fury.

"I'm, uh, Orson and this is..."

She planted a foot in his chest and kicked him away. "Leave me alone!"

"Hey. It's okay." Bernie said soothingly from the doorway. "We're here to help." She nodded to Ian. "Could you call an ambulance?"

The woman snapped her head around to shout at Bernie. "I don't need a fucking ambulance!"

"Okay, but we've got a guy downstairs who does. Can we call an ambulance for him?"

"Suit yourself." Her eagle talon earring swung with every movement of her head.

Ian started to pick up the desk phone but Bernie stopped him. "Could you call them from downstairs?"

Ian glanced at the woman, quickly averted his eyes and turned to leave.

Bernie turned to Orson. "Could you keep an eye on Des, keep him awake? He's in the gallery, and I'm betting he has a pretty serious concussion."

"Sure." Orson followed Ian downstairs.

Bernie unbuttoned the work shirt Ken had loaned her. Beneath the flannel, she was still wearing the T-shirt she'd started the day with. "My name is Bernie. What's your name?"

"Bernie? Short for Bernadette?"

"Yeah, but I really wish you'd call me Bernie."

"I know what you mean." She had her arms crossed over her chest, covering herself. There was a tattoo above the cuts on her left arm, two iterations of the symbol for woman, interconnected side by side. "My parents stuck me with Theresa, but that became Terri real fast."

"Okay, Terri, would you like to put this on?" Bernie slipped out of the shirt and held it out. "I mean, you're not really into this scene, are you?"

"Fuck, no!" Terri shook her head as she let Bernie drape the shirt around her shoulders. "Well," she shook her head a little less emphatically. "Not with him, anyway. What happened to Des?"

"Neault tried to bash his head in."

"That bastard has been busy, hasn't he?"

"Yeah. Where are your clothes?"

"Shredded. That motherless fuck from hell cut them off." She showed Bernie her left knee. Above and below the hinged knee-brace, her jeans had been cut off, leaving a sleeve of black denim underneath the metal support. "Sliced up my favorite jeans! Said he was going to do the same to my skin if I didn't talk, and, uh... I didn't." Terri tensed and looked worriedly around the room. "Where is Neault-nuts?"

"Locked up downstairs."

"Be careful. This whole place is a monument to that bastard's paranoia. He's got secret passageways everywhere."

"That's what we figured. He's handcuffed to a cell door in the basement."

"That doesn't matter. He probably has a key!"

"Don't worry, we've got him outnumbered. If he gets loose, we'll shoot him."

"Let's shoot him anyway." Terri looked at the gun on Bernie's hip before her eyes traveled up to her chest. "Who are you guys and what are you doing here?"

"A friend of ours has been kidnapped." Bernie glanced at the double-female tattoo on Terri's shoulder, "Actually, she's my girlfriend. We thought Paul was behind it and that she was here, but... hang on." Bernie adjusted the volume control over her left ear. "Ian?" She touched the boom microphone to her lips. "I missed that, what did you say?"

"An ambulance is on the way, but they said it'll take at least half an hour to get up here."

"Don't they have anybody closer?"

"The local EMTs are out of position, so they're sending a rescue unit from Oakland."

"Damn." Bernie thought for a moment. "We can get these guys to a hospital before the ambulance even gets here."

"Good idea. Ken, could you bring the car up to the courtyard?"

"On my way."

Terri was shaking her head. "I'll pass on the hospital, but I really am hungry."

"I could use a little protein myself." Bernie glanced at the talon earring hanging from Terri's left ear. "Don't you go to Cal? I'm sure I've seen you on campus."

"Business Administration." Terri slid her arm into one sleeve of the heavy shirt.

"Really?" Bernie helped Terri put the shirt on. "I'm in the architecture program."

"I went with an architect once. She was cute too." Terri eased her other arm into a sleeve, gasped, and pressed a hand against her shoulder. "Mother, that hurts! I'm going to kill that sonofabitch!" She let Bernie button the shirt for her.

"I don't blame you." Bernie slipped the last button into its hole. "What in the world did he want to know?"

"Paul thought I told, uh, my boss that he killed a cop, but he wasn't sure. Stupid fuck! Who else could have told him? He kept asking questions and cutting and asking..."

Terri hesitated. "I really need to take a piss." She started to move awkwardly, but stopped after a one step. "God dammit. My feet are asleep!" She tugged at the front of the shirt, glancing down to make sure it covered her. The checkered fabric almost reached her knees. "He cut me and he raped me but I didn't say a word, not one goddamned word. All the time he was hurting me, he kept telling me I liked it. That was the worst part. He kept saying I liked it and I needed it, that it was my nature to submit, and..." She shook her head and angrily hobbled to the bookcase behind the desk. She pulled on a section of the shelf, and a panel of books swung out to reveal another secret passage. The flick of a switch illuminated a large mirror-tiled bathroom. She started to step inside, but hesitated. "Wait for me, okay? I'll only be a second."

Bernie nodded reassuringly. "I'll be right here." She watched Terri close the panel before speaking into her microphone. "Orson? Is Des okay?"

"You were right about the concussion, but he's conscious. He keeps trying to throw up and his right eye is really dilated." Orson hesitated. "We're taking him out to the car now. Do you need a hand with the girl?"

"No, we'll be down in a minute."

"The faster the better."

"We'll be down as soon as we can."

When Terri stepped out of the bathroom just a few minutes later, she stumbled toward Bernie and almost fell into her arms. Bernie tried to steady her without putting too much pressure on her back or shoulders.

Terri held onto Bernie's arm. "I'm hungry."

"Me too." Bernie guided her toward the stairs. "We'll get something to eat at the hospital." She hesitated as they approached the passage through the bookshelf. "Did you have a purse, or anything?"

Terri laughed, "What the fuck would I want with a purse?" She pulled away from Bernie, turned toward the far end of the desk and tried to reach down for her backpack. "Ow!" Terri straightened up and held her arms out to lessen the pull across her shoulders. "My God that hurts!"

Bernie scooped up the backpack. "I've got it."

"Thanks."

"No problem." The stairs were narrow, but Terri was having trouble keeping her balance so Bernie stayed next to her, and Terri held onto her arm. Bernie said, "I know I've seen you at school, but I'm thinking I've seen you somewhere else too. Do you ever go to The Pentagram?"

"Hell yeah! I love that place. It can get intense but it's still intimate, you know?"

"'Intense, but intimate.' I like that. My ex's band plays there a lot. You must have seen 'em, the Smegheads?"

Terri nodded. "Oh yeah. I think the band stinks, but their singer is worth listening to."

"Nancy Betson, right?"

"Yeah. She's got the most incredible mouth. Terminally straight, but I can always hope, right?"

"Always." Bernie turned Terri down the gallery toward the main house. "Wasn't she going with the drummer, what was his name, Gil something?"

"Gil Stern." Terri wrinkled her face in disgust. "Rancid maggot. Nancy was going with him, but I think she's getting smart. She's been hanging with this cute little freshman named Joey."

"Have you seen them lately?"

"They played the Monkey last week."

"The Monkey? Is that a bar?"

"It's a dance club in the old Wards warehouse on East 14th. You know, "Monkey Wards"? They're gentrifying the shit out of it. Jesus Ruiz opened the Monkey a few months ago. It's huge, about half the first floor. The rest of the building is being turned into lofts and condos." Terri laughed. "It's like Jesus is becoming some kind of developer. You should see the crib he has on the seventh floor. Fabulous! The freight elevator is big enough for a car, so Jesus parks seven floors up, right in his own living room." Terri pressed her hand to her shoulder. "Ow."

"What about Gil?"

"What about him?"

"You said the Smegheads played there."

"Whenever Jesus can't get anyone better." Terri laughed. "Actually I don't think Jesus would let them play there at all if it weren't for Gil. He's been hanging with Jesus a lot."

"Really?" Bernie helped her through the door and down the brick steps to the courtyard. There was a white Lincoln Continental and a red Toyota minivan parked in the courtyard. "Were they playing there tonight?"

"Hell, I don't know. Wait." Terri let Bernie steer her toward the Lincoln. "Maybe; I think they had a gig tonight. It's still Wednesday night, isn't it?"

"Thursday morning."

"Shit. Oh well, I, uh…" Terri saw Ian and Orson standing next to the Lincoln and glanced down. Her knees were still covered by the shirt Bernie had given her.

Ian glanced at Terri as he adjusted his headset. "Are you okay?"

"I'm fine, how are you?" Terri sounded more sarcastic then she might have intended.

"Tired." He nodded to Bernie. "What's the closest hospital?"

"Alta Bates, off Ashby just above Telegraph." Bernie could hear Ian both directly and through her headset. She helped Terri into the backseat of the Lincoln. "Watch your head."

Terri's defensive expression softened when she saw Des. "Holy shit. What happened to you?"

"Paul…" Des started to open his door but started retching before he could lean out of the car. Fortunately he'd already thrown up everything in his stomach. He sagged back in the seat still holding the mass of bloody towels to the side of his head. "Ow."

"Hang in there buddy. I am definitely going to kill that motherless fuck! No," Terri clenched her teeth as she turned to put her hand on Des' shoulder. "I'm gonna kill him twice."

Bernie closed the door to the Lincoln and turned back to Ian. "I'll drop them off at Alta Bates. Then what?"

"Then we'll, uh," Ian's shoulders sagged and he shook his head sadly. "I don't know. She's not here. We've wasted … I don't know how many hours we've wasted, and she's not here! I almost killed that creep in the basement for nothing!"

"Not for nothing." Orson pointed to Terri and lowered his voice. "You saw the cuts on her arms and legs. That creep in the basement has to be the guy that killed your friend. That means we not only saved her, we've caught Mick's killer."

"Yeah," Ian sighed, "But we're further from finding Sandy than we were twelve hours ago!"

"Maybe not." Bernie raised an eyebrow and tilted her head toward the Lincoln. "That's Terri. Terri knows Gil."

Ian looked hopefully at the woman trying to make Des more comfortable in the back seat. "And Gil knows where Sandy is?"

"Exactly." Orson smiled approvingly at Bernie. "You know, I really liked the way you handled her. I couldn't help listening over the headset. You got a lot of information without making her suspicious at all. Nice technique."

"I'm just trying to find out where Sandy is." Bernie looked suddenly uncomfortable. "You make it sound so manipulative."

"Not a bad thing under the circumstances." Orson shrugged. "I just thought you handled the situation very well."

"Thanks." Bernie hesitated. "I think."

Ian shook his head. "Did I miss something?"

"Didn't you hear Bernie questioning Terri?"

Ian shook his head, "No."

"Terri thinks Gil may be at a bar called the Monkey."

"Well, let's go!" Ian looked to Bernie. "Where is it?"

"East 14th and, uh," Bernie thought for a moment. "29th Avenue."

"We can take the van." Ken got out of the Lincoln but as soon as he tried to stand on his bad foot, he grimaced and collapsed to the cobblestones. Cursing under his breath, Ken pulled himself up by the door handle and stood very carefully on his right foot. "I think I need to go with these guys."

"I'll drive." Bernie nodded to Orson. "Can you help him around to the other side?"

"Sure." Orson slipped his arm under Ken's shoulder, and half-helped, half-carried the shorter man around to the passenger side.

Bernie put a hand on Ian's arm. "I'll take these guys to Alta Bates. Where should I meet you?"

"I don't know. I'll..."

"Leave a message on my cell as soon as you figure it out, okay?"

"Yeah, that'll work." Ian leaned forward, hesitated, and then kissed her.

Bernie wrapped her arms around his waist and hugged him tightly. "Be careful. Gil wouldn't do anything like this alone."

Ian tried to smile reassuringly, but his eyes looked tired and uncertain. "Orson will keep an eye on me. If anything happens to me, he doesn't get paid."

"I like him." Bernie also forced a smile. "Just be careful, okay?"

"Okay." Ian kissed her again.

"You guys can knock that off any time. Ow!" Ken tried to hold his foot off the carpet. "You better get my keys from Des before we drive out of here."

Des jerked at the sound of his name. "What keys?"

"My keys!" Ken tried to look over his shoulder. "The keys to my Mom's van?"

"I don't know what you're talking about." Des absently searched his pockets.

"Great! Where'd you leave them?"

Des shouted, "I don't have any fucking keys!" as he stared at the keys dangling from his right hand.

Ken grabbed the keys and tossed them to Orson while Des studied his fingers.

"Thanks. Look;" Orson looked at Bernie and then at the three in the car. "They're gonna ask a lot of questions at the hospital and we really don't want anybody to know anything about Sandy until we find her, so if you guys could leave her out of anything you say, to anybody, it would be a great help."

Ken nodded and Des mimicked the gesture.

Terri just rolled her eyes. "I'm not talking to any cops!"

"Good." Orson said, "Thanks."

Ian gave Bernie a final squeeze and she reluctantly let him go. "Call me."

"I will." He bent down to look into the Lincoln. "Thanks for everything, Ken. Take care of that foot."

"Take care of my mom's van."

"You got it."

As Ian and Orson walked over to the Toyota, Orson handed Ian the keys. "You know, there's one thing we're overlooking, Gil didn't kidnap Sandy from Des because he wanted her. He wants what you were going to give Des to get her back."

"The cocaine I was supposed to bring back from Guadalajara." Ian opened the driver's side door as Orson opened the passenger side, and they climbed into the minivan together.

"Exactly." Orson pulled the seatbelt across his lap and buckled it. "So how does he make the trade? Gil can't get the cocaine if he doesn't get in touch with you, right?"

"Bernie said he wouldn't do something like this alone, and from what I saw of the prick this morning, I'm sure she's right."

"All right. My point is that Gil, or whoever he's working with, still has to contact you."

"All they have to do is call." Ian glanced over at the floodlit front door to Paul's house as he started the engine. "Shit. They'd call the cell because they'd have to get to me before I got back. They'd have to let me know that Des didn't have Sandy before I gave the coke to Des. Shit! I've had the damn thing on all day, and the battery is shot."

"Can we get another battery?"

Ian shook his head. "At this point, I need another phone."

"All right. If they couldn't get you on your cellular, they'd have to try you at home, or work or anywhere else they could think of, right? Have you checked your messages?"

Ian was following the Lincoln down the tree-lined driveway. "Yeah."

"When?"

"At the pizza parlor."

"Six hours ago?"

"Christ!" Ian looked at his watch. "It's almost two o'clock! We've got to find a phone."

"You can use mine." Orson also glanced at his watch. "When were you supposed to be back from Mexico?"

"Tomorrow morning, uh, make that this morning. About eight am."

"So they don't expect you for another six hours."

"Right. Damn! I've got to call Tony."

"The engineer?"

"Yeah. They'll be wondering where the hell I am and I don't know if they're in this with Gil or not."

"Now you're using your head. What are you going to tell Tony?"

"92 Whiskey is an old plane. I'll tell them we lost a fuel pump."

"Which one?"

"What difference does that...?" Ian smiled. "Okay. Right. The right fuel pump."

Orson pointed to the fuel gauge. "We also need some gas."

Ian glanced at the gauge. "Right."

At the next intersection Bernie went straight and Ian turned right, maneuvering the van down the winding residential streets to the broader avenues between the Berkeley hills and the bay. He pulled into the 24-hour station on University Avenue and parked next to the first pump. Orson stopped him as he started to get out.

"I'll get the gas." Orson handed Ian his phone and got out while Ian checked his messages.

Ian's recorded "Thank you" was followed by the familiar beep. Three seconds of dial tone were followed by a message from Carlos. "Ian, I tried your cellular, but I couldn't get through. I'm afraid I can't be much help to you north of the border, but if you can meet me here, I can get you anything you need. I've thought of a few options that may be worth exploring, but I don't know if I can do anything in time to really help. Call me as soon as you can. Good luck, my friend. Adios."

beep

"Good evening, Ian. This is Rashad. Mr. Quintero is quite worried and, I must confess, I am quite worried as well. Where have you been? Please call me as soon as you can. Thank you."

beep

"Ian, this is Tony again. We got tired of hanging around the airport so we moved across the street to the Holiday Inn." He gave the number for the hotel and said they were in room 283.

Ian listened to several messages from students trying to set up flights, and one student who wanted to know why Ian hadn't been at the airport for her lesson. Ian shook his head in frustration. "Sorry, Beth." There was nothing from anyone about Sandy.

Ian dialed the Holiday Inn outside of Tucson and asked for room 283.

"Hello?"

"Hi Cindy, this is Ian. I'm going to be delayed a bit; the right fuel pump seized on me."

"We were wondering what was taking so long. Can you get it fixed?"

"No, but we located another pump not too far from here and they've sent a driver to pick it up. Figure on at least ten hours before I'm ready to go."

"But you still want to go at night, right?"

"Right, we'll have to wait 'til after sunset. I'll call you tonight."

"We'll be here."

"Thanks." Ian hung up the phone.

Orson hung the nozzle back on the pump, and returned to his seat. "Anything?"

Ian relayed the conversation with Cindy. "Nothing on Sandy."

"Alright then. How do we get to East 14th?"

Thursday, 1:50 am - East 14th and 29th Avenue, Oakland

When Rock 'n' Roll was too new to have its own museum, Montgomery Wards was a major force in retail and its East Oakland warehouse was the epicenter of its west coast operation. The complex boasted multiple floors of retail space connected by moving stairways, an enormous seven-story warehouse that supplied stores throughout the West and the largest parking garage in California. By the turn of the millennium the city block of buildings had stood empty for over a decade. Another decade passed before a drug dealer with entrepreneurial aspirations bought the building and cobbled a loose association of D.J.s into a dance club in the southeast corner of the old department store. Made possible by equal parts free rent and optimism, the club didn't even have the same name from week to week until taggers spray-painted MONkEY in huge forest-themed letters over the south entrance.

Below the unauthorized artwork a circle of smokers chatted downwind of the club's main entrance. A party beat pounded out the open doors as the smokers talked about drugs and music and complained about life as they waited impatiently for the next distraction. When Orson stepped out of the noisy club half the group jerked to attention and watched him suspiciously. Orson nodded politely as he detoured around the smokers and made his way down the sidewalk. He took his time walking to the corner, pausing to look west along 29th Street before turning east and walking around the corner of the old warehouse. Once past the chipped concrete pillar, however, Orson sprinted to the first clump of water-starved bushes that clung to the side of the building. He crouched behind the dying plants, pressed himself against the dusty brown paint and waited.

The man following him hesitated after turning the corner. The rubber-heeled footsteps moved forward tentatively and then stopped for a moment before continuing down the sidewalk. Orson slipped silently behind the oblivious figure and followed him past an unlit loading dock. As they reached the corner at East 14th, Orson cleared his throat. "Weren't you going to wait in the van?"

Ian whirled around with his fists up, but quickly dropped his hands. "Sonofabitch, Orson! How'd you do that?"

"Trade secret." He pointed south, down East 14th Street. "Let's keep walking. There's a lot more guys with barely-concealed weapons wandering around in there than I would have expected in a dance club. What are you doing out here?"

"I wanted to see if the van I saw this morning was parked around here."

"What were you going to do if you ran into Gil?"

"You mean before or after I kill him?"

"I mean before we find your girlfriend. Did you find the van?"

"No, but there are half a dozen doors big enough to drive a van through."

"Okay, but the Smegheads weren't playing tonight. Nobody inside has seen Gil or anybody else in the band."

"I thought I heard a band."

"You did: 'Emergency Third Rail Power Trip.' The guy mixing sound for them told me the Smegheads didn't show. My first impulse would be to write this off as a dead end."

"Damn." Ian stopped next to the minivan. "What do we do now?"

"I'm not sure." Orson walked around to the driver's side and opened the door. "There's a chance that Gil will show up later. Terri said he was hanging out here, even without the band, and there's a lot more than dancing going on in there. We could go to your place and wait for them to call, but even if they call, you can't answer it."

"Why not?"

"Because you're supposed to be having mechanical trouble in Mexico, remember?" Orson scrunched down and slipped behind the wheel.

"Right. Christ! I knew that." Ian swung into the passenger seat and closed his door. "I'm really starting to lose it."

"We're both tired."

"What if they don't call?"

"They have to." Orson started the Toyota. "They can't take over from Des if they don't tell you they're taking over. How else would you know they had Sandra, or where to bring the cocaine?" He shifted the minivan into gear and pulled away from the sidewalk. "Personally, I doubt they'll call before morning."

"Then let's stake out The Monkey."

"On the off chance that Gil drops by?"

"Yeah, unless we can get a better line on him." Ian reached for the phone that was no longer in his shirt pocket. "Dammit!"

"What's the matter?"

"I never realized how much I take that phone for granted. Can I use yours? I need to check my messages, and I want to call Bernie to see if Terri told her anything else about Gil."

Orson handed Ian his cell. While Ian made his calls, Orson turned the van around and parked in front of the Shady Palms Hotel. An ancient sign in the office window advertised weekly, daily and hourly rates. Orson studied the cars in the hotel parking lot before glancing across the street at the 24-hour Burger Depot. A young man behind the counter was talking to a taxi driver whose cab was parked just outside the door. Orson watched the two men until Ian was finished. "Any news?"

"Nothing." Ian shook his head.

"Good. Like I said, Gil probably won't call 'til morning, but it doesn't hurt to check." Orson nodded at the Burger Depot. "You want some coffee?"

"No thanks."

"How about a soda or something?"

Ian shook his head. "No."

Orson studied Ian for a moment. "Look, you've got to have faith. She's going to be all right."

Ian shook his head. "Isn't there something we can do?"

"We're doing it. We're following leads, doing the leg-work, staking out a place where Gil may turn up, but we're no good to Sandy if you're too tired or too hungry to think straight." Orson opened his door. "What do you want on your burger?"

"I don't care!" Ian threw up his hands. "Hell! Whatever you're having is fine."

"Good. Two cholesterol specials coming up." Orson headed across the street to Burger Depot, returning a few minutes later with a bag of burgers and fries. He also brought two large milkshakes in a cardboard drink tray. Ian held the food while Orson drove around the block and headed back toward The Monkey. They parked under an overhanging oak tree that blocked most of the light from the streetlights and allowed them to watch the nightclub without being obvious about it.

Orson pulled out a napkin and spread it across his lap. He set a paper-wrapped burger on the napkin and handed one to Ian.

Ian set it on the seat between them.

"At least try a French fry."

Ian grudgingly opened the bag and fished out a fry.

"Thank you." Orson bit into his burger and a pinkish mixture of mayonnaise and ketchup dribbled into his beard. "Hey! This is really good." He used another napkin to wipe the sauce off his beard. "Messy, but good. Can I ask you something?"

Ian shrugged. "Sure."

"How did you get involved with two women who used to be involved with each other? That's a pretty big coincidence."

"I uh... I met Sandy at work. I met Bernie at a party at Mick's." Ian tried another fry.

"Mick was the undercover cop Paul killed?"

"Right. After my first date with Sandy, Bernie followed me home from Sandy's house. She noticed Mick's truck across the street from my house and applied for a job. I met her the day Mick hired her."

"What was she doing at Sandy's?"

"I guess you could say she was kind of stalking her."

"Kind of? That explains the coincidence, but it doesn't bode well for a happy ending."

"She said she loves me."

"And do you love her?"

"Yeah."

"What about Sandy?"

"I love her too."

Orson chuckled. "Life can be interesting."

"Lennon said, 'Life is what happens to you while you're busy making other plans.'" Ian sighed. "I used to think that was really funny."

"Not anymore?"

"It's too true."

"You may be right." Orson nodded thoughtfully. "So what made you decide to smuggle drugs?"

"Christ! What's with all the questions?" Ian picked up the second burger and started tearing of the wrapper.

"Hey, I'm sorry. You'd never guess I used to be a cop, would you?" Orson flashed a good-natured smile. "I'm just trying to understand."

"Join the club." Ian took a bite.

"So?"

"What?"

"What's your assessment so far?"

"My assessment? I'm an idiot."

"Seriously."

Ian swallowed. "I'm serious: I'm an idiot. I let greed flush my common sense. But it was a challenge, you know? It was dangerous and it was, I know this sounds so stupid, but it was an adventure. My whole life was grinding to a halt and along comes this opportunity to make everything right again. I didn't think."

"You did it twice, right?"

"Yeah. I felt alive, Orson. I didn't want that to stop."

"You've got ketchup on your chin."

"Thanks."

"Were you even considering the consequences?"

"I kept telling myself making drugs illegal was as stupid as prohibition."

"What about the addiction?"

"It's an abomination of everything this country stands for to put people in jail for being sick."

"That's a valid point, but what about the law?"

"It was a perfect plan; I didn't think about the law."

"What about the right and wrong?"

"What do you mean?"

"You don't use cocaine, do you?"

"No!"

"What about the morality of encouraging someone else's addiction?"

"I never even thought about the people using the stuff."

"Would you do it again?"

"No."

"Seriously?"

"Orson, I'll never run another fucking stop sign!"

"Good."

Ian crumpled up the paper wrapper as he swallowed his last bite. "So what do we do next?"

"We're doing it." Orson gathered their trash and stuffed it into the Burger Depot bag. "Actually, the best thing we could do right now is get some sleep. We can take turns watching The Monkey."

"There's no way I'm going to be able to sleep."

"Okay. You take the first watch. Wake me up in two hours."

"Right."

Orson settled down a few inches and tried to get comfortable. "You can wake me up sooner if you feel yourself dozing off, okay?"

"Don't worry."

Hours later, when the eastern sky was brightening with the coming dawn, Ian finished checking his messages and dialed Bernie's number. After four rings, punctuated by gentle snoring from the driver's seat, Bernie's voice-mail picked up. As he listened to Bernie's cheerful message Ian leaned his head against the cool window glass. "Hi, it's me again. I'm supposed to be catching some sleep but there's," he yawned, "there's no way I can sleep now so I'm letting Orson keep snoring. We're still parked on 28th, so when you get done at the hospital ... holy shit!" Ian jerked upright. "Gil and Nancy just drove by! I gotta go. Orson! Start the engine!" Ian closed the phone and pushed the door open. He stepped out of the minivan as though he was going to run them down on foot. The pale green Econoline with the crumpled right corner was already at the end of the block, but it slowed to a stop for a red light.

As the minivan's engine whined to life Orson shouted, "Get in!" and pulled into the street while Ian was still closing the door.

The signal ahead of the Econoline turned green and the van crossed East 14th, turning right halfway down the block. As Orson drove by they caught a glimpse of the van as it drove up the loading dock ramp and pulled into the warehouse. Ian watched the wide roll-up door trundle down as they reached the corner and turned back toward 29th.

"Well," Orson glanced over his shoulder, "That was anticlimactic!"

They were parked across from the Burger Depot when Bernie arrived and parked the Towncar in the space in front of them. Three doors opened simultaneously and the trio met at the Towncar's trunk.

"Hi," Bernie gave Ian a hug. "Any news? "

"Yeah." Ian hesitated, but put his arm around her shoulder. "About an hour ago, Gil and Nancy went by in that crappy van they were driving yesterday morning. They drove right into the warehouse."

"Okay then! " Bernie turned her attention to the Monkey. "So what do we do now?"

"Well, we've got a couple of options," Orson pulled a brown and gray gym bag out of the trunk. "We're still not positive that Sandy is in there but the odds are against her being anywhere else. We need confirmation, we need to find out where she is in the building and we need to know how many other people are inside."

Bernie let go of Ian. "Would plans of the building help?"

"Enormously, but where do we get plans?"

"From the Planning Commission; I should be able to get a copy of the permit blueprints."

"That would be great." Orson zipped the gym bag closed and slung it over his shoulder. "I'll snoop around a bit and see if I can learn anything more about The Monkey, Bernie will get us blueprints of the building and Ian..."

"I'm coming with you."

"Well it's your call, but," Orson pointed down the street at the old warehouse. "If Gil looks out one of those windows and sees you walking down East 14th Street, he'll know you're not in Mexico."

"Shit!" Ian shook his head in frustration. "So what do I do, wait in the van?"

"Why don't you take the rest of this gear and get us a room." He pointed at the Shady Palms Hotel. "We need someplace we can operate from, and I'm not the only one who could really use a shower."

"Done; I'll get us a hotel room."

Orson leaned into the trunk and dug some batteries out of a case to replace the cells in Ian and Bernie's headsets. They'd been wearing them, all but forgotten, around their necks. With the microphone booms tucked up along the headbands, the intercoms looked like old MP3 headphones. Orson dropped the old batteries into a vest pocket and tapped his headset. "Let me know what room we're in. I'll get this stuff set up and meet you there."

"Right."

Bernie grabbed Ian's left hand and raised it so she could look at the watch on his wrist. "A shower sounds good. The planning commission won't be open for a couple of hours." She was still wearing the shorts and T-shirt she'd started work with the previous day.

Orson had started toward the sidewalk, but turned back. "I forgot to ask about the hospital? How did it go?"

"Tedious and frustrating." Bernie sighed. "Everybody had to make jokes about giving us a group rate, and then it took forever to get through all the paperwork. God, I hate hospitals! Terri should be all right; they're mostly worried about infection. The skin specialist was on the way when I left."

"Did Terri say anything else about Gil that might help?"

"Nothing more than you heard." Bernie glanced at Orson. "You were right about Ken's foot. It was broken in three places."

"How could he walk?"

"Willpower, I guess." Bernie shrugged. "Ken is pretty amazing. He still wanted to come with me, even when the doctor said he could cause nerve damage if he didn't get it set properly. I finally convinced him to stay put. They're keeping him overnight for surgery in the morning.

They've got to put the bones back in the right places before they can put a cast on it."

Ian shook his head. "Unbelievable."

"Yeah." Orson nodded his agreement, "What about Des?"

"He's in ICU with multiple skull fractures. They won't know anything about brain damage until he wakes up, but they said something about keeping him unconscious for a bit to prevent any more swelling."

Orson nodded. "At least we don't have to worry about him making any phone calls."

"A couple of cops showed up and started asking the nurses about the way Terri was cut, so I split."

"The better part of valor." Orson stepped up on the curb. "I'd better get going. I'll meet you both at the hotel. Oh, and Ian? Don't use your real name."

Ian and Bernie watched Orson walk innocently down the sidewalk toward the warehouse, then they turned toward the Shady Palms. They checked in as Mr. and Mrs. Anderson, paid cash for one week, and carried the rest of Orson's hardware up the outside stairs to room twenty-three.

By the time Orson opened the door to room 23, the air was thick with steam from Bernie's shower, but she'd already left. Ian was sitting on the edge of the far bed with his back to the room's tiny bathroom. On the old nightstand between the double beds was an actual phone book and a grimy, putty-colored phone. The three cases Orson had brought from Las Vegas lay stacked next to the room's incongruously new-looking armchair.

Ian looked up when Orson opened the door.

"You should keep this locked." Orson closed and locked the door. "Have you checked your voicemail?"

Ian nodded. "Nothing."

"It's early yet. They'll call." Orson looked at his watch. "You know, I only got a few hours sleep in the van, but I feel a hell of a lot better than you look. Why don't you at least try to get some sleep?"

"I'm not tired." Ian leaned back and swung his legs up onto the bed.

Orson set his gym bag on the other bed and started pulling out the few pieces of equipment that were still left inside it. "I've set up some microphones and a few cameras, one on each side of the building and one on the front of the club. These microphones are really amazing. They're very sensitive, but they're also directional. They'll only pick up sound from the windows they're aimed at. The cameras are cheap black and whites, but they're small, so they're easy to hide, and easy to replace." Orson glanced up from his bag. "I don't know if we..." He stopped talking. Ian was asleep.

Thursday, 11:51 am - Room 23,
Shady Palms Motel, Oakland

Ian woke to the thumping sound of a car stereo trying to rap its way free of its mounts and escape. Bernie was standing at the window holding the drapes back just enough to look out. Outside the heavy bass faded and a siren could be heard winding down as an ambulance pulled into the Burger Depot parking lot. Ian pushed off the bedspread and sat up. He was still dressed except for his shoes, which were on the floor next to the bed. Ian rubbed his eyes and glanced at his bare wrist. "Uh, what time is it?"

"Hey there!" Bernie dropped the drape and walked over to him. "I think it's about one o'clock, but your watch is right there next to the phone." She pointed at the nightstand.

Ian glanced at the watch as he slid it onto his wrist. "Wow." He scooped up the keys, change, billfold and comb that had been lying next to his watch.

Bernie sat next to him. "How are you feeling?"

"Okay." Ian noticed her concerned expression. "Hey, I'm fine, really." He finished putting away his pocket litter, but her expression didn't change. "What?"

"You didn't seem to be sleeping very well."

"Weird nightmare. We were in a 747 and it started breaking apart. Sandy jumped, but she didn't have a para-chute. I dove after her with an extra 'chute, but I couldn't find her. There was this huge storm and..." Ian hesitated. "I had no idea I could be so afraid of falling."

"We'll get her back."

"Yeah..." Ian searched her face. "Then what?"

"What do you mean?"

"I mean what then? How do you see the three of us sorting this out?"

"A step at a time?" Bernie shrugged. "I don't know. We live in interesting times." She leaned over to the other bed and adjusted one of dozens of tiny knobs on a green phone-book-sized box.

"What are you doing?"

"Turning up the volume. I thought I heard something, but..." Bernie tapped her headset as she shook her head. "I'm listening to seventeen different offices across the street, but there's nothing going on right now."

"Have you heard anything at all?"

"Occasionally. I heard one guy yelling at another to let him sleep. Sounded like he had a hangover."

Ian glanced around the room. "Where's Orson?"

"Shopping. He took a look at the plans as soon as I got back and said we needed more equipment."

"More?" Ian glanced at the cases next to the room's old TV, and then at the screen itself. "Hey! That's the warehouse, isn't it?"

"Right. That's the south side." Bernie changed the channel. "That's the west side, and this," she changed channels again, "is the east side. Orson said there weren't any doors on the north side, so he didn't put any cameras over there."

"That's pretty good." Ian changed the channel back to the west side of the building. "Where are the cameras?"

"Two are on telephone poles, and the third is on the roof of the Goodwill store." Bernie pointed to a white plastic hard hat with the AT&T logo on each side. "Evidently you can do a lot in broad daylight with the right props. Along with the cameras, he put up some more directional microphones and that's what I've been listening to. We've got microphones focused on some of the windows where we heard people earlier. Most of the activity is on the first and 7th floors. Not much in between and nothing on the eighth floor. There's a guy named Jesus on the 7th floor who seems to be in charge, at least everybody else jumps whenever he wants anything. Terri said that Gil was hanging out with Jesus so we're definitely on the right track here."

"Nothing conclusive though."

"No." Bernie reluctantly shook her head. "Not yet."

Ian started putting on his shoes. "I'd better check my..."

There was a knock at the door and Bernie went to answer it. After glancing through the peephole, she opened the door and Orson came in carrying a cardboard box and two shopping bags. The heavy paper bags had "Alphonse's Military Surplus" stenciled on their sides.

"Greetings." Orson pushed the door closed with his foot. "Any news?"

Bernie shook her head. "Nobody's said anything about Sandy, and I haven't heard anything about Gil or Nancy either."

"Well, we've only got microphones on some of the outer offices and if she is over there, they wouldn't keep her any place that had a window. Still, we might get a whisper." Orson set the box and bags on the bed. "Take a look at these." He reached into one of the bags and pulled out a pair of thick goggles that looked like a cross between sunglasses and a diving mask. He handed the first pair to Bernie and dug out another set for Ian. "Go ahead, put them on."

"What are they?" Ian slid the elastic strap back over his head as Orson reached for the light switch next to the door.

"PNVGs."

"Pee what?"

"Panoramic night vision goggles." Orson looked from Ian to Bernie and back again. "What do you think?"

Ian raised the goggles to look at Orson. "I don't see that much difference."

Bernie nodded. "Everything looks green."

"There's too much light coming through the drapes. Come here." Grabbing a third pair for himself, Orson ushered them into the tiny bathroom and closed the door. "Well?"

"Definitely green." Standing in the shower stall, Ian shrugged, unimpressed. When he started to take the goggles off, Ian realized what Orson was trying to show them. With the door closed, the bathroom was darker than a moonless night. "Holy shit! These are great!" Ian slid the goggles back on and watched a greenish-white smile spread across Orson's face.

"Pretty neat, huh?" Orson led them out of the crowded bathroom and set his goggles next to the bags on the bed.

Ian looked reluctant to set his down. "How do these work?"

"They amplify visible light, but they also supplement the image with infrared. There's a processor onboard that enhances the image to give the best possible picture." Orson continued unpacking. "PNVGs can resolve an image in a mineshaft using the heat radiated from your body." He set a trio of headsets on the bed. "The goggles could be a great help, but these are what I really wanted to get from Alf. I didn't like the way the 3/4 watt intercoms kept breaking up, even after we got the new batteries. These three watt units are much more powerful and they're actually a little lighter."

"Great." Ian nodded. "What's in the box?"

"Tranquilizer guns." Orson retrieved the box and took out an air-powered pistol. "These will let you reach out and touch someone from as far as twenty meters away."

"How long does it take for someone to pass out once they're hit?"

"About ten to thirty seconds."

Ian shook his head skeptically. "That's an awfully long time."

"True. They're not perfect, but I think they're worth having. I don't want to hurt anybody if we don't have to." Orson glanced down at Ian and Bernie's feet. Ian was wearing black socks and black leather shoes, but Bernie had on white cross-trainers. Orson nodded to Bernie. "You need to get some black shoes."

"Why?"

Orson opened the second Alphonse's bag and pulled out a pair of black fatigue pants. "Camouflage." He handed Bernie the pants and dug out a matching shirt. He gave Ian a larger version of the same outfit. "When was the last time you checked your messages?"

"Hours." Ian pointed to the old phone on the nightstand. "There's something wrong with the 2. I can't access my messages. Orson, can I borrow your cell?" Ian set the fatigues on the bed.

"Here." Bernie reached down to the outlet under the window and unplugged a silver cell phone from its charger. "Try this."

Ian studied the cheap plastic phone for a moment. "Where'd this come from?" He punched in his home number and pressed send.

"I picked up three of them. It took the city a couple hours to copy the plans for me, but there was a Radio Shack right across the street. I thought it would be good to have some back-up communication."

"Damn good idea." Ian punched in the code to skip his outgoing message.

"Ian, this is Sandy. Could you call me on my cell? As soon as possible? I'm ..." Three short beeps indicated that there weren't any more new messages.

"Sonofabitch! She's on her cell phone!" Ian pressed end, and glanced at Bernie as he started dialing Sandy's number. "They've got her cell phone. Goddamn it! I could have called her yesterday!" Before he could press send, Orson stepped over and wrapped his hand around the phone, covering the keypad.

Ian tried to pull the phone away. "For Christ's sake, Orson! She's expecting me to call."

"I know, Ian. I know. But so is Gil. Let's just take a few minutes to figure out what you're going to say. All right?"

Ian reluctantly let go of the phone. "All right."

"How old is her cellular?

"Hell, I don't know! What difference...?"

"It's a long shot, but if they expect you to call, then they must have her phone turned on. If it's a newer model, it will automatically be keeping the cellular system updated with its position. That lets the system forward calls faster when the phone roams out of the home area."

"So?"

"So, if her phone is telling the system which cell tower it's closest to, then we can get a little more information about where she is. Okay?"

"Okay."

"Which cellular company is she with?"

Ian shrugged and shook his head, but Bernie answered, "GTE Mobilenet." She pointed to the phone in Orson's hand. "Just dial star 611."

"Okay." Orson punched in the number.

Bernie pointed to the display. "You have to clear Sandy's number, then dial star 611 and press send."

Orson followed her instructions and after a few minutes of menus and music on hold he was talking with a customer service representative. "Hi. My name's Orson Douglas and I'm with the Las Vegas Police Department. I'm trying to find a missing person and I'd like you to trace her phone ... Really? ... No, I was hoping you could tell me which repeater tower her phone is closest to." Orson listened, then nodded disappointedly. "No, I didn't know that. I understand. Thank you." He looked at the phone for a moment and then pressed end. "Damn. You have to be on the account for them to give you the phone's location. If you're just a cop you need a court order." Orson tossed the phone on the bed.

"But if you're on the account they'll tell you?"

Orson met Bernie's gaze. "Yeah, but you'd need to be able to prove ..." He watched her pick up the phone and dial *611.

Bernie waited through the same messages and music Orson had endured before getting a live person. "Hi. My name is Bernadette Selleca and I'm trying to locate my cell phone. Can you help me? ... No, it hasn't been stolen, but I think my roommate grabbed it this morning by mistake. If I give you the number, can you tell me where the last call was made from?"

Bernie spelled her name and gave the representative her social security number, but when she was asked for her address, she recited Sandy's address in San Francisco. After only a few more minutes of music on hold, Bernie got an answer. "Oakland? Can you be a little more specific? I know you guys must have more than one antenna in Oakland ... Well, if you're not allowed to give me the address of the transmitter, can you at just give me a rough idea of the neighborhood? An intersection, maybe? ... Foothill and 21st? Thank you." Bernie smiled triumphantly as she broke the connection. "That's ten blocks from here. She's gotta be in that warehouse."

"Or at least her cell phone is, but hang on a second. Why are you on Sandy's cell phone account?"

"I gave it to her."

Nine minutes later, when Ian finished dialing Sandy's number, Bernie and Orson were listening to headsets plugged into a tiny voice recorder. The recorder was, in turn, connected to the cell phone in Ian's hand. Sandy's phone rang only once before a young voice answered. "Hello?"

"Uh... is Sandra Taylor there?"

"Who's this?"

"Ian MacAran, who's this?"

"Just a minute."

Ian looked at Orson. "It's a kid!"

"It sure sounds like it." Orson shook his head.

Bernie said, "Jeez."

In their ears, an older voice said, "Thanks, Jamaal," before speaking directly into Sandy's phone, "Hi, is this Ian?"

"Yes. Can I talk to Sandy?"

"Of course. You haven't met with Des yet, have you?"

"Not yet. Who is this?"

"All in good time, Ian. I was worried you might meet with Des before we could explain the new situation, but I see we've caught you in time. You can relax. Miss Taylor is quite safe with me, so you obviously don't need to bother with Des anymore."

"Is this Gil?"

"Fuck no!" The man sounded insulted, but then he laughed. "I'd introduce myself, but cell phones aren't exactly private. For now, just keep your end of the deal and all will be well."

"What deal?"

"Let's just stick to the basics, Ian. You and Des had a deal. Now you have a deal with me."

"Who...?" Ian paused. "Let me talk to Sandy."

"I've already sent someone to get her. We weren't expecting your call so soon. Are you back in Oakland?"

Ian pulled the drapes back and looked down the street at the eight-story warehouse. "No. I'm still stuck in Mexico."

"When will you be back?"

"I'm not sure. They're bringing a replacement fuel pump up from Guadalajara. It shouldn't take too much longer, but we'll have to wait for sunset before we head back." Ian looked at the floor. "Look, this plan is not fool-proof. If I don't make it back, you'll get nothing. I've got 11 million dollars here. That's every dollar I've got. Just let Sandy go and it's yours."

"I'm sorry, there's really a lot of static on this end; these phones can be so temperamental. Maybe somebody else is on the same frequency. If you can still hear me, Ian, just finish our business and get back as soon as you can. Are you still there, Ian?"

"Yeah, I'm here."

"These phones are amazing, aren't they? Would you like to talk to Sandra?"

"Yes. Please."

"Ian?" Sandy sounded angry.

"Sandy! Are you okay?"

"I'm fine, Ian but Mike Nesmith is going to be pissed. Could you call my secretary and have him reschedule the meeting?"

"Of course. Listen, I'm really sorry about this whole mess, Sandy. I..."

"I'm okay Ian, really. I've got more room than my cubicle at OHI, and all the Shaggy's I..."

"So, Ian, when are you going to be back?" It was the man who wasn't Gil.

Ian choked back his anger. "Right now it looks like late tonight, maybe early tomorrow morning. It depends on how soon I can get that fuel pump installed."

"Then we'll just have to wait. Look there's a complication you need to know about. Where are Ross and Lenny?"

"What?"

"Your baby-sitters. Where are they?"

"Uh... Ross is asleep and Lenny's in the bathroom."

"Figures; amateurs! Just don't tell them anything, understand? They don't work for me."

Ian looked at Orson and shrugged. "Even those morons will notice something eventually."

"We'll take care of them. You take care of our merchandise."

"Where do we meet when I get back?"

"Just give your girlfriend a call when you get back and we'll set it up."

"Can I talk to... damn!" Ian jabbed end and tossed the phone on the bed. "He hung up."

Bernie pointed at the phone and looked at Orson. "That sounded like Jesus, didn't it?"

Orson nodded, but he was looking suspiciously at Ian. "You didn't tell me you had a million of your own money in this deal."

"I don't." Ian shook his head in frustration. "I offered Des the money Mick gave me if he would just let Sandy go. Des agreed. I dug the cash out of the insulation in the attic and then Des thanked me for the loan."

"Well, it sounds like Jesus believes you're still in Mexico. That buys us some time." Orson unplugged his headset from the Y-connector in the tape recorder and plugged it into the patch board. He adjusted the volume before continuing. "Isn't Shaggy's the pizza parlor we were at last night?"

"It's a chain. There're probably a hundred of them throughout Northern California."

Bernie nodded. "But there's one right down the street, right?"

"Right. She may be trying to tell us where they're holding her."

"She's got to be at The Monkey." Ian was still looking at the warehouse.

Bernie looked at Orson. "Sandy certainly doesn't work in a 'cubicle'. She's got her own office."

"What's it like?"

"Well it's a lot bigger than any cubicle. She was real happy about getting an office with a window."

Ian nodded to Bernie. "Let's call her secretary."

"Right." Bernie picked up the cell phone and started dialing.

"Wait, it just hit me." Orson chuckled. "You guys don't remember Michael Nesmith, do you?"

Ian and Bernie both shook their heads.

"He's a music producer or some such but he used to be a guitar player. One of The Monkees."

"She's there." Ian smiled at Bernie. "She's definitely there." As he turned to Orson, Ian's expression became almost predatory. "How do we get her out?"

Orson glanced around the room. "Where are the plans?"

Bernie pulled the blueprints out from under Ian's bed and rolled them out across the rumpled blankets. "The warehouse is actually four buildings, built one after the other: basically just filling up the block." She peeled back the first few sheets until she came to a plan view of the entire complex. "The buildings are interconnected, but the old walls between them are still there."

"This is good." Orson studied the sheet for a moment and then pointed to the west side of the building. "Okay. If we approach through this loading dock, we should ... hang on." Orson picked up the headphones Bernie had been wearing and handed them to her. "There's a woman talking, and it's not Nancy."

Bernie put on the headphones but disappointedly shook her head. "I don't hear anything."

Orson hastily unplugged her headset from the tape recorder and jammed the plug into the patch board.

Bernie listened for a few seconds. "It's Sandy!" Bernie smiled at Ian. "They're asking her what she wants from McDonald's. She's telling them she wants pizza. She sounds okay but she's moving away. Damnit! They're moving her back to her room."

Digging through the various components scattered across the bed, Orson found a small speaker, plugged it into the patch board and switched it on.

"Why are you such a kiss-ass with her?"

Bernie pointed at the speaker. "That's Gil."

"Hey, it's a nice ass."

"And that's Jesus."

Orson nodded to Ian. "Jesus is the one you just talked to."

Gil was saying something that ended with, "... cold bitch who needs to be taught a lesson."

Jesus laughed, "By you?"

"Damn right by me!"

"You're just pissed because she kicked your ass."

"She kicked me in the balls!"

"And whose fault was that?" Jesus laughed. "I don't give a shit what you do when this is over, but there's a lot at stake right here, right now. Stop fucking around! You wait until I say this is over before you worry about getting your rocks off or I'll cut 'em off and shove 'em down your throat."

"Come on man! I need to teach that bitch some respect, you know? I still can't walk straight!"

"Deal with it." Jesus chuckled. "Look, Yuri wants me to make sure the pilot hasn't talked to anyone else, and our Miss Taylor is the best leverage we've got. As long as she talks nice to him, MacAran will come right to us. You just keep your fucking pants on until we've got the coke and the pilot. Understood?"

"Yeah. And then I can have her, right?"

"Hell, you can have them both! Just don't touch her until we know everything MacAran knows, understand? I want her all vulnerable and lady-like so I can make him talk."

Bernie ground her teeth together. "Bastards."

Orson nodded. "Negotiation is obviously not an option. These guys will agree to anything we ask until they get Ian. Then it's over." He pointed to the plans for the warehouse. "Let's see what we can come up with."

"Right." Bernie turned her attention to the plans, but Ian was looking at a calculator-sized gray block that lay amidst the odds and ends Orson had bought at Alfonso's. Wrapped in clear plastic, the tiny brick looked like modeling clay.

Ian started to pick it up, hesitated, and finally just pointed to it. "Is that, uh…"

"C-4."

"Plastic explosive?"

"Exactly." Orson smiled. "I think we have the beginnings of a plan."

Friday, 2:52 am – Loading Dock on the Backside of the MonKey

At each corner of the old Wards warehouse, windowed stairwells rose like sentry towers above the top floor to provide access to the roof. Moonlight reflecting off the few unbroken windows looked like flickering torches. On the sidewalk below the southwest tower, Ian strolled past a long loading dock that had once handled boxcars full of furniture and lingerie. Bits of wood and a few tie plates were all that was left of the tracks that used to parallel the four foot tall loading platform. Wearing black fatigues and black rubber-soled shoes, Ian looked like a soldier or a SWAT cop. He walked carefully, thoughtfully, staggering every few steps and struggling not to fall over. Occasionally he stopped to stare stupidly at the construction debris on the dock before moving unsteadily on.

Concealed between a row of boxes and a stack of cable reels, a young man in a high-backed executive chair leaned forward and picked up a portable radio. The chair creaked, and Ian jerked his head toward the noise.

"Holy shit! You scared me." Ian put both elbows on the dock and looked up at the seated teenager. "Do you have a phone I could use?"

The kid shook his head. "No."

"I need to call a cab." Ian reached into his pocket and the punk snapped his hand down to his waist. When Ian pulled out his key ring, the kid relaxed. Ian held up the keys and smiled expansively. "I've got a car, but I'm way too bombed to drive. Is there a phone anywhere?" Ian dropped the keys. "Damn." He bent down to pick them up. After a moment, Ian pulled himself up just far enough to get his head above the edge of the dock. "Do you have a flashlight? I can't find my keys."

"Stupid shit." The kid set the radio down on the plywood and picked up a cheap D-cell flashlight. Flipping the light on, he rose, stretched, and walked over to the edge of the dock. "Here ya go." He aimed the beam over the edge.

Slipping silently out of the shadows, Orson cupped his left hand over the startled sentry's mouth. The teenager dropped his flashlight and grabbed Orson's wrist as Orson lifted him off the concrete. Dingy boots kicked frantically as Orson shoved a gun against the teenager's neck and fired. The dart emptied with a hiss and in seconds, the boots stopped kicking. Hands and feet twitched before going limp with the rest of the kid's body.

As he carried the sentry back to his chair, Orson spoke softly into the microphone attached to his headset. "Got him."

Behind him, Bernie scooped up the kid's flashlight and moved to get his radio. "That stuff works fast."

"Sometimes; he's not that big." Orson lowered the kid into his chair and started patting him down.

Ian pulled himself up onto the dock, took his backpack from Bernie and dug out his goggles. As he slipped on the PNVGs, everything on the dark shadowy dock blossomed into gray-green clarity. Ian glanced over to see Orson still leaning over the sleeping sentry. He said, "Something wrong?"

Orson had pulled the dart out of the kid's neck and was checking his pulse. "I just want to make sure he's okay."

"Is he?"

"Yep, he's fine." Orson joined Ian and Bernie as they came to a door marked Shipping and Receiving. There was no handle on the outside of the metal door, just a key slot. Orson slipped his dart gun into the thigh pocket of his fatigues and pulled a lock pick out of his vest. He was about to slip the pick into the lock when he noticed that the door had been blocked open with a small piece of wood.

"Well that was easy." Orson put the lock-pick away and carefully examined the edges of the door. He looked at Bernie and Ian. Bernie held her tranquilizer gun in both hands, pointed at the ceiling. The antenna from the sentry's radio poked out of the main compartment of her backpack. Ian held his air-gun one-handed, pointed at the floor. His backpack had the plastic stock of his shotgun sticking out the top.

Orson drew his Beretta. "Ready?"

Ian and Bernie both nodded.

"Right." The door made a soft grating sound as Orson pulled it open. He glanced inside and then flashed Ian and Bernie an "Okay". Orson went first, Bernie followed, and Ian left the door as they'd found it, blocked open with the small piece of wood.

Shipping and Receiving was an empty shell that opened to the warehouse on one side and to a wide corridor on the other. Bernie nudged the curled-up edge of a linoleum tile with her toe. "These glasses make every-thing look kind of virtual."

"Virtual?"

"Yeah. Like everything around us is a video game."

Ian lifted his PNVGs and held out his hand. He was startled when he bumped his fingers into the wall. With the goggles back in place, he could read fuzzy numbers on the price tag stapled to Bernie's pocket. Ian nodded. "I see what you mean."

Orson was already twenty paces down the hall. He whistled softly into his microphone. "Any time you guys are ready."

Catching up, Bernie and Ian followed Orson around the corner. Old linoleum gave way to moldy carpet when they turned left down another corridor. Orson paused at each empty office to cautiously check inside.

Following Bernie, Ian divided his attention between the corridor behind them and Orson's quick inspection of each successive office. As they approached the last few offices, Orson glanced at Bernie and nodded toward the end of the hall. "This doesn't look right."

"No. It doesn't." Bernie stared at the smooth wall just beyond the last office door. "This hallway should con-tinue through to the next building."

"Are we in the right hallway?" Ian was also studying the blank wall.

"I think so. Maybe they walled this off to separate the warehouse from the offices or something." Bernie looked back the way they'd come. "We'll probably find a lot of changes from the original drawings, but the basic

---

structure can't be that different. I'm sure there's still an opening in the concrete wall. They've just covered it over. All we have to do to get into Building Two is break through the sheet rock."

Orson shook his head. "Too noisy."

Bernie pointed back down the hall. "Let's try the scenic route." She started back the way they'd come, but Orson stopped her.

"I'll take point."

"Point?"

Orson pointed down the hall. "Let me go first."

"You're the expert." Bernie followed Orson back down the hall, and Ian fell in behind them. Bernie paused to get her bearings, and then nodded down the hall. "The stairs will be on the right, just past the corridor where we came in."

"Okay." When they reached the corridor, Orson checked it with the same caution he'd used on the offices they'd passed. On the other side of the corridor, the pattern of open doors and empty offices continued into the fuzzy green distance. The third passage on the right, however, was closed off by two doors with wire-reinforced windows. Orson pushed through the fire-doors, keeping his Beretta in front of him as he headed up the stairs. Bernie followed and Ian brought up the rear, keeping his dart gun pointed down the stairs.

On the second floor, Orson started to open the doors into the hall, but Bernie stopped him. "Orson, wait. We need to go higher."

"Why?"

"The second floors in this building and in Building Two aren't at the same level, remember? This building is all offices. Building Two is all warehouse space with much higher ceilings. The fourth floor in this building lines up with the third floor in Building Two. If four doesn't work, we'll have to try the roof."

"Right." When they reached the fourth floor, Orson wrinkled his nose as the carpet squished beneath his boots. "This place really stinks."

"Yeah." Bernie followed him onto the moldy carpet. "Composition roofs don't last like concrete walls."

The trio made their way down the hall, retracing the route they had followed three floors below. As on the first floor, the corridor ended at the dividing line between the two buildings, but the fourth floor hadn't been sealed off from the warehouse. The hallway opened into a vast, empty storage area where evenly spaced concrete pillars rose eighteen feet from the debris-strewn floor to the coffered concrete ceiling. Orson passed a huge freight elevator with a faded 'three' painted next to the door, and led the way into another stairwell.

They moved past the fourth and fifth floor landings with no delay, but there was light coming from the sixth floor. Orson spent more time checking that corridor before returning to the stairwell and he moved up the stairs as though unspeakable horrors waited around the corner at each new flight. Like the sixth floor, the seventh floor was lit by a scattering of fluorescent tubes. Before moving out onto seven, Orson glanced around the corner at the flight up to the eighth floor. He waved Bernie back against the wall behind him and held out one finger. Bernie repeated the gesture but Ian was looking down the stairs behind them. Bernie whispered, "Ian! There's someone on the stairs."

"Ahead?" Ian looked up at her. "There's somebody coming up behind us, too!"

"Damn." Bernie glanced up just as Orson slipped around the corner. When she looked back down, Ian was crouched next to the wall with his dart gun pointed at the landing below them. The sixth and seventh floors were lit, but the stairwell was black. Bernie aimed her dart gun down the stairs and watched the circle of a flashlight beam creep up the far wall of the staircase. Her goggles smoothly adjusted to the increase in background light as the circle widened, but when the flashlight swung around the corner, the image became a solid sheet of bright green. Bernie heard the hiss of Ian's dart gun as she pushed the goggles up and tried to see without them.

"Ow!" A kid wearing his pants impossibly low on his hips was pointing a flashlight at Ian. "Holy shit!"

Ian knocked the flashlight to the floor and pushed the kid off balance, spinning him toward the far wall. The flashlight broke and Bernie had to jerk her goggles down to see. The kid was reaching for something in his pants pocket, but the pocket was too far down his leg. The kid steadied himself against the wall and bent down to reach into his pants. Ian grabbed the kid's wrist and pinned his arm against his side. Before he could cry out Ian cupped his other hand over the kid's mouth. For a moment the teenager tried to bite Ian's hand and get at his pocket, but then he shifted his weight and hammered his elbow back into Ian's ribs.

Bernie rushed down the stairs as Ian fought to keep the kid from sounding an alarm. The assault on his rib cage slowed and the power behind each jab faded. By the time Bernie could get a clear shot at the kid's throat, she realized that another dart wasn't needed. Ian lowered the unconscious guard to the floor. "Is Orson okay?"

Orson answered for himself. "Orson is fine. The kid never even woke up. You guys okay?"

"Oh yeah." Ian pulled the dart out of the guard's shoulder. "I wish this one had been asleep."

Orson poked his head around the corner at the top of the stairs. "Well, he's out now. Bring him up here and we'll leave him with the other one."

Bernie and Ian each took an arm and they started carrying the guard up to the eighth floor. Ian stopped on the seventh floor landing and looked out through the stairwell doors. "Is that music?"

"Sorry." Orson joined them on the landing and grabbed the guard's feet. "I was humming 'Flight of the Valkyries'."

"No, this is something else. Don't you guys hear that?"

Orson and Bernie listened for a moment, glanced at each other and shook their heads.

"Well, I hear it."

They stretched the kid out next to the other unconscious guard. Orson swung an Uzi machine pistol off his shoulder and checked to see if a cartridge was chambered. "Be careful. Theses guys have a lot more than handguns up here. I got this off Sleeping Beauty there." Orson glanced at the shotgun poking out of Ian's backpack and then handed the gun to Bernie. "This is a nine millimeter Uzi. The safety is on the side, here. Right now it's on and the gun won't work. Move it to here," Orson demonstrated. "Now it's all set. If you have to use it, aim low because the recoil will kick the barrel up before you know what's happening. Don't hold the trigger down. Just use short bursts: a second or two at a time." Orson slid the safety back on and handed the gun to Bernie.

She looped the Uzi's strap over her shoulder and hefted her dart gun. "I'll try this first."

"If you have time."

Bernie nodded. "If I have time."

Orson led the way down and out of the stairwell onto seven. Evenly spaced across the concrete floor, the steel-reinforced columns only rose sixteen feet to the concrete ceiling. Of the hundreds of eight-foot fluorescent tubes that had once illuminated every corner of the space, only a dozen or so still worked. They stayed close to the north wall, moving east, toward Building One.

Building Two's east wall was actually the old outside wall of Building One. Faded letters from ancient bill-boards surrounded the two doors that had been cut in the wall to let forklifts pass between the buildings. The doors were on opposite ends of the wall, and though there was light coming through both, the south door looked much brighter. There was some kind of fusion-punk-death metal blasting through the doors. Defying the rhythm, someone with more attitude than talent was randomly screaming, "I'm better than you, and I'm smarter than you, and I'd've kicked your fuckin' ass if I wanted to, so fuck you! Fuck you! Fuck you! Fuck you!"

"Now I hear it." Orson looked at Ian. "I'm not sure it's music."

Ian nodded. "So much for the surprise them in their sleep theory."

"Oh, they'll be surprised." Orson pulled a small transmitter out of a fatigue pocket, turned it on and pressed the only button on the aluminum case. The chorus of "Fuck you!" continued unabated.

Ian was watching the north door to Building One. "Whenever you're ready, Orson."

"Damn." Orson turned the transmitter off, then on and pressed the button again. "I, uh..."

"Here." Bernie took the transmitter. "All the rebar is probably blocking the signal." She looked across the warehouse to the windows on the far side, glanced at the first brightly lit door into the next building and jogged off toward the windows.

"Bernie!" Ian started to go after her, but Orson stopped him.

"It's easier to cover her from here." Orson, Ian and Bernie had been whispering, but the next voice they heard didn't come through their headsets.

"Hey Spike, What's up?" Another teenager with over-size pants appeared in the north door and watched Bernie run past. "Spike? Is that you?" He watched the dark form with a puzzled expression until Bernie jogged under one of the fluorescent lights. "Hey!" He swung his Uzi up into both hands and started running after Bernie.

Ian and Orson fired simultaneously, but the kid kept running. As he raised his gun to aim at Bernie, the gun's nylon strap slipped off his shoulder and his pants inched down past his hips. Ian reloaded his dart gun while Orson reached for his Beretta, but suddenly the young man's pants dropped down around his knees and he sprawled face-first onto the concrete. His gun skittered away into the shadows. "Goddamn it! Link! Benji! There's some-body up here!" Blood poured from the kid's nose as he scrambled to his feet and tried to pull his pants up. He managed two more steps before he lost his balance and fell back to the concrete. "Ow! Link!"

Bernie had almost reached the far wall when a man wearing new Levis belted sensibly around his waist, stepped through the far door from Building One. "Hey! Hold it right there!" He walked after her. "I said, FREEZE!"

Bernie froze a few feet from the windows, her arms held out. She slowly turned to face the authoritative voice. She turned so her right hand swung closer to the window. Glancing at the assault rifle the man cradled in both hands, Bernie forced a smile. "Want to see a magic trick?"

The man smiled back. "Just keep your hands where I can see them and start walking this way." With the rifle, he motioned toward the passage to building one. "Come on, move!"

"Whatever you say." Bernie pressed the button on Orson's transmitter. The explosion in the sub-station below them sounded like far-off thunder. Orson had placed plastique on each of the main electrical cables and the blast severed all power to the building. As the shock-wave rumbled through the concrete beneath their feet, the amplified expletives stopped and all the lights in the building went out.

Through the PNVGs, the muzzle flashes from the assault rifle seemed even brighter than the fluorescent lights had been. The thug was firing at the last place Bernie had been, but she had ducked and started running the instant she triggered the blast. She raced to keep behind him as she pulled her revolver out of its holster. The gunman turned toward her, filling the space around him with semi-automatic fire. Just as Bernie noticed a bright red dot behind his ear, the dot blossomed into a 9mm hole. The man pivoted to the floor, cracking his empty head on the concrete.

Bernie looked back and saw Orson still aiming the laser sight at the fallen gunman. The Beretta sagged toward the floor and the little red dot zipped across the concrete toward its source. Before the dot reached Orson's feet, however, he flicked off the laser. The butt of the tranquilizer gun hung awkwardly out of the thigh pocket of his fatigues.

"Damn." Orson said it very quietly, still staring at the fallen guard, forty meters away.

Ian was looking in the same direction. "Bernie! Are you okay?"

"Yeah." She angled her head toward the dark doorway into the older building. "Let's find Sandy." Bernie disappeared through the far connecting passage.

Glancing at Orson, Ian tapped him on the shoulder. "Are you all right?"

"Yeah." Orson pulled his eyes away from the dead guard. "I'm okay."

"Then come on."

"Right." Orson followed Ian through the first door into Building One. As they slipped through the doorway, a teen with a flashlight came running toward them. The girl kept the flashlight aimed at the floor ahead of her and when Ian and Orson stepped to the side, she ran past them into Building Two. There were several other flashlights moving around in the southeast corner of Building One, but none of them were pointed toward Ian and Orson.

"Bernie, where are you?" Ian was looking down the long wall between the buildings. The door Bernie had come through was a dark green rectangle in the lighter green of the wall.

"I'm next to the car by the windows."

"Car?"

"Yeah, it's a big puke-colored Intrigue, you can't miss it. I don't see Sandy anywhere, but I can see you guys. I'll have to sneak around some of these jerks to get to you."

"She's right there." Orson tapped Ian's shoulder and pointed to where Bernie was crouched. Halfway between the two men and Bernie was a pair of spiky-haired teens. One swept a long, orange flashlight across the warehouse floor as the other followed the fuzzy circle of light with his machine pistol. Flicking from pillar to pillar, the light and the gun were both swinging toward Bernie.

Orson flicked on the Beretta's laser sight and leveled it at the one with the flashlight. As soon as the red beam swept across a pillar next to the teens, the gun and the flashlight snapped around toward Orson. The PNVGs filled with amplified light and the punks started shooting at the Beretta's bright red laser. Orson ducked behind the column next to him as Ian dove for the opposite pillar.

"Holy shit, that was stupid!" Orson hastily shut off the sight as dozens of bullets pelted into the column. More zipped past him on either side.

The machine gun bursts drew fire from other quarters and for a few seconds gunfire erupted throughout the building. When Ian looked back toward the Intrigue, he saw one of the spike-heads crouched over the other, but he couldn't see Bernie. The spike-head on the floor wasn't moving.

"Bernie, are you okay?"

"Yeah." Bernie sounded surprised. "These guys are shooting each other!"

On the other side of the warehouse somebody was yelling, "Cease fire, you fucking idiots! Stop shooting!" The fire didn't cease.

"Stay put, we'll be right there." Ian moved from pillar to pillar as Orson did the same, one row over.

"Ian, Sandy's not over here. It's just punks and…"

"Bernie?" Ian stopped and tried to find her. "Bernie!"

"I'm almost there." She was whispering. "I feel like I'm invisible. A guy just walked right past me!"

He looked over at Orson. "Regroup and start searching, right?"

"Right. As soon as the shooting stops." Orson holstered his Beretta and swung the Uzi off his shoulder. He made sure it had a cartridge chambered. He stood with his back against a concrete column, holding the machine gun in his left hand. Another flashlight beam swept across the other side of the pillar and Orson swung the gun toward the source. The circle of light kept going to the next pillar, and Orson let the man carrying the flashlight run past.

"Orson!" Ian started running after the guy. "That was Gil!"

"Who?" Orson stepped away from the pillar to cover Ian's back.

"The Smeghead that kidnapped Sandy!" Ian glanced back over his shoulder.

Orson waved him on. "I'm right behind you."

Gil ran down the row of empty offices along the north side of the building until he came to one with a closed door and a wide-eyed guard. When Gil angled the flashlight up at his own face, the kid looked relieved to see someone he recognized. He lowered his gun. Gil shoved him aside and stepped into the office. The guard had just enough time to mutter, "Fucking Smeghead," before Ian covered his mouth and fired a dart into his throat.

Over the intercom, Orson whispered, "Ian, we're right behind you. Uh ... damn. Somebody just started the car. They've got the headlights on and they're moving this way."

Bernie was only a few meters from Orson. "Ian, is Sandy in there?"

"I don't know." Ian saw the beam of Gil's flashlight flick out through the office door and a second later Gil pushed Sandy out ahead of him. Her hair was pulled straight back in a didn't look scared, she looked furious.

Gil held a gun to her head as he swung the flashlight in a nervous arc. The beam illuminated Bernie and Orson in quick succession. "Back off!" Gil briefly swung the light further around toward the east wall, but Ian had stepped back next to the office door. With his arm around Sandy's waist, Gil couldn't swing the light around far enough to see Ian.

"Put the guns down and back off!" Gil swung the beam back to Bernie and Orson and started edging away from them. "I'll blow her fucking brains out if you don't start doing what I say right now!"

Orson held his hands out. "Come on, take it easy, okay?" He motioned for Bernie to move back as he took a step away from Gil and Sandy.

"Put the fucking guns down!"

"Anything you say." Orson set his Uzi on the concrete, but Bernie hesitated.

Ian tossed his dart gun out to the left and stepped to the right, behind Gil. The air pistol clattered across the concrete and Gil swung both his flashlight and his Uzi toward the sound. Ian grabbed the gun, but Gil held on to it. He swung the flashlight around toward his assailant, partially releasing his hold on Sandy. She stepped to the side and slammed her heel down onto the top of Gil's foot. Gil screamed as the broken bones in his foot ground against each other, unable to support his weight. He fell to the floor as Ian jerked the Uzi from his grasp and twisted away.

Sandy started to run but stopped when she realized she couldn't see anything.

Struggling up onto his knees, Gil swung his flashlight wildly as he pulled a pistol from the waistband of his pants. The light caught Sandy and as she held up her hand to block the glare Gil took aim. The burst from Bernie's Uzi caught Gil in the stomach, chest and head. The flashlight and the gun dropped harmlessly to the floor.

Sandy scooped up the flashlight and pointed it at the nearest black-suited figure. "Ian?"

Wincing at the sudden brightness, Ian slid the PNVGs up onto his forehead. "Yeah, it's me. Are you okay?"

Sandy threw her arms around Ian and kissed him.

He pulled her close. "Turn the light off, okay?"

"Right." Sandy flicked the switch off. "Why?"

"So nobody shoots us." Even with the flashlight off, Ian realized he could see without the goggles. The shooting had stopped and the car had moved a third of the way across the warehouse floor. "Orson, we're losing our cover."

"I know. They're using the car's headlights to sweep the warehouse." Orson picked up his Uzi and moved off toward the slowly advancing Intrigue. "I'll take care of it."

"Sandy, are you okay?"

Sandy jumped at the sound before recognizing the voice. "Bernie?"

"Are you hurt?"

Sandy shook her head, "No, I'm fine. I just can't see you very well." She pulled the two black-clad figures close and hugged them. "I'm okay."

"We need to get moving." Ian made sure the microphone was still next to his mouth. "Orson?"

Orson said, "I'll meet you at the southwest stairwell."

"We're on our way." Ian took Sandy's hand. "Come on."

"Here." Sandy tried to push the flashlight into Ian's hand, but he held onto her fingers.

"Hang onto it, but don't turn it on unless you absolutely have to, okay?"

"But I can't see anything!"

"Hang on." Ian tugged her toward Building Two. "We'll be out of here in a few minutes."

Sandy held onto Ian's hand as Bernie led the way out.

The Intrigue was moving slowly to let the thugs on either side check for intruders behind every pillar. It had just reached the middle of the warehouse when Orson shot out the left headlight. The right headlight was blocked by an intervening pillar, so Orson shot out the left amber running light as the car lurched to a stop. Orson stepped to the right, took aim and fired at the right running light just as someone ran in front of him. The bullet hit the car's amber light and Orson spun around, leveling the Beretta at a four and a half foot tall kid.

Jamaal had seen the muzzle flash as the Beretta went off bare inches from his chest. He had Keenan's revolver out and he kept the gun in front of him as he whirled to face the black form silhouetted by the Intrigue's remaining headlight. Orson saw the revolver, but hesitated. Jamaal shot him, once in the arm and once in the center of his chest. Orson sagged back, lowering his gun for a second before flicking on the laser and raising the Beretta again. Jamaal saw the laser and dove behind the nearest pillar. The little dot danced after the boy, but Jamaal was gone.

"Sonofabitch." Orson held his wounded left arm tight against his body, his hand over the hole in his fatigues. He tried to feel through the fabric to assess the damage, but his fingers were numb. "He shot me."

"Orson?"

"He shot me!" Orson tried to take shallow breaths to lessen the pain in his chest. "The fucking munchkin shot me!"

"Orson, where are you?"

"I'll meet you at the stairs." Orson jogged back toward the east side of the building.

"Are you all right?"

"I'm fine, Ian. Just meet me at the stairs, okay?" Orson passed three columns before ducking behind a fourth. When he looked out from behind the pillar, the car had also moved closer to the east side of the building. Flashlights were searching the space ahead of the car. With a quick trio of shots Orson took out the car's remaining headlight, leaving a few flashlights, and the car's taillights as the only sources of illumination in the building. The taillights cast a red pall over the figures near the rear of the Intrigue. Orson was trying to take deeper breaths when he realized all three flashlights had swung toward the post he was hiding behind.

"Orson?" Ian gasped, "Where the hell are you?"

"Punching their lights out." Bullets pinged off the other side of the column and Orson winced as he tried to take another deep breath. "I'll be right behind you, Ian. Just watch your backs, cover each other and keep moving."

A shotgun erupted several columns to Orson's left. He looked over to see Ian pumping the action and firing again. The flashlights and Uzis swung toward the column Ian was hiding behind, but the shells he had fired were the miniature smoke grenades and the flashlights were quickly obscured by the smoke. That didn't keep the men around the car from firing wildly through the expanding cloud. One bullet caught Ian in the side as he rushed toward Orson.

Sliding to a stop next to Orson, Ian pressed his hand against his side. "Ow!"

"Dammit, Ian. You guys were supposed to stay together!"

"And you were supposed to stay..." Ian saw the wet streak down Orson's arm. Through the goggles, the blood looked like transmission fluid. "Oh, shit. We need to get some pressure on that. Can you walk?"

"Of course I can walk. Didn't I tell you I'd meet you at the stairs?"

"Are you hit anywhere else?"

"No."

"All right, let's go." Ian grimaced as he stood up. "God damn that hurts!"

"Hang on, are you all right?" Orson looked at the spot Ian was rubbing. "Looks like you got hit, but it didn't penetrate the Kevlar."

"Then why does it hurt so much?"

"If somebody hit you with a hammer, it wouldn't have to tear your shirt for it to hurt."

Ian noticed the Beretta in Orson's right hand. "Look, you've got to put that thing away and keep some pressure on this hole in your arm or you'll bleed to death." Ian helped Orson holster his Beretta and then guided Orson's hand to his left arm. "Just keep pressure on it. We'll get it bandaged as soon as we can. Bernie, where are you?"

"We're at the stairs."

"Which stairs?"

"Southwest corner on eight."

"Any problems?"

"Not so far."

"Okay, we'll meet you there." Ian fed another smoke grenade into the shotgun as he surveyed the floor around them. He turned south, away from the smoke and the flashlights and toward the door Bernie had come through to get into Building One. "This way."

Orson followed, but he was looking back toward the Intrigue and the guys circling around it. Someone was standing on the roof of the car screaming, "Find them, God Dammit! Find them!" Orson let go of his arm long enough to adjust his microphone. "They've figured out that we found Sandy."

"Tough. There's nothing they can do about it now." Ian pulled a cell-phone out of his thigh pocket with his left hand, and punched speed dial #1. He glanced at the windows along the south wall as he pressed send. Ian crossed through the doorway into building two with Orson right behind him.

Behind them, someone yelled, "They're over here!"

Ian whirled at the sound and fired the shotgun single handed, like a pistol. The smoke grenade thumped into the stomach of a guy holding a 9 volt lantern. As the young man doubled over, the burbling canister slipped to the floor, surrounding him with smoke. The light from the lantern disappeared in the cloud. Without turning it off, Ian dropped the cell phone into his right shirt pocket so he could pump the shotgun's slide. They ran.

Halfway across Building Two, Ian glanced back to see Orson trailing about five meters behind him. Behind Orson, the Intrigue's backup lights were flickering through the pillars between the windows and the next aisle. Ian stopped behind the next pillar he came to.

"Don't stop now, you idiot!" Orson caught up with Ian and stopped.

Ian waved him on. "Keep going. I'll be right behind you!" He leaned past the pillar and fired the last three smoke grenades at the Intrigue. He caught up with Orson at the southwest stairwell and they joined up with Bernie and Sandy on the eighth floor landing.

Sandy was the first to start down the stairs, but there was someone yelling on the floor below and then she saw a flicker of light. Bernie tugged her arm and together the four hurried up the stairs to the roof. As soon as Bernie pushed open the emergency door at the top of the stairs, they were blasted by the wind and dust swirling around the southwest tower.

Sandy was the only one who seemed startled. "What's that noise?"

"That's Rashad!" Ian was digging out shotgun shells much deadlier than the miniature smoke grenades he'd run out of.

Bernie clarified. "It's a helicopter." She pointed to the nondescript darkness over the warehouse roof.

"Where?" Sandy could barely see the outline of Bernie's outstretched hand.

"Come on." Bernie pulled Sandy onto the roof and toward the center of the thumping whirlwind.

Orson had drawn his Beretta and was covering the stairs back down to the warehouse. Blood was again pumping out of the bullet hole in his left arm. He hesitated.

"Go on Orson. I'll be right behind you." Ian shoved a third long red shell into the shotgun. "Let me know when you're all aboard."

Orson nodded, holstered his gun and followed Bernie and Sandy. Ian made sure Orson was moving and then turned back to watch the stairs. Ian was ready to blast the first person who came up the stairs, but he wasn't ready for them to come around the landing shooting blind. As chips of concrete sliced through the air all around him, Ian scrambled through the roof door to escape the hail of bullets. Rolling to his feet, he turned back toward the door. Jesus Ruiz was charging up the stairs, still shooting at the shadows above him when Ian fired.

The grenade hit the opposite wall and exploded less than a meter above Jesus' head. Phosphor white light filled the stairwell, setting off the sprinkler system and blinding Ruiz. Ian fired another flash grenade into the fire sprinkler rain before making a dash for the helicopter twenty meters away. The second shell exploded with the same intensity as the first, and for a moment the stairwell flared brighter than the sun.

The skids of the Army Reserve Blackhawk rested lightly on the tar and gravel roof, but most of the helicopter's weight was supported by the rotors whirling above it. Ian glanced back at the stairwell as he scrambled into the passenger compartment. Smoke and steam were pouring out the doorway, but no one was shooting at them.

"Welcome aboard!" Rashad shouted over the engine and rotor noise. "Is everyone here?"

Ian flashed Rashad a 'thumbs up' and shouted, "Let's go!" He slid the side door shut as Rashad raised the Blackhawk off the roof.

Bernie was shining Sandy's flashlight on Orson's upper arm while Sandy wrapped army green tape around it. Like Orson's arm, Sandy's fingers were covered in bright red blood.

At a thousand feet, Rashad turned on the interior and exterior lights. Ian pushed off his goggles and the tiny intercom headset, and leaned forward into the cockpit. "Isn't Summit the closest hospital?"

"Yes." Rashad shook his head. "But their helipad is occupied. I have radioed Alta Bates that we are inbound with a gunshot victim and that we will be there in less than five minutes. They need to know Mr. Douglas' vital signs. How is he?"

Ian turned back into the passenger compartment. "How are you doing, Orson?" When Orson didn't answer, Ian shook his shoulder. "Orson?"

Orson's head sagged forward toward his chest.

Friday, 5:53 am – Sunrise, Alta
Bates Hospital, Berkeley

Three hours after they'd snuck into the dank old warehouse, Ian was seated in Alta Bates' brightly lit, antiseptically clean fourth floor waiting lounge. Head in hands and elbows on knees, he was staring at the speckled floor when his view shifted to black boots and an olive drab flightsuit. He recognized the cheerful expression below the National Guard cap immediately. "Hi, Rashad."

"Good morning."

"It's not allowed to be morning until I get some sleep."

"Fair enough, but the sun is coming up. I wanted to make sure Mr. Douglas would be alright before I go. Will he be alright?"

"His vital signs are all strong, but they're worried about his arm. The nurse told me to talk to the neurologist, but he won't be out of surgery for a couple hours."

"Do they think there may be nerve damage?"

"I think that's what they're afraid of, but they don't know yet."

"I see." Rashad looked around but he didn't see Bernie or Sandy. "Miss Taylor?"

"Ladies room. She'll be fine."

"Good. I am sorry but I really have to go. The hospital has only one landing pad. I have been trying to clear it since we landed, but the police have only now finished with their questions." Rashad started toward the stairs. "Tell Mr. Douglas I wish him a quick recovery."

"Hang on." Ian stood. "I'll walk you up."

They climbed the four flights to the roof and Ian stayed with Rashad as he started walking around the big helicopter. The sun had begun to light up the eastern sky but it hadn't cleared the East Bay hills and much of the Blackhawk was still in shadow. Rashad had his flashlight out to make sure he could see everything he needed to.

Checking the big helicopter for damage as well as airworthiness Rashad found himself smiling. "You know, your Bernie is not at all the person I had imagined."

"What do you mean?"

"A joke, I was imagining a Bernard sort of Bernie. You know: big muscles and a thick mustache. Now that I have met Bernadette, I believe I understand what you were saying in Cabo San Lucas."

"Maybe you can explain it to me someday." Ian followed him around the helicopter. "When we were in Cabo I thought I'd stumbled into some magical twist of fate."

"Is it not? How else could the three of you have stumbled into each other?"

"It wasn't fate. Bernie set the whole thing up."

"Set it up? How could she set it up?"

"She was watching Sandy. Basically Bernie was stalking her. When I showed up she followed me home and she got close to me to get back with Sandy."

"How does getting close to you…?"

"I think deep down she was hoping to get between us and I think its working."

"I do not believe that. The three of you are destined to be together."

"Sandy wouldn't say more than two words to me, Rashad, but she hasn't stopped talking to Bernie."

"That may not be a good sign."

"No." Ian agreed. "Look, Rashad, I didn't get a chance to thank you when we were rushing Orson downstairs. Thank you." He held out his hand. "Thank you for everything."

Rashad shook Ian's hand. "I am delighted that I finally got you up in a helicopter."

"Don't remind me!" Ian looked up at the interconnected rods and bearings and associated connectors that made up the rotor mast and shook his head. "I owe my life to this thing." He nodded to Rashad. "And to you. I wish I could think of something more to say than "Thank you," but I mean it with all my heart. You risked an awful lot for me, Rashad."

"I was not the one they were shooting at." Rashad started to climb into the helicopter. "Will I see you on Monday?"

"If I'm not in jail."

"Good point." Rashad grabbed the big side door, but didn't slide it closed. "You know you are my friend and if you stand against the universe then I stand with you, but please tell me you are done with drugs."

"Yes." Ian nodded, ashamed. "Absolutely."

"Good. Risking one's license to feed another's addiction can not be good karma."

"You're right. Thanks again, Rashad."

"You are most welcome." Rashad slid the side door closed and Ian retreated behind the double doors labeled

Emergency Personnel Only. When the Blackhawk's starter whined, Ian turned to watch. The long blades seemed to crawl at first, but they gathered speed and quickly blurred into a translucent disk. Ian could see Rashad turning his head this way and that, checking the helicopter's various systems. After a few moments, he glanced out, noticed Ian watching and threw him a quick salute.

Ian returned the gesture. The turbines whined a little louder and the helicopter rose gracefully off the deck. It flew west at first, but then turned south, and as it climbed above the tops of the surrounding hills the morning sun lit it up like a recruiting poster for the Army Reserve. Ian's gaze drifted from the departing machine to the San Francisco skyline and soon he found himself staring out past the Golden Gate Bridge toward the Farallon Islands.

Three hours later, Ian was asleep. He'd nodded off waiting for Barrett Hogue to finish questioning Orson. Bernie was on a couch across from Ian and Sandy was leaning back in an armchair in the far corner. Bernie was snoring.

"MacAran!" Hogue's gravelly voice woke all three of them.

Sandy yawned as Bernie swung her feet to the floor and sat up straight.

"Come on, MacAran, I don't have all day. Wake up!"

"I am awake." Ian blinked his eyes as he looked up at the captain. "What?"

"You said you left Neault in his basement yesterday morning?"

"Yeah, at about one a.m."

"He isn't there! My guys found a cell in the basement, but they didn't find Neault."

"Who...?"

"I sent my guys up there with some of Berkeley's finest to check your story." Hogue glared at Ian. "Dammit, MacAran, you should have called me before you went charging in there!"

Ian rubbed his eyes. "Have you found the leak in your department yet?"

Hogue briefly looked around the waiting room. A uniformed officer was talking to a nurse on the other side of the waiting room, but he wasn't close enough to have heard the question or Barrett's answer. "No."

"So if I had called you, somebody else could have called Neault or Ruiz and Sandy might have gotten killed. Right?"

"That's not the point." Hogue glanced at Sandy, and then shook his head. "All right, maybe that is the point, but you've given Neault a thirty-two hour head start on us. He could be anywhere!"

"That may be true," Sandy said, "But thirty-two hours ago you didn't even know who you were looking for, did you?"

"No." Hogue took a deep breath and let it out slowly. "Moisin has already posted Neault on the Internet. We'll catch Neault, and we'll catch the bastard that's been feeding him information."

Ian sighed. "What if that bastard is Moisin?"

"MacAran!" Hogue shook his head, exasperated. "Don't worry about Moisin."

Bernie didn't seem convinced. "If Moisin is working with Neault, he wouldn't tell you he'd found him, would he?"

"Will you give me some credit for Christ' sake? I haven't narrowed the list of suspects down to one person but I have made some progress. Not only do I know Moisin and trust him, but he didn't even know Mick was working for us, let alone that he was a cop." Hogue looked at his watch. "Christ! Mossberg!"

"Yes, sir!" The uniformed officer snapped his head toward Hogue.

"Get the car."

"Yes, sir."

"If I think of anything else, MacAran, I'll be in touch. I'd like you to stay in town where I can reach you."

"Captain Hogue," Sandy stood up but the Captain still towered over her. "Mr. MacAran is a charter pilot. Are you suggesting he quit his job?"

"I'm suggesting he cooperate with our investigation into the murder of a police officer!"

"I'm sure nothing is more important to him, Captain, but…"

"Ms. Taylor, I really don't care what's important to any of you! This is my second trip to this hospital in as many days and I'm no closer to nailing the slime ball that killed my friend than I was last week!"

"I was just going to say that Ian has a very good cell phone and that you can probably reach him at any hour, anywhere in the U. S. Wouldn't that be acceptable?"

Hogue started to glare at Sandy, but his expression quickly softened. "Okay. That'll work." He looked at Ian. "I'll call you. Don't leave the country." Hogue turned on his heel and crossed the lobby to join Officer Mossberg at the elevators.

Sandy leaned close to Ian. "Be careful what you say to him, all right?"

"Hogue?"

"And anyone else who asks questions." Sandy considered. "We need to sit down and discuss what you do and do not want to say, but to do that right I really need to get some sleep first. For now just keep your mouth shut, okay?"

"Okay." Ian sounded resigned, but then he smiled. "Does that mean you're still my lawyer?"

Sandy hesitated, and then nodded. "Yeah, I'm still your lawyer."

"Good." Bernie stood up. "Let's go see how Orson's doing." She led the way down the hall.

Orson raised his fingers just enough to wave as Ian and Sandy followed Bernie into the room..

Bernie waved back. "Good morning! Are you up for some company?"

"Sure." Orson's voice was weak. He smiled at Sandy. "Miss Taylor, I presume?"

"Mr. Douglas." Sandy extended her hand. "Call me Sandy, please."

"If you'll call me Orson." He took her hand in a friendly grip. "How are you doing?"

"I'm fine, thanks to you." Sandy smiled. "Ian and Bernie both said they couldn't have gotten me out of there without you. Thank you."

"All part of the..." Orson closed his eyes for a moment, then smiled. "Wow. I don't know what they've got me on but it's definitely disorienting." He blinked. "I'm sorry. "

"I'm grateful. I'm sure I'll remember what you did for me for the rest of my life."

Orson nodded toward Ian and Bernie. "I had some help."

"Yeah." Sandy nodded. "I won't forget them either."

"Fair enough."

Ian looked at the cast that covered Orson's left arm. "How are you doing, Orson?"

"Great! Can't feel a thing." Orson winked. "We had a long talk about you, buddy. I like your Captain."

"Hogue?"

"Yeah, that's him. Good man. In-credibliciously-intense, but his heart's in the right place."

"What?" Sandy was still holding Orson's hand. "Okay, what did you talk about?"

"Barrett wanted to know everything I knew about you guys, especially Ian. Did you know that Mick and Barrett were in Kosovo together?" Orson glanced at the ceiling for a second, and then looked at Bernie. "Wow, I just remembered. Is Ben okay?"

Puzzled, Bernie looked at Ian and Sandy before shaking her head. "Ben?"

"The guy who leaped to your rescue?"

"Oh, Ken!" Bernie smiled. "Ken's great. They're releasing him today."

"That's good, I like Ken." Orson smiled, "What about Miss Turner?"

"Sleeping. The nurse said she isn't running a fever or anything that would indicate an infection, but they want to keep her for another few days. I think she'll be fine."

"Good. I like her too. What about Piroshki?"

"Orson?"

"I guess I'm hungry. What's his name, Desperate or something? The little prick that caused this whole mess! Him I don't like!"

"Des Pierrot." Bernie nodded. "Not great: he's in intensive care. They're pretty sure he'll live but they're not sure how much he'll remember."

"Pity." Orson closed his eyes and muttered, "Hard to learn anything from something you don't remember."

After a moment Sandy touched his shoulder. "Orson?"

"Yeah?" Orson opened his eyes.

"What did you and Hogue talk about?"

"Barrett does not like being kept out of the loop. He was pissed that Terri wouldn't talk to him, even though she had the same wounds as Mick; Des couldn't talk to him 'cause Des can't talk to anyone and Ken kept saying he didn't know anything about the other two even though all three were checked in by the same person." Orson nodded toward Bernie. "He wants to trust Ian because Ian is a likable enough guy and because Barrett has a sense that Ian is playing it straight with him, but Barrett's sense has been wrong before. There's some trust issues there. He really doesn't like being wrong about people 'cause it makes him feel betrayed, you know?"

Ian looked dubious. "He said that?"

"Yeah, well; actually he just said you'd better be playing it straight with him or you're dead meat. To get the rest of it you have to kind of read between the lines. Anyway, I told him I thought you guys were good people, and then we talked about his department, and my old department and..." Orson stared at them for a moment, then yawned. "You know, you guys should get some sleep. You look terrible."

Bernie laughed. "Look who's talking."

Orson's grin was a little exaggerated by the drugs.

Bernie nodded to Sandy. "We should get you home."

Sandy shook her head. "I don't want to go home Orson. What else did you and Captain Hogue talk about?"

Orson yawned. "I think that was it."

Sandy started to ask something else but found herself yawning instead. "Excuse me."

"Orson's right, hon." Bernie put her arm around Sandy's shoulder. "We all need to get some sleep. Let's take you home. We can come back if..."

"I don't want to go home!" Sandy shrugged Bernie's arm off her shoulder. "Look, I just don't want to go home right now, okay?"

"Okay, whatever you say." Bernie reassured her, "You know, we could just crash at my place, its right down the street."

Sandy glanced at Ian, "All of us?"

Bernie also glanced at Ian. "If that's what you want, yeah."

"That's what I want, *yeah.*" Sandy yawned. "You know, I'm really not that tired."

"Right." Ian held the door for Sandy and Bernie. "Good night, Orson."

"It's morning," Orson tilted his head toward the window as he settled back into the pillows.

Friday, 9:54 am - Intensive Care, Alta Bates Hospital

As soon as the south elevator doors opened, Officer Gunn started assessing the men who stepped out. One wore green scrubs, a white coat and a Hospital ID with a photo that matched his long gray beard, tanned skin, and turban-wrapped hair. The other could have been an accountant except for the bulge of a shoulder holster under his suit. The Berkeley cop casually lowered his hand to his holster as the Oakland detective moved his jacket to the side to reveal the badge on his belt. The two exchanged greetings while the doctor stopped at the nurse's station to ask about the trauma victim the cop was guarding.

The detective extended his hand. "Kendrick, OPD."

"Gunn, BPD."

They shook hands and Kendrick explained. "Doctor Chandra has agreed to see if he can help us."

"Okay." The cop watched the two make their way to Des Pierrot's room and then returned to his conversation with the nurse who'd just come on duty. "Where were we?"

"You were talking about ordering pizza, but I'm wondering why all the fuss over this patient." She'd pulled a file off the desk and was reading about Des' last MRI. "Is police protection like this normal?"

"Not really." Gunn shrugged. "We're trying to help Oakland find a cop killer, so nothing's normal."

As the door to Des' room closed, Paul Neault scratched his neck under the very expensive beard and cursed. "Damnit this thing is irritating!" He walked to Des' bedside and gently lifted Des' hand away from the side of the bed and the nurse's call button. He pulled the blanket over Des' arm and then sat down on the edge of the bed. Glancing at the detective-turned-secretary, Paul pulled a short .38 revolver from his jacket pocket. "Desmond?" Paul thumped the barrel of the gun against the bandages wrapped around Desmond's head.

Des grimaced, his eyes opened half way and he tried to raise his hands. One arm was tangled up in I. V. tubes and the other was pinned under the blanket, trapped by Paul's weight on the covers.

"Do wake up, Desmond, I haven't much time." Paul tapped the bandages again.

"Ow! Hey!" Des opened his eyes briefly, but quickly closed them against the bright light. "What?"

"Shush, keep your voice down."

"Okay." Des whispered. "What do you want?"

"I want my money. Where is it?"

Des forced his eyes open a little wider and tried to focus. "Who are you?"

"Underneath all this theatrical crap, it's me, Paul."

"Who?"

"Since the police and my psychotic former associate are both hunting the old me, I've had to assume a new identity. New driver's license, new credit cards, new HMO. I won't bore you with the details, but it's been very annoying." The former professor gazed down at Des, savoring his frightened expression. "For now, just think of me as the Angel of Death."

"I don't understand."

"That's an understatement, you moron." Paul thumped the gun against the bandages and Des winced. "I'm an imaginative man but I simply cannot fathom how stupid you've been. You were warned to stay away from MacAran but you didn't. When he refused your reckless scheme, you should have let it go. Instead, in a stroke of pure insanity, you kidnapped his girlfriend! Did you honestly expect him to just meekly do whatever you asked? Have you learned nothing from history? From film? From literature? Presuming, of course that you actually read. When in the whole of human history has kidnapping someone ever gotten anybody what they wanted?"

"What are you talking about?"

"Coercion doesn't work! Not in the long term. You open yourself up to far too many variables when you try to force people to do what you know they don't want to do. " Paul's anger became something more sadistic. "In the short term, however, I think coercion can yield very positive results." Paul pointed the revolver at the ceiling and released the cylinder. Six short brass cartridges with hollow point bullets fell onto Des' chest. Paul scooped them up and dropped them into his coat pocket. Pointing the gun away from Des so that he could see the empty chambers, Paul reached back into his pocket. "I almost forgot." He slid one cartridge back into the gun and spun the cylinder. While it was still spinning, Paul snapped it into place with a flick of his wrist. Pulling the hammer back, Paul pressed the gun against Des' forehead. "Now, I'd like to ask you a few questions."

"Ow! That hurts!" Des tried to move his head away from the gun, but Paul kept it pressed against his skin.

"Because of you, the police believe that I killed their detective and Yuri thinks I've skipped town with his cocaine. Because of you, I am now homeless and on the run, and I will exact my revenge when I have enough time to properly enjoy it. For now, I just need to know where my money is."

"What money?" Des glanced up at the ceiling. "Who's Desmond?"

Paul pulled the trigger. Click.

Des tried to scream but Paul held his hand over Des' mouth and whispered in his ear. "That's one." Paul cocked the gun again, advancing the cylinder to the next chamber. "The question, for those who weren't paying attention, is this: where is my money?"

"I don't know what you're talking about..."

Click.

"Please, I don't know!"

"That's two." Paul pulled the hammer back.

"I don't have your money, I swear. I can't give you what I don't have! I..." Des gasped for air. "Who are you?"

Click.

"This will make four." Paul pressed his hand over the terrified man's mouth as Des tried to call out for help. Click. "Since I haven't been spinning the cylinder with each turn, I believe there now remains a fifty percent chance that this next chamber has your bullet in it. Now where is my money?" Paul glanced back over his shoulder at the nurse's station and lifted his hand off Des' mouth.

"I don't know what you're talking about! Why are you doing this to me?"

"You really don't know who I am?"

"No!"

"Fascinating." As Paul studied Des' face the Professor's own expression softened and he lowered the gun. "Okay, Des: Let's try some easier questions, and if you answer one question right, just one, we'll leave you alone. How's that sound?"

Des was shaking with fear, but he nodded. "Okay."

"What's your name?"

"Des?"

"I think you're actually guessing. Who's the president?"

"Jed Bartlett?"

"What year is this?"

"1984?"

"What's the square root of 16?"

"What's a square…?"

Paul paused, considering. "How old are you?"

"Uh, 16?"

"What do you want to be when you grow up?

"A fireman," Des said with new found conviction. "I want to be a fireman."

"Pity." Paul pressed the gun back against Des's forehead. "Not one right answer."

"But I do want to be a fireman. I do!" There were tears in his eyes.

Click.

"My goodness, you're a lucky man! I was almost certain the bullet was in the fifth chamber." Paul leaned close. "Last chance, where's my money?"

Des sniffed. "I want to be a fireman."

"And I want my money!" Paul hissed.

Click.

Des stared at Paul in wide-eyed disbelief as the professor opened the gun and pulled out the cartridge. He held up the empty brass casing so Des could see that it held no bullet. "I'll kill you eventually, of course, but not with all these people around." Paul turned toward the detective at the foot of the bed. "Let's try a different tack. Maybe the pilot can be more helpful."

"MacAran told Hogue he'd be staying in Berkeley." Bob Kendrick was opening a file in his PDA. "Moisin gave me the address, and uh, here it is, but look; these guys are pretty heavily armed."

"So are we." Neault raised his hands and shrugged, "And we're smarter."

"I just thought…"

"Have faith." Paul glared at Des. "We'll be seeing you again, Desmond."

Watching his tormentor leave, the former business major whispered the only thing he was really sure of, "I want to be a fireman."

CHAPTER TEN

Friday, 10:55 am – Bernadette
Selleca's Residence, Berkeley

Slouched into Bernie's couch, Ian's head was back but his eyes weren't closed. Every time he tried to keep his eyes closed, he ended up staring into space or focusing on the texture of the ceiling. He was still wearing the black fatigues Orson had given him, but without the thick Kevlar beneath it, his shirt was loose and baggy. The vest lay on the coffee table with Bernie's vest on top of it.

Bernie nudged his arm and tried to hand him a steaming mug. "Have some coffee."

Ian waved it away. "Not right now, thanks."

Bernie had changed into jeans and a maroon sweatshirt. She set the mug next to the vests. "You know you could head home. Get some rest; have a shower? I'll keep an eye on her."

Ian glanced up toward the loft where Sandy was still sleeping. "I just want to talk to her, you know? Make sure she's okay."

"Sandy's gonna be fine. She's been through a lot and it'll take some time to process it all, but she'll be fine." Bernie considered him for a moment. "What about you?"

"Me?"

"Are you gonna be okay?"

Ian started to laugh but ended up shaking his head. "I have no idea."

Bernie nodded sympathetically. "You'll be okay. Have you thought about what you're…?"

They were interrupted by an authoritative pounding on the door.

"Christ! What now?" Bernie glared at the door as she walked around the couch. "Who is it?"

"Detective Kendrick, Ma'am: Captain Hogue had a few more questions."

"Terrific." Bernie sighed. She unlocked the deadbolt, but before she could slip the chain off its track, the doorknob turned and the door was shoved open the few inches the chain would allow. Bernie yelled, "Hey!"

"Sorry." Kendrick's apology sounded sincere enough, but he was holding a shotgun almost out of view behind his back. "Just a few questions?"

When she saw the barrel of another shotgun and the bearded man holding it Bernie shoved the door closed and turned the deadbolt. "Ian!"

The lock was new but the door was old and the two men on the other side were determined. When they kicked the door in unison the frame gave way and the splintering crunch seemed to shake the whole building. Bernie fell back into a stack of paintings as Ian came over the couch into the entryway.

"Freeze!"

Ian stopped inches from the barrel of Kendrick's gun as a man in a turban followed him into the studio. Paul moved the shotgun to his left hand so he could close the door with his right. A piece of the splintered door jamb had gotten wedged under the door and it wouldn't close. Paul kicked the splinter free and slammed the door. The door bounced off the shattered jam, and Paul patiently pushed it closed.

Kendrick quickly had Ian and Bernie up against the wall and was searching them for weapons.

Paul glanced around the apartment and then asked Kendrick, "Anything?'

"Wallet, keys, some pocket change."

"Any weapons?"

"No."

Paul smiled at Ian. "Where's all the fancy commando gear?"

Ian tried to see the face behind the beard. "Neault?"

Paul poked him in the ribs with the butt of his shotgun. "I asked you a question."

"Confiscated." Ian gritted his teeth. "The police have it."

Paul looked at his detective. "How come you didn't know that?'

Kendrick shrugged.

Ian was still studying Paul's disguise. "What do you want?"

Paul sighed. "What I want is complex and far beyond your comprehension but we'll try small words: where is my money?"

Ian didn't make the connection. "What the hell are you talking about?"

"The money Desmond gave you was stolen from me and I want it back."

"That's your money?" Ian glanced at Kendrick. "Fair enough: pick a place to meet and I'll bring it to you."

"So you do still have it?"

"You were guessing?"

"I was hoping." Paul shrugged, "Where is it?"

"Pick a place to meet and I'll bring it to you."

"You're getting on my nerves, MacAran." Paul jabbed Ian in the ribs with the gun barrel and then pressed it to his throat. "You've broken into my house, assaulted me, and left me chained in the dark in my own basement! Of course you managed to leave every other light in the house burning."

"What?" Bernie tsked. "You're worried about your power bill?"

Neault glared at Bernie, "Cute."

Bernie glared back, "So how'd you get loose?"

"Kendrick keeps his appointments." Paul's shotgun was still pointed at Ian. "Where is my money?"

"Just pick a place to meet and I'll bring it to you."

"Unacceptable. Tell me where the money is or we'll start putting bullets into your friend here."

"And risk having the neighbors call the police?" Ian glanced at the door. "If they haven't already."

Neault shook his head and pointed to the earpiece Kendrick was wearing. "If the police dispatch anyone to this address, we'll know about it."

"I don't have any choice." Ian sighed. "You're right about that. But if I tell you who has the money you could kill us and go after them and there wouldn't be anything I could do about it. The only way I can be sure we get out of this alive is if you let me deliver the cash later."

"If you give me my money, what motive would I have to harm you?"

"Aside from your power bill?" There was no humor in Ian's expression, "I saw what you did to Mick; and Terri."

Paul shrugged. "Everybody needs a hobby." He nodded to Kendrick. "Shoot her in the foot."

"Wait!"

Kendrick had taken aim at Bernie's bare foot, but he paused and looked expectantly at Paul.

Ian looked at Paul. "How much money are we talking about?"

"You didn't count it?" Paul looked amused. "What difference does it make? I want it back."

"And I want to give it to you, but Des gave me a lot of money. I know some of it came from cashing out his stocks so how much of it was yours?"

Paul hesitated. "Two million."

"Fair enough. That's your property and I'll give it back to you, but we're not doing this at gun point." Ian looked from Neault to Kendrick and back. "I've got another eight million that Des gave me. Would you like that, too?"

"Why would you give up eight million dollars?" Paul looked suspicious. "Why not just offer us another million?"

"Because I don't want the money. It's the goddamned money that got me into this mess in the first place. Now, do you want it or not?"

Paul glanced at Kendrick and smiled. "I want it very much."

"Then leave her alone. Pick a place to meet and I'll bring you ten million dollars."

Paul shrugged. "Two million, ten million, nothing has changed. We'll leave both of you alone if you tell us where the money is." Paul narrowed his eyes. "All of it."

Ian met Paul's arrogant expression with a grimly determined stare. "If I tell you where the money is, I have nothing left to bargain with. I have to assume you're planning to kill us anyway, so I can't tell you who's holding it for me, no matter what you do. But if you leave right now, I'll give you all ten million dollars. If you wait one more minute, you get nine million. Another minute and it drops to eight million."

Paul laughed. "You won't trust me; why in the world should I trust you?"

"Because you know where we live! You'll be back if you don't get what you want and I do not want you coming back."

"True." Paul seemed to consider the offer.

"You don't have much time to think about it, Paul. Leave right now and you get ten million dollars."

"What's to keep me from coming back after you deliver the money?"

"I don't think you're that mad at me, are you?" Ian glanced at his watch. "I'd think nine million dollars would buy a lot of electricity."

Kendrick was quick to correct him. "Ten million."

Ian shook his head. "The last sixty seconds cost you a million dollars. I am now willing to deliver nine million dollars anywhere you want; anywhere in the world." Ian looked at his watch. "But you have to be out of here in forty-five seconds."

Kendrick raised his gun and pointed it at Bernie's head. "MacAran, you stupid fuck! You have no idea who you're dealing with."

"That's true." Ian kept his eyes on Paul. "But even a stupid fuck has to realize that splitting nine million dollars is better than splitting nothing. I'm assuming you'd be splitting it fifty-fifty." He glanced at Kendrick. "Wouldn't you? How much are you paying your partner, Paul?"

"Not your worry, MacAran. We're not stupid, and we're not... odd." Paul was looking past Ian at the purse on the breakfast counter. He looked at Bernie, glanced around the studio and then walked around Ian to the purse. "This isn't your purse, Miss Selleca, is it?"

"Yeah," Bernie nodded. "Why?"

"It's the only pastel thing in this apartment." Paul opened the main compartment, took out a checkbook and read the name on the checks. "Sandra Taylor." He dropped the checkbook on the counter and looked at Ian. "The woman you were looking for, yes?"

Paul glanced at the beams above the kitchen and realized there were stairs that led up to a loft. He walked over to the stairs and started up.

"The money isn't upstairs, Professor," Ian looked at Kendrick. "But you guys are down to eight million dollars."

"Come on, Professor!" Kendrick gestured toward the door with his gun.

"Patience." When Paul rounded the top of the stairs, he could see that the French doors to the loft's tiny balcony had been opened. He crossed the floor and started to step out onto the narrow metal landing, but he stepped back, reached over and swung the left door closed. "Miss Taylor, I presume?"

Sandy had been hiding behind the door, in the small triangle of carpet between the open door and the corner. She nodded resignedly, but she had one arm behind her back. Paul motioned her toward the stairs with his gun. "Let's join the others, shall we?"

Downstairs a voice much deeper than Kendrick's yelled. "Police! Freeze!"

As Paul turned toward the sound, Sandy whipped her hand from behind her back and sprayed Bernie's favorite perfume into Paul's face. Gunshots echoed through the studio as Paul raised a hand to his eyes. He blindly swung his gun toward Sandy and fired, but she ducked under his arm and grabbed his wrist. Adding her weight to his motion, she stepped toward him and swung him into the glass door. The shotgun broke through the glass and when Paul tried to pull away the broken glass cut into his arm. He dropped the gun.

The door Sandy had been hiding behind was closed, but the other door was still open. As Paul jerked his arm free, Sandy bent her knees, lowered her shoulders and shoved him out onto the balcony. Paul scrambled to keep his feet under him, but his momentum carried him over the railing.

Sandy turned away from the edge before Neault landed and rushed toward the stairs. Meeting Ian at the top, she said, "Are you all right?" in the same moment that Ian said, "Are you okay?" Both nodded.

Glancing down into the entryway, Sandy saw Barrett Hogue pulling a gun out of Kendrick's shoulder holster. Kendrick was lying face down on the floor with Barrett's knee in the middle of his back. Ian looked past Sandy at the empty loft.

"Where's Neault?"

Sandy pointed to the open door. Ian crossed the loft, leaned out through the doorway and looked down. Moison and Nagant's tan sedan was parked in the red zone in front of the apartment building. Paul Neault was embedded in the roof.

Friday, 11:56 am - Third Floor, Alta Bates Hospital

"I'm going to kill him; I'm going to kill him and then I'm going to kill him again." Terri looked anxiously at Yuri, "You don't have a problem with me killing him do you?"

Yuri hesitated, "I have concerns about the timing." He changed the subject, "What did he knock you out with?"

"I don't know what it was, but it was fast. Half a glass of apple juice and I was out cold." Terri shifted toward Yuri to lift her shoulder off the pillow. Yuri was standing next to her bed with his hands crossed in front of him, but when she winced with the effort he quickly reached across to move the pillow for her. A bulky TV mounted high in the corner of the room hovered protectively over Jamaal who was curled up in the big comfy chair beneath it. The room's other bed was empty, but Jamaal was deep asleep in the recliner. Terri grimaced as she leaned back into the pillows. "I can't believe he took me out so easily. I even brought the juice!"

Yuri raised an eyebrow. "Then how did he get the drug into the glass?"

"Ice. Paul insisted on getting me a glass of ice."

"Always the congenial host."

"Yeah, well, he's going to be one deceased fucking host as soon as I get out of here. I'm going to kill him."

"You mentioned that."

"Twice."

"Agreed, but we have to take care of business first. The police didn't find anything at Paul's house, but that doesn't mean our product isn't there. Not that I have any desire to search the place myself. If he won't pay for it, we need Paul to tell us where those 20 kilos are. After we've recovered our product we can dispose of him." Yuri looked at the bandages covering Terri's shoulders and upper arms. "I still don't understand why he did this to you."

"He figured out that I told you about the cop."

"How could he know it was you?"

"He knew you wouldn't deal with Des and I was the only other person who knew Mick was a cop. Paul said by talking to you and going independent with Des I'd betrayed him. The sanctimonious asshole said he was willing to forgive me, though. He told me he'd stop cutting me if I told him everything I knew about your end of the business."

"I am so sorry, Terri." Yuri sighed. "What did you tell him?"

"I laughed at him." Terri adjusted the pillow behind her head, wincing with the exertion. "I called him a liar and a fraud and I asked him where all his sex slaves were."

"Sex slaves? Paul?"

"Oh yeah! He loved to tell his grad students how these rich women would pay him to let them clean his house naked. He said they catered to his every whim but we all knew it was bullshit. Anyway, he asked me about you and Ruiz and he started braiding my skin. He'd ask a question, make a cut, ask again, and trim my skin back a little ..." Terri gingerly touched her arm. "It was really intense. Of course Paul didn't think it up by himself; he saw it at an S&M demonstration. He said he'd wanted to try it ever since. He tried it on the cop, but he didn't get to see how the scars looked. That's the whole point when it's consensual."

"Consensual?"

"Yeah. You let the skin heal with the strips braided across each other and it leaves a fantastic scar."

Yuri shuddered. "I'm sure the doctors here will be able to keep that from happening."

"No way." Terri shook her head. "I mean they could if I wanted them to, but Neault-nuts actually did a pretty good job. The strips are balanced and symmetrical and I think the scars will be pretty cool. They make a good trophy."

"You want something to remind you of Paul?"

"Damn right! I beat him, Mr. Milanov! I didn't tell him anything he wanted to know and that means I won." Terri smiled proudly. "I also want something to remind me of my favorite professor after I feed him his intestines. I can deal with the knife work, you know? But that bastard raped me! He raped me and then he laughed about how he wasn't going to kill me. He was going to keep me alive as long as I 'continued to amuse him.' He said he was going to watch how my skin healed, and he kept telling me I liked it." She reached up to wipe at the tears that had suddenly filled her eyes. "I didn't."

Yuri offered her a handkerchief, but the tears had already stopped. Terri gave him a determined smile. "You know, I didn't tell him a goddamned thing, Mr. Milanov. Neault-nuts knows nothing."

"That's helpful, Terri, but I'm honestly much more concerned with your welfare than with how much Paul knows. Of course it simplifies our reorganization if he can't warn anyone, but we're adaptable. You've done well. Quite well." Yuri looked at her for a moment, studying her. "It's been an eventful week, Terri. On top of everything else, I've lost Jesus. That means I need someone I can trust to handle the East Bay. Can I trust you?"

"Of course." Terri nodded. "Yes, absolutely."

"You'll make the same percentage as Jesus, with the same bonuses."

"Paid vacation?"

Yuri smiled. "And health insurance."

"Thank you Mr. Milanov. I won't let you down. I just need to take care of Paul first."

"You don't need to be so formal. 'Yuri' will do nicely. As for finding Paul: we have some competition, and the police have a lot more resources than we do. On the other hand, we're not as limited in our methodology, so there's a chance we'll get to him first, but you can't afford to wait around until that happens. You have work to do. When we find Paul, you can take a day or two of that vacation time. Just remember to get the information we need before you do anything irreversible."

"Business before pleasure?"

"I prefer to think of business as pleasure." Yuri glanced over at Jamaal, sleeping peacefully in the corner. "What about our young friend? Aren't his parents worried about him?"

Terri shook her head. "He lives with his aunt, but she's got her own problems. Jamaal is really on his own, but he's a smart kid. He can work for me as long as..."

"Terri," Yuri was shaking his head. "Like you, the boy has moxie, and I admire that. He's been through more in his few years than many see in a lifetime, but he's still a child, and we don't do business with children."

"But I don't see why we..."

"Terri. Why take away what little childhood he has left?"

"But..."

Yuri held up his hand. "This is not negotiable. Take care of him, find him a good school, make sure he has everything he needs to succeed, but do not involve him in our business. Is that clear?"

"Yes sir."

"You can even adopt him if you wish, but he can not work for us in any capacity."

"I understand."

"Good." Yuri nodded.

There was a polite knock at the door and Yuri's chauffeur stepped into the room. He nodded to Terri as he walked over to whisper something to Yuri. Jamaal looked up, recognized Travis, and went back to sleep.

"Really?" Yuri looked pleasantly surprised, "What happened?"

Travis whispered something else and Yuri laughed out loud.

"That was good." Yuri was still chuckling, the lines around his eyes crinkled with amusement. "Thank you, Travis. See if you can get any more information, but don't be obvious about it."

"Right away, Mr. Milanov." Travis headed back out to the hallway.

Yuri explained, "Travis was trying to spare your feelings, but I think you'll like this. The police have apprehended our wayward professor, but this cloud has a silver lining."

Terri looked disappointed. "What's the good news?"

"As we speak, Paul is recovering from surgery only two floors above us."

"Surgery? What happened?"

"He's been admitted for multiple injuries including a broken leg, and a fractured pelvis." Yuri laughed. "As Travis put it, he got himself defenestrated."

"Dee…?"

"A fitting reference to nobility and the French Revolution; he was thrown out of a window."

Terri grinned. "I like it."

"I thought you might." Yuri studied the bandages covering her arms. "I would imagine he's in quite a lot of pain."

"You hope." Terri threw her covers off and sat up. "I think we should make sure."

"Unfortunately he's in police custody which means at least one cop outside his door."

"True, but we may not get a better chance to talk to him before the cops do."

Yuri nodded. "We need a plan."

"I have an idea, but, uh…" Terri looked over at Jamaal. "You're not going to like it."

Yuri shrugged philosophically. "Persuade me."

Friday, 5:57 pm - Fourth Floor, Alta Bates Hospital

For a man whose left arm was immobilized by a wrist to shoulder cast and suspended from bars above his hospital bed, Orson looked pretty comfortable. Supported by a mountain of pillows, he glanced from Ian to Bernie to Sandy, as he shook his head in amused disbelief. "But why did they bring Neault here?"

"He's hurt too bad to go anywhere else." Ian shrugged. "The police have him under guard on the next floor. Hogue said they'll probably move him to the county jail tomorrow."

"That makes sense, but how did Barrett know about Neault in the first place?"

"He had Kendrick followed. When Kendrick picked up Neault, Moisin called Barrett and they followed Neault to Bernie's."

"Wasn't Kendrick Hogue's secretary?"

Sandy nodded. "He was actually a detective on what they call Temporary Modified Duty. Barrett said he'd killed an old woman in a shoot-out and wasn't sure he could use his gun again. He was supposedly working it out in therapy..."

"And his shrink was Paul Neault, right?"

"Of course." Sandy nodded.

Orson looked at Ian and his expression got serious. "What about you?"

"What about me?"

"Are you going to jail? Are you turning State's Evidence?" Orson paused. "Are you going to get through this?"

Ian glanced at Sandy, "My lawyer maintains that Mick was a cop and the fact that he repeatedly refused to take 'no' for an answer constitutes entrapment."

"Really?" Orson looked at Sandy. "Nice work."

Sandy looked uncertain but she said, "From a legal standpoint it was over as soon as Mick started exerting undue influence."

"That may be true," Ian sighed, "but I'm still the one who's responsible for all this."

"True;" Orson nodded agreement. "Would you do it again?"

"God no!"

"Then you've learned something." Orson shifted a bit and winced as he jostled his shoulder.

Sandy winced sympathetically, "Is your arm going to be okay?"

"Oh yeah. It'll be stiff for a while but physical therapy will make it good as new. Hey!" Orson leaned to one side to sort through the debris on the bedside table. "Does anybody have a pen?"

Sandy looked in her purse, but Bernie pulled a felt-tip out of her pocket. "Here." She tried to hand it to Orson but he pointed to the cast on his arm.

"I want you guys to start the autographs."

"Sure." Bernie surveyed the curve of the cast where it bent around his elbow, then started drawing.

"Bobby said it helps the bone heal." Orson watched the image taking shape on his temporary exoskeleton. "What are you drawing?"

"A knight in shining armor. Who's Bobby?"

"A very cute nurse." Orson watched Bernie's pen carve a graceful arc across the plaster. "The doctor doesn't think I'll be skiing any time soon, but I think they're being far too conservative."

Ian moved closer to watch Bernie draw. "You ski?"

"God yes, whenever I get the chance." Orson smiled. "Swoosh!"

Ian looked at him quizzically. "You're still on pain meds, aren't you?"

"Oh my, yes!" Orson nodded enthusiastically. "Best drugs the insurance company would approve."

"Look, I'm really sorry about your arm. If there's..."

"Don't go there!" Orson waved the apology away with his free hand. "I was glad to help, glad for the experience, and I'd do it all again in a heartbeat."

"I'm just saying..."

"You don't realize it was fate that brought you to me; do you?"

"Fate?" Ian sounded skeptical.

"Yes; fate. You could have gone to any gun shop in Nevada but you came to me. Why? Fate!"

"How many other gun shops are right across the street from the airport?"

"Not the point. For the first time in my life I was tested in actual combat!"

Ian shook his head resignedly. "You're on more than pain meds."

Orson laughed. Bernie finished her knight, initialed the sketch and handed the pen to Sandy.

After writing, "Thank you", Sandy underlined each word. She drew a heart around the words and signed her name.

"My pleasure." Orson smiled, but his enthusiasm suddenly faded. "I'm sorry. You probably weren't glad for the experience at all, were you?"

"No." Sandy shook her head as she handed the pen to Ian. "Not at all."

Ian hesitated, wrote, "Get well soon," and signed his name.

"You're so sentimental." Orson laughed. "I want to get Ken's autograph too. Is he still here?"

Bernie shook her head. "He checked out this morning. His mom picked him up."

"She got her van back?"

Bernie nodded.

"Good. How's Pierrot doing?"

"He's pretty screwed up. This morning he got up, got dressed and tried to walk out of the hospital. The nurse I talked to said he was hysterical. They've got him sedated and they've upgraded him from critical to stable condition, but they won't know how extensive the brain damage is for a while."

"What about the castaways?"

Bernie glanced at Ian, who said, "The Coast Guard should've picked them up by now."

"Did you ever tell the computer guy that he could come home?"

Ian nodded. "Tony and Cindy are honeymooning in Tuscan."

"Boring!" Orson pretended to yawn. "Well, maybe not if you don't live there."

Ian looked at his watch. "We still have to go to Hayward."

Orson looked puzzled. "What's in Hayward?"

"Do you ever stop asking questions?"

"I'm a detective, remember? What's in Hayward?"

"My airplane, remember? I have to return the Towncar and pick up the PBY."

"And I need to drop Ken's truck off at his house." Bernie said.

Orson looked puzzled. "Ken has a truck?"

"Yeah. I left it at the Airport after I followed Ian and Des to the PBY." Bernie sighed. "God was that just yesterday?" She started toward the door.

"Day before." Ian shook Orson's good hand and moved to follow Bernie. "I'll check in on you tomorrow, Orson."

Sandy seemed reluctant to leave. She looked from Orson to the door and back again. "I guess I should pick up my car from Ian's. Thank you, Orson." She kissed him on the cheek. "Thanks for everything."

Bernie was holding the door open. "See you tomorrow." She waved cheerfully.

Orson raised his hand and wiggled his fingers weakly. "Bye kids!"

At the end of the hall Bernie pressed the up button for the elevator, realized her mistake and quickly pressed the down button as well. She watched Ian watching Sandy impatiently checking her watch. "So," Bernie cleared her throat. "We'll go to Ian's first so Sandy can get her car?"

Sandy and Ian both nodded. Bernie reached out to touch Sandy's shoulder. "Are you okay to drive?"

"I'm fine!" Sandy opened her purse, "Would you stop hovering?" She dug out her cell and busied herself checking messages.

The middle elevator pinged but the arrow above the car pointed up. When the doors opened, Jamaal glanced out at the three grumpy adults and quickly pressed the already glowing 5th floor button. He wanted as few people as possible to see him carrying the stupid teddy bear. He pressed 5 again, but the doors didn't close until he pressed the door-close button. When the doors finally opened on the 5th floor, Jamaal stepped out of the elevator wearing pirate pajamas from the gift shop and Terri's hospital slippers. At first he carried the stuffed bear securely under his arm, as if it were a football and he started down the hall with the self-assured stride of a man twice his age. That all changed when he saw the police officer. Jamaal slowed down and made his steps nervous and unsure. He changed his grip on the bear so that it dangled pathetically by one paw, and he tried to think of something that could make him cry. He thought about the last time he and Richard had been with the X-men.

Across the hall from Paul Neault's room, Officer Lazzeroni was sitting in a chair reading Newsweek. He'd chosen a post that gave him a clear view of the elevators, most of the hall and the suspect's room, or at least the door to Neault's room. He thought it was stupid to be guarding a cop-killer from the other side of the door, but hospital staff insisted Neault be given a chance to recover from surgery undisturbed. The same medical staff assured him that Neault wouldn't be able to get out of bed for weeks and might never walk, let alone pose a flight risk, so Lazzeroni could as easily guard the prisoner from a beach in New Zealand. After three and a half hours of watching nurses and doctors check on the immobile patient, Lazzeroni was inclined to agree.

Jamaal slowly walked up to the officer and stared at the floor underneath the chair.

"Well, hi there." Lazzeroni smiled as he closed his magazine.

Jamaal looked up just long enough for the officer to see the fear and uncertainty on his face. He lowered his eyes. "Hi."

"You don't look too happy there, little guy. What's wrong?"

"I can't find my mom."

"Sounds just like the kind of problem I'm trained to take care of." The officer smiled. "My name's Walter, what's yours?"

Jamaal looked like he was about to cry. "I want to go home."

"That's a funny name, but I know exactly how you feel. I want to go home too." Walter stood and set his magazine on the chair. "Let's go check with the nurses. I'm sure they can help us find your mom." He held out his hand. Jamaal hesitated, then switched the bear to his left hand. He took Walter's hand with his right and let him lead the way down the hall.

As they turned the corner, Jamaal tugged on the officer's hand and pointed past the nurses' station toward the men's room. Looking first at Jamaal and then down the hall, Walter noticed the orderly with the eagle talon earring passing behind him, but he didn't pay her any attention. As Terri slipped into Paul's room, Jamaal pointed even further down the hall and yelled, "Hey, there she is. Mom, wait!" He ran a few doors down the hall then stopped. He looked every way he could think of then slowly turned back toward Lazzeroni. A tear pooled at the corner of one eye.

Walter closed the distance between them and dropped to one knee. "Wasn't that her?" He glanced into the empty room and quickly surveyed the hall but there was nobody to be seen.

Jamaal stared at the floor and dejectedly shook his head.

"Hey come on! We'll find her!" Walter stood up and held out his hand. "Let's just…"

The cold metal against the back of his neck didn't feel anything like the plastic practice guns they used in Judo but Lazzeroni's reflexes spun him around in a textbook perfect reverse attack. His black belt almost got him killed. Fortunately Travis was cool enough to not shoot him and quick enough to use Lazzeroni's spin to pull him off balance and into the empty hospital room. In moments he and Yuri had the officer cuffed to a chair with a pillowcase over his head, ten grand in his vest pocket and the assurance that he would survive to spend his "inconvenience fee" as long as he didn't move for the next half hour. Over the next decades Lazzeroni's priest would tell more people about the money and the murder than Walter Lazzeroni, but still, for all practical purposes, the secret would remain safe.

Travis caught Yuri's eye and nodded toward Jamaal. "He is really good."

Yuri nodded agreement but said, "No."

"But he just helped us…"

Yuri held up his hand. "An exception that proves the rule doesn't mean a change in policy."

"When he's twenty-one?"

Yuri considered. "When he finishes college."

Meanwhile, all remained quiet in Paul's room. The drapes were drawn; the room was in shadow and Paul's chest moved up and down with each peaceful breath. Terri stood in the private room's bathroom holding a black doctor's bag at her side. When the phone in her stolen orderly's shirt vibrated, Terri looked at the text on the tiny screen. The cop was taken care of.

Moving to the side of Paul's bed, Terri pulled several restraints out of the black bag and looped one around Paul's wrist. She gently fastened his arm to the railing along the side of the bed and pulled the strap tight. Paul slept on, even as Terri limped around the bed and immobilized his other wrist. He didn't seem to notice when she turned on the bedside light but she got a response when she dropped the hand-respirator on his chest.

"What…?" Neault's voice was groggy and slurred.

"Good evening, Neault-nuts." Terri slipped a plastic bag over the top of Paul's head. The clear polypropylene covering his hair looked like a shower cap.

"Terri? What the hell?"

Terri pressed her hand over his mouth. "Now hush, Professor. We don't want to be interrupted." She laid a syringe with a very long needle on Paul's stomach and next to that she set a tiny bottle of clear liquid.

The needle looked scary but the little bottle was what made Neault's eyes widen. Beneath her hand, he managed to ask, "What's that?"

"You mean this?" Bernie held the bottle up and grinned. "Adrenalin. Have you ever seen Pulp Fiction?"

Neault tried to shake his head.

"Well, depending on how cooperative you decide to be, we might get to reenact my favorite part." Terri leaned close and whispered directly into his ear. "It's the scene where the very sexy heroine O.D.s and they bring her back with a shot of adrenalin straight into her heart. Can you imagine? How's your heart Professor?"

"Terri, I…"

"Shush. Save your strength. You are *so* going to need it." Terri smiled. "I just want you to know that you didn't break me, Professor. I didn't tell you anything I didn't want to. I didn't tell you that Yuri has been planning to shut you down for months. I didn't tell you that I've been working for him, and that he knows everything I know about you." Terri considered. "Actually, he knows a lot more. He knows the police didn't find any coke or any money when they searched your house. What he doesn't know is how you're planning to pay for the 20 keys from prison. Which is why I'm here."

"Tell Yuri I'll settle with him when I get out of here. Now, piss off!"

"I spent some time thinking about how I was going to hurt you. Then you got yourself all busted up and beat me to it. The nurses said you're on all kinds of pain killers, so my original plan probably wouldn't even hurt." Terri smiled. "I was going to cut your balls off and stuff them down your throat. You'd probably suffocate, but you wouldn't really get the full effect, if you know what I mean."

Paul didn't answer.

"That's when it hit me: you don't have to feel anything to suffocate. So, this is me asking you all nice and civilized: where is Mr. Milanov's money?"

"Go to hell."

Terri grabbed both sides of the plastic bag and pulled it down over Neault's face. As she gathered the bag tight around his neck, she said, "As they say in the movies: you first."

The plastic squeezed against Paul's face as he tried to inhale, then billowed out as he tried to get the carbon dioxide-charged air out of his lungs. Fighting the wrist restraints, Neault's eyes filled with panic. He tried to scream for help but he had no air in his lungs and the faint sounds that squeaked out were muffled by the plastic. Mist from the moisture in his breath started to form on the inside of the bag. After a few minutes, Neault weakened. Another minute passed and he stopped struggling, just staring at Terri as the life faded from his eyes. The plastic hung motionless from the tip of his nose to the stubble on his chin.

Terri checked his pulse and then pushed the plastic up off his face. Placing the respirator over his nose and mouth, Terri squeezed several breaths into him, and then checked for a pulse. Raising her arm above her head she pounded her fist into the center of his chest. Neault gasped for air, the terror in his eyes more desperate than the fear he'd felt before his heart stopped.

"Help." His voice was hoarse and weak.

"Now shush." Terri put her hand over his mouth and a finger over her lips. "Just breathe."

Paul nodded and Terri uncovered his mouth. He took a deeper breath and started to shout, but Terri slipped the plastic down over his face. She shook her head. "You just don't play well with others, do you?"

Neault shook his head from side to side and strained against the straps holding his arms. The bed squeaked each time Neault jerked against his bonds, but it soon fell silent as Neault's strength faded.

Terri slid the bag back to the top of Neault's head and he sucked in a deep breath of air. When his panicked panting settled down Terri asked him again, "Where's the money?"

"Des stole the money he was supposed to take to Yuri. The pilot has it, Ian MacAran. I haven't had a chance to sell the coke."

"Okay, so give it back. Where is it?"

The plastic crinkled as Neault shook his head. "I need it to start over. I'll get Yuri his money. Tell him..."

Terri reached for the plastic bag.

"Wait! You kill me and you won't get anything!"

Terri pretended to consider before she nodded, "I'm okay with that."

Neault tried to call out as Terri slid the plastic over his face. Then he tried holding his breath, but that only lasted half a minute. He stared at Terri and she smiled back as he faded. When he stopped struggling, Terri pushed the plastic out of the way and started pumping fresh air into Neault's lungs. She checked his pulse, thumped his chest, checked his pulse and thumped his chest again before dropping the respirator and picking up the hypodermic. Jabbing the needle into the tiny bottle of adrenalin, Terri filled the syringe and dropped the empty bottle on Neault's stomach. She raised her hand above her head, squeezed a few drops of fluid out of the needle, then hammered the hypo through his breastbone and into his heart. Terri mashed the plunger down. After a long second Paul gasped for air.

Neault blinked, his eyes focusing horrifically aware on Terri's face.

"Welcome back shit-head." Terri pulled the needle out of Neault's chest but he didn't seem to feel it. "Here's a new topic for discussion: what's it like being dead?"

Neault focused on breathing.

Terri checked his pulse. "Whoa, your heart is really going! By the way, I'm keeping the braids you sadistic worthless fuck. A small token of my complete victory over your pathetic psyche."

Neault coughed, trying to clear his throat. "What do you want?"

"A synopsis then: in your last incarnation we were talking about cocaine. Mr. Milanov would prefer cash but we'll settle for the return of his twenty kilos."

"It's in a storage locker. I can show you..." Neault was having trouble getting enough air into his lungs.

"Is the money there too?"

"What money?"

"The money you were going to use to pay for it."

"I told you: Des took that. He ... wait!"

Terri slipped the bag over Neault's face and watched him struggle to stay alive. Before he passed out, however, she pulled the bag up enough to give him a single breath of air. "Where exactly is this storage locker?"

"U-Store-It," Neault gasped. "Shattuck Avenue. Number 314."

"Good." Terri pulled the bag back down over Neault's face. She smiled at him as he jerked back and forth, trying to free his arms. She lifted the bag again, allowing one more breath. "Where's the key?"

Neault managed to look defiant. "You're going to kill me anyway!"

"Not if you play nice. Unlike you, I have a sense of honor and I know how to win gracefully. I promised myself I'd kill you twice, but I seem to have done exactly that already. I've killed you. Twice." Terri smiled as she pushed the plastic further up onto the top of his head. "I must say I enjoyed it more than I thought

I would. Not a good thing, perhaps, but very liberating. Tell me: what's it like? Did you see any bright lights?"

"No."

"The gates of hell?"

"Very funny."

"You must have seen something."

"I didn't see anything."

"Nothing?" Terri looked genuinely disappointed. "That's too bad. Where is the key?"

Paul shook his head and clenched his jaw.

"Get over yourself Professor, I don't need to kill you; I've proved my point: I've beaten you. I've proven that I'm stronger than you. In fact I'm so much stronger that I can forgive you. In fact, I *want* you to live. You're going to prison, Neault-nuts, as a cop-killer no less and I want you to spend a long miserable life knowing each and every day that I kicked your sanctimonious ass. Just tell me what I want to know and everything will be settled between us. Otherwise..." Terri reached for the edge of the plastic bag still bunched up above Paul's forehead.

"Wait! Please. It doesn't have a key, it's a combination: 36-17-28."

"And that's at the U-Store-It on Shattuck?"

Paul nodded.

"Which locker?"

"314."

"Locker 314?"

"Yes!"

"And that combination was?"

Neault repeated it.

"Well thank you very much." Terri glanced over her shoulder at the door. "Now all I have to do is get out of here." She pulled out her cell phone and dialed Jamaal's number. When he answered she asked, "All clear?" She smiled at his reply and closed her phone.

"I really enjoyed our talk Neault-nuts, but I must be off." Terri smiled at Neault as she gathered everything back into the black bag.

Paul just glared at her until she reached for the bag over his head. When she tugged it toward his chin instead of pulling it off he yelled, "But you said..." The plastic muffled the rest of his objection.

Terri watched him struggle against his restraints. "Things are totally settled between you and me, Professor and I forgive you, I really do. I'd love to leave you stewing in your inadequacy but I work for Yuri. Did I mention he said I could call him Yuri?" She smiled as Paul began dying for the third time. "Yuri has more..." she searched for the right word, "*practical* criteria for closure."

Friday, 6:58 pm - Highway 880 - Going South

Bernie stared out the window as clusters of bright orange safety cones blipped past. Beyond the cones, bulldozers and graders shared the dirt shoulder with trucks, cranes and paving machines. Some of the cranes had their booms raised high, dangling tools and trailers too awkward to carry home and too valuable to trust to the weekend. Generators and welding machines swayed like bait waiting to be cast into the stream of traffic. Above the construction zone, wispy clouds glowed pink and red in the fading sun.

Ian was driving. Bernie glanced at him occasionally but if he noticed he didn't show it. Neither had said a word since they'd dropped Sandy off at her car ten minutes ago. Sandy hadn't said much more since the hospital. As they reached the exit for Oakland Airport, Bernie broke the silence.

"Are you exhausted or just lost in thought?"

Ian shrugged but then tried to stifle a yawn. "A little of both, I guess."

When Ian didn't say anything more, she tried another tack. "What do we do next?"

"You take Ken's truck back to Ken and I go get the Catalina."

"After that?

"Sleep."

"Amen." Bernie looked at him nervously. "And after that?"

Ian considered, "After that I have no idea."

"Are you going to call Sandy?"

"She doesn't want anything to do with me."

"Yeah. She hasn't been too thrilled with me either." Bernie shifted her weight a little to turn toward him, "Look: Yesterday she didn't want to be alone; today she wants some space. Give her some time."

"It's not that simple. Sandy's eleven kinds of hurt, pissed and disappointed in me and I can't blame her."

"So you're giving up?"

"What do you expect me to do; stalk her?"

"That was mean. I expect you to not give up!"

"Easy for you to say."

"Not really." Bernie sighed. "This is your future. You should never let anyone else or anything else keep you from doing what you want to do. You have the power, you have the strength, and you have the wisdom, but you're the one who has to use them to change your life!"

"What?" Ian studied her suspiciously. "Are you seriously quoting Chuck Williamson at me?"

"Well," Bernie hesitated, "It isn't bad advice."

Ian turned into the parking lot and maneuvered the Towncar into a space across from Ken's pickup truck. He glanced at Bernie as he shut off the car. "What exactly are you trying to do?"

"What do you mean?"

"I keep thinking about everything I could have done or should have done and I realize you're the only one who seems to have a plan." Ian considered her for a moment. "Am I completely paranoid? Is it just coincidence that everything is working out so you and Sandy can end up living happily ever after?"

"Dammit Ian!" Bernie got out of the car and leaned back in to yell at him. "Yes, you're completely paranoid! No, things are not working out! I'm not trying to make anybody do anything they don't want to do!" She slammed the door and shouted. "This isn't about me!"

"This isn't about you?" Ian had stepped out the other side and was following her toward Ken's truck. "You're the one who was stalking Sandy! You're the one who followed me home and you're the one who maneuvered your way into my life – into our lives. You must've been planning something! This is totally all about you!"

Bernie whirled around to face him. "I was not stalking her and I did not *maneuver* anybody! I'm not the one who was smuggling drugs. I'm not the one who got Sandy kidnapped and I'm sure as hell not the one who almost got her killed!"

"You're right." Ian's anger was completely eclipsed by guilt. "I could've gotten us all killed! God! I can't believe how completely I've screwed things up."

"You have at that." Bernie studied him for a moment and her angry expression softened. "But we made it right, Ian. Together we made it right."

" And now she won't talk to me!"

"She's not talking to either one of us right now. Like I said before: give her time." Bernie considered. "I told you I didn't have a plan, but I do have a hope. Your paranoia just got it backwards."

"You weren't trying to break us up?"

"No, just the opposite."

"Why?"

"Because you're the only hope I have of being a part of Sandy's life."

"Wouldn't that be a lot easier if I wasn't around?"

"Of course." Bernie nodded. "And that's what I thought when I decided I had to meet you, but getting to know you showed me just how totally crazy complicated this thing is. More than I could ever have imagined. And then I fell in love with you too."

"What about Sandy?"

"If you weren't around I wouldn't be either. We tried. Just because I need her doesn't mean she needs me. She thinks she needs you and I think she's right." Bernie paused. "I am so screwed. I'm like the ocean getting dragged from shore to shore every time the Moon passes overhead and even when she's on the other side of the planet I can still feel her pull."

"Sandy's the moon?"

Bernie nodded, "Since the day we met. But it's never been the same for her."

"I know the feeling."

"You know the feeling?" She mocked, "There was a time when I wished you knew the feeling you lucky bastard, but trust me: you don't have a god-damned clue!"

"But I…"

"Look: If I'm the ocean and Sandy's the Moon in this cosmic train-wreck of a metaphor what do you think that makes you?"

"Uh, the Earth?"

"The Earth?" Bernie rolled her eyes. "Jesus freaking… You are such a moron!"

"What?"

"You light her up, Ian! Like dawn on a beach in the Bahamas: You're the Sun! Whenever she talks about you she gets all… she just…" Bernie clenched her fists in frustration. "You stupid, lucky, impossible idiot; she thinks you're the one, Ian! She thinks you're soul mates!" Her rant trailed to a whisper. "Jackass."

"And she's right." Bernie sighed. "And I know it."

Saturday, 6:59 pm - Yuri's Jaguar,
Mission District, San Francisco

The long silver Jaguar turned off Mission and onto 16th street. In the back, Yuri Milanov poured champagne into two long-stemmed glasses while Terri poured 7-Up into a third. Jamaal reluctantly took the glass from her. "I don't see why I can't drink champagne."

"Don't spoil the moment." Yuri splashed a little champagne into Jamaal's 7-Up before sliding the bottle back into its bucket of ice. He picked up the glasses and handed one to Terri. "To my newest associate." The three clinked their glasses together.

The car turned another corner and rolled to a stop on Valencia. Over his shoulder, Yuri's driver said, "We're here, Mister Milanov."

"Thank you, Travis." Yuri glanced out at multicolored apartment building. He looked at Terri. "You're sure you don't want us to wait?"

Terri shook her head. "Thanks, but I can handle this. I'll see you Monday."

Yuri nodded. "As you wish."

Travis opened Terri's door, but she hesitated, checking her jeans pocket for her keys. She looked at Jamaal. "I gave you the keys, right?"

Jamaal jangled his jacket pocket and nodded.

"Good. I'll be home in a few hours, Jamaal." Terri levered herself out of the car, said, "Thanks," to Travis and stepped up onto the sidewalk. She paused to look up at a pair of windows on the third floor, two apartments from the corner. Behind her the Jaguar eased into traffic and drifted up Valencia Street.

Terri limped into the entryway and picked up the intercom phone. She dialed the apartment and crossed her fingers as the dial tone clicked off and Stacia's phone started ringing.

"Hello?"

"Stacia, this is Terri. I just wanted to…"

click

Terri sighed, "That was predictable." She broke the connection and started to dial again, but a woman with a Doberman and a handful of plastic bags came out of the building and Terri caught the door before it closed. She said, "I'm on my way," into the dead handset, nodded at the woman with the dog and slipped into the building.

Terri stopped outside Apt. 306. She raised her hand to knock but hesitated, then reached down to adjust the brace around her knee. Taking a deep breath Terri softly knocked on the door. When she heard movement within the apartment she couldn't help glancing down the hall at the emergency exit.

"Who is it?" The distorted light leaking through the door's spyglass was obscured for a moment, then, "Damn it, Terri. Go away!"

Terri reached inside her leather jacket, "I'm sorry about sneaking into the building but you couldn't hear me if I stayed downstairs."

"I don't want to hear you! Just go away or I'll call the police."

"Just give me one minute, please. You don't even have to open the door. I just want to apologize. Please?" Terri watched the spyglass darken.

"I've got nothing to say to you, Terri."

"Okay, just listen. All I want to say is that I'm sorry. I was totally out of line. I hurt you. I took advantage of you, and I uh… I hurt you and I'm really, really sorry." She pulled a flower out of her inside pocket and held it up to the spyglass. "I brought you a yellow rose, you know, to symbolize friendship and starting over and stuff, but uh; I'll totally understand if you don't want to see me again."

The spyglass brightened briefly, but the lens darkened as Stacia returned to it. "I don't ever want to see you again."

"Right." Terri smiled nervously. "You said you hated dead flowers, so I got you a plastic one. It'll stay 'fresh' forever."

Stacia said nothing.

"I'll just leave it here. Okay?" Terri coiled the wire stem around Stacia's doorknob and nodded at the spyglass. "So, uh, goodbye. I won't bother you again." She zipped her jacket closed. "I promise." Terri turned away from the door and limped down the hall toward the elevator.

Saturday, 12:00 pm – Gate A11 Boarding Area, SFO

The 326 passengers waiting for the red-eye flight to London formed an oasis of life in the otherwise deserted terminal. The boarding area couldn't hold as many people as a sold out 777, so the adjacent gates were also filled with travelers waiting for the 11-hour flight. Most looked tired or bored, or both; trying to stay awake when they would normally be sleeping. The duty free shops, newsstands and restaurants wouldn't reopen until 6:00 am, but flat screen TVs hanging throughout the terminal provided some distraction. Sandy usually ignored the kaleidoscope of ads and news and flight information, but she turned toward the closest screen when she heard the name of a familiar company.

> *"Silicon Valley's Daga Kabt has been shut down amid allegations that the highly publicized 'T-minus Chip' was actually a hoax. Investigators believe DKI executives may have rigged elaborate demonstrations and set up phony benchmarks to convince investors and employees alike that the new technology was viable. Since the test results and performance data were largely or completely fabricated, it is extremely unlikely that the so-called 'Negative Time Chip' could ever actually work."*

Sandy glanced at the clock over the check-in counter and noticed Ian walking toward the gate. His uniform reminded her of the day they met. As she looked away she realized he'd probably seen her and when she looked back he was making his way toward her through the crowd.

> *"Investigators with the Securities Exchange Commission became suspicious when they learned that DKI executives had started selling their shares in the company. DKI shares had more than tripled in value over the past few weeks on rumors that their new chip would revolutionize the computer industry. Shares reached a high of 169 5/8 this morning, only to plummet when news of the scheme reached the press. The SEC suspended trading in DKI shares this afternoon, after the value of the stock crashed to less than a dollar a share.*
>
> *"I'm Wendy Wallace and you're watching News Break."*

Ian stopped a few feet away and smiled self-consciously. "Hi."

Sandy's smile was diplomatic. "How did you find me?"

"You told Orson you had a 12:45 flight and there are only two out of SFO. London seemed a lot more likely than Cincinnati."

"Maybe I should have gone to Cincinnati. How'd you get through security?"

"Pilot, remember?" Ian pointed to his FAA ID Badge. "Can we talk?"

"We do need to talk, I mean I'd like to talk, but I was hoping to get a little perspective first. Can we do this another time? I really think I need a little time away."

"Right." Ian nodded. "I just wanted to tell you I'm sorry for putting you in danger."

"We already had this discussion. You didn't kidnap me. You rescued me and I'm really, really grateful for that."

A woman in a pink running suit looked toward Sandy when she heard 'kidnap' and 'rescued' but the three year old at her feet quickly recaptured her attention.

Ian looked around to see if anyone else was listening but no one seemed interested. "I also wanted to apologize for the whole thing with Bernie. I still don't know what I was thinking. I knew how I felt about you from the moment we met and I…" He paused when Sandy held up her hand.

"Bernie wasn't your fault. She seduced both of us and I was just as gullible as you were. She has some issues, but she means well. She was there for me with you and Orson and I think that makes up for a little machination, don't you?"

"Ladies and Gentlemen, we're ready to begin boarding flight 1231 to London, England. At this time we'd like to welcome our Upper Class passengers aboard. Now boarding flight 1231 at gate a11"

"That's me." Sandy bent down to pick up her carry-on.

Ian glanced left and right at the passengers shuffling together, closing the gaps between them as they queued toward the Jetway, "Look, could I come with you? We could talk on the plane. I could take the next flight back if that's what you want."

Sandy glanced at the check-in counter and shook her head. "I think the flight's full."

"Dispatch cleared me to jump-seat," Ian hesitated, "I mean, if it's okay with you. That's why I was cleared through security."

"That explains the uniform. You're so resourceful." She started to smile, but the impulse faded. "No, Ian. Please. I just want some time away to think about all this."

"You're not mad at me for almost getting you killed and you're not mad at me for Bernie, but you're getting on a plane and you don't want me to come along. I don't understand."

"You don't understand?" Sandy glared at him. "What I don't understand is how a guy like you could do something so despicable!"

"Despicable?"

"You smuggled drugs, Ian!"

"You said you didn't care about that. You said it didn't matter! 'Whatever happens' you said, 'I'm on your side.'"

"I thought there was an explanation. I thought there would be extenuating circumstances. I didn't think you were just guilty!"

"Ladies and gentlemen, we'd like to welcome our business and upper class passengers aboard. business and upper class now boarding flight 1231 at gate a11"

The pink running suit picked up her toddler, but hesitated. She seemed torn between eavesdropping and getting an early chance at the overhead storage. She wasn't the only passenger waiting for Ian's response, but Ian didn't reply.

Sandy lowered her voice and said, "You also lied to me."

Ian had been looking at the floor but his eyes flashed up to meet her gaze. "How did I lie to you?"

"You didn't tell me what you were doing with Mick and that's the same thing."

"Not telling you something is the same as lying to you?"

"If it goes to who you are it is! You had to know it was something I'd want to know about. You had to know it was crucially important and you chose to not tell me. That's the same as lying."

"That's not fair! What was I supposed to say? 'Hi. My name's Ian and I'm in the middle of making the biggest mistake of my life?' From the moment we met I wanted to tell you everything I've ever done, or felt or imagined, but we only met a month ago! I started to tell you the last night you came over, but we ended up talking about Bernie and then Des showed up."

She looked at him critically. "Why didn't you just say 'no' the first time Mick brought it up?"

"It's not that simple."

"It's exactly that simple, Ian! I've been trying to wrap my head around the usual excuses: nobody's perfect, everybody steals paper clips from work, speed limits are just guidelines…" Sandy shook her head. "It's all rationalization! Laws are contracts. They're promises between members of society and when you break those promises you break your connection with everybody else! And with me." Sandy sighed. "And we're certainly not talking about paper clips here."

The woman with the three year old was still hovering within earshot but the gate agent invited all Economy passengers to board and she reluctantly carried her child toward the Jetway.

"I never meant to hurt anybody."

"But you did. The 'war-on-drugs' may be the worst mismanagement of a public health crisis since prohibition but it's still a crisis. Being addicted to something shouldn't be a crime, but making money off that addiction is far worse than criminal!"

Ian looked stunned and Sandy took a deep breath.

"I'm sorry." She said, "Maybe that was a bit harsh. I didn't want to talk about this before I had a chance to think and I told you I wanted some time but you wouldn't take the hint."

"Ladies and gentlemen, this is your last call for flight 1231 to London, England. We'd like to welcome all passengers aboard. Last call for flight 1231 at gate a11"

Sandy sighed, "I've got to go, Ian."

"I know." He walked with her to the Jetway. "Will you call me when you get back?"

"I'm not thinking that far ahead, but uh," Sandy nodded, "Alright, I'll call you." She handed her boarding pass to the gate agent.

"Sandy, I love you."

"I…" Sandy hesitated, but she reached out to touch Ian's arm. "I love you too, Ian."

He reached for her hand but Sandy stepped back and shook her head. "I really do love you, I mean that. I just don't know if that's enough." She turned and started down the Jetway.

Ian started to follow her but the gate agent stopped him. She recognized the uniform and said, "May I have your pass Captain?"

Ian automatically reached for the boarding pass in his shirt pocket, but he said, "I'm uh, I'm not going." Ian's hand dropped to his side as he watched Sandy walk down the windowless tunnel and round the corner toward the airplane. She didn't look back.

When she disappeared from view Ian moved to the window and searched the front of the 777 but he couldn't see anything distinct through the tiny windows. He moved along the window until he could see the other side of the plane but he still couldn't see Sandy. He watched the ground crew secure the access doors and back the container lifts away from the plane. The last catering truck withdrew and then a squat double-ended tractor pushed the jet back from the gate. When the tug disconnected and left the plane on the taxiway, the blue taxi lights behind the jet began to shimmer in the heat from the engines. Moments later the plane was following the taxiway out toward the runway.

"Sir?"

Ian turned away from the window. The gate agents were gone and behind the young police officer the vast transit cathedral was empty.

The cop seemed sympathetic, "Did you miss your flight, sir?"

"Yeah." Ian looked back outside at the empty ramp. "I missed my flight."

Epilog – Hundred to One Odds

Rashad Rehman eased the power back on the left engine and said, "Gear down."

Jeannie Douglas moved the gear selector to down, waited a moment and then shook her head. "Nose and left main are locked, but the right main isn't moving. I'm recycling."

"Roger." They were descending toward Patterson Ranch, a grass strip the GPS had offered as an emergency field just before it failed with the rest of the navigation instruments. For the last three minutes Rashad had been descending through the clouds on a compass heading based on a wind correction angle his copilot had calculated in her head.

"We're not even getting the right transition light. It's hanging up. Emergency gear extension?"

"Not enough time."

"Go around?"

"Not on one poxy engine. Hold on." Rashad eased the wheel forward and the plane accelerated toward the valley floor. When he jerked the wheel back the Citation pushed them into their seats as everything in the plane including the right wheel suddenly weighed three times more than normal. The right main annunciator flipped from amber to red, which was actually an improvement: It meant the gear was somewhere between up and down and that it was moving. As their airspeed dropped back to best glide, Rashad leveled off and resumed their descent toward Patterson Ranch. As they strained to see through the mist surrounding them, the LED switched from red to green.

"You shook it loose!" Jeannie flashed him a thumbs up. "Three green! Gear down and locked."

"Prepare for landing."

Just before the secondary electrical buss failed and they lost the landing lights, Rashad saw the dark outline of a grass runway slightly right of the nose. He turned to line up with the strip and smoothly brought their remaining engine back to idle. When the lights failed and he lost sight of the runway, Rashad took a deep breath and kept scanning the backup instruments. He still couldn't see a thing outside the window, but he knew their heading, their altitude and their speed. He held their course and descent rate steady. When they were fifty feet above the published elevation of the grass strip he brought the nose up a little, waited a heartbeat and then smoothly pulled the wheel back to his chest.

Even though the runway's "surface" was supposed to be grass, the sound effects were rubber on concrete. Two chirps announced the mains touching down and then the plane settled onto all three wheels. Rashad gingerly pressed the brakes and eased the Citation to a stop.

"Yes!" Jeannie shouted, "You did it!"

"We did it, Jeannie! We did it. Good job!" He let out his breath as though he'd been holding it for the last half hour. "Fantastic job, Jeannie. After-landing checklist, please."

"Roger." While Jeannie cleaned up the airplane, resetting the simulator for the next crew, Rashad turned around to look at the facility's senior check pilot.

Shaking his head in disbelief, Bert Stroud whispered, "Son of a bitch."

"Well put, Mister Stroud, but we are on the ground, right side up, and in one piece. I believe you owe us one thousand dollars." Rashad grinned as he glanced at Jeannie. "Each."